REMORSE STABBED AT MADDIE.

The Knight family had given her so much, and what had she given them? Lies.

Her throat tightened in anguish. She wasn't Amelia. She was Madeline Beecher, the deceitful daughter of a scoundrel. "I didn't mean to sound ungrateful. I truly am grateful—for everything. More than you'll ever know."

"I understand." Blaine's palm moved from her chin to the side of her face. His touch was gentle, reassuring. She closed her eyes and leaned into his hand, savoring the feel of his rough fingers against her skin, wishing with all her heart that she could be liked as herself instead of as the girl they thought she was.

"Amelia." The husky plea in Blaine's voice brought her head up. He moved closer to her; his fingers tensed on her jaw. His eyes burned with some inner secret that made her heart thump heavily.

She stared up at him wordlessly, waiting.

LINDA O'BRIEN

Promised to a Stranger

To Pat
With best wishes -
Linda O'Brien
Troutonius

AVON BOOKS ◆ NEW YORK

This is a work of fiction. Names, characters, places, and incidents either are the product of the author's imagination or are used fictitiously. Any resemblance to actual events, locales, organizations, or persons, living or dead, is entirely coincidental and beyond the intent of either the author or the publisher.

AVON BOOKS, INC.
1350 Avenue of the Americas
New York, New York 10019

Copyright © 1998 by Linda Eberhardt
Inside cover author photo by Edda Taylor Photographie
Published by arrangement with the author
Visit our website at **http://www.AvonBooks.com**
Library of Congress Catalog Card Number: 98-92770
ISBN: 0-380-80206-6

First Avon Books Printing: October 1998

AVON TRADEMARK REG. U.S. PAT. OFF. AND IN OTHER COUNTRIES, MARCA REGISTRADA, HECHO EN U.S.A.

Printed in the U.S.A.

WCD   10 9 8 7 6 5 4 3 2 1

To my husband Jim,
my very own
"Knight" in shining armor
who inspired my muse
to do her best.

To my editor
Micki Nuding,
for her tenacity
and kindred love for Maddie.

To Cindy and Anne,
to whom I will be eternally grateful.

And, as always, to the two
I cherish with my whole heart,
Jason and Julie.

Chapter 1

Indiana, 1880

There was no warning, just the sudden and prolonged screech of metal brakes against iron track as the monstrous steam locomotive barreled across the wooden bridge. Madeline flew forward, hitting the seat in front of her. "Amelia, hold on to me!" she cried, groping for her companion's hand. "The bridge must be out!"

And then she was pitched head-first over the seat as the giant engine hurtled off the bridge and plunged into the ravine below, dragging all twenty cars to their doom.

"Maddie!" she heard Amelia cry, but any further words were drowned by the sounds of groaning metal and screaming passengers.

Please, God, let Amelia live through this! Maddie prayed as she clung to the leg of a seat. *She has so much to live for.*

The cars hit bottom with a thunderous roar, followed by the tremendous explosion of the boiler,

1

spewing flames, burning coals, clouds of dust, and debris a mile high into the air. Maddie had a moment of consciousness before something heavy hit her on the back of the head, and then her world went black.

It was the acrid smell of smoke that finally roused her. Maddie struggled to open her eyes, her head feeling as if it had swollen to twice its size, her body battered and stiff. She gazed blankly at the mangled roof of the train car overhead, trying to make sense of what had happened. The silence around her was ominous.

And then she remembered.

"Amelia," she called weakly, pushing herself to her elbows. The movement caused a severe pounding in her head. She clenched her teeth and sat up to look around.

There was no longer an aisle down the center of the narrow car. Most of the cushioned seats had pulled loose and were lying haphazardly on the floor. Hatboxes, valises, and bags of all sorts had opened, their contents scattered everywhere. Shards of glass, pieces of coal, and splinters of painted wood covered every surface. The floor had pulled away from the sides of the car, and in some spots there were only gaping holes. It seemed a miracle the car had even stayed in one piece.

Maddie heard groans from somewhere close by. An arm dangled lifelessly from a twisted seat in front of her. She rose on shaking limbs and looked over the seat, shrinking back with a gasp at the unseeing eyes that stared up at her.

Thank God it wasn't Amelia. Maddie swayed unsteadily as a wave of dizziness swept over her, then she forced herself to move on, past that vacant gaze.

"Help me," someone moaned. "Please, help me."

Maddie carefully picked her way over debris and dead bodies, following the sound of the moans. The smell of smoke was getting stronger and she could hear the unmistakable crackle of wood from somewhere close by. Soon, she knew, the whole car would be ablaze.

An old woman was lying on the floor, her leg twisted awkwardly beneath her. "Help me," the woman whispered, looking up at Maddie with pleading eyes. Maddie lifted her to her feet, one arm around the woman's frail waist, and supported her as the woman hopped slowly to the jagged hole at the end of the car. Maddie's head throbbed fiercely as she lowered the woman to the ground. She straightened slowly, fighting dizziness, and turned back.

"Don't go back in there!" The woman coughed and struggled to breathe. "You'll be burned alive!"

Maddie ignored her and kept going, stepping over more bodies, more broken seats. She had to find Amelia.

She had met Amelia Baker only that morning after boarding the train in Philadelphia. For reasons of her own, Maddie had not wanted to strike up a friendship with the young woman, but Amelia had radiated such genuine kindness and compassion that it would have been impossible not to like her. In fact, Amelia reminded Maddie very much of her own mother in her younger years: wistful, hopelessly romantic, and always a lady.

Amelia was traveling from New York to Indiana to meet a fiancé she'd never seen, but knew through letters. She had been orphaned at the age of six and raised by nuns in a convent north of New York City, living a very sheltered, restricted life. She had spent the last four years working for a seamstress as a pattern cutter in New York, and had taken a job as a corresponding secretary for an art patron in the evenings to make ends meet. She'd never had a beau and thought she had few prospects of meeting one. And then she had answered a letter from an unknown artist in Indiana.

Amelia had corresponded with Jeremy Knight weekly for over a year after that, and then he'd asked her to marry him. For a young woman with little hopes of a good marriage, it had been a dream come true.

Maddie caught a glimpse of navy material on the floor several yards ahead and her heart began to thud heavily. Amelia's dress had been navy.

"Oh, dear God, Amelia!" Maddie shoved a heavy bench aside and dropped to her knees beside the crumpled form of the young woman. She cradled the lifeless body in her arms, her tears falling thickly on the navy bodice. "Why her?" she cried bitterly, gazing heavenward. "Why Amelia?"

"Miss," the conductor called from the open end of the car, "you've got to come out. The train's on fire."

Maddie rocked back and forth, weeping silently, holding Amelia in her arms. Amelia, who was to begin a brand-new life, who was finally to have a family of her own, was dead. "It should have been me," Maddie sobbed. "Why wasn't it me?"

The front of the car burst into flames. "Miss!" the man shouted from outside. "Please! You've got to get out!"

Maddie gazed down at the peaceful face of the

dead girl, wishing it were her own. Amelia's black drawstring handbag lay beside her. In it was the most recent letter from her fiancé. He had sent it with a miniature of himself, which Amelia now wore in a locket around her neck. The other letters she carried in the smaller of two worn brown satchels under her seat.

Maddie knew all about Jeremy Knight and his wealthy family's vast spread of farmland. She knew about Jeremy's dream of becoming a famous artist and about his nervous condition as well. In fact, she thought ruefully, she probably knew as much about Jeremy and Amelia as they did about each other. There had been nothing else for the two young women to talk about; Maddie hadn't offered any information about herself.

Bright orange flames licked the side walls of the car and thick black smoke curled insidiously closer. Maddie stared at it unseeingly. If someone had to die, why hadn't it been her instead of Amelia? Death would have been preferable to living in constant fear. She knew for certain that only her death would stop *him* from hunting her down like an animal.

Only her death.

Maddie stilled. A plan, a hope, flickered inside her. She reached for Amelia's drawstring bag, then quickly drew her hand back. *Could she do it? Did she have the courage?* She closed her eyes tightly, took a deep breath, and exhaled. *Yes. She could do it.*

Quickly, Maddie tore her smaller handbag off her wrist and dropped it beside the girl's body. There was nothing of value in it anyway; what little money she had was tucked safely in her bodice. She took Amelia's larger bag and looped the drawstring cord around her hand, then unfastened the gold chain around the girl's neck and shoved it in her skirt pocket.

Gazing down at Amelia for the last time, Maddie smoothed the auburn hair away from her peaceful face and adjusted the black bonnet which had come loose in the fall. She pressed a soft kiss on her forehead and laid the girl gently on the floor. She pushed to her feet, looked around for the satchel containing Jeremy's letters, and saw it wedged under an overturned seat. Her own bag seemed to have disappeared in the chaos. There was no time to search for her belongings; she would have to forfeit them to save Jeremy's letters.

"Miss, hurry! This car's about to go!"

Sweat ran in a rivulet between Maddie's breasts as she desperately struggled to free the bag. The heat was intense and the smoke so thick she could barely see the opening at the end of the car. She gave the bag one more hard tug and it pulled free. She clenched her teeth against the hammering pain in her head, hardly daring to draw a breath for fear of suffocating, and belly-crawled through the smoke-filled compartment. She threw herself to the ground outside just as the rest of the car erupted in a volcano of fire.

The train conductor pulled her away, and together they helped the old woman get across the ravine, where other survivors sat staring at the wreck—some weeping openly, others in stunned silence. Maddie sat with them, watching the train car burn to cinders, and all her worldly possessions with it.

Madeline Anne Beecher was no more.

*   *   *

"Dammit to hell, she's gone!"

The tall, craggy-faced man lashed out with an expensively booted foot, kicking the crude wooden table across the tiny kitchen. He seized a chair and threw it as hard as he could. The chair hit the ancient coal stove on the opposite wall and broke into several pieces.

His companion, a squat, muscular, pug-nosed man nicknamed Bull, leaned against the door frame and calmly picked meat from his small flat teeth with the point of his pocket knife. "Maybe she just stepped out to the market."

"Her clothes are gone. *Dammit!*" Vincent Slade turned with a jerk and strode out of the house. He stood on the stoop and stared down the long line of cheap rowhouses as Bull swaggered out behind him. "Get over to Broad Street Station. See if someone matching her description left here this morning. If that doesn't pan out, check Grover Lane Station, or Reading."

"She could be hiding in town."

"She'd be too frightened to stay in Philadelphia. But have a couple of the boys check around just in case." Slade's hand curled into a fist. "I *will* find her, Bull. I *have to find her*. If that girl gets her hands on Crandall's letter, I'm finished."

Blaine Knight opened the door of the attic room and quietly stood watching his younger brother paint. Jeremy's back was to the door, but it was evident from the relaxed set of his shoulders, the dip and sway of his right arm, that he was in deep concentration.

Even so, the sound of the door opening registered

somewhere in his mind. "L-leave it on the t-table," he called absently.

"It's me, Jer."

There was an immediate tensing of his shoulders. His arm stilled. His voice, as he spoke, was flat. "Has there been more n-news?"

Blaine let out his breath. "It wasn't as bad as what was first reported, Jer. Twenty people survived the train wreck. They were taken to the county hospital."

Jeremy turned slowly. His crystal-blue eyes were bleak, agonized. "Do they have a l-list of n-names?"

Blaine looked down at his dusty boots. He had never been able to stand seeing his brother in pain. "No names yet. But Amelia could be alive."

Jeremy stared at him desolately, as if he knew the chances were slim. "D-do you think we should go?"

"Yes. We should leave right away. It'll take a good two hours to get there."

Jeremy turned back to his easel and stared at it, his shoulders slumped. Blaine watched a moment longer, then abruptly turned away. "We'll take the surrey instead of the buggy—just in case. I'll see to it."

Blaine swore to himself as he jogged down the staircase. He'd been counting on this marriage as much as Jeremy had—more, perhaps—although initially he hadn't been keen on the match. His natural wariness had made him suspicious of a female who would accept the proposal of a man she'd never met. He worried that she'd be homely or mentally slow, or, worse, a fortune-hunter, out to dupe a painfully shy, naive young man. But his brother had insisted that he knew all he needed to know about

Amelia. Jeremy's only concern was that *he* would disappoint *her*.

Because of his stutter and extreme shyness, Jeremy had never had the courage to court a girl in person. But courting through letters had come easily to him. On paper he was able to express sentiments he'd never be able to say to a young lady directly for fear of sounding foolish.

Blaine strode down the long hallway toward the back of the house, stopping briefly in the kitchen to alert the cook and housekeeper to the situation before heading toward the barn. Only a day ago he had stood on the wooden platform at the depot and watched Jeremy pace back and forth as he anxiously awaited Amelia's arrival. Only a day ago he had believed his *own* dreams had finally come within reach. Then the wire had come through about the train wreck. Just a short wire, which had altered both of their lives forever.

Blaine led the big farm horse out of its stall. The news of the wreck had devastated Jeremy. He'd sat in the buggy in shocked silence all the way back to the farm and then retreated to his attic room, where he'd stayed until now, lost in his painting.

Blaine prayed that Amelia had survived—for if she were truly dead, Jeremy would probably never marry.

More important, if Amelia Baker were dead, Blaine would never get out of Marshall County.

Cursing under his breath, he hitched the horse to the surrey and led it around to the front of the house. He hadn't wanted to come back home from the army to manage the farm in the first place. It was Jeremy's land, handed down to him when Oliver Knight died. Blaine had never expected to share in it. His stepfather had made that clear to him from the moment of Jeremy's birth to the time of his own death. But when the farm had started to flounder, Blaine's mother had turned to him—once again.

Yet there was still a slim chance the girl was alive. If he was lucky.

Chapter 2

Maddie sat on the edge of a cot in the women's ward of the Marshall County Hospital, reading through the stack of letters from Amelia's brown satchel. She was grateful that she'd saved them. They told her details about Amelia's fiancé and his family and even Amelia herself that she hadn't mentioned.

"The name of the orphanage," Maddie whispered furtively, digging through the stack of letters. "What was the name of the orphanage?" It was a fact she should know, since she was supposed to have been raised there. But all she found was a reference to the nuns who had raised Amelia.

Please extend an invitation to Sister Mary Josephetta and Sister Mary Margaret to visit us as they journey to Chicago in the autumn, Jeremy had written. *I am certain they would welcome the chance to see you and your new home.*

Maddie repeated the sisters' names several times to memorize them. As she tied the letters with string and set them aside, she wondered if Amelia had extended the invitation as Jeremy had requested—and if she had, what the chances were of the sisters actually showing up. She tried to figure the odds but her head hurt too much to concentrate. She'd worry about it later.

Maddie had done little that day but sleep, sip the strong beef broth brought to her every two hours, and study the letters. Her body was bruised from head to toe, her head ached constantly, and it was only by sheer will that she was able to put the pain out of her mind and concentrate on the task at hand.

She lay back on the bed, closed her eyes, and mentally recited the list she'd made for herself. *Jeremy David Knight: twenty-four years old, birthday—October twenty-third; owns the farm; paints landscapes and still lifes.* She chewed her lip thoughtfully. She'd never met a painter before.

She remembered Amelia telling her how she had "met" Jeremy while working as corresponding secretary for Mrs. Harrington of New York, a grand lady who considered herself a patron of the arts. Mrs. Harrington had seen one of Jeremy's paintings at a mutual acquaintance's house, and was so impressed by his talent that she had arranged a display of his work in an art gallery.

Mrs. Harrington had even made two trips to Indiana to try to convince Jeremy to move to New York, where she could help him get established. Both times Jeremy had politely put her off, but, as Amelia had put it, Mrs. Harrington wasn't the type to give up. In other words, Maddie thought with a frown, Mrs. Harrington would try to bully him into leaving his farm.

"Not if I have anything to say about it," Maddie muttered.

Amelia's first letter to Jeremy had been merely for business purposes, but they had soon struck up a friendship that later blossomed into something much deeper.

"He's so sweet and sensitive," Amelia had told her only that morning. *"And he has such deep feelings. I've never heard a man express himself with such poetic beauty as Jeremy."*

Maddie had never heard a man express himself with *any* poetic beauty. The only men she'd ever spent much time around had either been issuing orders or drunkenly accosting her as she walked past the rowhouses of South Philadelphia. Hardly what anyone would call poetic.

And because she'd spent her early years moving from town to town, she'd gotten a late start in school and had been older than most of her classmates. Any boys in whom she might have taken an interest had dropped out by fifteen to work in the factories. Later, she'd had no time to think about boys. She'd been too busy working.

Maddie pulled her thoughts together and began to recite again. "Mother's name is Evelyn; father, deceased, Oliver. Brother, Blaine, thirty years old, unmarried, spent four years as an officer in the army, runs the farm. The family claims Methodist affiliations and has made arrangements for Amelia to be converted from Catholicism before the wedding."

Maddie paused and looked up with a puzzled frown. How was she to convert from Catholicism when she wasn't a Catholic to begin with? The only knowledge she had of Catholicism was what she had learned at the free Quaker school she'd attended, and that was only that the Quakers renounced "Papism" and its practice of the "terrible confessional."

She shrugged her shoulders. She would just have to pretend to be very glad to leave it behind.

"The house is built in typical farmhouse style, with six rooms on the main floor: front and back parlor, kitchen, dining room, sewing room, and a small bedroom behind the kitchen for the cook, Mrs. Small." It wasn't nearly as big as the houses where she'd worked, Maddie thought. Still, it was a darn sight better than the meager, two-room rowhouse where she'd lived the past four years.

"There are two girls who come each day to help with the cooking and cleaning. On the second floor are six bedrooms. The housekeeper, Mrs. MacLeod, has a room on the third floor, which is also where Jeremy does his painting."

Maddie tried to imagine what her own room might look like—or rather, the room they had prepared for Amelia. She pictured a big feather bed so high off the ground it took three steps to reach it. Naturally it would have a fancy canopy and side draperies in a rich velvet. And of course there would be a long, carved oak bureau with a triple mirror above and a fancy silver toilette set on top.

In one corner of the room there would be a reclining couch covered with pale green damask, and a fancy crystal lamp on the delicate scroll-leg table beside it. Occupying a wall all by itself would be a large bow window, with a window seat full of lacy white pillows where she could sit and look out at the vast farmlands. Oh, and there had to be a dressing room! A dressing room filled with more clothing than she could wear in a lifetime.

Maddie had seen a room like it once—it had only

been a week ago, she realized in surprise—when she'd been ordered to take a message upstairs to *him*. She shuddered, remembering how Vincent Slade's icy gray eyes had slid over her and his thin, cruel mouth had curved up in a leer. She'd never in her life taken such an immediate and instinctive dislike to someone, or felt such an unreasonable fear of them, until that moment.

"*What's your name?*" Slade had demanded, advancing steadily across his room toward her.

"*Madeline,*" she'd blurted nervously, her usually glib tongue deserting her.

"*Madeline what?*"

"*Beecher.*"

He had stared at her with mouth agape. "*Beecher? Are you Fast Freddy's daughter?*"

Maddie had winced at the unflattering term and nodded, her throat too dry to reply.

"*Yes, I should say so. You have his eyes, and that incredible red hair . . .*" Slade had reached out for a silky wisp lying loose on her neck and rubbed it between his fingers. "*Your father hoodwinked me out of nearly a hundred dollars; did you know that?*"

Maddie had shaken her head unhappily, lowering her lashes to hide the fear in her eyes.

"*No, you probably were only a child. You're new here, aren't you, Madeline Beecher?*"

Maddie had only nodded, trying to still the trembling in her limbs. She had wanted desperately to run, but she had been paralyzed with fear.

"*Well, Madeline,*" Slade had said, his silvery voice making her skin crawl, "*if you prove to be a capable girl in the kitchen, I just might have you promoted to the second floor.*" He'd placed the strand of hair carefully on her shoulder, then let his fingers trail down over her breast. *"Would you like that, Madeline? Would you like serving me?"*

And then his wife had walked in.

"Vincent, what is that kitchen girl doing here?"

Maddie had jumped back guiltily, and thrust the folded paper at Mrs. Slade. In a trembling voice she replied, *"I was told to bring this message upstairs to Mr. Slade."*

Slade had snatched it from her fingers, then turned to his wife with an angry glare. *"Did you want something, Millicent?"*

"I rang for tea over five minutes ago. Girl, go fetch it immediately."

Maddie had done as instructed and returned hastily, slipping quickly past *his* suite and darting into his wife's. Carrying the tea tray across the sumptuous room to the bedside table, Maddie couldn't help but gape at the beautiful furnishings. She would never forget the beauty of that room.

Nor the evil in the other.

Maddie shook off the ugly memory and forced her mind back to the letters. She had to know every detail backward and forward if she were going to fool Jeremy. *Jeremy.* How familiar his name sounded, almost as if she really did know him.

Maddie swallowed hard. She *didn't* know Jeremy. She wasn't even sure she would like him. What kind of man would ask a woman who lived hundreds of miles away to marry him sight unseen? He could very easily be cruel, or insane. Yet in a month's time, just after the fall harvest, she would be marrying him—a virtual stranger. A stranger who thought he knew her.

Her mother would be so appalled by her deceit. Maddie blinked rapidly at the sudden sting of tears.

"I'm sorry, Mother," she whispered raggedly. "Perhaps you were right. Perhaps Freddy's blood does run too deep in my veins."

Perhaps she was doomed to follow in her father's footsteps after all.

Frederick K. Beecher, or Fast Freddy as he was widely known, had been the smoothest con man in Pennsylvania until he went to prison ten years before. When Maddie was eleven years old her mother had left him because, as she had said over and over again, "*He's a bad influence on you, Maddie. A leaf never falls far from the tree.*"

Poor Mother, Maddie thought with a sigh. She had tried so hard to make a lady out of her wayward daughter. "*You don't have to have money to act like a lady,*" was Sarah Beecher's favorite saying. But Maddie had never taken to household skills. Sewing bored her; she was too impatient to do tedious needlework; and she hated Sundays when her mother would make her sit at their shabby table and have tea with her as if they were in some fancy tearoom, dressed in their finery.

Yet Maddie had sat through it all, knowing how important it was for Sarah to believe that someday her daughter would turn out to be a lady; knowing, too, that she didn't ever want to be like her father. Maddie had pitied her mother, because Sarah had been conned by Fast Freddy, too, and had run away from a solid, middle-class home to marry him. When Sarah had finally discovered the truth about her charming, deceitful husband, she had been too ashamed to go home.

Maddie remembered little from her early childhood other than that they'd never stayed in one place long—not until her mother had had enough of Freddy's deceiving ways. And then Sarah had made her way alone, supporting young Madeline by working as a kitchen helper for the wealthy, until her death only a year ago.

From the age of eleven Maddie had pretty much had to look after herself, but it had made her resourceful and independent, and determined to prove that she was not like her father. Yet here she was, posing as a quiet, unaffected orphan girl from New York whose only dream was of a kind husband and a home of her very own.

Maddie sighed unhappily and pushed a lock of red hair away from her face. What other choice did she have? She could never go back to Philadelphia. And even if she continued on to St. Louis and then to California, as she had planned, Vincent Slade would eventually track her down.

And then he would kill her.

She took the locket from her skirt pocket and opened it, staring at the faint image inside. She had to marry Jeremy. He was her only escape. She would be safe as Amelia Knight. No one would ever think of looking for Madeline Beecher in a little Indiana farm town, especially when it appeared that Madeline had perished in the train wreck.

She fastened the locket around her neck, vowing to be a good wife to Jeremy, just as Amelia would have been, and to be the lady her mother had always wanted her to be, too. And once she was safely married, she would never tell another lie. She would not live a life of deceit, as her father had. She would not hurt innocent people.

It was an unbelievable stroke of fate that had brought her and Amelia together. They had been the same age, nearly the same height, and even their eye color was close—although Maddie would call hers more gray than green. She worried about her hair, though. Amelia's had been a medium brown with red highlights, while Maddie's was definitely a deep cinnamon red. But Jeremy had never seen Amelia, she reminded herself.

She tucked the letters safely away and dug through Amelia's few belongings. She pulled out a white nightgown made of cambric, embroidered at the cuffs and hem with rows of blue fleur-de-lis. Her wedding nightgown?

Maddie quickly stuffed it back inside and removed two dresses: a serviceable one-piece costume of light blue serge, and a gray-and-white suit of checked ladies' cloth. She replaced the suit and kept out the blue dress to wear. A lavender-scented handkerchief was tucked in the bodice of the dress. Maddie wrinkled her nose. Her own taste ran to lighter scents. She noticed initials embroidered on the corner: AMB. What did the M stand for? she wondered. Mary? Martha? Margaret? Mabel?

She frowned thoughtfully. If anyone asked, she would say it stood for Madeline. She prayed Amelia had never told Jeremy what her middle name was.

She glanced inside the satchel once more. There were no undergarments, no toiletries, not even a pair of stockings. She thought longingly of her own satchel, which she'd been forced to leave. Bother! She'd just have to make do. After all, she had escaped with her most important possession—her life.

A nurse walked toward her, smiling broadly. "Miss Baker? Your fiancé has come. Would you like to change before you see him?"

Maddie suddenly felt faint. Jeremy had come! She

didn't feel at all ready to face him. She looked down at her charred brown dress and nodded. "Please," she said, her voice hoarse from the caustic smoke. Anything to delay the inevitable.

Chapter 3

<svg>⎯⎯⎯◯◯⎯⎯⎯</svg>

Blaine leaned one shoulder against the wall and watched Jeremy pace the narrow corridor of the women's ward.

"I still c-can't believe it," Jeremy said. "Amelia is alive! *Alive*, Blaine! And I was s-so sure..." He stopped suddenly and swung to face his brother. "What shall I s-say to her? Do I look all right? I didn't even s-stop to change. I never expected—this."

Neither had Blaine. He wanted to shout out his good fortune: Jeremy was going to be married after all. "Calm down. You look fine. She's probably just as nervous as you are, if she's not in a state of shock from the accident."

Jeremy looked remorseful. "You're right. How could I think only of m-myself after what she's been through?"

The door to the women's ward opened suddenly and both men turned. A nurse stepped out, followed by a young woman in a pale blue dress that was a little short at the wrists and ankles and much

21

too tight across the bust. She paused just outside the doorway and stared at Jeremy apprehensively, her slender hands knotted in fists at her sides.

Blaine's stomach tightened as his eyes raked over her, moving from her stunning deep red hair and sultry coral lips down to the slim ankles showing beneath the hem of her dress and slender feet encased in soot-covered high-button shoes. It seemed impossible that Jeremy had found this young woman through a chance letter; even more impossible to believe she had not been snatched up by some wealthy man looking for a mistress—for if anyone was born to the role, it was this provocative creature.

His gaze moved slowly up again, over her hips to her small waist, pausing at the full breasts constricted by an ill-fitting bodice. She had shoulders that were a little wider than was considered the height of femininity, but it only made her waist seem narrower. She had a graceful neck, and her long, richly hued hair had been pulled back and tied tightly with a ribbon, as if she were afraid of its wild nature.

She had a smooth, creamy complexion and a straight nose, perhaps a bit too long to be fashionable. But her mouth was sensuously curved and her eyes were an incredible mixture of light green and silvery gray, framed by a sweep of dark lashes.

Blaine saw those silver-green eyes shift suddenly to focus on him and his heart began to thud heavily. Her gaze was guarded yet curious, and a slight furrow appeared between her eyebrows, as if she were trying to place him in the order of things. He met her stare evenly. *Damn, she was beautiful.* He couldn't seem to pull his gaze away.

As he watched her, something flickered in those depths that put all his senses on alert. Something very much like fear. His eyes narrowed as he studied her, and his wariness returned. A plain, retiring, impoverished woman might leave behind everything familiar to travel halfway across the country to marry a man she'd never met, but not a beautiful one—not unless she had a very powerful reason to do so. A reason like love. Or escape. And his gut feeling told him that Amelia Baker's reason had nothing to do with love.

At his insistent stare, a blush colored her cheeks. Abruptly, her gaze shifted to his brother. "Jeremy?" she asked in a tentative voice.

Blaine had to restrain himself from jumping to Jeremy's aid as his brother struggled with his rehearsed speech, his mouth contorting, his fair face turning a painful red. "H-hello, Amelia. I'm s-so g-glad you're f-finally here."

The girl hesitated, as if stunned by his reticence. Blaine clenched his jaw, praying she would say nothing to humiliate him. Then she walked up to Jeremy and smiled at him, touching his sleeve gently, as if he were a child. "Thank you, Jeremy. I'm *very* glad to be here."

At her understatement they both laughed, Jeremy with embarrassment, breaking some of the tension between them.

"Are you all r-right?" he asked, risking a glance at her. "Were you b-badly hurt?"

"I suffered a concussion, but I'm better now."

Blaine could hear the rawness in her voice, probably caused by the smoke, and knew it must hurt her to talk.

The nurse spoke to Jeremy. "She's had a few

dizzy spells and she's terribly bruised. You'll need to watch her for several days. If the headaches and dizzy spells continue, have a doctor look at her." She smiled fondly at her patient. "Amelia is a lucky young woman. Only twenty passengers out of one hundred forty survived."

"I'm the l-lucky one," Jeremy replied, blushing harder. He cast a glance over his shoulder at Blaine as if he wasn't sure what to say next.

Blaine pushed himself away from the wall. "I think we're ready to go home."

"Don't forget your bag," the nurse called to Amelia as they walked away. She held out a worn brown satchel.

Amelia turned back for it, but Blaine took it from the nurse before she could reach it. Her surprised silver-green gaze met his dark eyes and for the span of a single heartbeat neither one moved. Tendrils of heat curled inside Blaine as he stared at her.

"Thank you," she said in a hoarse whisper.

Blaine couldn't hear his own reply. His blood was pounding too loudly in his ears.

Bull knocked twice and opened the heavy, eight-paneled door, peering into the richly furnished office beyond. He closed the door behind him and smiled crookedly at the craggy-faced man watching him expectantly from behind the massive ebony desk. "I found her."

Vincent Slade clenched his teeth. "Where is she?"

"Chicago. She took a train out of Broad Street Station early yesterday morning. One of the ticket clerks remembered selling her a ticket. She was asking questions about Chicago."

"She does have a way of impressing herself in the

memory," Vincent murmured thoughtfully. He lifted the lid of the gold case on his desk and removed a cigar. It was too bad Nate Crandall had told Madeline where he had hidden his blackmail letter. Madeline would have made a damn fine bed partner. Vincent sighed regretfully. If it had only been Crandall's murder she had witnessed, he wouldn't have concerned himself with finding her. After all, who would take the word of a con man's daughter over his? But with the evidence to back up her story, that was another matter.

Vincent clipped the end of the fat cigar, lit it, and puffed slowly until the tip glowed orange. "Take one of the boys and bring her back."

Bull grinned. "Sure thing." He swaggered toward the door.

"One reminder."

Bull paused, his thick-fingered hand on the brass door handle. "Yeah?"

"Don't hurt her." Vincent blew a large puff of smoke from his thin lips. "Save that pleasure for me."

Seated on the front bench of the surrey next to her soon-to-be brother-in-law, Maddie stared dismally at the seemingly endless stretch of rutted dirt road ahead. She shifted, trying to find a more comfortable position, but she was too bruised for it to make any difference. If she turned her head slightly she could see Jeremy sitting stiffly on the bench behind her, his face turned away, as if he were afraid to look in her direction. Maddie sighed inwardly.

Jeremy Knight was nothing like the man Amelia had described to her. If Jeremy was capable of deep feelings or poetic thought, then it must be that he could only express them on paper, for in person he surely didn't show it. Painfully shy, he would hardly look at her for longer than a second, and when he spoke to her, his stutter was so great that she had a hard time understanding him.

His clothing, as well as his brother's, had been a second surprise. Since they were men of some means, she had expected to see them wearing suits or frock coats, at the very least boiled shirts with linen collars and cuffs, and waistcoats with trousers. And above all, hats. Gentlemen always wore hats, her mother had told her, especially when meeting a lady.

These men wore simple, unbleached cotton shirts with no collars, and work pants in a light tan cotton held up by plain brown suspenders. Their boots were dusty, unpolished brown leather, and only Jeremy wore a hat—though the floppy brim and crushed crown barely resembled anything she had ever seen before. She was beginning to wonder if Amelia had been duped.

At a particularly jarring bump, she winced in pain, and when she opened her eyes she found Jeremy's brother's piercing gaze on her.

Blaine. The soldier. She stifled a shiver of apprehension. He frightened her with his brooding countenance and cold, distrustful gaze, so different from Jeremy's shy blue one. She felt naked before him, as if he could strip her with his eyes and see down to her soul, down to the guilty secrets hidden there.

Blaine Knight was a big man. Even seated, he seemed tall and very broad in the shoulders. His plain cotton shirt clung to his strong arms and outlined a muscular chest. His legs seemed cramped in the narrow space in front of him, and she couldn't prevent her eyes from traveling up the dusty boots and long, slim pants to his trim middle, and then to the glimpse of dark hair at the open neck of his shirt. A tingle ran down her spine, settling somewhere deep inside her.

Maddie quickly glanced at his face to see if he was watching, but his gaze was focused on the road in front of them, giving her an opportunity to study him further. He had thick, nearly black hair that parted neatly on the right, except for an unruly lock which drooped lazily onto his forehead. His mouth was firm and his nose long and straight. His eyebrows were black and there was the dark shadow of a beard on his tanned face.

The two brothers didn't look much alike. Jeremy was much fairer-complected, but perhaps that was because he spent his time indoors, painting. Jeremy was almost as tall as Blaine, but not as muscular—again, probably due to his occupation. His mouth was more generous, his nose a little wider, and his hair a medium brown. Of the two, Blaine was much more handsome, but there was something about him that unsettled her, that made her feel as if he knew she was an impostor.

There had been no conversation for the past fifteen minutes and Maddie was glad of it. She had spent the first half hour of the trip answering Blaine's questions about the train wreck. Jeremy had listened intently to her replies, seeming inordinately fascinated by it, and he'd even mentioned that he might take his easel back to the ravine to paint it. Maddie had shuddered at that. She didn't ever want to see the ravine again. Thankfully, both men now seemed content to let her sit quietly without talking.

She turned her head to the side and closed her eyes, wishing she could lie down and sleep. Her head ached from the bumpy country roads and her stomach growled from lack of food.

"Are you dizzy?" Blaine asked suddenly, startling her.

She opened her eyes and met his penetrating gaze. "No, it's only a headache. I'll be all right once I rest."

"We've traveled almost half the distance already. Another hour and we'll be home, and then Mrs. MacLeod can put you to bed."

Maddie turned her head to gaze out over the farmland. Home. They were taking her home. To a room prepared just for her. She smiled to herself.

Blaine's deep, husky voice cut through her reverie once again. "I'll have Mrs. Small brew some herb tea for your throat."

He must have heard the rasp in her voice. Somehow she was not surprised. "Thank you," Maddie said quietly. When he continued to study her, she looked away.

Maddie wasn't aware she had fallen asleep until the surrey jerked to a stop. Her head snapped up and her eyes flew open. Blaine had already stepped down and was tying the horse's reins to an iron hitching ring. She glanced to her right and her eyes widened in surprise.

Amelia had not been duped. The Knights were definitely people of means. Maddie had never imagined a farmhouse so large or so welcoming.

It was a three-story, white frame house with rows of green-shuttered windows across its face and a wide veranda that wrapped around the front and one side. Two white wicker rocking chairs and a matching settee, draped with a colorful patchwork quilt, sat facing the long, tree-lined lane to the road. Pots of bright red geraniums lined both sides of the steps and pink impatiens spilled over clay pots onto small wicker tables between the chairs. Maddie blinked back a prickle of tears. This was the home Amelia had always wanted.

Jeremy stepped down and waited to assist her. Maddie took his hand as she lifted her skirt and stepped onto hard-packed dirt. She ignored his heated blush and gazed around in fascination. She'd never been on a farm in her life. This one was a very pleasant surprise.

The front door opened and a petite, silver-haired woman in a simple lavender gingham dress floated across the veranda, a black lace shawl draped gracefully around her shoulders.

"Mother," came Blaine's husky voice from behind, "this is Amelia."

Maddie stared curiously at the person who would soon be her mother-in-law. Evelyn Knight was a far cry from what she had supposed a farm wife to look like. This lady had neither the sturdy build nor the ruddy cheeks and raw manners of Maddie's vision. Rather she was fair-complected and fine-boned and spoke in the quiet, genteel voice one would expect of a highborn lady.

"Amelia, my dear child!" The woman moved swiftly toward her and enfolded her in a delicate embrace. Maddie hugged her in return, gladdened by her warm reception.

Evelyn Knight leaned back and smiled sympathetically. "We were all so concerned about you—thank heavens you came through that ordeal. Come inside and have some tea. You can tell me all about it."

"She's had a concussion," Blaine explained. "We need to let her rest."

"A concussion!" Evelyn stared at Maddie in genuine horror. "Good heavens, Blaine. Don't you think we should send for the doctor?"

"The nurse's instructions were to watch her for several days and call the doctor if her head wasn't better."

Maddie suppressed a shiver at the deep voice so near her ear. Evelyn hooked her arm through Maddie's and walked with her across the porch. "Then that's exactly what we'll do. Mrs. MacLeod has a room all made up for you. Jeremy will see you there now and I'll have a tray of food sent up. We'll have plenty of time to talk in the morning. Coming, Jeremy?"

Maddie glanced over her shoulder to see Blaine leaning against the surrey watching her with those dark, wary eyes. She turned back, her mouth pursed. Thank heavens it was Jeremy she was to marry and not Blaine.

"I'll b-be r-right there, M-mother," her fiancé managed.

Maddie winced and wondered if she had been too hasty in thanking the heavens. But it could be far worse, she told herself. She could still be running for her life.

"What do you think?" Blaine asked his brother as they walked across the wide veranda together.

"She's l-lovely. N-not at all what I expected. In her letters, she described herself as p-plain-looking."

Blaine laughed. "That's quite an understatement, wouldn't you say?" He glanced at his brother's concerned face and frowned. Jeremy's stammer had been much more pronounced than usual, something that only happened when he was agitated. "What's bothering you?"

Jeremy shrugged. "I c-can't put my finger on it. J-just a feeling that something's off-kilter."

"Amelia has certainly made you very nervous."

Jeremy sighed miserably. "I had h-hoped because we'd been corresponding that it wouldn't h-happen. But in p-person she seems so . . ." He shrugged unhappily. "I don't know, d-different, somehow."

"It's been a long, emotional week for you, Jer. After a good night's sleep you'll be back to normal." Blaine put his hand on his brother's shoulder. "Tomorrow you can start teaching Amelia about the farm."

Jeremy stuffed his hands in his pockets and looked down. "I c-can't, Blaine. I n-need time to get reacquainted with her."

"Jeremy, we don't have time. Your wedding is in a month and there's a lot for her to learn."

Jeremy looked up imploringly. "Would you t-teach her?"

"Me?" Blaine asked, startled. He remembered his reaction to Amelia and a feeling of apprehension swept through him at the thought of working closely with her. "Look, Jer, I—"

"You're a m-much better teacher than I ever could be. Besides, I still haven't learned everything I need to know. And I know nothing at all about keeping the b-books. Do it for h-her sake, if not for mine. Please?"

Blaine gave Jeremy a disgruntled look, but it

didn't seem to affect his brother one bit. In truth, Blaine had to admit that Jeremy was right. He *would* be a lousy teacher and he still had a lot to learn about the farm himself. Blaine sighed. "All right, Jeremy. I'll teach Amelia."

The relief on Jeremy's face almost made Blaine forget his apprehensiveness.

Once again, though, he was coming to Jeremy's rescue.

Chapter 4

❧∽◦◦∽❧

Maddie balanced on her heels on the very edge of the bed, took a deep breath, closed her eyes, and fell backward, landing in a cloud of down. A smile curved her mouth as she raised her arms above her head and stretched languidly. It *was* a feather bed! And it was covered with a thick down comforter, as well. She sighed, not even minding that her head hurt from the fall. Her stomach was full, her throat felt better from the soothing tea, she'd had a hot bath, and now she had a big, soft feather bed all to herself.

An oil lamp glowed softly on the table beside her, casting shadows on the pink-flowered wallpaper. The bedroom wasn't as large as she'd envisioned, nor was there a bow window with a window seat, or a reclining couch, or even a dressing room. But there was a delicate scroll-leg writing desk with a matching chair, a pink slipper chair beside the bed, a tall, brass-framed cheval glass in one corner, and a huge armoire for her clothes, such as they were.

With a contented sigh, Maddie rolled to a sitting

33

position and swung her legs over the side of the bed. Her toes touched the smoothly varnished wood of the bedside steps and she stood, swaying momentarily as sudden dizziness swept through her. She waited until it had passed, then she stepped down and carried the small satchel to the bed. She pulled out the checked two-piece suit and laid it neatly over the back of the pink slipper chair. The stack of letters and her small coin purse she tucked safely inside a drawer in the armoire.

She yawned as she untied the sash of the plaid flannel wrapper Mrs. MacLeod had lent her. The sleeves hung down to her knees, and she'd had to wrap the material nearly twice around her body, but it was soft and clean and felt much better than Amelia's too-small dress. She dropped the robe on the chair where she'd laid her undergarments and gently massaged her aching breasts, wondering how she could tactfully request new clothing.

She unfolded the white nightgown with its tiny blue fleur-de-lis embellishments and held it up, but decided against wearing it. It seemed too personal. Amelia had no doubt designed it for her wedding night. She would wear her own chemise to bed instead.

Maddie had just slipped it over her head when a sudden knock sent her scurrying to the door, clasping the wrapper in front of her. She opened it a crack, then smiled in relief and swung it wide to admit the housekeeper.

"I brought ye a warm glass of honeyed milk," Mrs. MacLeod said in her soft Scottish burr. "Just the thing to put ye straight off t' the land o' nod."

"Thank you," Maddie said, slipping on the wrapper. "The food was delicious." She had to slide back a sleeve to accept the glass. She took a long swallow and licked her upper lip, sighing in contentment.

Maddie liked Mrs. MacLeod. There was something comforting about her cheerful round face and twinkling blue eyes. She was a big woman with an ample bosom, thickset waist, and wide hips, yet she wore her gray dress, with its white collar and cuffs, with an air of dignity.

Mrs. MacLeod smiled as she tucked a wisp of gray hair under her white mobcap. "If there's anythin' else ye'll be wantin', just give a tug on the pull over there."

Maddie's gaze followed her finger to a long, flat embroidered ribbon which hung near her bed. A bellpull! She smiled in delight. She hadn't expected such a luxury in a farmhouse.

Mrs. MacLeod's eyes brimmed with humor, as if she had read Maddie's thoughts. "Mrs. Knight had it installed only last year. She's one for the fripperies, ye know. Trouble is, Mr. Blaine can't be bothered to use it. His hollering nearly drives the poor woman off her trolley." Mrs. MacLeod peered around her. "I couldn't help but notice ye've only the one bag. Did the rest burn, then?"

Maddie tensed and looked away. "I didn't have time to save the rest."

"Ye don't even have a bonnet for your head?"

She shook her head. "It was scorched by burning cinders."

"Poor lass. I'm certain Mr. Blaine will be happy to order some material for ye. I'll mention it to him in the mornin'. And ye can borrow a bonnet from Mrs. Knight until we can get ye a few of your own."

"Thank you, Mrs. MacLeod."

The housekeeper smiled again and turned toward the door.

"Mrs. MacLeod," Maddie began hesitantly, twisting the sash around her fingers, "is Jeremy always so painfully shy?"

The housekeeper sighed sadly and shook her head. "Aye, lass, as shy as they come. When he gets flustered he stutters somethin' terrible. He's been like that since he was in breeches, poor lad." She carried the empty glass to the door, paused, and turned. "Don't ye worry now, lass. Once the two of ye get better acquainted, he'll come out of the worst of it. Sleep well."

"Good night, Mrs. MacLeod." Maddie closed the door and leaned against it, feeling somewhat relieved. She couldn't imagine being married to a man who was unable to hold a conversation with her.

She crossed to the open window and knelt down, propping her elbows on the sill, trying to make out shapes in the darkness. Her window faced the backyard, so she knew the barn was out there, as well as the convenience, which the Knights referred to as the backhouse. The backhouse, she had discovered, was a rather crude version of the water closets she had seen in the wealthy Philadelphia homes. But it was better than having to carry a smelly porcelain pot to the open sewers every morning, as she'd had to do at the rowhouse.

She took a deep breath of country air and slowly let it out. The farmhouse already felt like home. She'd only had a minute to glance into the front parlor, but even in that brief glimpse she'd seen the love and warmth of a family. The room wasn't nearly as fancy as the Slade home, but it did have a tall ceiling, a richly carpeted floor, upholstered furniture in warm, cozy colors, lace-covered tables full of photographs and knickknacks, and lots of space. She'd never feel boxed in as she did in her little house.

And then there was the kitchen. She smiled and closed her eyes, recalling the delicious aroma of roasted hen that had greeted her. Tall white cabinets filled one whole wall, from the wooden floor to the beamed ceiling. In the center of the room, six ladderback chairs with red-checked seat cushions surrounded a long pine table, and in a corner two oak rockers sat facing a cozy stove. Near the gigantic black range was a wide window framed with matching red-checked material, and hanging from the beams overhead were bundles of dried herbs. There was a pantry, too, where she had taken her bath, behind the privacy of a red-checked curtain.

Maddie sighed wistfully. She couldn't wait to explore the rest of the house. She felt like a child at a candy counter. *Yes, that's exactly how I feel. Like a child.* For the first time in over ten years, Maddie had no responsibilities other than to pretend to be a lady. For the first time in her adult life she felt completely carefree.

A shadowy movement caught her eye and she peered more closely at the ground below. Was someone standing down there watching her? Her heart began to pound. She stood abruptly, pulled the heavy overdrape shut, and backed away, then instantly felt foolish for her reaction. She had nothing to fear here. *He* would never find her here.

The long day combined with a full stomach finally took its toll. With another yawn, Maddie extinguished the lamp and crawled under the down comforter. "Thank you, Amelia," she whispered as her eyelids drifted shut.

Blaine waited until he saw the light go out, then he let out his breath and strode toward the kitchen. He was hot, dusty, and tired, and now, on top of everything else, aroused. He'd spent the evening chopping firewood behind the barn in an effort to get his mind off Jeremy's fiancée. And then he'd come striding toward the house to find her window draperies open and her slender form clearly outlined by lamplight.

He paused on the back stoop and closed his eyes, seeing in his mind's eye her graceful hands running over her naked breasts. *Damn, she was beautiful.* But she was also Jeremy's. Just as everything else was. He could never let himself forget that.

Soon, he told himself, very soon, it wouldn't matter. Jeremy and his new bride would take over the duties of the farm—and he would be free at last.

"Miss Baker? Wake up now, lass. 'Tis well past mornin'. Lass, can ye hear me?"

Maddie came slowly from her dream. A woman was calling for Amelia, searching through the burning train wreck for her. Maddie groped her way through the black smoke, following the sound of her voice. She had to warn her that Amelia was dead, but she couldn't see her. "No," she moaned. "You've got to get out. The fire—"

"Miss Baker, don't fret now. There's no fire. 'Tis just me, Mrs. MacLeod."

Maddie's eyelids fluttered open and slowly focused on the ruddy, round face of the housekeeper.

"There's a good lass. Ye gave us fright, Miss

Baker, sleepin' so long. Mr. Blaine said we should have had someone sit with ye last night, due to your head injury and all."

Maddie attempted to clear her throat, but her voice came out in a rasp anyway. "Mr. Blaine?"

Mrs. MacLeod nodded, her cheeks puffing as she smiled. "When ye didn't come down for breakfast, he came up to check on ye. 'Twas my idea to bring up the food in case ye were still sufferin' from your dizzy spells and couldn't make it downstairs. I brought more herb tea for your throat, as well. I'll send one of the girls to fetch the empty tray later. If ye be needin' anything else, just give a tug."

"Thank you. That's very kind." Maddie sat up too quickly and braced her hands on either side of her as a wave of dizziness swept over her. "Where's Jeremy?"

Mrs. MacLeod plumped up several pillows behind her. "Mr. Jeremy is up in the attic, paintin'. He'll want to come see ye as soon as you're respectable. Eat up now, lass. Ye look a mite peaked. I've got to bustle right down now and give Mr. Blaine a report on ye before I start my chores."

She started for the door. "Ach, I nearly forgot. Mr. Blaine is sending Zebediah to town for material for your new wardrobe. He'll be back later this afternoon. We'll bring it up and ye can choose whatever ye fancy."

The door closed and the room was suddenly silent. Maddie glanced down at the tray on her lap and her mouth watered. She'd never eaten breakfast in bed before, and here she was, sitting in a down bed holding a tray full of the most delicious-looking food she'd ever seen.

She attacked it with a vengeance, pondering Mrs.

MacLeod's words. Blaine had been to check on her. Mrs. MacLeod had said she'd given him a fright. Was it possible that the cold, mistrustful Blaine Knight was actually worried about her?

She ate until she couldn't stuff another bite in her mouth, then leaned back against the pillow with a sigh. She certainly couldn't eat like that at each meal or she'd weigh as much as a horse in a week's time. She set the tray aside and eyed the checked suit on the chair with distaste, remembering the constricting bodice of the blue dress.

"Oh, bother!" she said with a scowl, and thrust her legs out from beneath the comforter, groaning at the aches in her muscles. She found the steps and eased herself down gently so as not to jar her head. She laced up her stays, fastened her petticoats at her waist, and slipped into the bodice of the two-piece outfit, sucking in her breath in order to fasten the toggles down the front. The skirt fastened easily, but was much too short at the hem.

Standing in front of the cheval glass, Maddie studied her image, wrinkling her nose first at the suit, then at the sight of her unruly hair. She needed more than just material for clothing. She needed pins and combs and ribbons, too. All she had was the sooty black ribbon she'd had on when she left Philadelphia. And she needed a new chemise as well, since hers had several holes burned into it. She glanced at the bellpull as she ran her fingers through her hair, and, on impulse, tugged it once.

In a few moments, there was a light rap on her door. "Come in," she called, trying to use an authoritative voice.

A girl of about seventeen opened the door and bobbed politely. "You called for me, miss?"

"I thought Mrs. MacLeod would come."

"Mrs. MacLeod doesn't answer summons, miss."

"I see. Then could you show me where she is?"

The girl bobbed again and, with no warning, started away. Maddie hurried after her and was halfway down the staircase when she remembered she hadn't tied back her hair. Hastily she ran her fingers through it again, wincing at a snarl. "Add a brush to that list," she grumbled to herself, then turned the corner at the bottom and came face to face with Blaine.

"Oh!" she gasped, stepping back in surprise.

Blaine had on his tan cotton work pants, dusty boots, and a blue denim shirt, opened at the collarless neck and rolled back at the sleeves, exposing tanned, muscular forearms. His dark hair was neatly combed to the side, except for that one thick lock that drooped onto his forehead. His dark eyes, as they raked over her, were probing, fathomless—wary.

"What list is that?"

Maddie felt her cheeks grow hot. "A few items I lost in the train wreck."

She saw him silently appraising her hair. "A brush being one of them?"

Maddie ignored the sarcasm. "I was on my way to find Mrs. MacLeod. She said someone named Zebediah was going to town. I thought perhaps he could buy a brush for me. I have some money—"

"Zeb's gone already."

"Oh." Maddie looked down at her high-button shoes, noticing belatedly that they, too, were covered with soot. "Perhaps the next time he goes to town, then." She spun and hurried toward the stairs, relieved to be away from those cold, piercing eyes.

"We'd better see about new shoes while we're at it."

Maddie turned to stare at Blaine in surprise. "While we're at what?"

"I understand you need a hat, as well. I'll take you to town myself. I need to order some supplies anyway."

Maddie nibbled her lower lip. "Should I see if Jeremy would like to go with us?"

Blaine seemed to think her question amusing. "If you like."

Maddie glanced up the staircase, wondering where to find him.

"Third floor. Far north room. Don't bother knocking; he won't pay any attention to it."

She hurried up the stairs, aware of Blaine's eyes on her. Jeremy *had* to go with them—she didn't want to be alone with Blaine Knight.

"Jeremy?" Maddie moved quietly across the varnished floorboards, not wanting to disturb his concentration. She stopped behind him and studied his work. It was a painting of a river, cold and crystal blue, winding its way through a meadow of wildflowers. The flowers seemed so real she wanted to reach out and pluck one. "It's beautiful," she breathed.

Jeremy turned in surprise, his face immediately coloring a deep red. "I d-didn't hear you come in." He stared at her helplessly, then quickly looked down at his feet. "Are you b-better t-today?"

"Some better, thank you."

Jeremy looked around the room, his features strained. "You should be s-sitting d-down. You don't want to t-tire yourself." He shoved a pile of books from a chair and plopped the wooden seat in front of her.

Maddie hated to be rude, so she sat. "Your painting is breathtaking, Jeremy. I had no idea you were so talented."

He looked so completely devastated by her statement that Maddie was startled. What had she said?

Jeremy quickly dropped his gaze, staring at the floor as if he hoped it would open up and swallow him. "B-but you saw Mrs. Harrington's d-display, Amelia. Didn't you l-like it?"

Maddie closed her eyes and clenched her teeth. How could she have forgotten such an important detail? She cast about for a plausible excuse for her blunder.

Suddenly Jeremy raised his head and smiled, a smile that spread from ear to ear. "You're teasing me, aren't you? That's j-just like you, Amelia."

Maddie's shoulders sagged in relief. "Will you show me more, Jeremy? You don't know how much I've longed to see your most recent works, especially—" She paused to remember exactly how Jeremy had described it in his letter. "—especially your *Hummingbird and Morning Glories*."

Jeremy's face and neck turned beet-red, yet he seemed extremely pleased. "How like you t-to remember. It's right over here. I only f-finished it last week."

Maddie walked through his attic studio with him, marveling over his paintings. He was clearly a gifted painter, and when he talked about them, his shyness was completely gone. How sad, she thought, that he wasn't courageous enough to go to New York, or even Paris, to sell his work. She remembered Amelia saying he suffered from nerves and always feared he would be a complete failure if he left home to strike out on his own. Nerves, then, was how he described his shyness.

"Would you like to go to town with me, Jeremy?" she asked as they returned to his easel. "Your brother was kind enough to offer to take me so I can purchase a few things I lost in the wreck."

He bent to examine a minuscule flower at the bottom of the painting. "If you'd l-like," he said, but by his tone, Maddie knew it would be a miserable ride for him, struggling to think of things to say to her. And though it meant spending the morning with Blaine, she took pity on him.

"I'll tell you what," she said cheerfully. "Since it's bound to be boring for you—I take forever to pick out hair ribbons—I'll go to town with Blaine, and when I come back you can show me around the farm."

His entire body seemed to relax. "I'd l-like that, Amelia," he said, giving her a grateful look.

Maddie left quietly and closed the door behind her, wondering if the real Amelia would have been as disappointed in Jeremy as she was. She hoped Mrs. MacLeod's prediction was true, because if Jeremy was always going to be that shy around her, it would make for a very dull marriage.

Chapter 5

Maddie held onto the straw hat Evelyn Knight had given her and glanced covertly at Blaine as the buggy bounced along the crude dirt road. He didn't seem quite as frightening today as he had at first. Still, he made her uncomfortable, and for some reason Maddie was beginning to think it was done purposefully.

"Jeremy didn't want to go, I take it?" Blaine's mouth quirked at one corner.

Maddie lifted her chin and sat straighter. "You knew he wouldn't come, didn't you?"

"Jeremy paints, Miss Baker. That's about the extent of it. He eats occasionally, farms when he has to, and attends church whenever the preacher comes to town. Other than that, he paints."

"And writes letters," she reminded him, annoyed by his derisive tone. "Don't you approve of his painting?"

"I'm not his father. It's not my place to approve or disapprove."

"Yet it is your place to run everything."

45

Maddie saw the muscle in his jaw tense and wondered if she had touched a sore spot.

"Not for long," Blaine told her. "Once you're married, you and Jeremy will have to shoulder the responsibilities for the farm."

"You're the older brother. Shouldn't they be your responsibility?"

"I'm the half-brother, Miss Baker. A poor relation. Jeremy is the heir. I'm simply here to teach him how to manage his inheritance so that I can leave, which will be in another month, I believe." He glanced at her. "You're having a fall wedding, as I remember it, just after the harvest. Right?"

Maddie ignored his question. "You said yourself Jeremy *paints*. Do you really expect him to give that up to run the farm?"

Blaine took a deep breath and let it out slowly, as if striving to keep his patience. "It doesn't matter what I expect. My mother expects Jeremy to fulfill his duty. To do that he needs a capable helpmate. That's where you come in."

She gave him a wary glance. "What do you mean?"

"Jeremy said you were a capable girl, holding down two jobs. You should be able to help him run the farm."

Maddie stared at him in astonishment. Had Amelia known of Blaine's plans for her? Surely she would have mentioned it if she had. Maddie wondered if *Jeremy* even knew what his brother was planning.

"I'm hardly capable enough to run a farm."

"You won't be running it by yourself. You'll handle the bookkeeping, banking, and inside duties and Jeremy will handle the outside work."

"But when will he paint?"

Blaine almost smiled at that. "Jeremy will find time, never fear."

"Why can't your mother help him manage the farm?"

Blaine turned his head to gaze at her speculatively. "You haven't had much contact with my mother yet, have you? She can manage a house, Miss Baker, but that's as far as her capabilities extend."

At Maddie's skeptical look, Blaine explained. "My mother comes from a monied family on *her* mother's side. They had servants to take care of their every need. Her father's story was quite different. He was a penniless, struggling artist who had been lucky enough to catch the fancy of a wealthy socialite. They married and had two children. The first, a boy, died in infancy. My mother was the second and became the family pet. She especially adored her father; unfortunately, no one else did and his paintings never caught on. He drank himself to death at an early age and my mother never quite got over it. Can you ride?"

Maddie was having a hard time keeping up with his train of thought. "Ride?"

"A horse."

"Of course not. I used the trolley at home."

"You'll have to learn." Blaine's gaze slid down to her waist, following the line of her dress to her ankles. "We'll pick up some pants in town for you to wear."

"Pants!" Maddie exclaimed, horrified. "I'll wear a split skirt!"

"That will have to be made by Mrs. MacLeod. In the meantime, we should be able to find some boys' pants that will fit. You can't ride rutted fields side-saddle. You need to know how to ride like a man and not twisted at the spine in some perverted attempt to look ladylike."

Maddie folded her arms across her chest, simmering silently, hating his ruthless manner, his scorn.

"Can you keep books?"

She looked the other way. "No."

"Cipher?"

"Yes."

"Write?"

"How do you suppose I answered your brother's letters?" She cast a quick glance at him and saw a flicker of a grin appear on his hard face.

"At least the good sisters taught you a few things."

"They also taught me it was rude to pry."

Blaine gave her a quizzical look. "Is that what you think I'm doing?"

"You're interrogating me."

His eyes grew cold, distant, almost haunted. "You don't know the meaning of the word, Miss Baker. I merely thought that since you will be running things around here, it would be wise for me to find out if you're as smart as you've led Jeremy to believe."

Maddie rounded on him, furious that he dared to cast such aspersions on Amelia's character when he had no idea what she was like. "I *led* him to believe? Are you saying I purposefully *mis*led him? Why in heaven's name would I do that?"

"You're an orphan. You had no dowry and probably no prospects of a good marriage until a naive, idealistic, *wealthy* farmer fell in love with your letters. If Jeremy were your brother, what would you think, Miss Baker?"

Maddie stared into those wary brown eyes and all the fight drained out of her. She would have thought exactly what Blaine was thinking. The tragedy was that he had no way of knowing how genuine Amelia had been. Especially when the girl he was quizzing was an impostor.

The buggy hit a deep hole, causing Maddie to bounce hard on the bench. She grimaced and pressed her hands to her temples. When she opened her eyes, he was watching her.

"Dizziness or headache?"

"Both."

"I'll try to be more careful."

She wondered if he meant his driving or his prying.

The town of Collinsville was little more than two cross streets lined with a few shops. The general store was the largest of these establishments, followed by a rambling, two-story boardinghouse/restaurant which sat diagonally opposite it at the intersection of the two streets.

Feeling as though she had just stepped off a ship in a foreign country, Maddie eagerly absorbed every detail of the town. She followed Blaine across the wooden sidewalk and into the large store, where she gazed with childlike anticipation down the long aisles crammed with merchandise. Blaine led her to the back of the store, where a glass counter held an array of fancy buckles, buttons, button hooks, fans, gloves, and jewelry. On the wall behind the counter were shelves stocked with material.

"Clem, this is Jeremy's fiancée, Amelia Baker," Blaine announced in a loud voice to the stoop-shouldered, gray-haired man behind the counter. "Miss Baker," he said more softly, his dark eyes on Maddie, "Clement Spriggs, the owner."

"How do, Miss Baker?" the shopkeeper called loudly.

Blaine leaned closer to Maddie and muttered, "He's nearly deaf."

"How do you do, Mr. Spriggs?" she offered in reply, her voice breaking from the effort of speaking loudly.

"You're the one almost killed in the train accident, ain't you?"

"Yes, she is. And her voice is still raw from the smoke."

" 'Course it would be. Shoulda figured that. Jeremy painting?"

"What else? We'd like to see hair combs and ribbons, Clem." Blaine glanced at Maddie's hair. "And a sturdy hairbrush." He lowered his voice to ask her, "Anything else on that list?"

Maddie dropped her gaze and blushed, too embarrassed to mention to a virtual stranger that she also needed undergarments, especially when she knew Blaine would have to shout the words to Mr. Spriggs.

As if he understood her thoughts, Blaine reached for a piece of paper and pencil lying on the counter and handed it to her. "Why don't you write down what you need?"

Maddie scribbled furiously as Clem brought out a tray of hair combs and ribbons and set them down in front of her. She thrust the paper at the shopkeeper. "Here are a few more things I need," she said in as loud a voice as she could manage. She was relieved when he took the list and disappeared through a curtained doorway. She leaned over the tray to examine the combs and chose a serviceable pair in bone.

Blaine reached across her and picked up a pair of iridescent white mother-of-pearl combs cut in the shape of oyster shells. He held them out to her on his open palm. "These would be prettier."

Maddie eyed the combs enviously. "They're beautiful." She sighed. "But too expensive."

His voice grew softer, huskier. "My treat."

Maddie looked up, wondering why he was suddenly being so kind, but his expression gave no clue to his thoughts. She carefully picked them up from his open palm, her fingertips brushing the warm, vibrant skin there. A tremor raced through her, the intimate contact somehow erotic, arousing.

Her gaze slid up to his once more, colliding with his penetrating one. Her breath caught in her throat and she quickly looked down at the combs. She didn't know exactly what she had seen flickering in those dark, shadowy depths. She only knew it left her weak-kneed and breathless.

"Here's them other things," Mr. Spriggs said, coming through the curtains from the back room.

Grateful for the interruption, Maddie turned to attend to business.

The shopkeeper gave her a gap-toothed smile. "I wasn't certain of your size, but bein' such a bitty thing you'd probably take a small." He placed the underclothing on the counter and waited expectantly.

Mortified that such intimate apparel was in full view of her future brother-in-law, Maddie risked a sidelong glance at Blaine. To her surprise, he, too, seemed to be speechless. She saw his Adam's apple bob as his gaze moved over the garments, then he quickly turned his back.

Maddie licked her dry lips. On top of the pile lay a peach-colored chemise made from fine cambric, the likes of which she had never seen before. It had delicate ivory lace scallops across the bodice and thin satin straps at the shoulders and had to be, in Maddie's opinion, the most beautiful chemise ever made. She eagerly reached out to run her fingers over the exquisite fabric, never imagining that she would have anything so splendid to call her own.

Blaine swallowed hard as he imagined Amelia wearing the delicate finery. He had seen that lithe, beautiful form unclothed. His blood thickened, and his body responded accordingly. Those delicate shoulders, the curve of her breasts, the narrowing of her waist, the gentle flare of her hips . . . His breath escaped between his teeth in a lusting, longing sigh. He turned in frustration to see if she was done, and as his eyes met hers, the sudden awareness he saw in hers made his neck and ears redden. Quickly he turned his attention back to the shopkeeper.

"I'm sure these garments will be fine, Clem," he said in a gruff voice. "Wrap them up, please."

As Clem turned to cut a length of the brown wrapping paper, Maddie pretended to study the combs under the glass. Though Blaine's expression had startled her, she felt almost exultant about the silent exchange that had just taken place. From the intensity of his gaze and the way he had instantly turned away from her, she knew she wasn't the only one with something to hide.

She followed the shopkeeper to another counter where she was shown a variety of straw hats and bonnets, both fancy and plain. She tried each one on at her leisure, studying her image before an oval mirror on a stand, turning her head from side to side, while Blaine leaned against the counter and watched with apparent disinterest. Only now she knew better.

Clem went to the front window and brought back a feathered creation on a hat stand. "Here's a new one just come in yesterday, made by them Frenchies."

It was a black brimless hat decorated with a trim of gold braid and a fan of pink ostrich feathers which stuck straight up from the front. The feathered fan was punctuated by a butterfly brooch at its center, and was, without a doubt, the ugliest hat Maddie had ever seen. She gave Clem a dubious look. He was beaming at her as if he had made it himself, so she picked it up and tried it on.

"That's surely somethin', ain't it?" the shopkeeper remarked.

"Yes, it surely is." Maddie looked at her reflection and tried not to cringe. Through the oval glass she could see Blaine watching her, his eyes brimming with suppressed laughter. Her own eyes narrowed. She turned back to Clem and smiled. "I'll take it."

Maddie heard a choked sound behind her. She turned and fixed Blaine with an innocent look. "Don't you like it?"

"What's that?" Clem said in a loud voice. "You say you don't like it?"

Maddie smiled at Clem. "Oh, I like it just fine, Mr. Spriggs. I was asking Mr. Knight for his opinion."

They both turned to regard Blaine, who straightened and cleared his throat, his face turning a deep red. "It's certainly unusual, Clem."

The shopkeeper beamed. "Ain't it though?"

Maddie gave Blaine an ingenuous smile. "Then you think I should buy it?"

Blaine's wary eyes met hers and she saw a sudden look of understanding flicker in those dark depths. He knew she was baiting him. Maddie swung back to the mirror, suppressing a grin. She was thoroughly enjoying teasing him, this dark, enigmatic man.

"On second thought, Mr. Spriggs," she said sweetly, "perhaps I should just buy the white straw hat I tried on earlier. I seem to remember Jeremy mentioning in one of his letters that he's bothered by feathers. They make him sneeze and break out in little red bumps." She settled the deep-brimmed straw hat on her head and tied the blue sash beneath her chin. "Yes, this will do just fine."

Once Maddie had selected her toiletries, she wandered away to explore the rest of the store while Blaine waited at the counter for Mr. Spriggs to wrap her purchases. She stopped at the candy counter and leaned over the glass top. A fat jar full of glossy red peppermint sticks caught her eye.

"What do you suppose is hiding in my vest pocket, Madeline?"

"Oh, Papa! A peppermint stick?"

"Ah, there's my quick girl. Did you miss me, pet?"

"I always miss you, Papa. But must you leave again so soon?"

"If I don't, who'll bring you another peppermint stick?"

Maddie straightened with a sigh, remembering

how eagerly she had looked forward to her father's simple gift. It was the only thing Freddy had ever done that had made her believe he really cared about her. The only good memory she had of her notorious father.

Blaine's deep voice behind her made her jump. "We're not finished yet." At her puzzled look, he added, "Your pants. Come with me."

He took her to the back corner of the store opposite the ladies' accessories where stacks of boys' overalls and brown canvas pants filled the wooden shelves. His gaze moved over several shelves, then he pulled out a pair of pants and turned. Squatting in front of her, he held them to her waist.

Maddie glanced over his dark head, her cheeks on fire. She hoped there were no customers to witness such an intimate, embarrassing scene.

"They seem long enough," Blaine said, straightening.

Maddie took the pants and held them out before her, wrinkling her nose in distaste. "I won't wear them."

"Would you rather have your bare limbs hanging down the horse's sides?" he asked pointedly.

Maddie weighed her options, then huffed in annoyance. If she had to ride a horse, she certainly did not want to expose her limbs. The problem was that she didn't like admitting she was wrong either. "I don't have anything to wear with them," she said petulantly.

"That's easily fixed. We'll buy you a shirt."

Blaine scanned another shelf, pulled out a blue cotton shirt, and handed it to her. "You'd better hold that one up yourself," he said with a crooked grin.

Maddie turned her back on him and held it up to her shoulders, glancing down at the front. She turned back. "It's too small."

Blaine's forehead wrinkled. "Too small? The sleeves are a mile long."

"That's not where it's small!" she whispered furiously.

Puzzled eyes moved to her tightly constrained bodice and then his face cleared. Not quite able to suppress a grin, he turned to take another shirt from the shelf and hand it to her. "This one's—uh—roomier. Mrs. MacLeod can shorten the sleeves for you."

As they waited for Mr. Spriggs to wrap her riding clothes, Blaine leaned against the counter and studied her, his gaze moving to her bodice and then away. Maddie's stomach tensed. She knew what he was thinking. Why were her dresses so small?

Be careful. Don't make a foolish mistake. She took a breath and tried to make her tone sound conversational. "I wish I'd had time to retrieve my larger satchel, the one carrying my good clothing. I hadn't expected to wear this old dress or the blue one until I'd refashioned them. I only had a minute to look, though, and the small satchel was the only one I could see. Unfortunately." Maddie's gaze slid guiltily away from Blaine's probing look.

"Here you go, Blaine," the shopkeeper called, to Maddie's immense relief. He handed Blaine the wrapped bundle and Maddie's handwritten list with prices penciled in beside each item. "Glad to make your acquaintance, Miss Baker."

She gave him a fleeting smile. "Thank you, Mr. Spriggs."

Blaine ushered her through the store and stopped

on the sidewalk outside. "While we're in town, is there anyone you want to wire? Anyone you want to let know you're all right?"

Maddie shook her head. "No one."

"Not even the nuns at the orphanage?"

Her fingers curled into her palms. She wished she knew how much Jeremy had told his family about her past. All she could do was take a chance he hadn't told them much. "I've lost contact with them over the years," she blurted.

"But they raised you, didn't they? Don't you think they'd appreciate knowing you're alive?"

"They weren't very kind to me." Maddie hid her gaze beneath the brim of her new hat so he wouldn't see the shame in her eyes.

"What about your employer? The seamstress."

"She probably wouldn't remember me." Maddie looked up at him with wide, guileless eyes. "There were so many of us."

Blaine studied her for a moment, and she thought she detected a glimmer of sympathy in his eyes.

"Let's go get your shoes."

The shoemaker's shop was across the street, two doors down from the boardinghouse. As Blaine escorted Maddie across the street, a woman stepped out onto the narrow, shaded veranda of the boardinghouse and watched their approach.

"Morning, Penny," Blaine called with an easy smile and nod of his head.

"Morning, Blaine."

The woman's honeyed tone made Maddie think there was something very personal between the two, and for some mysterious reason it irked her. Maddie observed her from beneath the wide brim of her white hat. Penny was an attractive woman with golden blonde hair, full pouting lips, and an extremely curvaceous figure. If Blaine liked that type of woman, Maddie thought with a scowl, it was no business of hers.

She guessed Penny's age to be several years older than her own, but with the heavy makeup on the woman's face it was hard to tell just how many. What was easy to tell, however, was that Penny had set her cap for Blaine.

Blaine took Maddie's elbow and pulled her to a stop in front of the house. "Miss Baker, this is Miss Penelope Tadwell, the owner of this establishment. Penny, this is Jeremy's fiancée, Miss Amelia Baker."

The woman's syrupy voice belied the chilly smile on her face. "Pleased to make your acquaintance, Miss Baker."

Maddie gave her a cool smile in return. "The same to you, Miss Tadwell."

"Jeremy is busy," Blaine explained, "so I brought Miss Baker into town to pick up some things she needed."

Penny looked her up and down so thoroughly that Maddie had to stifle the urge to tug the skirt of her dress lower to cover her ankles. "So sorry to hear about your misfortune, honey." And with that, the woman dismissed her presence entirely and turned to talk to Blaine.

Honey? Maddie scowled down at her sooty shoes in a silent simmer. She wasn't a child and she resented being treated like one, especially by a blonde hussy. She wasn't about to stand still for it either. "I'm going to the shoemaker's," she muttered sullenly, shooting Penny a contemptuous look.

"When are you coming to dinner again, Blaine?" she heard Penny say in a silky voice as she marched away. "I know it's been less than a week, but it seems like ages."

Maddie didn't wait to hear his reply. What Blaine did was his own damn business.

Chapter 6

$\sim \infty \sim$

When Blaine finally appeared at the shoe-maker's shop, Maddie was sitting on a chair in the middle of the store with at least ten pairs of slippers, shoes, and boots around her, while the shop owner's son, a young man with frizzy brown hair, freckles, and a red face, knelt at her feet, gazing up at her worshipfully.

Maddie looked up at Blaine, who stood glowering at her from the doorway, and gave him her sweetest smile. Mimicking Penny's silky voice, she said, "I found some shoes, *Blaine.*"

Maddie had a hard time keeping up with Blaine's fast stride as he stalked back to the buggy. She knew he was angry with her, but she thought it best not to ask why. She was still in shock over how many pairs of shoes he'd ordered for her. She hadn't really intended for him to buy everything she'd asked the clerk to bring out. She'd only done it to annoy him. But he'd ordered one of each kind, which, except for the ready-made boots Blaine now carried, wouldn't be done for a week.

Blaine tossed her package into the boot of the buggy, then held out his hand to help her up. Maddie settled herself without meeting his glare, but looked up, puzzled, when he strode back toward the general store.

"I'll be right back," he snapped. He returned a few moments later, but offered no explanation. He'd probably gone back to order those supplies he'd said he needed, she thought.

They were at least a mile out of town when Blaine finally spoke, and then it was in a tightly restrained voice. "I can't help but wonder what prompted you to be so rude to Penny."

Maddie untied the blue sash of her new hat and removed it. "I merely treated her in the same fashion that she treated me."

"You walked away from her."

Maddie turned her head to glare at him. "She called me 'honey.'"

"She calls everyone that."

"She didn't call *you* 'honey.'"

A muscle in Blaine's jaw twitched. "Penny was only trying to be kind."

"Ha," Maddie scoffed, and looked away.

Blaine urged the horse on faster. "If Mrs. Mac-Leod had called you 'honey,' you wouldn't take offense, would you?"

"Mrs. MacLeod would have called me 'lass.'"

The muscle twitched faster. "What difference does it make?" he said through gritted teeth.

"Are you seeing Penny?"

Blaine turned his head and narrowed his dark eyes at her. "Why?"

Maddie shrugged. "She's clearly enamored of you. You'd have to be blind not to notice that. Are you going to take her with you when you leave the farm?"

"I'm beginning to think the good sisters had a reason for treating you as they did."

"Shall I take that to mean yes?"

Blaine glowered at her. "I think it's time for your first lesson."

Maddie gave him a wary look. "What are you talking about?"

"You've got a lot to learn before you can help Jeremy run the farm. Pay attention. I'm going to quiz you at the end."

Maddie listened obdurately while Blaine told her how many acres Jeremy owned, how much they paid for seed, what crops were planted, and what people they employed. Then, as he'd promised, he quizzed her on it until she could recite all the information back to him without error.

"Lesson number two tomorrow morning," he said. "Wear your pants."

Maddie sighed unhappily, thinking of all she had yet to learn and of how relentless Blaine would be in teaching her. She didn't want to run a farm and she seriously doubted Jeremy's capabilities to do anything but paint. How would they ever survive without Blaine there to manage things?

Maddie rubbed her temples. Her head hurt from concentrating and her stomach was growling from lack of food. They took a curve at a fast clip and suddenly it seemed as if the road were tilting beneath her. Maddie's fingers gripped the bench as a wave of dizziness hit her. She took deep gulps of breath to keep from passing out, but it didn't help. "Blaine," she whimpered, and then she fainted.

Blaine swore under his breath as he caught her.

He pulled the horse to the side of the road with his free hand, then slowly lowered Amelia to the bench. He felt her clammy forehead, then pressed his fingers against the rapid pulse in her neck, cursing himself for driving the buggy too fast. He opened the top two buttons of her checked suit. The bodice seemed so tight he wasn't sure how she could even draw a breath. He would have to see that she had a new dress by morning.

He thought back to what Amelia had told him about her good clothing being lost in the wreckage. Why, he wondered, had she put only those two undersized outfits in a separate satchel and nothing else?

"Amelia," he said, patting the side of her face, then picking up a slender hand and rubbing it between his own. "Amelia, wake up."

Amelia. Someone was calling for Amelia. Didn't he know Amelia was dead? The man in the cellar was dead, too. Tortured and killed so he couldn't tell his secrets. But she also knew the secrets. Crandall had told her before he'd been murdered. Now she would be the next one to die.

"No," she whimpered. "I don't want to die."

"You're not going to die. You only fainted."

She shook her head. "He'll find me."

"Who?"

Maddie saw Vincent Slade's face as she had that night from her hiding place in the cellar, glowing with a fiendishness that had stopped her blood cold. She tried to cover her eyes so she wouldn't see what he was doing to Crandall, but someone was holding onto her hands. *No. Stop! Please don't hurt me.*

The smell of burning flesh gagged her. The man's screams pierced her eardrums. Blood ran everywhere. She began to struggle, to fight for her life. *I don't know anything. Please don't kill me.* And then she was lifted up and held tightly against a hard chest, her hands pinned against her sides by strong arms to stop her struggles.

A gentle hand stroked her hair and a husky voice murmured soothing words in her ear. "You're out of the wreck. You're safe. I won't let him find you."

Maddie opened her eyes and saw the front of a blue shirt, Blaine's shirt, and she let out a sob of relief. She was Amelia now, not Madeline. *He* couldn't find her. She wrapped her arms tightly around Blaine's solid rib cage and pressed her face in the curve of his shoulder, breathing deeply of his clean, masculine smell, trying to still the trembling that shook her body. She was safe.

And then she remembered what Blaine had murmured. *"I won't let him find you."*

Maddie's eyes flew open. Dear God, what had she said aloud? She pushed away from Blaine and straightened her clothing, hastily fastening the top buttons of her bodice, belatedly trying to remember when she had unbuttoned them. She glanced quickly at Blaine and found his penetrating gaze on her.

"Are you all right?" he asked in a strained voice.

She rubbed her forehead. "I'm sorry. I must be dizzy from not eating."

"It's my fault. I should have let you eat before we left. And I was driving too fast on top of it."

"I've gone all day without eating before. I'm just not fully recovered from the concussion." Maddie didn't understand why she was making excuses.

"Lean against me if you start to feel dizzy again." Blaine clicked his tongue and the horse started off.

From the corner of his eye, Blaine could see Amelia sitting rigidly straight and knew she wouldn't lean against him even if she did feel dizzy. Rather than fault her for her stubbornness, however, he found himself admiring her for it. Obviously, being raised in an orphanage had taught her self-survival.

He was still shocked that Amelia had no one to contact, no one who cared whether she was alive or dead. He found it hard to believe the sisters at the convent would have no concern for her whatsoever. Also, he thought it highly improbable that the person who had employed Amelia for four years could forget her. She was not a young woman easily forgotten.

He glanced at her again, his gaze traveling from her features to the luxurious red hair cascading over her shoulders and down her back. His fingers itched to touch it, to tangle themselves in the silky waves, to memorize the feel of it. He imagined her wearing the mother-of-pearl combs and the new chemise and stockings he had bought for her. It gave him a measure of satisfaction to think that when she put them on, she would think of *him*, not Jeremy.

He thought of how she had clung to him only a few moments before, her soft curves pressed against his body, tormenting and tantalizing him. It reminded him of how she had looked standing nude, bathed in the golden glow of her bedside lamp. He swallowed hard, fighting the desire raging through him. His gaze fastened on the curve of her mouth. How he yearned to taste those sensuous lips, to explore the sweet hollows of her mouth, to glide his tongue down the smooth ivory column of her neck. But he couldn't. She was Jeremy's. He would not betray his brother.

When they reached the farmhouse, Blaine jumped down from the buggy and strode around to her side. Maddie rose and held out her hand to step down, but he swept her into his arms instead. He carried her into the house and up the staircase as if she weighed nothing at all, bellowing for Mrs. MacLeod as he went.

"I'll have a tray of food brought up for you." Blaine pushed open her door with a booted foot. "If you're feeling up to it later, Mrs. MacLeod can measure you for a new dress. You can't wear that one anymore." He placed her gently on top of the comforter and looked down at her, as if waiting for her reply.

But Maddie could think of nothing to say. She could only think of how good his arms felt around her, holding her so close she'd heard the steady, strong beat of his heart against her ear and felt the ripple of hard muscle beneath her cheek. She felt stunned, shaken, bewildered. She gazed up at him mutely, more aware than ever before of his dark handsomeness, of his size and strength, of his potent maleness. Nervously, she licked her upper lip.

Blaine's eyes seemed to grow darker as he watched her. He turned abruptly and strode toward the door. "If you're not better tomorrow," he called gruffly, "I'm going to send for the doctor."

As soon as the door had closed behind him, Maddie slid off the bed and paced to the window and back again, viciously chewing her thumbnail. She couldn't have such dangerous thoughts about Blaine. She didn't understand *why* she was having them. Blaine was her fiancé's brother. And he was certainly no gentleman. He was rude, mistrustful, and relentless, nothing like Jeremy.

Why, then, did his touch make her tingle with excitement? Why did she forget all about Jeremy when Blaine was near?

Maddie hurried across the room and pulled open the door. She would go see Jeremy; that would take her mind off Blaine. She started into the hallway and just avoided colliding with Mrs. MacLeod.

"Ach, ye frightened me to death, lass! Don't go chargin' off now. I've brought ye some food. Mr. Blaine said ye'd fainted from lack of it."

"Oh, thank you, Mrs. MacLeod!" Maddie exclaimed, taking the tray from her hands. She sat on the slipper chair, balanced the tray on her knees, and began shoveling the food in her mouth with a fork. "Is Jeremy still in the attic?" she mumbled through a mouthful of potatoes. "He promised to take me around to see the farm."

"Slow down, lass! Ye'll choke yourself, or I'll choke watchin' ye!"

Maddie swallowed hard. "I'm sorry. I was more hungry than I realized."

"That's better. Ye'll find Mr. Jeremy in the attic. Between farmin' chores it's where he spends all his free time, except when he takes his easel outdoors. If ever ye want him to go somewhere, tell him ye've found the perfect setting for a painting. He'll follow ye anywhere."

Maddie washed down the food with cold mint tea and handed the tray to the housekeeper. "I'll go find him right now."

"When ye come back, I'll take your measurements for a new dress. Mr. Blaine says it must be ready by morning."

Maddie stopped at the door and swung around. "Bother Mr. Blaine! I don't want anyone sitting up all night to work on a dress for me. I can wear this one another day."

Mrs. MacLeod shook her head. "Ye don't know Mr. Blaine, lass. When he says he wants something done, it had better be done or there's hell to pay."

"Then I'll just stay in my room tomorrow until the dress is ready." Maddie's eyes widened suddenly at the thought of the morning. "The pants! I won't even need the dress until noon, Mrs. MacLeod. Blaine is insisting I learn how to ride a horse—like a man, no less! He bought me boys' pants today and told me to wear them tomorrow morning."

"Pants." The housekeeper clucked her tongue in disapproval. "I hope Mrs. Knight doesn't catch sight of ye. The poor woman will have a fit of apoplexy. Run and see Mr. Jeremy now and I'll be back later to take your measurements."

Jeremy was standing ten feet from his easel, one long finger tapping his square chin as he contemplated his painting. Maddie stood just behind him, tilting her head to one side as she studied it with him. She jumped when he strode forward suddenly, wielding his palette knife as if he were going to slice the canvas to ribbons.

She gasped and ran around him to stand in front of the easel, arms outstretched. "Jeremy, no! You can't!"

He gazed at her in bewilderment. "Why not?"

"Because it's too lovely. You can't destroy it."

"B-but I can always p-paint another one."

"But it will take you weeks, months!"

"N-not at all. I can p-paint another in two minutes."

"You can?" Maddie moved aside as Jeremy applied his knife to the lower corner and sliced off a daisy. She pressed her hand against her mouth to suppress a laugh. He was only talking about a silly flower.

She perched on the wooden chair and watched as Jeremy deftly created a new one—watched and tried to imagine herself married to him. Her eyes moved from his brown hair down to his shoulders and arms. She closed her eyes, imagining those arms around her.

She inhaled slowly, smelling the clean, masculine smell of him, feeling the warmth and strength that radiated from him, imagining his firm lips moving over hers, his beard like fine sandpaper against her chin, his thick, dark hair like silk between her fingers. Desire coiled deep inside her, sweet and throbbing. *"You're out of the wreck. You're safe. I won't let him find you."*

"There. That should do it."

Maddie opened her eyes and stared at Jeremy with a sinking heart. It had not been his arms she had imagined, but his brother's.

Jeremy resumed his contemplative position and backed slowly away from the easel. Maddie saw the pile of books behind him and gasped.

"Jeremy, watch out!"

He fell backwards over the books and hit his head on the wooden floor. Maddie sprang off the chair and dropped onto her knees beside him, her heart in her throat. "Are you all right?"

His blue eyes focused dazedly on the ceiling for a moment and then drifted away. "Do you see all those d-dust motes in the air? I've never n-noticed them s-sparkle so b-before. Why do you suppose we don't feel them when we b-breathe?"

"I think you need fresh air, Jeremy. Can you stand? Perhaps we can take that walk now."

His eyes moved to her face and a blush slowly crept up his neck. "W-will y-you—" He took a deep breath. "Will you k-kiss me, Amelia?"

Maddie stared down at him in surprise. "Jeremy!"

He blushed harder and his stammer worsened. "You're so l-lovely, l-lovelier than I ever d-dreamed you'd be. I've wanted to k-kiss you since I first s-saw you at the h-hospital."

"Then why haven't you?"

"The c-c-con—" He paused to take a breath and try again. "The c-concussion."

"Oh. I see." Maddie gazed down at him, wondering if she should be so forward as to actually kiss him. Jeremy looked so utterly flustered that she slowly lowered her mouth to his and lightly touched his lips. They were warm and firm, and she thought they should have sparked some kind of response within her. But they didn't. His kiss did nothing for her at all.

She tried again, closing her eyes tightly to concentrate. Jeremy's arm slid around her back, pulling her closer, until she was chest to chest with him. Obviously it had sparked a response in him.

At that moment, heavy footsteps sounded in the hall outside and someone burst through the open doorway.

"What the hell?"

Maddie jerked her head up and stared straight into Blaine's angry, accusing eyes. Behind him came the two day girls, who gaped at her in amazement.

She jumped to her feet and hastily smoothed her skirts, her cheeks flaming with mortification. Blaine glanced over his shoulder and the girls quickly left the room. His dark gaze swung back to her red face.

"Jeremy fell," Maddie blurted, backing away guiltily, "over a pile of books."

"Hit my h-head, too," Jeremy added with a wince, rubbing the back of his head as he rolled to a sitting position.

"Was that your idea of first aid?" Blaine growled in a voice only Maddie could hear. "Or were the nuns remiss in teaching you the proper conduct of an *unmarried* lady?" He stalked across the room and helped his brother to his feet.

Maddie's fingers curled at her sides and she had to clench her teeth together to keep from giving him a piece of her mind. The only thing that stopped her was her mother's voice in her ear. "*A lady would never be caught in such a compromising position.*"

Bother! She couldn't remember to be a lady all the time. And Blaine didn't need to be so nasty about it, either. It wasn't as if she had thrown herself at Jeremy. Maddie took a deep breath, walked past Blaine, and took Jeremy's arm. "Are you feeling up to that walk now?"

Jeremy struggled to answer her, gave up, and nodded instead.

"Excuse us, won't you, Blaine?" Maddie said in a sweet voice. As she and Jeremy moved past him, she shot him a frosty glare. Blaine had no right to look at her as if she were out to seduce his brother. Jeremy was, after all, her fiancé. If she wanted to kiss him, then she would kiss him.

If only she *wanted* to kiss him.

Chapter 7

V incent Slade leaned back in his leather chair, propped his expensive calfskin shoes on his desk, drew on his cigar, and squinted his eyes at the newspaper reporter from the *Philadelphia Journal* sitting across from him, scribbling intently.

"One more question," the young reporter said, his shrewd brown eyes watching Vincent closely. "I'm sure you're aware that there are still rumors running around about the disappearance of Albert Anderson, one of Mr. Penrose's leading opponents in the upcoming election. What do you have to say to those who claim you were involved in his disappearance?"

Vincent narrowed his eyes. It was no secret he wanted Boies Penrose to be elected mayor of Philadelphia and he had gone to great lengths to ensure Penrose's success. He was within inches of controlling Penrose, and once that happened the city would be his. What was a secret, however, was how he had managed to get rid of one of Penrose's strongest opponents. His plan had been foolproof, too, until one of his own men, Crandall, had become greedy and started blackmailing him. And even then his secret would have been safe had it not been for Madeline's accidentally stumbling into his wine cellar that night.

Vincent blew smoke from his mouth, swung his feet to the floor, and sat forward. "I have only one thing to say to those charges: prove it!" He grinned complacently and sat back.

The reporter grinned with him and flipped his tablet closed. "Thanks, Mr. Slade," he said, extending his hand.

Vincent clasped it. "Do a good job on that article. I'll expect to see it in tomorrow's paper."

The reporter started for the door.

"One more thing."

The reporter swung around and stared at him curiously. "What's that?"

"How would you like to be editor of that rag?"

The reporter stared at him incredulously, then a knowing smile spread across his thin face. Without another word, he pulled open the door and swaggered out.

Vincent chuckled and swung his chair toward the window, puffing contentedly on his cigar.

"Hey, boss?"

He swiveled to see Bull's thick head peering around the door at him.

"Get in here and close the door," Vincent ground out. "Did you find her?"

Bull pulled his hat off his brown hair and hung his head ashamedly. "No."

Vincent was around the desk before Bull could look up. He pulled the little man up by the lapel of his cheap frock coat until they were nose to nose, and then he bared his teeth. "Don't ever tell me no."

Bull swallowed. "But she's disappeared! I checked every hotel and boardinghouse in Chicago. No one has heard of her, or even remembers seeing her."

"Did you check the train station in Chicago?"

Bull swallowed again. "I—I didn't think of that."

"You didn't think of that? You *imbecile*!"

Vincent dropped him on his heels and went back to his desk, where he began furiously shoving papers into folders. It wasn't by chance that he lived in one of the most expensive homes in Philadelphia. He'd worked hard to get where he was, clawing his way out of the slums, charming, wheedling, gambling, and even killing when necessary. He wasn't about to lose it all to some slip of a girl or an ugly little runt like Bull.

"Get over to the train station and buy two tickets to Chicago."

"Me and Potter are going back?"

Vincent looked up, his eyes cold and merciless. "No, you idiot. I'm going this time. If I want this done right, obviously I'll have to do it myself."

Maddie got as far as the kitchen, and then Jeremy decided they should have some tea before setting out on their walk. He sat at the long pine table where the cook prepared meals while Maddie filled the kettle and put it on the range to heat. She found a canister of tea on the shelf above and measured it into a china teapot.

"You c-certainly know your way around a kitchen," Jeremy remarked as he watched her.

Maddie barely heard him. Through the window she saw Blaine stalk across the yard toward the barn, and it reminded her of her upcoming riding lesson, as well as the fact that she'd have to face those accusing eyes again in the morning. "Jeremy, do you ride?" she asked suddenly.

"Of c-course."

Bother! Her hopes of Jeremy joining her for lessons evaporated.

"My f-father taught me when I was four. I don't ride much anymore, though. Mostly I take the b-buggy when I go out to paint. I may g-go out to the ravine early tomorrow morning before I start my chores." He paused and asked shyly, "Would you l-like to c-come along?"

Maddie shuddered as she turned to pour the boiling water into the teapot. "Thank you for asking, Jeremy, but I'd rather not."

When they'd finished their tea, Jeremy took Maddie out to see the grape arbor on the east side of the house, the setting for one of the paintings Mrs. Harrington had shown. From there he took her to a small pond where two large goldfish swam, also the setting for a painting.

Maddie marveled at the change that came over Jeremy when he talked of his paintings. His stammer disappeared and his voice softened and grew huskier, reminding her of Blaine's deep voice. But as soon as she asked him a personal question, his shyness returned. The only topic other than his painting that he seemed comfortable discussing was, unfortunately, the train wreck.

"D-did anyone else make it out of your car?" Jeremy asked as they walked back to the house together.

"Just an old woman whose leg was badly broken." Maddie shivered, picturing the scene in her mind, remembering the twisted bodies, the suffocating smoke, and intense heat of the orange flames. Remembering poor, broken Amelia.

"How did she get out?"

Maddie's throat tightened. "She didn't."

"I th-thought you said the old woman survived."

Maddie sucked in her breath. "She did survive. I helped her myself. I—I was thinking of someone else."

She braced herself for more questions as Jeremy shot her a puzzled glance. But he merely walked on beside her in silence until they reached the porch, and then he said quietly, "D-do you know what I think?"

Maddie's throat was so dry she couldn't swallow. "No."

His face turned bright red and he looked down in embarrassment. "I think I'd like to p-paint you, Amelia."

Maddie stared at Jeremy, horrified. "But you don't paint portraits."

"You'll be my f-first. If you consent."

"I thought you wanted to paint the train wreck."

"I'll p-paint your portrait afterward."

Maddie twisted her fingers together. "What will you do with the portrait?"

He seemed surprised by her question. "Hang it in the front p-parlor. Or the dining room."

"You won't sell it, will you?"

"Oh, no. Never."

The door squeaked open. "Here you are, Jeremy." Evelyn smiled as she sailed out onto the veranda. "Did you have a pleasant walk, Amelia?"

Maddie forced a smile. "Very pleasant."

"Good. Dinner will be served shortly. Would you like to freshen up before we eat?"

"Yes, thank you." Maddie moved past her and into the house, nibbling frantically on her lower lip. She had to talk Jeremy out of painting her portrait. She couldn't take the chance of anyone outside of Marshall County seeing her face.

The surprise waiting for Maddie in her room made her forget entirely about the portrait. She saw it as soon as she closed the door. It lay on her pillow, long and glossy and scrumptiously red.

A peppermint stick.

Maddie sat on the bed, tucked her legs beneath her, and contemplated its significance. It could only have been put there by Blaine. He'd seen her gazing at them at the store. That must have been what he'd gone back to buy. But why had he left it now? Especially after what he'd witnessed in the attic.

He'd probably put it there just before Jeremy had fallen. That would explain how he'd gotten to the third floor so quickly. Maddie was surprised he hadn't taken it back afterward to punish her. Or maybe he left it there just to make her feel guilty.

"Bother!" She picked up the candy and stuck it in her mouth, sucking forcefully on it. She didn't care what Blaine's motive was. The candy was delicious and she didn't feel one bit guilty.

From some distant place, Maddie heard the roosters crowing. She snuggled deeper into the bed, smiling contentedly, and drifted back to sleep. She was roused again a few moments later when the bed shook briefly, causing the headboard to creak. She ignored it and turned on her other side.

Then a cloth fell over her head, covering her nose and mouth. With a muffled cry, she snatched it off and sat bolt upright. Blaine stood at the end of her bed, his foot perched on the footboard, a satisfied grin on his face. He had on his customary blue shirt, tan work pants, and suspenders. One dark lock of hair fell dashingly over his forehead. A pair of boy's denim pants dangled from his fingers. Maddie looked down at the cloth in her hand. It was her new shirt.

"Lesson two. We rise at dawn." He tossed the pants and she caught them.

"I'm not one of your farmhands. You can't order me about." Maddie pushed the clothing to the floor, flung herself back onto the bed, and pulled the cotton sheet over her head.

"We *all* rise at dawn," she heard him say. "If you want anything to eat this morning, be downstairs for breakfast in fifteen minutes." She heard his footsteps cross the room. When she heard nothing further, she lowered the sheet just below her eyes to peek out. The bedroom was empty.

Grumbling about having to rise before the birds, Maddie threw back the sheet and slid down onto the bedside steps.

At that moment Blaine stuck his head back in the doorway. "Don't forget to . . ." His dark eyes widened as they took in her revealing clothing, lingering at a point below her chin.

Maddie glanced down. It seemed the lace scallops at the top of her new chemise revealed more of her breasts than they covered. She pulled the comforter in front of her and looked up with a furious scowl. "Don't forget to what?"

Blaine seemed momentarily flustered, then his face cleared. "To wear your pants."

"Ladies don't wear pants," she retorted.

"*Ladies* don't roll on the floor with their fiancés, either."

Maddie stiffened. "And *gentlemen* do not barge into a lady's room without knocking. And I ate your peppermint stick. All of it!"

A grin tugged at one corner of his mouth. "I thought you might." He strode from the room and in seconds she heard his footsteps on the stairs. "Fifteen minutes," he called back in warning.

Maddie flung the clothing to the floor and stamped on it. Hateful, odious man! *I thought you might.* Hah! She should have tossed the candy out the window. That's what she'd do if he ever bought her another one. She still didn't know why he'd bought that one for her.

"*Ladies don't roll on the floor with their fiancés.*" Oh, how she wanted to get even with him!

Maddie glared down at the clothing and, with a snort of annoyance, swooped it off the floor and began to change. *Just wait until Mrs. Knight sees me in these clothes. If the poor woman does have a fit of apoplexy, it would serve Blaine right!*

Maddie paused. A mischievous smile spread slowly across her face. Blaine wanted her to dress like a boy, did he? She ran to the bellpull and yanked twice, then spun around and studied her image in the looking glass. Quickly, she rolled up the sleeves of the soft blue shirt in imitation of Blaine's style and opened the top two buttons at her neck. *Oh, yes, she'd get even with Blaine Knight!*

At a soft tap on her door, she opened it and hurriedly gave the young girl instructions, then scooped up a handful of hairpins from the bureau and went to work.

Chapter 8

Blaine leaned back in his chair at the foot of the long, polished oak table and glanced at the porcelain clock on the sideboard in the dining room. More than fifteen minutes had passed since he'd left Amelia's room. Where the hell was she?

His brother was sitting at the table calmly wolfing down a plate of eggs and sausage. His mother daintily sipped tea from a china cup. Mrs. MacLeod adjusted and readjusted the plates of food on the sideboard. He saw her glance at the clock, too.

At the sound of a throat clearing, Blaine, Mrs. MacLeod, Jeremy, and Evelyn all turned their heads toward the doorway at once, then sat frozen in their seats as Amelia stood before them in her new riding costume.

The blue cotton shirt hugged softly rounded breasts unbound by stays and, where she'd opened it at the throat, a tantalizing wedge of creamy flesh beckoned seductively. Her sleeves had been rolled back to expose slender ivory forearms and slim wrists. From somewhere, God only knew where, she'd managed to procure a pair of navy suspenders which now lay against the very tips of her breasts and followed the curves down to her tiny waist, where a brown belt gathered the loose denim material tightly around her.

The pants themselves molded to her slender, shapely hips and compact little bottom and enhanced the long line of her legs. Her ankles were covered by thick wool stockings, and on her feet were the small leather boots he'd bought for her yesterday. His gaze moved back up over her curves to the most outrageous part of her outfit. A hat. A dusty brown wool boy's cap with a short brim in the front, perched at a jaunty angle on her head. She'd fastened her hair beneath it, except for a few stray wisps that had come loose around her face, making her look for all the world like a mischievous schoolboy.

Jeremy rose with a jerk, nearly toppling his chair. His mother made a tiny choking sound and set her cup in its saucer with a loud clatter. Mrs. MacLeod hurried to Evelyn's side, standing ready to catch her if she should faint.

Blaine couldn't move. He could only be grateful that the table hid his unfortunate reaction to her costume. He wished to God he'd never insisted she dress in boys' clothing, for rather than diminishing her sexuality, the shirt and pants only succeeded in emphasizing it further.

"Good morning, everyone," Amelia called in an overly cheerful voice. Only Jeremy replied, his stammer more pronounced than usual. She seemed not to notice that the others continued to stare at her dumbly. She walked straight to the sideboard and loaded her plate with food, then turned and studied the table with a puzzled frown, as if trying to determine which seat was hers.

Blushing hotly, Jeremy pulled out a chair for her. "Y-you can s-sit here, Amelia, n-next to me." As soon as she was seated, he scooted in her chair and returned to his own. "Is th-that your n-new riding outfit?" he asked, afraid to meet her gaze.

Amelia smiled dulcetly and glanced around the table, her silver-green eyes finally coming to rest on Blaine. "Yes, Jeremy, it is. Your brother picked it out for me."

Blaine flinched at his mother's horrified look. He knew he would get an earful later. His gaze shifted to Amelia and narrowed. She was trying to get him in trouble, her revenge for being awakened so abruptly.

"Y-you look w-wonderful in it, Amelia. Doesn't she, M-mother?"

Evelyn Knight had been in the process of trying once again to sip her tea, but at Jeremy's query, her hand wobbled, sloshing tea on the tablecloth. "You look very—unique, dear," she managed with a wavering smile.

Amelia smiled back. "Thank you. I've never had to wear boys' clothing before. But it's actually quite comfortable. No stiff stays or layers of petticoats to bother with."

Evelyn's cup clattered to the saucer. "I think I'd better see to—" Her hand fluttered in the air. "—something. Come with me, Mrs. MacLeod." She rose from the table and hurried off, the housekeeper following in her wake.

Jeremy wiped his chin with his napkin and rose. "W-will you p-pardon me, Amelia? I m-must get to the ravine b-before the good light fades. G-good luck with your riding lesson."

The door closed behind him, leaving only Maddie and Blaine in the room.

The porcelain clock ticked loudly on the sideboard. Maddie slowly lifted her gaze to Blaine's face. He was leaning nonchalantly against the back of his chair, his eyes calmly watching her, yet she had the feeling that underneath his placid exterior, he was exerting the utmost control over his temper.

Let him stew, she thought. It was his own fault. She hadn't wanted to wear the silly pants in the first place. And if the truth were known, she'd enjoyed immensely seeing the shocked look on his face when she walked into the dining room.

Maddie picked up a fork and began to eat, but jumped when Blaine scraped back his chair and rose to his full, towering height. Her heart began to thump loudly as he moved toward her. She gasped as his hand shot out and snatched the cap off her head.

"Lesson three," he said in a low, dangerous voice. "No hats at the table." He tossed the cap on the sideboard and sauntered out, leaving her alone.

Mrs. MacLeod returned moments later. "Saints in heaven, lass, did ye have to wear the suspenders, too?"

"Of course not."

"Did ye not see the expression on Mr. Blaine's face?"

Maddie slanted her a look. "Why do you think I wore them, Mrs. MacLeod?"

The housekeeper stared at her dumbfounded, then her face turned red and her cheeks puffed out as laughter bubbled up inside her, erupting in a deep belly laugh. Maddie began laughing with her until both women were holding their sides, tears streaming down their cheeks.

"Oh, my," Mrs. MacLeod wheezed, collapsing onto a chair. "I haven't laughed like that in years." She wiped her eyes, gazing at Maddie fondly. "Ye're good for this house, lass. It needs some shaking up."

The clock chimed seven-thirty and Mrs. MacLeod jumped up. "Oh, lass, finish your food quickly and dash outside to the barn. I almost forgot. Mr. Blaine is there waitin' for ye."

"Oh, bother Mr. Blaine," Maddie grumbled, but ate hurriedly nevertheless. There was no sense pushing her luck. The day had just begun.

Vincent Slade leaned down to the ticket window in Chicago and smiled at the clerk behind the glass, discreetly shoving a ten-dollar bill through the opening. Bull stood silently behind him, his short, heavy arms crossed in front of his chest.

"I understand you were on duty this past Monday evening," Vincent said to the clerk with a practiced smile. "I'm hoping you can help me. I'm looking for my daughter. Her train was due in Monday night from Philadelphia. She may have bought a ticket west. You'd remember her if you saw her. About twenty years old, beautiful face, red hair. Traveling light and alone. Seen anyone like her?"

The thin, middle-aged man removed his wire spectacles and polished them. "Nope. Can't say that I have."

"Are you sure? Take your time and think about it."

The clerk snatched the money and stuffed it in his pocket. "I'm sure."

Vincent's smile dissolved. He swung around and motioned for Bull to follow him. "Bastard," he hissed under his breath.

"From Philadelphia, you say?" the clerk called suddenly.

Vincent turned back. "Yes."

"Monday evening?"

"Yes, Monday evening. You remember her?"

The clerk shook his head. "Your daughter, you say. Sorry to hear that. The train from Philly derailed that night. Hundred forty passengers died."

Vincent strode up to the window and hunkered down to talk through the opening. "Are you sure it happened Monday night?"

" 'Course I'm sure."

"Were there any survivors?"

"Twenty or so. They were put on a train out the next day. Would've arrived here at—" He paused to look down at his schedule. "—six o'clock Tuesday eve. But I was on duty that night and didn't see any girl like you described come through."

"Do you have a list of the survivors?"

"Should have in a day or two. Takes time to check out these things, you know."

"I'll be back the day after tomorrow."

Bull hurried after Vincent as he left the station. "You think she survived the wreck? Twenty out of a hundred forty ain't good odds."

"It's possible, isn't it?' Vincent snapped. "And if Madeline Beecher *is* one of the survivors, I'll find her."

*   *   *

Maddie stood on the back porch and adjusted the cap on her head. "Time for lesson four—the riding lesson," she muttered resolutely and set off across the dusty ground toward the barn, passing a small herb garden along the way. A pretty rippled-leaf plant caught her eye and she stopped to examine it, rubbing one of the textured leaves between her fingers. She sniffed her fingers and smiled. Mint! She plucked the leaf and popped it in her mouth, slowly crushing it with her teeth to savor the tangy flavor.

Maddie started off again and noticed Blaine leaning against the side of the barn watching her, his arms folded across his chest. Tied to a fence post beside him was the tallest, widest horse she'd ever seen. Even the animal's hooves were gigantic. She came to a dead stop.

Blaine pushed himself away from the barn with a scowl. "What are you waiting for?"

"I'm not riding that beast!" Maddie swung around and marched back toward the house.

"Amelia, come back here."

Maddie ignored him. She'd just made the porch when a steely arm wrapped around her middle and yanked her off her feet.

"Let go!" she cried, struggling to get loose. She was about to kick him in the shin when she was turned around and tossed over his shoulder.

"I'll tell your mother you're mistreating me!" Maddie blinked rapidly as the blood flowed too quickly to her head, making her dizzy again. "Blaine," she called breathlessly, "I think I'm going to faint."

Blaine muttered a few choice words under his breath as he pulled her over his shoulder and into his arms, kneeling carefully to lower her to the ground. "Take shallow breaths." He looked around and spotted one of the farmhands going into the barn. "Zeb, pump some water and bring it here. Hurry."

In a few moments Zeb arrived with a dipper full of water. Blaine supported Maddie's shoulders and raised her to a sitting position to drink. She swallowed thirstily, peering at Blaine's concerned face over the edge of the dipper. An idea jumped into her mind. She handed the dipper back and wiped her mouth with the back of her hand. "I don't think it would be safe for me to sit on that big horse. I might get dizzy again and fall off."

Blaine searched her features with his intense gaze. "You're right."

Maddie smiled to herself as Blaine helped her to her feet. That had been easy enough. "I'll see you back at the house," she called, only to have strong fingers grip her wrist and lead her back toward the horse.

"You just said I didn't have to ride!" she cried as Blaine picked her up by the waist and placed her on the saddle.

"I only agreed that you might get dizzy and fall off." He swung up behind Maddie, adjusted her to sit between his legs and put his arms around her to take the reins. "I'll be right here to see that you don't." He pulled on the reins and led the big farm horse away from the barn.

Maddie did a slow burn as he walked the animal down the lane in front of the house. She was coming to the conclusion that it was nearly impossible to outfox Blaine Knight.

"Take the reins now," he directed. "Get a feel for them. When you want the horse to go left, guide his head by tugging this way. To go right, pull the other way. To stop, pull back firmly and say 'Whoa.' This is a farm horse, used to pulling a plow. He knows a few verbal commands, but you still have to show him a firm hand. And if you sit that stiffly in the saddle all morning, you'll have one hell of a backache tonight."

Maddie took the reins from him, but didn't alter her position. She'd rather suffer a backache than lean into that hard chest. It was bad enough having his thighs around her, knowing that her backside was sitting snugly against his groin, without also having his chest to deal with. Why, just the sound of that low, husky voice in her ear was causing gooseflesh all over her body. She clenched her teeth resolutely. She would *not* think about Blaine Knight that way.

"Okay, let's go back the other direction," he instructed. "Turn his head. That's it."

Maddie was amazed when the horse obeyed her commands. She tried again, turning the horse away from the farm, then she laughed aloud. "I did it!"

But then the horse came to an abrupt halt and lowered his head to nibble at the long grass under a tree. Maddie jiggled the reins and kicked his sides, but the horse didn't respond.

"What's wrong with the silly creature?"

"Firm hand," Blaine reminded her.

Maddie pulled back on the horse's head, but the animal only snorted in annoyance and pulled harder the other way.

"Oh, bother! Eat the grass then!"

Blaine laughed as he took the reins from her and gave a firm yank, clicking his tongue at the horse. Obediently, it started walking.

Maddie frowned. "I knew this wouldn't work."

"You'll learn. This horse is just too big for you."

"Can we go back, then?"

"I want to show you the property first." He clicked his tongue again and the horse set off at an ambling trot. Maddie bounced on his lap and had to hold the cap on her head so it wouldn't fly off.

"My head," she complained. "It's going to start hurting."

Blaine responded by sending the horse into a gallop. Maddie grabbed for the pommel with white-knuckled hands, sure she would be thrown off. The cap flew off her head and over Blaine's shoulder, but she was too frightened to turn her head to look for it. When Blaine's arms tightened around her, she realized that she was leaning back against his chest with all her might. She sighed resignedly. Anything was better than falling off.

She was taken to see the various fields that had been planted in the spring, with Blaine pointing out the particularly bountiful corn crop. She met the men working in the long rows, picking off the bugs by hand and tilling the soil with heavy hoes, and the women and children tending their own plots at their homes scattered around the countryside.

Indeed, Blaine introduced her to so many people that her head began to ache, but Maddie was determined not to mention it. Better to save it as an excuse when she really needed it, she decided, and resolutely set her mind to ignore it.

"I think you've seen enough for one morning." Blaine helped Maddie into the saddle, watching her closely. "How long has your head been hurting?"

"My head isn't hurting."

"It's interesting the way your forehead wrinkles when you're lying." He swung up behind her. "We'll stop in the apple orchard to eat."

Maddie probed her forehead for the telltale wrinkle. "You brought food?"

"I didn't want you to faint again."

When they reached the apple grove, Blaine dismounted near a large old apple tree set away from the others and helped Maddie to the ground. The grove was situated on a low hill, with fields of oat and wheat on all sides. Maddie leaned against the tree trunk and watched curiously as Blaine spread a blanket, removed several wrapped bundles from the saddlebags, and knelt to open them.

"I suppose there's no reason to leave my hair pinned so tightly now that my cap is gone," she remarked. At his unconcerned grunt, Maddie began to remove the pins in her hair. "You know, there's a lot to be said for wearing pants."

"I've always thought so."

She shook her hair free, dropping her head back to massage her scalp. Her eyes focused on the sturdy limbs above her. "Why, I could even climb a tree in pants."

"I wouldn't advise it," he murmured absently. "That tree is old. The limbs may not be sturdy. We're going to take it down come fall."

"Oh, bother. It's still a good climbing tree."

Blaine began to divide the food Mrs. Small had prepared, placing half of each item on napkins of heavy, red-checked cloth. "Here's yours," he said, turning toward her.

The blanket was empty. Leaves rustled over his head.

"Blaine," Maddie cried from somewhere above him. "Look out!"

Chapter 9

~~~ ◦◦ ~~~

Blaine tilted his head back to look up into the tree just as an apple fell straight toward him. He ducked as the fruit landed a foot away, then he glared up at her, his hands on his hips. "What the hell are you doing?"

She sat on a perch high above him. "I told you to look *out*, not *up!*"

"Come down before you slip and give yourself another concussion."

"Oh, Blaine, don't be such a stick-in-the-mud. The view is beautiful from up here."

Muttering obscenities, Blaine climbed onto the lowest branch. "If you fall, everyone will blame me for buying you the blasted pants in the first place." He pulled himself up to the second branch. "Now we'll probably both fall from this old tree and break our necks."

"I'd almost forgotten what fun it is to climb a tree," he heard Amelia call merrily.

Blaine hoisted himself onto another branch and looked up. She was still one branch above him and smiling as she had when he'd seen her gazing at the peppermint candy through the glass. "The sisters let you climb trees?"

Amelia's smile dissolved as quick as butter on a hot skillet. It was becoming clear that her past was something she did not like to remember. Blaine wished now he hadn't brought it up. He climbed up beside her and gazed out at the view below.

From his vantage point he could see acres of rolling fields in all directions. A brook meandered lazily along one edge of the wheat field, dividing it from a field of oats. Farther back, Blaine could just make out the cornfield.

It *was* a beautiful view, and always had been. But it was also a bittersweet view, because everything as far as the eye could see and beyond was Jeremy's. Including the girl next to him.

"You've done all that."

The awe in her voice made Blaine turn his head to look at her. Yes, he *had* done it all. The only reason the Knight farm was profitable was because he'd poured his own blood, sweat, and tears into it.

Her soft voice cut into his thoughts. "You should be proud."

Blaine's gaze dropped to her sensuous coraltinged mouth, and from there to the inviting glimpse of creamy flesh at her throat. He wished she didn't look so damned appealing in those clinging clothes. He wished he could put his arms around her and kiss her.

Blaine clenched his jaw and forced his gaze away from her to look out at the fields. "It'll all be yours in a matter of weeks."

"I can hardly wait."

The sarcasm in her voice surprised him. Blaine

turned his head to find her climbing down. "Hold on a minute. Let me help you." He swung down and was at the bottom before her to lift her from the last branch. He set her down slowly, staring deep into her silver-green eyes, feeling the familiar heaviness in his groin.

Damn, he wanted to kiss her. To lay her down on the blanket and hold her in his arms. To bury his face in her red hair and inhale its sweet perfume. To bury himself inside her.

Blaine abruptly released her and strode to the blanket, keeping his back to her as he knelt by the food. "You'd better eat before it spoils," he said gruffly.

Maddie stared at his broad back, shaken by the feelings he aroused in her, confused by the sudden change in his mood. She sat on the blanket, picked up a chicken leg, and stared at it. She was disappointed that he hadn't kissed her. Disappointed that her fiancé's brother hadn't *wanted* to kiss her. *Dear God, what's wrong with me?*

Maddie closed her eyes and turned her head away. She was Amelia Baker, not Madeline Beecher. She could not allow any feelings but Amelia's to dictate her life. She couldn't fall in love with anyone but Jeremy.

"Is something wrong with the chicken?"

Maddie looked up at Blaine and shook her head guiltily. She bit into the leg and began to chew, the juicy, salty taste of the meat reviving her appetite. She saw Blaine turn his head to gaze out at the fields as he ate. As she watched him she saw his features relax and the tension drain from his body. She remembered how proud he had been of the fields as he showed them to her, and sudden realization washed over her. Blaine didn't want to leave the farm. He loved it.

And he resented Jeremy for inheriting it.

Blaine leaned back on one elbow and brought the piece of chicken to his mouth. "Haven't you forgotten something?" he asked.

Maddie looked around at the food spread out over the blanket. "What?"

"Grace."

"Grace?"

He turned his head to look at her. "Prayers. Didn't the sisters insist on it?"

Oh, bother, they would have insisted on a prayer before meals. "I suppose I've gotten out of the habit since I've been on my own." She started to raise the meat to her mouth once more, but he was still watching her.

"Well?" he asked.

"Well, what?"

"Now that you've been reminded, why don't you go ahead and say grace?"

Maddie stared at him blankly. How did the Catholics pray? It couldn't be too different from the way her mother had taught her, could it? She shut her eyes and folded her fingers together. "Thank you, Lord, for the food which we are about to receive." She started to unfold her fingers, then added a hasty "Amen" before delving into the cheese and bread.

"You don't cross yourself?"

"I beg your pardon?" she mumbled, her mouth full of food.

Blaine touched his forehead, chest, then each shoulder as Maddie stared at him. She resumed chewing and swallowed hard. "I don't always do that."

"You don't?"

She licked her upper lip. "Not when I'm—outdoors."

"I see."

Maddie looked around for something to wipe her hands on. She reached into her pants pocket and removed Amelia's dainty embroidered handkerchief.

"Here." Blaine handed her his cotton handkerchief. "Don't ruin your pretty handkerchief."

She met his frank gaze with a smile. "Thank you."

Her throat had healed, Blaine noted, leaving a voice which had a low velvety quality that made his insides quiver. He rose and busied himself with picking two apples from the tree. "There's something I've been meaning to ask you." He used his sleeve to polish the apples, then handed her the reddest of the two. "Who were you hiding from on the train?"

He saw her lips freeze on the apple. She pulled it away from her mouth. "Hiding?"

"Yesterday you mentioned that you were afraid of someone finding you." Blaine sat down again, took a bite, and slowly chewed, waiting for her answer.

"I'm not hiding from anyone."

He watched as she nibbled upon the apple and swallowed hard. The little wrinkle in her forehead was back. He stretched out on the blanket and folded his arms behind his head. Amelia was lying.

She followed his example and lay back on the blanket. Blaine munched his apple and stared at the wispy clouds overhead, contemplating a possible reason for her lie. Who could be looking for her? A jilted lover? A bill collector? The law? He pondered the possibilities for a few moments, then turned his head and found she'd fallen asleep.

He remembered how she had looked that morning lying on the bed, covered only by a thin sheet, one arm flung above her head, the outline of her slender body clearly revealed. Her glorious red hair had been fanned out around her, as it was now. As he watched her he felt himself harden with desire. Desire that could go nowhere.

Blaine tore his gaze away, fighting the passion raging within him. He focused once more on the feathery clouds and let his thoughts drift. He didn't like the idea of someone looking for Amelia, especially if it were a jilted lover. Amelia's life had been difficult enough. It would be best to find out who it was, so he could determine what to do about it.

Blaine rolled to a sitting position. He caught sight of the delicate handkerchief at his side and picked it up, inhaling the fragrance that clung to it. He grimaced at the heavy lavender scent, then noticed the letters AMB embroidered in one corner. What did the M stand for? Mischief?

Blaine glanced up, gauging the position of the sun in the sky. He knew they should head back, but Amelia was sleeping so peacefully that he hated to wake her. He reached out a hand, wanting to touch a silken cheek, but withdrew it again.

"If you were mine," he murmured softly, leaning over her, "I wouldn't be holding a paintbrush in my hand staring at the wreckage of a train. I'd be making love to you right here under this tree."

But she wasn't his. She was Jeremy's.

"Miss Baker," he said, gently shaking her arm. She sighed and stretched languidly, bringing on a rise of desire so fierce Blaine had to grit his teeth to fight it. Slowly, her lashes lifted and she looked at him. She was so close he could count the green flecks in the silver background of her eyes. He heard her sharp intake of breath, and then she hurriedly sat up.

"Did I fall asleep?"

"Just for a moment. Here's your handkerchief." Blaine dropped it in her lap and got to his feet. He glanced over at her as he began to pack the saddlebags. "What does the M stand for?"

"I beg your pardon?"

"The M on your handkerchief."

"Madeline," she answered instantly.

"Your mother's name?"

"Grandmother's."

"Madeline," Blaine said, trying out the name. "It suits you." He turned to look at her. "Much more than Amelia does."

Blaine led the horse back toward the blanket. Amelia was watching him, her lower lip between her teeth. He frowned. "Is something wrong?"

"Oh, no! I was just wondering something." A vivid blush stained her cheeks. She rose to her feet and stuck her hands in her pockets. "Since I'm shortly to be your sister-in-law, would you mind—" She hesitated, then licked her upper lip. "Would you mind calling me Maddie instead of Amelia? My friends called me Maddie; I much prefer it to Amelia. The sisters used Amelia."

Blaine stopped before her and studied her anxious features. "No, I don't mind. That's fine with me." He picked her up by the waist, lifted her to the horse's back, and swung up behind her.

"All right, Maddie. Are you ready to gallop?" At

her happy nod, he took the reins, clicked his tongue, and pressed the horse's flanks with his boots. The old horse took off at hard run. Blaine held Maddie securely against him, thinking about her request. *Maddie*. He didn't mind that at all. In fact, he liked it very much. He wondered if Jeremy knew she preferred it.

Jeremy. Blaine suddenly realized he was holding Maddie much too tightly and immediately loosened his arms. *She was Jeremy's.* It was becoming harder and harder to remember it.

The buggy was back in its stall when Blaine took the horse to the barn. He wondered if Jeremy had noticed how long his fiancée had been gone. Guiltily, he sought Jeremy out in the attic.

"How did it go? Was there enough of a wreck left to paint?"

Jeremy was seated at a small drafting table, busily working on sketches. "What's that? Oh, it's you, Blaine. It didn't g-go well. I can't paint it; it's too tragic. It's a m-miracle Amelia even survived."

"What are you working on?"

"I'm trying out some ideas. I'm g-going to paint Amelia's portrait, but I haven't decided the kind of background that would suit her."

Blaine looked over his brother's shoulder at the charcoal sketches. "Did she ever mention to you that she prefers to be called Maddie?"

Jeremy looked around, a puzzled expression on his sunburned face. "Maddie?"

"It's short for Madeline, her middle name."

Jeremy smiled. "Her middle name is Margaret. She was named after her mother. You must have misunderstood her. Maybe she said Maggie."

Blaine scowled at the sketches. "Are you sure her middle name is Margaret?"

"Not one hundred percent, but I can check. Her l-letters are in the rolltop desk." He bent his head over his drawings. "It doesn't matter. She'll always be Amelia to me."

Blaine pondered the matter as he returned downstairs. He was certain Amelia had said Maddie. He distinctly remembered her saying she was named Madeline after her grandmother. But even if she had said Maggie rather than Maddie, why hadn't she ever mentioned it to Jeremy? Why wouldn't she have wanted her intended to call her by the name she was used to, rather than one she obviously disliked?

Something wasn't right about the whole situation. He was beginning to think he should take a look at her letters himself.

The hall clock chimed three as Blaine passed it. He had three hours before supper. Plenty of time to ride out to Sam Hackett's place and back. He imagined Maddie's—or Maggie's—reaction when she saw what he planned to buy her, and he grinned.

"Oh, Blaine, wait a moment, please."

Blaine stopped and turned. His mother came toward him, a calendar in her hand.

"I think we should have a social evening to welcome Amelia to Marshall County. Do you think two weeks from Saturday would be too soon?"

"Will that give Mrs. MacLeod and Mrs. Small enough time to prepare?"

"I'm sure it will. But that wasn't exactly what I meant."

"What did you mean?"

"Amelia is a lovely girl, but her manners are a bit

rough around the edges. The preacher is due in next week for her religious instruction. I was thinking perhaps I would give her some help in the social graces at the same time. Do you think she would be offended if I suggested it?"

"Not if you were tactful about it."

Evelyn smiled. "Oh, I can be very tactful." She sailed blithely up the hallway. "If anyone needs me, I'll be in the study making out the guest list."

Blaine shook his head and continued down the hall to the back door, trying to imagine his mother explaining to Maddie/Maggie—dammit, he was sure she'd said Maddie—that she lacked social skills. As he passed the kitchen, he heard Maddie's voice and stopped just outside the door to listen. She was talking to Mrs. MacLeod, but he couldn't make out her words. At the housekeeper's deep belly laugh, he stepped into the room to investigate.

The curtain was pulled across the doorway of the pantry. Beneath the hem of the red-checked material he saw Mrs. MacLeod's sensible brown shoes walk past. He heard the sound of water splashing and realized Maddie was taking a bath. The curtain was closed only when the galvanized tub was in use.

He decided to have some fun with Maddie.

"Mrs. MacLeod," he called, and grinned when he heard two startled gasps.

The housekeeper hurried through the curtain, then pulled it tightly closed behind her as she stood before him. "Can I fetch ye somethin', Mr. Blaine?"

He advanced toward her. "I have a sudden hankering for watermelon pickles. Are there any left in the pantry?"

He thoroughly enjoyed the shriek of terror that

came from behind the curtain. Mrs. MacLeod braced her hands against his chest. "You know we ran out of watermelon pickles last month, Mr. Blaine."

He winked down at her. "They may be on a high shelf where you can't see them. I'll just take a look myself."

"Blaine Knight," Maddie called angrily, "if you come in here, I'll drown you. I swear I will!"

Blaine jumped back as something hit the curtain from Maddie's side and slid to the floor. A bar of Ivory soap skittered out, spun around, and came to a stop in a sudsy puddle in front of the pantry.

At that moment Blaine heard footsteps in the hall and swung around just as Jeremy rounded the corner, muttering to himself in his usual absentminded way. Before Blaine or Mrs. MacLeod had time to warn him, he stepped squarely on the soap. His foot slid forward and his arms windmilled the air. In desperation he grasped the curtain and fell, pulling the red material down with him, rod and all.

Blaine caught a glimpse of Maddie's startled face just before half the curtain dropped on top of her. As Mrs. MacLeod scurried toward the tub, and Maddie spluttered and fought to get out from beneath the sodden material, Blaine began to laugh.

"Blaine Knight, I'll get even with you if it's the last thing I ever do!" Maddie cried.

"But I didn't do anything!" Blaine protested as he helped Jeremy to his feet. "Come on, Jer, let's leave before I get blamed for something else."

Still laughing, Blaine strode out to the barn. Damn, it felt good to laugh again.

Chapter 10

Maddie turned in a full circle before the tall cheval glass, glancing over her shoulder to see the back of her new outfit. It had been sitting on the slipper chair when she returned from her bath, put there, no doubt, by Mrs. MacLeod. There was even a pair of bloomers to go with it.

The outfit was a two-piece dress in a soft mint green calico. It was a plain country dress with a back-buttoned bodice and a simple bell-shaped skirt, its only decorations being deep ruffled caps of white crocheted lace at the shoulders of the wide leg-of-mutton sleeves and another width of lace running across the bosom. Country people apparently had no use for the many embellishments city ladies found so necessary in their toilettes.

Still, she thought, lifting the hem to admire the lace-edged bloomers, the dress was becoming. The mint green seemed to bring out the green in her eyes and make her fair skin glow. And the cut of the dress emphasized her narrow waist and slender neck. She couldn't wait to see Blaine's face when she wore it in to dinner.

Maddie sat down heavily on the bed. *Not Blaine's face. Jeremy's face. She was marrying Jeremy.* She rose impatiently and went to the bureau to put up her hair. She had to stop thinking about Blaine.

But the mother-of-pearl combs she tucked in the back of the chignon only reminded her of their trip to the store and of the peppermint stick he had secretly bought her. And then she remembered the surprised look on his face when the apple nearly hit him. She giggled.

Blaine had come right up to get her, too, and had lifted her down so she wouldn't fall. She sighed, recalling the look in his dark eyes as he'd leaned over her on the blanket. If he had kissed her she wouldn't have minded a bit. She was surprised she'd ever been frightened of him. Now she was frightened only of her growing feelings for him.

If only she felt for Jeremy what she felt for Blaine.

"Miss Amelia, I've brought more material for ye," Mrs. MacLeod called out.

Maddie heaved a wistful sigh. "Come in, Mrs. MacLeod."

"What's this, then? A sad face? And in such a bonny dress, too. Turn around and let me see. There's the girl. My, and what a sight ye are, lass. Mr. Jeremy's eyes will pop clear out of his head and into his soup. Ah, there's the smile. Look what Mr. Blaine ordered. A fair selection, wouldn't ye say? Come, let's pick out the best of the lot."

Maddie impulsively threw her arms around the housekeeper's neck and hugged her.

"What's this now, lass?" the woman asked, her voice husky with emotion.

"I just wanted to hug you."

The housekeeper clasped her tightly to her

bosom, patted her on the back twice, and turned to the material, swiping at her eyes with the back of her hand. "Will ye look at this apricot color? Just the shade to go with your hair. Oh, and look at this robin's egg blue."

By suppertime Maddie's spirits had lifted. She had selected material for eight toilettes, as well as two gowns for special occasions and a split skirt for riding. For the first time in her life, she was going to have a wardrobe. She stopped in the hall outside the dining room and wiggled to adjust the top of her stays. After wearing boys' clothing all day her corset felt uncomfortably stiff, but there was nothing she could do about that.

This time when she entered there were no shocked faces, and she was pleased to see the frank admiration in Blaine's dark eyes. Both men rose gallantly, making her feel like the lady her mother had always wanted her to be.

"Good evening," she said in a suddenly shy voice.

Jeremy pulled out a chair at his side, his face bright pink. His mother smiled at her from the head of the table. "Your dress is lovely, Amelia. What a marvelous color for you."

"Thank you." She cast a quick glance at Blaine and found his gaze on her hair, and she knew he was looking at the combs she had used to secure her chignon.

"We're ready, Sophie," Evelyn said to the servant standing at her elbow. The girl hurried to the kitchen and came out with a tray laden with soup bowls, followed by another servant with bread, freshly churned butter, and pitchers of milk.

Evelyn dipped her spoon in her bowl. "Amelia,

I've planned a social evening here in two weeks. We thought it would be best to introduce you to Jeremy's neighbors before the wedding."

Maddie stared at her, stunned, touched by their kindness. A party in her honor.

"I'm sure you would like to make friends with some of the other young wives your age. Jeremy told us how often you'd commented in your letters that you missed having friends."

Tears prickled the backs of her eyelids. The party was not in her honor. It was in Amelia's honor. For the girl they thought she was: a warm, sweet, lonely orphan girl raised by nuns. A girl who would never deceive people who treated her with such kindness.

"What's the matter, dear?" Evelyn asked in alarm. "You don't look at all happy about it."

Maddie blinked back tears. "Oh, no, I'm—I'm grateful, Mrs. Knight. It's just that I—" She glanced around at the three faces watching her expectantly and she burst into tears. She was appalled. She'd never resorted to tears in her life. She pushed back her chair and dashed from the room, holding her hands over her face.

Blaine and Jeremy jumped to their feet at the same time. Swearing silently, Blaine checked himself and sat down while Jeremy went to find her. Maddie wasn't his responsibility.

He heard Jeremy's footsteps overhead and his fingers closed around the arms of his chair, his knuckles turning white. What did Jeremy know about his fiancée? Did he know she liked shiny red peppermint sticks? Did he know her shoe size or her chemise size? Had he ever seen her sigh in her sleep or call out fearfully from a bad dream? Hell, Jeremy hadn't even known that Amelia didn't like her name! All Jeremy knew about his fiancée was what was in the letters.

It was almost as if Jeremy had fallen in love with the letters themselves, and now that the genuine article had arrived, he couldn't equate the two.

At a timid knock, Maddie wiped her eyes and rose from the bed to open the door. Jeremy stood in the open doorway, his hands stuffed in his pockets, looking perplexed and unhappy.

"Amelia?" he said hesitatingly.

Maddie gave him a wavering smile. "I'm all right, Jeremy. You didn't need to interrupt your dinner to come up here."

"I w-wanted to s-see if I could help."

"That was very sweet of you, Jeremy."

He turned a deep, unflattering shade of red. "If you're uncomfortable m-meeting the n-neighbors, we don't have to have a s-social."

Maddie shook her head. "It's not that. It's just that everyone has treated me with such warmth and kindness that sometimes it overwhelms me."

"W-what would you like us to do about the s-social?"

"Whatever you've planned will be fine."

Jeremy's shoulders relaxed and he looked visibly relieved. "I'll g-go down and tell M-mother."

"Jeremy."

He glanced at her sidelong. "Yes, Amelia?"

"Do you think you could take a walk with me after supper?"

He nodded. "I w-wanted to confer with you anyway about your p-portrait. Shall I wait while you fr-freshen your face?"

"No, you go on and finish your dinner. I don't have much of an appetite."

"Your h-head isn't hurting, is it?"

"No, my head hasn't hurt all day."

He looked at her as if he wanted to say more, but couldn't find the words. He shrugged instead. "I'll c-come for you in an hour."

After he'd gone, Maddie went to the window. Deceiving the Knights was the most difficult thing she'd ever done. She was behaving just as her father would have, duping innocent people. She hated herself for it.

But if she wanted to live, she had no alternative.

Blaine prowled the downstairs hallways, alternately rubbing the back of his neck and stopping to glance out the nearest window as he waited for Jeremy and Maddie to leave the house. He had to get into Jeremy's desk and find Amelia's letters. He was determined to discover what was in those damn things.

Blaine heard the sound of Maddie's voice, and stood out of sight beside the study window until he saw her and Jeremy walk down the drive together. Then he casually climbed the stairs to the attic and slipped into Jeremy's workroom. He searched the rolltop desk and found the bundled letters in a cubbyhole. Shoving them beneath his shirt, he slipped out again and went to the privacy of his own room to read them.

The letters were arranged in chronological order, enabling Blaine to follow the blooming relationship between Amelia and his brother. The earliest were very businesslike and concerned the paintings which Josephine Harrington had ordered for her art show. After that the letters became slightly more personal as the two exchanged interesting bits of news and opinions on topics of current events.

Amelia's viewpoints came across as sweetly naive and extremely conservative in the letters, in keeping with someone raised in a convent. It seemed at odds with the girl Blaine was beginning to know. He wondered if Jeremy felt it, too.

In one letter she described herself for Jeremy as a plain girl with reddish-brown hair and green eyes. Blaine looked up, puzzled. He could understand Maddie viewing herself as plain. In the sisters' eyes, vanity would have been a sin. And she did have green in her eyes, although she also had an equal mixture of silvery gray. But reddish hair? Her hair was a deep, rich cinnamon red. Reddish would be an understatement.

He skimmed through the rest of the letter and put it down on the growing pile at his elbow. He was looking for information about someone whom she might have feared, someone who might be looking for her still. What he found was something totally unexpected.

I had the most dreadful experience this afternoon, Amelia wrote in one letter. *Mrs. H. sent me to her lady friend's house across the river to deliver an important letter. She bade me use her driver and the landau, whose top had been put down to better catch the evening breeze, and what do you suppose happened? We were stuck in a traffic snarl* on the bridge! *Do you know I nearly swooned, having a most awful fear of heights?*

Blaine stared at the paragraph for a long moment, remembering Maddie's scramble up the apple tree. *"Oh, Blaine, don't be such a stick-in-the-mud. The view is beautiful from up here!"* There hadn't been an ounce of fear in her. Had she made up the story about her fear of heights to elicit sympathy from his brother? Had she thought it a way into Jeremy's heart?

He frowned as he refolded the letter. Fear of heights didn't fit with the girl who'd sat on a high branch happily dangling her legs as she gazed out over the fields. He glanced at the clock on his bureau, surprised to see an hour had passed, and quickly tied the letters together with the string.

From Jeremy's attic window, Blaine looked down to the front of the house and saw the two strolling up the lane, Maddie's hand hooked through his brother's arm. A surge of jealousy coursed through him, causing his fists to clench at his side.

Blaine swung away from the window and looked around the attic room at the stacks of canvases leaning against the walls. What had Jeremy ever done to deserve Maddie? What had Jeremy ever done to deserve the farm? What had Jeremy ever done besides paint? He grabbed a bottle of ink on the desk and curled his fingers tightly around it. He wanted to hurl it at the easel. He wanted to destroy the beautiful painting sitting there!

Then Blaine's shoulders sagged, and he set the bottle on the desk. He could never hurt his brother, not after a lifetime of protecting him. It wasn't Jeremy's fault he'd inherited his father's estate. Jeremy hadn't asked for it; it was his by rights. And the sooner Blaine left Marshall County for good, the sooner he could forget it.

Maddie retired early that evening, then lay in her feather bed with her hands folded on her stomach and her eyes scrunched shut, willing herself to sleep. Her conscience bothered her. Her walk with Jeremy had not eased it.

Jeremy, she was learning, was as straightforward and as innocent as his letters had been. He was an idealist and rarely saw the bad in anything. He probably would understand if she told him the terrible thing she'd done. He also probably wouldn't marry her.

Maddie sighed, wishing, as she had so many times, that she could go back to the night of the dinner party and change the events that had led to her frantic escape, and thus to her deception. If only she hadn't been so curious. If only she'd gone straight to the police with her information.

She scowled and turned on her side, staring into the darkness. The police would never take the word of Fast Freddy's daughter over an upstanding, wealthy political boss like Vincent Slade. If anyone were to believe her story, she would first have to find the letter Crandall had used to blackmail Slade and the two thousand dollars Slade had paid him to keep quiet. But they were hidden in a barn on Crandalls' parents' farm west of Philadelphia, and she didn't dare return to look for it.

Maddie closed her eyes tightly as the events of that night replayed themselves in her mind. She heard Crandall's screams of agony as Slade and one of his men slowly tortured him, and she felt his pain as if it were happening to her. She began to shake, remembering the sinister sound of Slade's voice.

"Did you tell anyone else about your blackmail scheme?"

And then she had heard Crandall's voice whisper the answer that would incriminate her, that would condemn her to death. *"I—told—the girl."*

"What girl?"

"S-servant—girl."

"One of my servants knows?"

"Yes."

"She knows where this evidence is that you claim to have?"

"Yes."

"What's the girl's name?"

"Don't—know."

"Damn it, Crandall, where is the evidence? Where did you hide it?"

There had been another long, agonized scream. And then Crandall's voice, weaker than before. *"Parents'—farm."*

"Where on your parents' farm? Where, damn you!"

There had been no reply, only Slade's sound of disgust. Maddie had known then that Crandall was dead. And that Vincent Slade would interrogate each servant in the house until he had discovered who Crandall had told.

Maddie's stomach twisted in fear and her heart began to pound just as it had that night in her hiding place deep in the bowels of the house. She sat up, driving herself back against the headboard, drawing her knees up and wrapping her arms around them as she rocked herself back and forth, sobbing hysterically. Vincent Slade was going to find her. She was going to suffer as Crandall had suffered, painfully, horribly, until she died.

"Miss Amelia, I knocked twice but ye didn't hear me . . . Ach, lass, what is it?" Mrs. MacLeod hurried across the room and set the oil lamp and a glass of milk on the bedside table. She wrapped her sturdy arms around Maddie and held her to her bosom, crooning softly in her ear. "There now, lass. Nairne

MacLeod's here now. Hush now, lass. It can't be all that bad. Hush now."

Maddie sobbed harder, unable to speak of the cause of her terror. She clung to the housekeeper's neck as if it were her lifeline.

Blaine walked silently through the darkened house and up the stairs. He'd ridden hard all evening trying to outrun his jealousy. Now he just wanted to fall into his bed and sleep a dreamless sleep.

At the top of the stairs he heard a woman sobbing and started down the hallway, knowing it was Maddie. His gut twisted at the heart-wrenching sound. He stopped just outside the open door and listened as Mrs. MacLeod talked to her, calming her down. "Can ye tell me what frightened ye so, lass?"

Blaine strained to hear the hoarse reply.

"I can't."

"Was it naught but a nightmare then?"

"Yes."

"Drink some of the honeyed milk I brought ye. It'll help put ye straight off to sleep."

"I don't want to sleep. I'm afraid to go to sleep."

"Nothin' will harm ye here in this house, lass, God willin'. Drink up now. Every drop. There's my girl. Would ye like me to sit with ye tonight, lass?"

Maddie's voice was desolate, resigned. "No, you need your rest. I'll be all right soon. I'll read until I feel sleepy."

"Are ye sure? Won't be the first time I've sat up with a young one, ye know."

"Do you have children of your own, Mrs. MacLeod?" Maddie asked in a little girl's voice.

"That I do, all grown now, of course, but I was

also referrin' to Mr. Blaine and Mr. Jeremy."

Blaine heard a shaky sigh, and then Maddie said softly, "They're very good men, aren't they?"

"As decent and honorable as any man I've ever met."

There was a long silence, and then Maddie's voice again. "They don't tolerate dishonesty, do they?"

"Not at all, lass. Not at all."

Blaine heard Maddie yawn, heard the covers rustle, heard her sleepy voice. "Mrs. MacLeod, would you do me a favor?"

"Anythin', lass."

"Would you call me Maddie?"

"Maddie, is it? Wherever did ye get that name?"

"From my grandmother. Madeline is my middle name. My friends called me Maddie."

Blaine's fists tightened. It *was* Madeline. Jeremy had been wrong.

Or Maddie was lying.

"Have you told Mr. Jeremy this?" Mrs. MacLeod asked.

Maddie's voice grew quiet, melancholy. "I don't think he'd like Maddie. I think he'd prefer Amelia."

Blaine frowned in the darkened hallway. It had almost sounded as if Maddie were talking about herself, and not her name.

Chapter 11

Vincent Slade slid a five-dollar bill through the opening in the cage and repeated the story to the Chicago clerk that he had used two days before.

The young man behind the window eyed the money as if it were an insult. "I'll check on that for you." He turned around to look at a log attached to the wall behind him, removed one of the papers, and brought it back to the window. "The train derailed in central Indiana. The official death toll was one hundred forty-one."

"Is that the list of the dead?" Slade asked, nodding his head at the paper in the man's hand.

"These are the survivors."

"May I take a look at it?"

The clerk handed it through the opening. Slade pulled a pair of wire-rimmed spectacles from his coat pocket and put them on, his gaze moving rapidly down the list of names. "Adamson, Andover, Aswell, Baker, Banbury, *Christenson*." He swung around to show Bull, stabbing the list with his index finger. "Madeline Beecher isn't on here."

Bull cleaned his dirty thumbnail with his pocketknife. "I guess that finishes it then, doesn't it, boss?"

Slade turned back to the clerk. "Where did they take the bodies?"

"Most were buried in a local cemetery."

"And the survivors came through here?"

"That's right."

"Were you on duty at this window the night that train came in?"

"That would have been Frank Pomeroy."

"And where is this Mr. Pomeroy?"

The clerk checked his pocket watch. "He's due in at four o'clock this afternoon."

"Thank you very much, sir."

"What are you thinkin' now, boss?" Bull asked in a quiet voice as they proceeded through the train depot. "The girl is dead."

"The girl is also Fast Freddy's daughter, Bull. I've got to be sure she didn't slip through somehow and take a train out of Chicago."

"What are we gonna do?"

"Talk to Frank Pomeroy. If Madeline Beecher came through this depot, he'll remember her."

Maddie awoke as soon as the roosters began crowing. With a groan, she flung back the light sheet she had used to cover herself and slowly sat up. Her eyes felt heavy and swollen from crying, and had she not feared Blaine would chide her for sleeping in, she would have crawled back under the covers and slept until noon.

Another dress had been finished for her and now lay draped across the slipper chair. It was a pink-checked day dress with a white collar and cuffs that came down only as far as the elbows, a perfect outfit for a warm August day. But she found little joy in her new clothing this morning. She dressed mechanically and plodded down the stairs and into the dining room, where she found only Blaine and his mother eating.

"Good morning, dear," Evelyn called in her usual cheerful voice. Maddie found herself wondering if the woman ever had a glum moment. She had never seen Blaine's mother with anything but a smile on her face.

"Good morning," she replied in a subdued voice. She walked to the long marble-topped sideboard to help herself to the food there. She took her customary seat next to Jeremy's chair and spread her linen napkin on her lap before meeting Blaine's questioning gaze.

"Didn't sleep well?" he asked, a look of genuine concern on his face.

Maddie looked away. "I think I dreamed about the train wreck."

Evelyn clucked sympathetically. "You poor dear. Well, there's nothing to do but put that tragic event out of your thoughts. Blaine, we must do something to help her forget."

Blaine leaned back and folded his arms across his chest. "Such as?"

"Oh, you'll think of something, dear. You always do." Evelyn frowned thoughtfully, then looked up with a smile. "Blaine, do you remember the time Jeremy had the mumps and you tried to cheer him up by walking past his window on stilts and making faces at him?"

Blaine winced. "How could I forget?"

Evelyn smiled at Maddie. "Blaine fell in the rosebushes. It took Mrs. MacLeod hours to pull the thorns from his—"

"Mother," Blaine quickly interjected, "spare me a little dignity."

"Oh, nonsense, Blaine. I was only going to say she pulled them from your backside."

Blaine dropped his head to his hands as Maddie giggled. "Thorns? That must have hurt terribly."

Blaine gave her a scowl. "You don't have to look so pleased about it."

"When the doctor came to check on Jeremy," Evelyn concluded, "he thought Blaine had the measles. We had the hardest time convincing him the red bumps were thorn pricks."

Maddie laughed. "I wish I could have seen you fall in the bushes."

Blaine lifted a dark eyebrow. "I suppose you've never done anything so foolhardy."

Maddie gave him an impish grin in return. "I did climb out my bedroom window once. I tried to jump to the tree next to the hou—uh—convent, but the branch broke and I fell to the ground. It knocked the wind clear out of me."

Blaine toyed with his fork. "Is that when your fear of heights started?"

"Fear of heights?" Maddie gave him a puzzled look. "I don't—" At Blaine's sudden alertness, she hesitated. *Oh, bother, did Amelia have a fear of heights?* "—remember. It's possible, I suppose."

His gaze was intense, probing, belying the casualness of his voice. "By the way you climbed the apple tree yesterday, it appears you've outgrown it."

"Yes, I suppose I have." Maddie began to eat, hoping it would put an end to the questions.

Blaine wiped his mouth and tossed the napkin on the table. "Are you ready for your next lesson?" For his mother's benefit he added, "Amelia is learning about the farm."

Evelyn's face lit up and she turned to Maddie with a smile. "Oh, that's wonderful, dear! I'm so happy you're showing an interest in it. And Blaine is the perfect person to teach you. Jeremy needs a capable wife to help him, you know. He has no head for figures and such."

Maddie scratched her nose. There was that word again. Capable. She was damn sick of it.

Blaine scraped back his chair and glanced at Maddie. "I'll be out by the barn. Come out when you're done. And wear your riding outfit."

Maddie narrowed her eyes at him. "I'm not going to have to ride that big farm horse again, am I?"

Blaine lifted an eyebrow. "How else do you expect to learn how to ride?"

"Bother! Why can't I just learn how to handle the buggy?"

"In an emergency, you'll need to know how to ride. Fast." Blaine glanced at Evelyn. "Isn't that right, Mother?" He winked at her and left.

Evelyn reached over and patted Maddie's hand. "It is true, dear. Even I learned how to ride, although you'll never catch me at it. But pay no attention to Blaine's gruff manner. He always was obstinate—nothing like our Jeremy. Jeremy was the sweetest, most obedient child there ever was. But I suppose that's to be expected. Blaine is so like his father, my first husband."

Maddie scooted her chair in closer. "May I ask what happened to your first husband, Mrs. Knight?"

"Of course you may, dear," she replied with a kind smile. Her gaze shifted to Maddie's left, toward the window. "He was killed in the war—the battle of Gettysburg. We had married just two months before he enlisted. Blaine was born nine months later. The poor boy never knew his father." She sighed, her eyes misting. Even in her sadness, she smiled.

"Such a dashing man, Blaine's father was. Tall, dark-haired, with magnificent eyes. How I loved that man. I would have done anything for him." Evelyn stopped to dab her napkin beneath her eyes. "I had always thought we would grow old together—" Her voice broke. Maddie looked down, unable to bear the pain in her eyes.

"He died a hero," Evelyn finished in a whisper. She blinked to clear her vision, then picked up her teacup and took a sip. After a moment, she continued. "When Blaine left home to fight in the Indian Wars I thought I'd lose my mind. It was just like the first time all over again. Thank heavens he made it safely back, and decorated as a hero, too, just like his father."

Maddie propped her elbow on the table and leaned her chin on her hand, hungry for any information about Blaine. "Where did he fight?"

"South Dakota. He was a second lieutenant. He fought the Sioux at Wounded Knee. He'd still be in the army if we hadn't called him home."

"You called him home?" No wonder Blaine was eager to teach her everything, Maddie thought. He couldn't wait to get back to soldiering.

"Yes. You see, Jeremy's father passed on suddenly and it threw us into a turmoil. Jeremy, the poor dear, hadn't taken much interest in the day-to-day running of a farm, and all I'd ever dealt with were the household matters. Oh, I know I should have insisted that Jeremy learn so that when the time came he'd be able to step into his father's shoes, but Blaine had always been there, you see, and for him it seemed to come so naturally. So I didn't worry about it." Evelyn sighed unhappily. "I suppose we all thought Blaine would stay here forever."

"If Jeremy would rather paint than farm, then why did his father leave the farm to him instead of to Blaine?"

Evelyn looked flustered. "Why, because the farm rightfully belongs to Jeremy, as his father's only heir. Besides, farming is a man's life work. Painting is merely a—" She fluttered her hand in the air. "—a hobby. It should never be taken so seriously that it causes—well, it should never be taken seriously, that's all. Jeremy's duty is to run the farm, as his father did." She looked down at her hands on her lap and shook her head, as though having a private dialogue with herself. With a resigned sigh she said, "I can't take Blaine's dream away from him, either. Jeremy will just have to learn to manage the farm on his own." She glanced up and gave Maddie an embarrassed smile. "I mean with your help, dear, of course."

"Did Mr. Knight adopt Blaine?" Maddie asked, trying to turn the subject back to the one she was most curious about.

Evelyn nodded, a thoughtful look on her face. "Blaine was four when I married again. Mr. Knight was kind enough to suggest he adopt the boy to make it easier for us. He never did treat him as his own, though. I suppose that's only natural since Blaine wasn't his own blood."

Maddie suddenly remembered that Jeremy hadn't come down for breakfast. She blushed guiltily and looked down at her plate. She had forgotten him the moment she'd walked into the room and seen Blaine. "Where is Jeremy this morning?"

"Probably still in the attic, though it's time he was outside doing his chores. He gets so caught up in his painting that he forgets where his first responsibility lies. I'll have to send one of the girls to fetch him. I believe he's working on ideas for the background of your portrait."

Maddie sighed heavily. She didn't want Jeremy to paint her, but she couldn't think of a reasonable excuse for him not to.

Evelyn fidgeted with her napkin. "There's something I need to talk to you about, dear." At her hesitant manner, Maddie tensed, fearing she had made another slip.

"Reverend Williams will be by here in a few days to begin your religious instruction. I thought perhaps you'd also like some instruction in—well, dancing, that sort of thing—before the social. Jeremy said you'd never learned to dance."

Maddie started to protest, but caught herself in time. Her mother had taught her to dance when she was thirteen—not that she remembered much of it, for she'd never had occasion to use it. But of course she couldn't admit that to Evelyn. She smiled graciously. "That would be very kind of you."

"It's very kind of you to agree to convert to Methodism, Amelia. Catholics are still looked on with some degree of hostility in this part of the country."

"That's no bother at all," Maddie assured her.

"I'm glad to leave it behind." She quickly excused herself to go change into her riding clothes, wanting to avoid further discussion on the subject.

Maddie felt sinfully wicked as she removed the stiff corset and slipped into the soft shirt and comfortable pants. She almost regretted that one day soon she would actually have a proper riding skirt. Anything deemed proper just had to be uncomfortable. She finished buttoning the shirt and smoothed the sleeves with a satisfied sigh. If she didn't have to sit on the wide back of that big, contrary farm horse, she might actually enjoy herself.

She thought of stopping to visit Jeremy, but then decided he'd probably be on his way outside as well, so she headed straight downstairs. She walked past the kitchen and smiled in at Mrs. Small, who was already preparing the stew and biscuits for lunch. She pushed the back door open and let it swing shut like Blaine did, then tucked her hands in her pockets and sauntered across the hard-packed ground toward the barn, stopping to pluck a mint leaf on her way.

She saw Zeb repairing the top rail of a fence outside the barn and stopped to speak to him. "Have you seen Blaine?"

He jerked his head toward the big double doors. "Last I saw he was in the barn."

Maddie opened one of the doors partway and slipped inside, letting her eyes adjust to the dim light. It was cool inside the barn and it smelled of hay and animals. Farm tools lined the walls on either side of the double doors and sacks of grain stood beneath them on the straw that covered the floor. Maddie remembered suddenly that Crandall's evidence was hidden in a barn. She looked around curiously, wondering where a logical hiding place would be.

"Over here," she heard Blaine call. She spotted his dark head and broad shoulders above the first stall.

"What are you doing?" she asked.

"Come see."

Maddie stood in the doorway and watched Blaine brush the smooth back of a tall, powerfully built chestnut gelding. "I've never seen that horse before. Is he yours?"

"I bought him yesterday." Blaine grinned as he worked the brush over the animal's sleek flank. "I haven't had a horse since I left the army. I decided I'd better get one if I wanted to keep up with you." He looked around at her.

Maddie laughed dryly. "I doubt you'll have a problem keeping up with me."

"I wouldn't be so sure." With a mischievous grin, Blaine ushered her to the next stall and opened the door. Maddie stared in dismay at the small charcoal-and-white horse inside.

He had bought her a horse, too.

Remorse stabbed at her. The Knights had given her so much, and what had she given them? Lies. "You didn't need to do this. I could have managed with the farm horse."

"The farm horse was too wide for you. This one is just your size." Blaine watched her expectantly and she knew he was waiting for some display of happiness, but all she felt was guilt.

"Does that scowl mean you don't like her?"

Maddie ran her hand over the spotted coat and stroked the coarse black mane. "She's beautiful, but surely she cost too much."

"Cost isn't a concern. You're better off learning on a horse you can handle easily. This one is three years old, smart and very gentle."

"But Jeremy doesn't even have his own horse."

"Jeremy has never liked to ride and my mother prefers a buggy."

"But—"

"Maddie." Blaine cupped her chin. His penetrating gaze searched her face. "Don't you want the horse?"

"It's not that." She lowered her gaze so he wouldn't see the shame. "I'm not accustomed to so much kindness, is all."

"It's not a kindness. You're a part of this family now. You're entitled to your own horse."

Maddie's throat tightened in anguish. She was entitled to nothing. She wasn't Amelia. She was Madeline Beecher, the deceitful daughter of a scoundrel. "I didn't mean to sound ungrateful. I truly am grateful—for everything. More grateful than you'll ever know."

"I understand." Blaine's palm moved from her chin to the side of her face. His touch was gentle, reassuring. She closed her eyes and leaned into his hand, savoring the feel of his rough fingers against her skin, wishing with all her heart that she could be liked as herself instead of as the girl they thought she was.

"Maddie." The husky plea in his voice brought her head up. He moved closer to her. His fingers tensed on her jaw. His eyes burned with some inner secret that made her heart thump heavily. She stared up at him wordlessly, waiting.

But before he could say anything more, the barn door swung open and Zeb stepped inside. Blaine pulled his hand away and stepped back, distancing himself from her.

What had he meant to say?

Maddie watched, puzzled, as he removed a small leather saddle from a peg.

"Do you know how to saddle a horse?" He stopped in front of her, holding the saddle between them. His voice was gruff now and abrupt. She searched his dark gaze, but it revealed no clues to his previous thoughts.

"I didn't know how to ride a horse until yesterday. What on earth makes you think I can saddle one?"

"I thought perhaps when you weren't falling out of trees someone at the convent might have taught you." His mouth quirked at one corner. He handed her the heavy saddle. "Lesson five: how to saddle a horse."

Blaine watched Maddie canter the horse around the paddock next to the barn. Her long red hair had been tied low at the nape with a black hair ribbon, but a few stray wisps had come loose and now blew about her face. Her smile was one of childlike delight.

"Look!" she called happily. "She even responds to my commands!"

Her eyes were still slightly swollen from crying. Blaine remembered the pitiful sound of Maddie's heart-wrenching sobs and wondered how long into the night she had lain awake. Several times he'd been ready to steal down the hallway to check on her, but each time he had talked himself out of it. He knew better than to try to comfort her. Once she was in his arms, he wouldn't be able to stop until he'd made her his.

A shudder rippled through him as he wondered what she would have done. Surely it would have troubled her, and he had no wish to cause her more anguish.

Somehow he had to get a hold of Jeremy's letters again. Finding the source of Maddie's fear was becoming an obsession. He was sure it was the reason for her lies. And Blaine was certain now she was lying.

The question he could not answer was why she would have made up the story about the bridge at all. Had she concocted the easily frightened, friendless, plain-featured Amelia for Jeremy's benefit, believing he'd never fall in love with a free-spirited, headstrong nymph nicknamed Maddie?

Had she even grown up in an orphanage?

He was beginning to doubt that, as well. He'd fought side by side with men of all faiths, and had never heard such a ridiculous excuse as the one she'd told of crossing herself only when she was indoors. He'd had a hard time keeping a straight face at that story.

There was one sure way to find out: to ask the sisters who raised her. He knew they had been invited to visit, but if they came after the wedding, it might be too late. He had to make sure they visited *before* the wedding—just in case.

He almost felt guilty about checking into her background. But if Maddie had invented her elaborate stories because of her fear of this unknown man, then Blaine wanted to know his identity in order to protect her. If, on the other hand, it was simply to fool Jeremy . . .

Blaine cursed under his breath as he swung up on his horse. What would he do in that case? Tell his brother his intended was a phony and run the risk of Jeremy calling off the wedding? Or would he keep the information to himself so he could leave the farm?

What would he do?

Chapter 12

~~~~~OO~~~~~

Blaine spent the rest of the morning taking Maddie around to see the outbuildings, explaining the proper use and care of the smokehouse, the root cellar, the icehouse, and the grain silo, and even taking her inside the chicken coop to show her how to hunt for eggs.

She learned rapidly and with surprising eagerness. She had a knack of soaking up information and putting it right to use. But by lunchtime Blaine could tell she was tiring, no doubt due to her sleepless night. "Why don't you go on back to the house and I'll rub down your mare?"

Maddie shot him a wary glance. "Aren't I going to have to learn how to do that as well?"

"I'll let you off the hook today. You might want to go put your feet up until we eat. You look like you're ready to fall asleep."

He saw that stubborn lift of her chin and knew his suggestion was worthless. "I'm perfectly fine. Show me what I have to do."

Blaine shook his head. "All right, Miss Baker. Lesson six coming up."

129

* * *

Blaine heard the dinner bell ring and walked to the little mare's stall to wait for Maddie to finish. "What are you going to name your horse?"

She chewed on a lush lower lip. "I'll have to think about it. I want her to have a special name."

"What about your mother's name?"

Maddie shook her head and laughed. "Sarah wouldn't suit her at all. Perhaps Ash. She looks as if she were sprinkled with spots of ash."

"Or pepper." Sarah—Jeremy had said her mother's name was Margaret. It was another fact he would have to verify.

"Pepper." She frowned in concentration. "Yes, I think I like Pepper. It sounds frisky, like her." Maddie stroked the mare's smooth nose. "Your name is Pepper. How do you like it?" She tilted her head as if the horse were whispering to her then turned to smile at Blaine. "Oh, she likes it very much. But she said since you picked out her name, that I should pick out your horse's name."

"She did, did she?" Blaine shut the stall door behind her and walked through the barn with Maddie. "I didn't know you could speak to horses."

Maddie gave him a playful grin. "There's a lot you don't know about me, Blaine Knight."

He grinned back. There was a lot he'd *like* to know about her. And not all of it concerned her background.

She stopped at the door and turned to survey the interior. "If you were going to hide something in a barn so that no one could find it, where would you put it?"

He shot her a questioning look. "Why? Did you rob a bank?"

"No, you goose. I was just wondering."

Blaine's gaze swept the barn. "The hayloft, I suppose."

"But wouldn't that be too obvious?"

Blaine rubbed his jaw. She was right. The hayloft would be the first place someone would think to look. "I suppose if I really didn't want anyone to find it, I'd hide it in the most difficult place to get to."

"Such as?"

Blaine considered the problem. "Such as—under a floorboard in the corner of an occupied stall perhaps."

Maddie glanced around at the interior. "Yes, that would be logical." She gave him a smile and strolled out into the sunshine.

Blaine stared after her for a long moment. What the hell was she up to now?

"Frank Pomeroy?"

"Yes, sir. What can I do for you?"

Vincent Slade launched into his well-rehearsed speech. He was not very optimistic that the ticket clerk could help him. Frank Pomeroy had to be seventy if he was a day and his eyesight was probably as poor as his hearing. All Slade could hope for was that even an old man would be awestruck by a beauty like Madeline Beecher.

The clerk listened to Slade's story, then scratched his thinning gray hair. "Can't say that I do remember seeing a girl like that. 'Course, that's not to say she didn't come through here. No, sir. I guess the man you need to see is the conductor."

Slade's heart began to race. "The conductor of the train?"

"Yes, sir."

"He survived the wreck?"

"Yes, sir. One of the few."

Slade nearly rubbed his hands together in glee. "And where might I find this conductor?"

"On his run, most likely."

"What run is that?"

"Whatever he's assigned to."

"Is there any way you can find out?" A five-dollar bill slid silently through the window.

"I can wire Philly for you. 'Course, you'll have to wait until I get off duty. Can't leave my window, you see."

Slade clenched his fists impatiently. "How long will that be, Mr. Pomeroy?"

The old man took out his pocket watch with annoying slowness. "Two hours, sir."

"I'll be back in two hours, Mr. Pomeroy." Slade stalked away, gnashing his teeth, with Bull close on his heels. "Dammit, I'm supposed to be in Philadelphia for a meeting tomorrow morning."

"Want me to wait around for the information?"

Slade swung on him. "Good idea. I'll catch the five-thirty for Pennsylvania; you get the next train out and report to me after my meeting tomorrow."

Bull chuckled. "Who woulda thought such a stupid girl could give us all this grief, huh, boss?"

Slade stabbed his long index finger into Bull's chest. "If it wasn't for *your* stupidity, we wouldn't be in this mess in the first place."

Bull took a step back, rubbing his chest. "You never told me there was a door into the wine cellar from the cold storage."

"Just remember one thing, my friend. If that girl

is alive and if she finds the evidence before we find her, I'll see that you hang right beside me."

As soon as the noon luncheon was over, Jeremy quietly excused himself to resume his chores. Blaine rose from the table soon after and followed his brother to the barn. He had to convince Jeremy to take Maddie away from the house so he could resume his investigation of her letters without either of them knowing.

Blaine walked up behind his brother, who was raking fresh straw into one of the stalls. "You've accomplished quite a bit this morning."

At the unexpected sound of Blaine's voice, Jeremy straightened and turned with a gasp, striking the hayfork against the side of the stall. Blaine took a quick step back to avoid being hit. "Sorry, Jer. I didn't mean to startle you."

Jeremy let out his breath. Shaking his head in consternation, he propped the fork against one wall. "I was thinking about Amelia's p-portrait. I guess I should have been paying attention to what I was doing."

"No harm done. Speaking of Amelia, Jer, why not take an hour or two to do something with her? She's going to think you don't like her."

Jeremy looked startled. "D-do you think so?"

"If I had traveled all the way from New York, almost getting killed in the process, and then was virtually left to my own devices every day, yes, I'd think so."

"B-but you've been showing her around."

"She's *your* fiancée. Go do something with her."

"I d-don't know what to do," he confessed miserably.

Blaine put his arm around Jeremy's shoulders as they walked to his room. "Jer, you fell in love with this girl. What did you talk about in your letters?"

"Oh, this and that, a little of everything." He heaved a sad sigh. "But it's not the same."

Blaine searched his brother's somber profile. "How, Jer? How is it not the same?"

"I'm not certain. She's different somehow. More—" He cast about for the right word.

"Spirited?" Blaine supplied.

"Yes . . . Perhaps . . . I don't know, Blaine. I can't describe it. Maybe it's m-me. Maybe she's d-disappointed in me. I knew I should have t-told her about my s-stammer."

"That's all so much spilt milk, isn't it, Jer? She's here now. You can't hide from her. She'll be your—" Blaine's fingers curled at his sides. "—your *wife* soon. She's probably sitting on the porch right now hoping you'll go for a walk with her. Why don't you take her out to the stream? She might like to follow it into the copse of trees. Maybe you'll see some deer. She'd like that."

Jeremy brightened at the prospect. "There's a p-portion of it that flows over a bed of good-sized rocks. Be a wonderful painting. Yes, I'll take her there right away."

Blaine rolled his eyes as Jeremy started back toward the house. Then his brother stopped and turned around.

"Did I tell you I'm going to paint her?"

"You mentioned it. I didn't know you had an interest in doing portraits."

"I've never had a s-subject like Amelia before." He came striding back, warming to his topic. "At first I thought I'd paint her outdoors in a n-natural setting, but the more I see her, the more I think a simple interior backdrop would better show off her magnificent coloring. A rich velvet drape, gold perhaps.''

Blaine pictured Maddie seated primly on a straight-backed chair, wearing a high-necked ivory blouse and black skirt, her hands folded demurely in her lap, her deep red hair in a conservative pompadour, prim pearls on her delicate earlobes, gold velvet drapery behind her. He winced at the thought. Stiff collars, hard chairs, and velvet curtains would definitely not suit Maddie.

Then he imagined her lying on her side on a pristine bed of white, propped languidly on one elbow, the other arm resting on a slim hip, a sheet draped modestly over her silken nakedness. Her deep red hair would cascade over her creamy shoulders. Her silver-green eyes would be heavy-lidded with desire, and her sensuous, coral-tinted mouth would be parted ever so slightly, revealing a glimpse of pearly teeth. He clenched his jaw as his body responded to the image in his mind.

"What do you think?" Jeremy asked.

"About what?"

"The velvet curtains."

"Overdone."

"I'll have to g-give it more thought then."

To occupy himself until Jeremy and Maddie were well away from the house, Blaine went down to the study and drafted a letter to the sisters at the convent, inquiring as to the time of their visit. All that was left was to learn their address. When he'd finished, he tucked the draft in a drawer, returned to the attic, and removed the letters, taking them back to his room as he'd done before. He shuffled through the stack, locating the spot where he'd left off, and began to read.

His investigation paid off in the fourth letter. In it, Amelia mentioned the name of the order, the Sisters of the Holy Sacraments, located in a convent well outside of New York City. He jotted down the name and address and continued. And the more he read, the surer he became that Maddie had invented Amelia. Yet he found it difficult to reconcile the clever creature who had concocted such a well-drawn character with the ingenuous girl he knew better each day. Was Maddie so good at deception that she had him fooled, as well?

He jumped at an insistent knock on his door and quickly bundled the letters together. "Who is it?"

"Mrs. MacLeod, sir."

He left the letters on the bed and went to the door. "Yes?"

The housekeeper was wringing her hands, a distraught look on her round face. "Mr. Jeremy has had an accident."

"Not again. Where?"

"Down at the stream. Miss Maddie came back to fetch help."

"Have you told my mother yet?"

"I came straight up here."

"Did Jeremy take the buggy?"

"Yes, sir, but Miss Maddie didn't bring it back with her."

Blaine glanced back at the letters on the bed. He had to get them back to Jeremy's desk before he left. "Have someone bring my horse around. I'll be down in a minute."

When he strode onto the veranda, Maddie was

pacing next to his horse, a worried frown on her face. She had on her pink-and-white dress from the morning, and he saw that the lower third was sopping wet. Her new boots, too, looked sodden. Her expression cleared when she saw him.

"Oh, Blaine, hurry! Jeremy is in a great deal of pain. I think he may have broken his ankle."

Blaine released the reins from the post ring and swung up on his horse. "Where is he?"

"I'll show you." She held out her arms to him. "Lift me up."

Blaine remembered the feel of her warm, womanly body against his on the occasion of her first riding lesson and he balked. There was no sense tormenting himself needlessly, especially when he would have to face his brother at the ride's end. "You're all wet. You'll catch a chill."

"No, I won't. Besides, you need me to drive the buggy home. Jeremy won't be able to manage."

"You can't ride in that outfit."

"I'll hitch up my skirt."

"Not on your life." He glowered at Maddie as he pulled her up to sit sideways in front of him. There was no sane reason for taking her back to the stream. He was perfectly able to find Jeremy on his own, and he could have one of the hands walk out to bring back the buggy. So why was he giving in to her?

Blaine reached around her to take the reins. "Hold on. We're going to gallop."

Maddie gasped as the horse leaped into action. She had nothing to secure her position on the saddle except the iron-hewn arm around her waist as she sat before him. His hard thighs were warm against her buttocks, and she had the strongest urge to put her head on his shoulder and slip an arm around his ribs.

She inhaled the clean spicy smell of him. He had on his usual blue cotton shirt and tan work pants, and there was a dark shadow of a beard on his lean, hard face. A stark contrast to pale, gentle Jeremy. She remembered how shocked she had been at first at their manner of dressing. Now she couldn't imagine Blaine wearing a stiff suit. In fact, thinking back to their first meeting, she also couldn't imagine why she had ever felt frightened of him.

Indeed, of all the people in the house, Maddie suddenly realized that it was Blaine to whom she felt closest, even above Mrs. MacLeod. Even above her own fiancé, although she was ashamed to admit it. With Blaine she felt like a carefree schoolgirl, something she had never experienced in her own childhood. Yet at the same time, he had a way of looking at her that made her feel very much a woman. Even when he was cross with her he made her feel vibrantly alive. She prayed fervently he would change his mind about leaving the farm. She couldn't imagine life without him there.

He spoke suddenly, his deep voice rumbling in her ear. "Why is it Jeremy has more falls when you're around?"

"What do you mean by that?" Maddie turned her head and found his dark eyes brimming with amusement. She glowered. "That wasn't funny at all. I had nothing to do with Jeremy's fall. He was intent on reaching the other side of the stream and slipped on the rocks."

"And how did you get wet?"

"I pulled him out." At Blaine's incredulous look, Maddie retorted, "Well, someone had to do it!"

"You've ruined your new boots in the process. What do you suppose you're going to wear tomorrow? We've thrown out those old sooty shoes of yours."

"How foolish of me. I should have left Jeremy in the water to catch his death of cold so my boots wouldn't get wet."

"You could have taken them off first."

"Oh, bother! There was no time to sit and think about it. He fell. I went after him. Turn the horse to the right; we're over there by that stand of trees. Oh, look, there's poor Jeremy now. He's pulled himself back to lean against the trunk. Does he fall often?"

"Often enough to be annoying. I'll see to Jeremy," Blaine told her. "You bring around the buggy."

He reined in the horse beside the buggy and lowered Maddie to the ground before trotting over to where Jeremy sat. Jeremy stared up at him, his features white and pinched with pain.

"Sorry to b-bother you, Blaine."

"Don't be silly. Can you hop to the buggy if I support you?"

"I think so."

Blaine crouched down at his side, propped Jeremy's arm around his shoulders, and raised him to one foot. Maddie walked the horse past him until the men were even with the buggy and held the horse steady as Blaine helped Jeremy hop inside. Jeremy sank onto the bench with a groan and gingerly stretched out his injured foot, resting it on the seat beside him.

Maddie stood with her hands on her hips, contemplating how she was going to sit on the short bench with Jeremy sprawled across it.

"Well?" Blaine called down from atop his horse.

She looked up at him. "It looks like we're going to have to lead the horse and buggy back to the house."

"We?"

Maddie gathered the other horse's reins and handed them up to Blaine. "I'd rather not make another trip back in my wet boots. I'll have to ride with you again."

He eyed her slender form uncomfortably. "Take off the boots and walk barefoot."

"Blaine, you wouldn't dare make me walk all that way barefoot!"

They both glanced back at the buggy as Jeremy moaned.

"Blaine, hurry!" Maddie implored.

She couldn't decipher the look on his face. "It'll only take you about half an hour to get back."

"Oh, bother!" Maddie swung around and set off at an angry march along the edge of the stream, heading for the lane that ran along one side of the wheat field. Her feet made squishing noises inside her boots and she huffed furiously. If Blaine was going to be mule-headed, she'd just walk back in her wet boots and catch her death of cold. If she died, she would at least have the satisfaction of knowing it was all his fault.

Chapter 13

⸻ ꧁꧂ ⸻

"**C**ome back here," Blaine called impatiently. "I was only teasing."

"Well, I'm not laughing." Maddie heard the muffled clop of horse's hooves on the grassy ground and knew he was behind her.

"Maddie, I swear I'll drop you headfirst in that stream if you don't come here and let me help you up."

Maddie smiled and kept walking, enjoying the contest of wills. But she hadn't taken ten more steps when she was whisked off her feet, carted back to the horse, and plopped onto the hard saddle. Her bottom throbbed and she shifted to ease it. "That hurt!"

Blaine swung up and wordlessly adjusted her body in front of him. He clicked his tongue and the horse began to walk. "Better than being dropped into the stream, isn't it?"

She twisted around to give him a frown. "Your mother was right."

"What did she say now?"

141

She turned her back on him, her mouth curving up mischievously. "Oh, look, there's my apple tree."

"What did my mother say?" Blaine repeated.

"Jeremy, are we going slowly enough?" Maddie called over Blaine's shoulder.

Blaine glared down at her. "You're not going to tell me, are you?"

"Perhaps I'll come out here after supper and pick myself an apple," she responded blithely.

"Then you'll do it alone. I'm going to town."

To town? What was there to do in town besides . . . Maddie's body stiffened with resentment at the thought of Blaine seeing the uppity, buxom Penny Tadwell. In her best imitation of Penny's honeyed voice she said, "Are you going to visit Penny tonight, *Blaine?*"

"Hold on, Jer," Blaine called back, purposely ignoring her question. "We're turning a corner."

Maddie did a slow simmer. Blaine had turned the tables on her again. Why could she never get the upper hand? And why did he have to go visit that hussy? Surely he could find someone better suited to him.

"She's not right for you."

"Who are you talking about?"

"You know very well who I'm talking about."

"Oh, *her.*" Blaine laughed.

"Yes, *her.*"

"Why don't you like Penny?"

"She treated me as though I were a child."

"You *are* a child. And as I remember it, you had on a dress that was a size too small. You even *looked* like a child."

Before Maddie could fire back a stinging retort,

she saw Blaine's dark gaze shift to a point beyond her head.

He sighed. "We have a welcoming committee."

Maddie turned her head. They were on the long lane approaching the house, and on the veranda stood Evelyn Knight, Mrs. MacLeod, Mrs. Small, the two day girls, Zebediah, and Earl.

Blaine leaned closer to her. "In the next several hours you're going to see more fussing over an injury than you ever thought possible."

They must have made an odd procession, Maddie thought. A tall, powerful horse carrying a man holding a woman, leading a horse and buggy with another man sprawled awkwardly across the buggy's seat.

Evelyn was the first to reach Jeremy. Blaine set Maddie down, then he, Earl, and Zebediah shouldered their way through the crowd of women to lift Jeremy and carry him into the house.

Maddie trailed behind as the party moved down the hallway to the back parlor, where they had set up a makeshift bedroom for him. Once they had disappeared inside, Maddie removed her soggy boots and stockings and padded barefoot to the kitchen.

When Mrs. Small returned fifteen minutes later, Maddie's boots were sitting near the oven to dry and Maddie was carrying a bucket of hot water into the pantry to dump into the galvanized tub.

"Oh, now, miss, you oughtn't do that yourself. We've got a sturdy girl for that work."

"It's no bother. I'm used to it, Mrs. Small."

The large woman planted her broad, work-roughened hands on her hips and shook her head. "It just ain't right for the intended of the master of the house to haul her own bathwater. Why, just look at you! Wet as the Monday wash. Strip out of them clothes this minute and I'll have Daisy see to the water." She turned and bellowed loudly, "Daisy? Where are you?"

Maddie pulled the curtain and began unbuttoning the bodice of her dress. She felt guilty for putting an additional burden on the kitchen help. She knew firsthand how hard the work was. It was how she had survived after her mother died.

In a few moments, the beleaguered Daisy scurried in with another bucket of hot water, followed by several more of cool water. When the tub was halfway filled, Maddie sank gratefully into it and leaned her head against the back. She closed her eyes and listened to Mrs. Small and Mrs. MacLeod fuss over a tray of food to be taken to their new patient.

Poor Jeremy. He truly was clumsy when it came to anything but painting. And now he was anxious to start her portrait. With a frown, she thought of her first sitting, scheduled for the next day. She hoped his injury would put a crimp in his plans.

Maddie paused, remembering her walk with Jeremy along the stream. With the right beau it could have been such a romantic walk. With Jeremy, it was, well, a walk. Until Blaine had come, Maddie had considered the entire afternoon a boring waste of time.

Her eyes closed and a dreamy smile appeared on her face as she remembered the feel of Blaine's arms around her. But at the sound of his voice on the other side of the curtain, her eyes opened wide and she held her breath.

"I'm going to town, Mrs. Small. Don't set a place for me at dinner."

"Dining at the boardinghouse, are you, Mr. Blaine?" the cook asked, and Maddie could almost see the conspiratorial grin on her face. Maddie sat forward with a jerk, causing the water to lap noisily against the sides of the tub. She froze, praying the splashes would not draw Blaine's attention.

"I'll be back around dusk."

Maddie sank down again with a frown. Blaine *was* going to visit Penny at her boardinghouse.

"Anything you want from town, Maddie?"

Startled, Maddie gasped and instinctively crossed her hands over her breasts. "No!" she blurted, then instantly changed her mind. "Oh, wait! There *is* something I need."

His shadow loomed large on the curtain. "What do you need?"

"Toilet water. And I'll pay you when you get back."

"Lavender?"

"No! Anything but lavender."

There was a long pause. And then, in a low, husky voice that made her insides quiver, he asked, "Anything else I can do for you?"

The warmth of his voice melted away any feelings of guilt. With a wistful smile, Maddie closed her eyes and imagined herself responding in like tone, "*Well, I am having somewhat of a time washing my back. If it wouldn't be too much trouble, would you mind . . .*"

"Did you fall asleep in there, Maddie?"

Lost in her daydream, it took a moment for Maddie to realize that Blaine was talking to her, and yet another moment to realize the folly of her fantasies.

"Nothing else, thank you," she replied with a melancholy sigh.

In an instant, his shadow receded and she heard the back door shut. She lathered her hands with soap, her mouth curving up at the corners. Wouldn't that have been a sight, she thought, to see the proud, willful Blaine Knight on his knees by the tub scrubbing her back.

Actually, she wouldn't mind that one bit.

Blaine stood outside the back door and took a deep breath to collect himself. He was painfully and, much to his embarrassment, quite obviously aroused. The thought of Maddie in the nude, separated from him by a mere curtain, had been his undoing. He glanced around the yard. Thank goodness no one was around to witness the evidence of his weakness.

As he started for the barn at a fast stride, he couldn't help remembering how Maddie had felt in his arms as he took her to find his brother. His step slowed as he imagined how she would have felt if he had lifted her from the tub and carried her to his bed.

"Damnation," he muttered. If he kept having such thoughts he'd have to have his pants retailored.

After supper, Maddie wandered out to the barn to visit Pepper. The evening seemed to be plodding by and she found herself at loose ends. There was no sense paying Jeremy a visit. Among his mother, Mrs. Small, and Mrs. MacLeod, he had all the attention he needed.

The truth was she missed Blaine. Maddie hadn't

realized how much she counted on his presence until he was absent from the dinner table. She and Evelyn had eaten alone, and Evelyn had chattered so unceasingly about her plans for their social evening that Maddie had found herself fighting yawns.

She could summon no enthusiasm for the coming event. The only socials she'd ever attended were ones in which she had worked in the kitchen. And the last one had turned out to be a nightmare.

Maddie wandered through the herb garden, stopping to sample various interesting-looking leaves. She would never in a thousand years forget the dinner party at Vincent Slade's house. The mayor had been in attendance that night, along with the president of the Pennsylvania Railroad and several other prominent community leaders. She and the two other kitchen girls and the cook and pastry chef had worked for two days preparing the food for the dinner.

That night, all the lights in the magnificent Philadelphia mansion had been lit. Carriages had lined the street for blocks. Servants had bustled from kitchen to dining room, filling wineglasses, serving endless courses, making sure each guest had enough to eat and drink.

But Maddie had been stuck in the kitchen all evening, scraping dirty dishes and pumping endless buckets of water from the kitchen sink pump in which to wash them. Finally, when she could take the stifling heat of the kitchen no longer, she had slipped out the back door for a cool breath of air.

That was when she'd heard the moan.

It had seemed to be coming from the wine cellar, which was reached by either a narrow flight of stairs at the rear of the house or by a separate entrance from the yard behind the house. Quietly, she'd crept closer to the outside entrance to listen, and when she was sure the pitiful sounds were indeed coming from the cellar, she had lifted one side of the heavy wooden doors, batted aside the thick tangle of cobwebs, and crept down the stairs. She had come to the root cellar first, where she had stopped to listen before tiptoeing on, following the sound of the moans to the wine cellar.

Maddie shuddered violently, remembering the scene that had greeted her there. A man had been lashed to an old slat-back chair with a length of thick rope. His hands had been drawn behind the chair and bound with more rope, his mouth stuffed with a dirty rag. His manner of dress was poor, his face was unshaven and his hair crudely cut. His eyes were desolate and had turned upon her with a look of desperation. With a gasp of horror, Maddie had hurried to remove the gag. That was when he had begun to talk.

"Listen carefully, girl. Don't bother with the ropes. This is important. They'll be coming for me in a few minutes."

His harsh manner and gruff voice had frightened her, causing her to draw back. "Who will be coming?"

"Slade. Who do you think?"

"Then let me untie you so you can escape."

"There's no escape for me now. I've done myself in. But Slade will get his just desserts as well if you do as I say. I've been blackmailing him, you see. He paid me and Bull to murder Albert Anderson. I've got a letter from Slade to one of his political cronies telling everything, all the details. I was supposed to deliver it, but I got wise and kept it. I hid it and the two thousand Slade *paid me in my pa's barn in Havertown. The Crandall farm. Ask anyone around and they'll tell you how to get there. You got to get it, girl, and take it to the police. It's the only way they'll catch Slade."*

The man had stopped suddenly and turned his head toward the inner door. At the sound of heavy footsteps above, beads of sweat had broken out on his high, narrow forehead. *"Put the gag back, girl, and hide yourself well. He'll kill you, too, if he knows about you."*

"No!" Her voice came out in a frightened whisper. In the warm evening air, Maddie shuddered and hugged herself. She didn't want to remember the rest. It was bad enough that she dreamed about it constantly. She stopped suddenly and looked around in the growing dusk. She had walked all the way to the apple grove.

She found her tree and climbed it, then sat looking down at the rolling fields of wheat, letting her body relax, letting the memory of that terrible night fade away. Thanks to a twist of fate, Vincent Slade and the tragedy in his cellar were all behind her now. She closed her eyes and said a prayer for the girl who had exchanged lives with her.

Chapter 14

Blaine bent low over his horse as the sleek chestnut raced down the country lane. He was eager to get home, but it wasn't to find out how his brother was faring. He was imagining the look on Maddie's face when she saw what he'd brought her.

"Come on, boy, we're almost home." He'd be glad when the horse had a name. As yet, Maddie hadn't announced her choice.

Suddenly he brought his horse up short. Damn! He was behaving like a lovesick fool over his brother's fiancée. Racing home to see her, bringing her surprises. Letting her pick out the name of his horse, for God's sake.

"Fred," he snarled. "Your name is Fred." He cantered the horse the rest of the way, a stony look on his face.

When Blaine reached the barn, he turned the horse over to his farmhand Earl, removed the packages from his saddlebags, and stormed into the house. He turned the corner at the top of the stairs, stalked down the hall to Maddie's room, and rapped heavily on the door.

There was no answer. Muttering to himself, Blaine twisted the knob and opened the door. He glanced around the room, dropped the large package on the bed, and stalked out.

"How are you doing, Jer?" Blaine stood in the back parlor doorway, leaning against the door. Jeremy was propped up on the reclining couch, reading by the light of a lamp on the table nearby. His splinted ankle rested on three pillows.

"Not bad. It's just a sprain. The doctor said I have to s-stay off it for two weeks. But I should be able to do some painting tomorrow."

"For Amelia's portrait?" For some odd reason, Blaine wasn't able to use the nickname Maddie around Jeremy and his mother. He wasn't quite sure why.

"Yes, I p-promised A-amelia I w-would." As usual, any mention of his fiancée brought out his stutter.

Blaine walked closer to the couch. "I want to spend some time going over the books with her tomorrow."

"Will the afternoon d-do? I prefer to work in the morning light."

"That's fine. See you in the morning." He turned toward the door.

"Blaine?"

He paused and looked around. "Yes, Jer."

"You've b-been an awfully good s-sport about Amelia, taking time out of your day to s-spend with her."

Blaine could feel his ears turning red. "It's no bother."

"I w-want you to know—" Jeremy hesitated, then rushed on. "—I understand why you're doing it."

Blaine's stomach turned over as he stared mutely at his brother's earnest face. *Don't ask me, Jer. Don't ask about my feelings for her.* Because if his brother asked him directly, he would have to answer directly.

"It's because you know I'll never be able to teach her how to run things. I have a hard enough time t-talking to her about the weather." Jeremy gave Blaine a lopsided grin, then looked down, an expression of infinite sadness on his pale face. "I wish you weren't leaving, Blaine."

Blaine let out his breath. "The place is yours, Jer. There's nothing for me here."

"Can I tell you something? In confidence?"

"Of course."

"I'd give an eyetooth to change places with you."

Blaine stared at his younger brother in astonishment. With a fortune in inheritance, with a beautiful, desirable fiancée, why in God's name would he want to change places? He hadn't realized he'd spoken those thoughts aloud until Jeremy answered him.

"Because you're free to do whatever you like."

Blaine regarded his brother for a long moment, trying to see himself as Jeremy saw him. He had never thought of himself as lucky. It was Jeremy who had inherited the farm. Yet that same inheritance also tied him down. Blaine's responsibilities were temporary, Jeremy's were permanent.

Jeremy leaned his head against the back of the couch and turned his head toward the window, his face mirroring his distress. Blaine was utterly at a loss as to what to say to him. He'd always looked out for Jeremy, but he could not stay and run a farm that would bring him nothing. He'd played the role of dutiful son and protective brother all his life. It was time to live for himself.

Blaine stuck his hands in his pockets and looked down at his shoes. "I'm sorry, Jer." It was a woefully inadequate thing to say. Guiltily, he turned and walked out.

On the way to his bedroom, Blaine met Mrs. MacLeod coming down the stairs, a worried frown on her normally cheerful face.

"Oh, Mr. Blaine, have ye seen Miss Maddie?"

"Isn't she in the house?"

"I've checked all over for her. She went out just before dusk and I haven't seen her since."

"Where was she headed?"

"Toward the barn."

"I'll find her." Blaine strode quickly through the house and out the back door. Why would she be out in the dark?

Her horse was in the stall. He saddled his chestnut and galloped down the lane. The only place he could think to look was the apple grove, but what in hell would she be doing there at night?

"Maddie?" he called as he pulled up beside the grove.

"Sh-h-h!"

He heard a rustle of leaves in the tree she had climbed the day before and urged his horse forward. "Maddie, what the hell are you doing?"

"There's some kind of animal down there," she whispered. "I heard it grunting."

Blaine glanced around. "I don't see anything."

"I swear, Blaine, there was something down there."

"Probably a groundhog or a raccoon." He maneuvered the horse directly below the branch. "Climb down to the lowest limb. I'll catch you."

He could barely see her in the darkness. A shadowy shape moved lower in the tree. He held out his arms. "Jump, Maddie."

There was another rustle of leaves and then a heavy object landed against him with an "oomph." She immediately wrapped her arms around his neck and buried her head in his shoulder. He could feel her trembling.

"I thought I was going to have to stay up there all night," she muttered against his shirt.

Blaine struggled to hold back a laugh. He imagined how frightened she must have been, unable to see what kind of terrible beast she was facing and too far away to call for help. Any other female would have gone into hysterics. But not Maddie.

He closed his eyes and breathed in the scent of her hair. She was still trembling, but he could feel the warmth of her body seeping through his shirt, heating his blood. When he realized he was holding her as tightly as she was holding him, he had to force his arms to relax their grip.

He turned the horse around and headed for home. "Why did you come out here?"

"It's a good place to sit and think."

"What were you thinking about?"

Maddie sighed heavily. "A lot of things."

"Such as?" He felt her squirm.

"How was your dinner?"

"Don't evade the question."

"I'm not. I was thinking about how your dinner with Penny went."

"I didn't have time to eat."

She stiffened and pushed away from him, turning so she faced forward. "What's wrong now?" he asked.

"Nothing." She sat silently, sullenly, puzzling him by the swift change in her mood. It almost seemed as if she was jealous of Penny. But that was absurd. Why would she care whom he saw?

"I bought your toilet water."

"Oh, you did?" Maddie turned then to smile at him. "Thank you. How much did it cost?"

"Twenty-five cents."

"I'll pay you as soon as we get back."

Blaine rode up to the porch and let her down, where she was met by a worried Mrs. MacLeod. He watched as the housekeeper shepherded Maddie into the house, scolding her like a mother hen all the way. Just before she stepped inside, Maddie paused to glance back at him and smile. His heart turned over. With a wide grin, he urged the horse forward, imagining Maddie's surprise when she found the package on her bed.

Blaine's thoughts were still on Maddie as he sat in the leather chair behind the big desk in the study that night and sipped his whiskey. He kept remembering how she had clung to him, her arms wrapped trustingly around his neck, her womanly scent weaving its seductive spell on him.

In the short time she had been there, Maddie had become a vital part of his life, chipping away at his resolve to leave Marshall County. He was torn by his emotions, his feelings for Maddie vying with his need for independence.

Blaine's fingers slowly tightened on the glass in his hand. He was being a fool. Maddie was promised to his brother. There was only one solution to his dilemma. He had to leave soon.

With a heavy sigh, Blaine finished the drink and rose. The house was dark and silent as he moved quietly up the stairs. He paused outside Maddie's bedroom door and listened. He heard her moving around inside and raised his hand to knock.

But what reason did he have for disturbing her? He didn't expect her to pay for the toilet water. And God only knew he shouldn't be near her room tonight. What he should do was go back to the study and pour himself another drink. And try not to think about her.

His arm dropped limply to his side and he turned away. And then the door opened suddenly, spilling light and warmth into the hallway. He swung around and saw Maddie framed by the golden lamplight, wearing her baggy denim pants and blue shirt, her red hair wild and loose, her silver-green eyes wide and expectant. There was a look of surprise on her face.

"You went to town for my shoes."

Her softly spoken statement held a wealth of meaning. It said she'd thought he had gone to town to visit Penny. It said she was touched by his thoughtfulness and ashamed of her spiteful words. Tears misted her incredible eyes as she stood before him. She was so beautiful that Blaine couldn't tear his gaze away.

"I couldn't very well let you go barefoot." He heard the husky desire in his voice and wondered if she could hear it as well.

Maddie stared at him a moment longer, as if unsure what to say next. "I'll get your money," she said at last. She turned and walked into her room, stopping to look back at him questioningly when he didn't follow.

Cursing his foolishness, Blaine followed.

"Only three pairs were finished," he added lamely. He saw her bloomers, corset, and chemise draped across the slipper chair and realized with a sudden surge of heat that she wore little or nothing under her shirt and pants. He swallowed hard.

As if aware of the direction of his gaze, Maddie snatched up her undergarments as she moved past the chair and rolled them into a ball. Blaine watched as she opened the armoire, pushed the undergarments to the back, and removed a small purse from the bottom drawer. Inside the drawer he saw a tall ribbon-tied bundle of folded papers that looked vaguely familiar. It took another minute before he realized he was looking at the distinctive Knight stationery his brother and mother always used.

Jeremy's letters. Understanding washed over him like a frigid shower. He clenched his teeth. Maddie had saved the smaller satchel because they had contained Jeremy's letters. She'd sacrificed the majority of her clothing for his letters.

Blaine's insides burned with bitter jealousy.

"Here's twenty-five cents." With a smile, Maddie held out the money.

Blaine opened his palm to accept the coins as she placed them gently in the center. He stared at the money dumbly, his mind still absorbing the shock of the letters. His pulse thundered in his ears. He wanted to destroy them. He wanted to rid her of any thoughts of his brother. He wanted Maddie for himself, wanted her so much he could neither speak nor move.

Maddie tilted her head curiously. "I like the scent you chose." She stuck out her wrist. "It smells like genuine roses, don't you think?"

Slowly, Blaine raised his eyes to her wondering silver-green gaze. He took the proffered wrist and lifted it to his nose, closing his eyes as his lips brushed the satiny smooth skin that smelled sweetly of roses. He pressed his thumb in the center of her palm and felt her fingers curl around it. His blood coursed thickly through his body. He was hard and near senseless with desire. He felt the questioning pressure of her fingers around his thumb and opened his eyes, lifting his passion-clouded gaze to her confused one. Slowly, he pulled her toward him.

"Blaine," she whispered, panic in her voice.

"Sh-h-h, Maddie." He put his hand on the back of her head, tangling his fingers in the glorious red mass as he tilted her head back and lowered his mouth to hers. He could feel her trembling, but she didn't pull away as he lightly pressed his lips against hers, sampling the sweet taste of her mouth. He ran his hand down the curve of her back, drawing her against his body, letting her feel his desire.

Damn, Maddie, I want you. Don't marry Jeremy. Come away with me.

Blaine heard a soft moan deep in her throat and lifted his head to look at her. Her eyes were closed, her coral-tinted mouth moist and parted slightly. The coins fell to the floor as he slipped his arm around her back and pulled her tighter against him, molding the length of her supple body to his hard, angular one. Through the thin material of her shirt, he felt her nipples tighten in response. His kiss deepened, growing hungrier and more possessive. She was his, not Jeremy's. She would never be Jeremy's.

Maddie pushed against him suddenly to free herself, her head jerking toward the doorway. A small gasp escaped her lips. Blaine turned his head in time to see the hem of Mrs. MacLeod's dress as she hurried away. He turned back to look at Maddie. Her fingers were pressed to her swollen lips, her eyes wide, frightened, and guilty. His stomach knotted.

"I shouldn't have done that," she whispered, turning her back on him. "It was wrong."

"Maddie, it's my fault. I don't know what came over me. It was a mistake, a stupid mistake." Blaine stared at her stiff back for a moment, his thoughts churning wildly. He swung around and strode to the door. "I'll explain to Mrs. MacLeod."

In a moment, Maddie heard his footsteps on the stairs. She stared at her reflection in the looking glass above the bureau, her fingers still on her lips, remembering the feel of Blaine's mouth hot against hers, of his body touching hers intimately, seductively. She closed her eyes, squeezing a tear from the corner. Kissing him had been wrong.

But she had lied to Blaine again. She didn't regret it at all.

Chapter 15

In the morning, Maddie found yet another new outfit on her chair: an aqua-and-gray plaid dress with a single ruffle at the neck, leg-of-mutton sleeves, and a wide gray sash at the waist. Mrs. MacLeod had returned sometime in the night to leave it, sometime after she had witnessed the kiss.

"The kiss" was now how Maddie thought of what had happened in her bedroom. It made it seem more a tangible item rather than the earth-shaking experience it truly was, and thus less of a cause to feel that she had committed a terrible sin. The kiss wasn't something that would keep her from being friends with Blaine. He had meant nothing by it. As he had said, it was a mistake.

Yet, although she kept assuring herself that what happened between her and Blaine meant nothing, she was still reluctant to go down to breakfast, worrying that Mrs. MacLeod had informed Evelyn of the kiss, and that she, in turn, had immediately gone to tell Jeremy of his fiancée's infidelity. Would they turn her out? Could she convince Jeremy that it had meant nothing?

Maddie walked slowly down the staircase on trembling legs, her fingers gripping the stair railing, her heart thudding heavily against her ribs. She could hear Evelyn talking and paused just outside the door to listen. Mrs. MacLeod made a comment about the weather and Evelyn replied absently. Neither mentioned her name. She took a deep breath and stepped into the room, expecting both women to turn and stare at her with contempt.

"Good morning, dear," Evelyn called cheerily. "Come have some breakfast. Mrs. Small has made biscuits for us today with fresh raspberries in cream."

Maddie gave her a faltering smile and hurried to put food on her plate. Blaine was not there, but she was careful not to let her disappointment show. Mrs. MacLeod poured her a cup of tea and set it beside her place at the table. As Maddie sat down, she met the housekeeper's eyes. Sympathy and understanding shone in the topaz-blue depths. Mrs. MacLeod gave her a smile, letting her know everything was fine. Maddie blinked back a sting of tears. Mrs. MacLeod hadn't told Evelyn. Her secret was safe.

It made her wonder what Blaine had said to her by way of explanation.

"I understand Jeremy is to begin your portrait this morning," Evelyn commented, reaching for the sugar bowl.

"Yes, he's very excited about it." Maddie bit into the buttery biscuit, licking crumbs from her lips. "And I'm going to start learning how to keep the books this afternoon." With a blush, she glanced guiltily at Mrs. MacLeod, but the housekeeper kept busy at the sideboard.

"That's wonderful, dear. And your new dress is very becoming. You have a knack for selecting just the right colors and patterns. Working for a seamstress had its benefits, I see. Perhaps I should have you advise me on my wardrobe. How do your new shoes fit?"

Maddie wondered who had told her about the shoes. She scooted back her chair and raised one leg to show off the gray leather high-top shoes. "They fit perfectly." She wanted to mention Blaine's kindness in getting them for her, but she was afraid even speaking his name aloud would give her nervousness away.

"Very attractive. We'll have to decide shortly what you'll wear to the social. We've only a week and two days left." Evelyn stirred her tea, a thoughtful frown on her face. "Mrs. MacLeod, when are Amelia's two gowns to be finished?"

"On Monday, Mrs. Knight, and lovely they'll be, too. An emerald-green satin and a copper-colored watered silk."

Evelyn's forehead wrinkled. "Oh, dear. Monday is going to be a hectic day. Reverend Williams is due to come that afternoon for your religious instruction, Amelia, and I wanted to begin working on your dance lessons in the evening. Well, we'll just have to add the evaluation of your gowns to that list." She took a deep breath, then a smile spread across her face. "Are you excited about the social, dear?"

Maddie swallowed a bite of biscuit. "A little nervous, to tell the truth. I haven't had much practice at social evenings."

"I'll be glad to help you, dear. And remember,

Jeremy and I will be at your side the entire evening."

Maddie sighed morosely and took a sip of tea.

"Jeremy, are you ready for me?" Maddie peered around the open door into his makeshift bedroom.

"I was j-just about to s-send someone to find you." He was sitting on the reclining couch, his back cushioned by several pillows. A basket of painting tools sat next to him on one side and his easel on the other. His injured ankle was outstretched.

"Would you pull the green chair to the w-window?" he asked her. "Yes, that's it. Now turn it slightly to the left, please. Good."

Maddie sat down on the chair and adjusted her skirts around her. It still amazed her how Jeremy could change from a shy, somewhat clumsy young man to confident painter in the blink of an eye.

"Could you look toward me? Hold still now."

Maddie sat stiffly in the chair and held her breath, until she realized she'd probably pass out before he'd finished. Slowly, she let out her breath and drew it in again, trying not to move her chest. Having nothing to focus on, her thoughts began to wander. She wondered where Blaine had gone so early and what she'd say to him when she saw him next. Would she make light of the kiss and tease him about it, or pretend it had never happened?

"I don't like it." Jeremy ripped off the top sheet of paper and tossed it aside. "Perhaps if you turned the chair more to the left. Now look over your shoulder. That's better. Hold still."

Maddie held still until she couldn't tell if she was smiling or not. She wished she were brave enough to ask Mrs. MacLeod what Blaine had told her. He'd said last night the kiss was his fault, but it wasn't. She could have stopped him.

"No, that still isn't what I want." Jeremy sighed impatiently. "Perhaps it's the chair. You l-look uncomfortable." He tapped his square chin as he looked around the room. "Mother has a wicker settee on the porch that might work."

Maddie rose and stretched her stiff muscles. Jeremy was deep in thought, so she perched on the foot of the couch with her knees drawn up and stared out the window, hoping she wouldn't be stuck indoors all morning. It looked like a beautiful day outside. The sun was bright, but not too warm, and there was a gentle breeze that lifted the white under-draperies at the window, bringing with it the sweet smell of new-mown hay. With a wistful smile, Maddie wrapped her arms around her knees. As soon as Jeremy was finished she would go visit Pepper. Maybe she'd have time to ride before her lesson with Blaine.

Blaine. The memory of his warm, hungry lips against hers sent a tingle racing down her spine. Her kiss with Jeremy had been such a failure that she had been shocked to realize kissing a man could be so pleasurable. *Kissing Blaine*, she corrected. She glanced guiltily at Jeremy and found him staring at her, a frown of concentration on his face.

"Amelia, what were you thinking a m-minute before?"

Maddie's heart began to pound and her cheeks felt on fire. "I—I was thinking about what a beautiful day it was to go riding."

"Keep thinking it, then." He began to paint madly, muttering to himself. "This is going to be my finest work. A portrait unlike any other—reminiscent of the old masters. We won't tell anyone what we're doing."

Maddie's heart slowly stopped its frantic pace. He hadn't known that she was thinking about Blaine. And anyway, she chided herself, she *shouldn't* be thinking about Blaine.

Jeremy finished with a last, sure stroke of his brush and looked up with a triumphant smile. "Come look. Tell me what you think."

Maddie walked around the couch and peered over his shoulder. Her own face gazed back at her, wistful and dreamy-eyed, even though he had merely outlined her. Where the couch had been, there was a garden with tall stone columns and long vines of ivy winding around them. He had captured her likeness so well that she was frightened. "Jeremy, promise me you'll never sell the painting."

He looked suddenly unsure of himself. "All r-right, Amelia. I p-promise."

She leaned down and kissed his forehead, causing him to blush a bright pink. "Can I go now?"

"Yes. But t-tomorrow morning we start in earnest."

Maddie grimaced as she darted away. At least she could look forward to her lesson with Blaine.

Slade paced his office floor like a caged tiger, a cigar clamped between his teeth. He stopped every few minutes and glanced at the clock on his desk. At a sudden knock on the door, he snapped, "Come in!"

The door was thrust open and Bull swaggered into the room. Slade glowered at him. "My meeting ended hours ago. Where have you been?"

Bull plopped down in one of the custom-upholstered leather chairs in front of the desk, took out his silver-handled pocketknife, and spat on it, then began to polish it with his handkerchief. "I got things all set up for you, boss. Not only did I get the name of the conductor, I also found out where he lives."

Slade's lip curled back at the little man's crude habits, then he yanked out his desk chair and threw his bony frame into it. "All right, fill me in."

"His name is Walter Durwinski and he lives in South Philly."

"A damn Pole," Slade grumbled.

"He's on a run right now and is due back late tonight at the roundhouse."

Slade puffed furiously on his cigar, his heavy brows lowered in thought. "I don't want to be seen at his house. It might raise questions with nosy neighbors. When is his next run?"

"Tomorrow afternoon."

"Then we'll be at the depot tomorrow before he leaves. Got that?"

"Sure."

"Then get out." Slade swung to face the window and took a deep pull on his cigar. "One more thing," he said over his shoulder.

"What's that?"

"It's your job to know what the man looks like. Don't disappoint me."

Maddie hurried to her room to change into her denim pants. She had only an hour until the noon meal, and then her lesson with Blaine. She took an apple from the kitchen to feed to Pepper and strode lightheartedly toward the barn. In the field beyond the house she suddenly caught sight of Blaine. She stopped to admire him as he shouldered a heavy plow, guiding it along the ground as the draft horse plodded steadily forward. She tried to imagine Jeremy doing the same chore and shook her head.

"Jeremy paints, Miss Baker."

Blaine was right. Jeremy was a painter, not a farmer. And all she'd ever done, beside tend to her school studies, was keep house for her mother and work in a kitchen. How would they ever manage a farm on their own?

Pepper was in a frisky mood and it was all Maddie could do to keep her from galloping away. They trotted down the country road together, circling the fields, climbing the hill to the apple grove, and continued on, until the dappled gray's sides were heaving from the exertion. Maddie watered her at the stream, then let her walk back at her own pace, arriving at the farm shortly after noon.

She turned the horse over to one of the farmhands and hurried toward the house, stopping at the pump to splash water over her hot face. She dashed upstairs to change into a dress and hurried down to the dining room, her face flushed in the expectation of seeing Blaine. But only Evelyn was there to greet her.

"Where is—everyone?" she asked, catching herself before she said his name.

Evelyn smiled at her. "Oh, it's much too soon for Jeremy to be up and about. But perhaps tomorrow he can join us. And Blaine is around the farm somewhere, I'm sure. He should be in soon."

But by the end of the meal, Blaine still had not appeared. Maddie excused herself and went out on the veranda to sit in one of the rockers. Surely he would be back soon; her lesson was due to start shortly. And she couldn't wait to show him her new dress.

She waited all afternoon and he did not come, nor did he appear at the evening meal. Maddie went straight to her room afterwards and sat in the pink slipper chair, staring dismally through the window as the light faded. Blaine was avoiding her.

Maddie dropped her head to her hands and let the tears come. It was all her fault. She'd invited Blaine into her room. She'd given him the opportunity to kiss her. She hadn't resisted at all. And now he didn't want to see her, probably because he felt he had betrayed his brother.

She sniffed and wiped the tears off her cheeks. She had to prove to Blaine that there was no reason to avoid her. She had to show him that she would be a devoted wife to Jeremy. She had to show Blaine he had nothing to feel guilty about.

Better yet, she would tell him.

Blaine walked up to the pump in the backyard, stripped off his shirt, pumped the handle, and stuck his head under the spigot, letting the cool water cascade over his hair and neck. He straightened and shook his head, spraying water on the dusty ground around him, then ran his fingers through his hair, combing it back away from his face. He'd done harder physical labor that day than he'd done all summer. His muscles ached from the punishment. He was bone-tired from lack of sleep, as well. He hoped the combination of the two would let him fall asleep that night without thinking of Maddie.

He stopped in the kitchen for some food. Mrs.

Small had already retired to her room for the night, so he ate at the worktable in the semidarkness. When he finished he started down the long hallway toward the staircase at the front, stopping to peer into the back parlor, only to find Jeremy asleep. He glanced out the window as he rounded the corner to go upstairs, and as he did so, he caught a glimpse of red hair through the window.

Maddie. From the front parlor window he saw her sitting in one of the rocking chairs, staring out at the lane, her head resting against the chair's high back, her feet drawn up underneath her skirt. He cursed silently and started toward the door. She was waiting for him.

The screen door squeaked, bringing Maddie's head around with a jerk. She rose from the chair and smiled in relief. "I was beginning to worry. You've been gone all day."

Blaine scowled at her. "What are you doing out here?"

Her smile dimmed. "Waiting for you."

"You should be inside with Jeremy." He strode to the railing and stood looking out at the trees, his face set in a stony mask.

Maddie was stung by his harsh words. "Jeremy is asleep, and besides, I was with him all morning. You said we were going to have a lesson this afternoon."

Blaine shrugged. "It slipped my mind. I've got more important things to do."

Maddie knew he was being deliberately cruel. Her hand touched his bare arm, the heat of his tanned skin setting her nerves on fire. "Blaine, you're avoiding me because of the kiss, aren't you?"

He clenched his jaw. "We're not going to talk about it."

"We *have* to talk about it. I can't stand it when you're cold to me." She gripped his arm, trying to make him face her. "Blaine, please listen."

He stepped away from her. "Go to bed, Maddie."

"We can still be friends, Blaine. There's no reason why we—"

She drew back with a gasp as he turned on her, his body rigid with tension, his eyes as stormy as thunderclouds. He ground out each word slowly, deliberately. "We can't be friends anymore. Do you understand?"

Maddie stared at him a moment longer, her eyes filling with tears, then she whirled and ran down the veranda steps. It was her fault. She never should have invited Blaine into her room, never should have let him kiss her. And because she had, he couldn't stand the sight of her. She swiped tears from her cheeks as she ran blindly down the lane.

Blaine swore viciously as she faded from view in the growing darkness. "Dammit, Maddie, where do you think you're going?" He started after her at an angry pace.

"To the apple tree," she called back in a hurt voice.

He caught up with her at the end of the lane near the road and yanked her to a stop. "Do you remember what happened last time you went to the apple tree in the dark?"

"Yes. You rescued me." Maddie jerked her arm free and continued on.

"You're not going anywhere tonight but back to the house." He hauled Maddie around to face him, abashed by the sight of her tear-streaked face.

Her eyes flashed angrily. "You should be glad I'm going there. Maybe a bear will eat me and you won't have to tolerate the sight of me anymore."

"Tolerate the sight of you? What the hell are you talking about?"

Maddie's breath caught on a sob. "I know why you don't want to be friends anymore. You think you betrayed Jeremy, so you're punishing me. Well, you didn't betray him, *I* did. I could have stopped you from kissing me if I'd wanted to. But I didn't. And I'm sorry now. If I had known it would mean we couldn't be friends anymore, I *would* have stopped you. Friends make mistakes, and you said yourself that kiss was a mistake." Tears pooled in her eyes and ran down her cheeks. "I need you, Blaine," she said in a little voice. "Don't say we can't be friends."

Blaine stared at Maddie for a long moment, fighting a harsh battle with his conscience. How could he remain friends with her when he wanted so much more? How could he deny the passion he felt for her and keep his feelings neutral? But, dear God, how could he turn her down? He needed her, too.

Blaine pulled her against him and closed his eyes as Maddie laid her face against his bare chest and slipped both arms around his waist. He breathed in the sweet rose scent of her skin, holding her tightly as she wept, her tears hot against his chest. Her soft curves pressed against him, tormenting him, making him throb with desire. At that moment all Blaine could think about was how much he wanted to kiss away her pain. But he'd taken advantage of her trust already with that potent kiss in her bedroom. He could not do so again.

His hands gripped her upper arms and he leaned away from her. "You can't depend on me. You know I'll be leaving in a month."

The stricken expression in her eyes sent sharp pangs of guilt deep into his heart. "Don't go, Blaine," she pleaded. "Stay here with us."

He started to remove her arms from around his waist, but she gripped him tighter. "You love this farm," she told him in a desperate voice. "I've seen it in your eyes and in the way you speak of it. Jeremy can't run it and I can't do it alone. Please stay."

Blaine gritted his teeth, fighting strong emotions. "There's nothing in it for me. I want something of my own. My own place. My own—" He gazed down at her with desperate longing. "—wife. Can't you understand that, Maddie?"

A tear rolled silently down her cheek as she searched his eyes. "But what will I do when you leave?"

He couldn't think of that. Maddie wasn't his problem. Blaine pulled her arms loose and set her away from him. "You'll have a husband, Maddie."

She hugged herself and looked down remorsefully, as if she'd forgotten. "Yes, I'll have a husband."

Damn, Maddie, how I wish I could take you with me. But he could never hurt Jeremy that way. Jeremy had despaired of ever meeting a woman who would love him despite his handicaps. And Maddie wouldn't have sacrificed her belongings to save his letters if she didn't feel something for him.

He lifted her chin with his knuckle and gazed down into desolate eyes. Her lower lip quivered slightly and he ached to kiss it. He ran his thumb over the curve of her mouth, remembering the

warmth, the velvety texture of her lips against his.
"I'll be your friend, Maddie, if that's what you
want."

Relief shimmered in her eyes. She looked as
though she wanted to hug him, but he didn't trust
himself to hold her that close again. He put his arm
around her shoulder. "Let's go home."

They walked together without speaking up the
long, tree-lined lane. He opened the door for Maddie and walked her to the bottom of the stairs. "Tomorrow," he said firmly, looking down at her
lovely face, "you'll learn the books."

"Oh, bother the books!" she huffed in mock annoyance, then grinned mischievously and started
up the stairs. "Good night, Blaine," she called
softly.

He stood at the bottom and watched her go, his
heart in his throat. How could he ever leave her?
With a muttered curse he strode to the study for a
glass of whiskey. He *had* to leave. He had no choice
in the matter. He would never be able to stay after
she was married, knowing it was Jeremy's arms she
lay in each night and not his.

Chapter 16

〰️〰️◦◦〰️〰️

"Mr. Durwinski?"

The conductor swung to look behind him. "Do I know you, sir?"

"Vincent Slade." Slade offered his hand and clasped the conductor's hand firmly. "I understand you were on the train to Chicago that derailed in Indiana."

Walter Durwinski removed the blue hat of his uniform and rubbed his hand over a balding pate. "Terrible tragedy. I don't like to speak of it, sir."

"I understand." Slade gave him his smooth, practiced smile. "However, my stepdaughter was on that train and I was hoping you could put my mind at ease a bit."

"If I can, I will."

"I was told she died in the crash. I've been hoping she died instantly and did not—" He looked down and pressed his fingers to his thin lips. "—suffer in the fire." He waited a moment, as though trying to compose himself, then sighed heavily and looked up. "I wonder if you might remember her. Her

174

name was Madeline Beecher. Twenty years old, pretty girl, delicate features—"

"Yes, sir," the conductor said before Slade could finish. "I do remember her. A sweet, kind girl."

Slade's eyes widened. "You do?"

"To put your mind at ease, sir, she died in the crash, not in the fire."

Slade glanced over his shoulder at Bull. "You're sure, Mr. Durwinski."

"She didn't suffer." He took out his pocket watch and snapped it open, then shut it and tucked it back in his waistcoat pocket. "Her friend took her death pretty hard, though. I feel for you, sir. I have a daughter of my own."

Slade tensed. "Her friend?"

"Yes, sir. The young lady your stepdaughter was traveling with, a red-haired girl. I had a hard time getting her out of the train. She didn't want to leave your stepdaughter behind."

Slade's fingers twitched at his sides. "I didn't know my stepdaughter was traveling with anyone. You're sure we're speaking of Madeline Beecher."

"Yes, sir. About twenty, fair of face, brown hair. Kind of shy from what I remember."

"And the other girl, this *red-haired* girl?"

"Kept to herself most of the way. Surprised me at the end, though. Helped rescue an elderly passenger. Quite a brave girl. Unspoiled for such a beauty."

Slade could barely speak for the rage choking him. *Madeline was alive, goddammit! And somehow she had managed to keep her name off the list of survivors.*

"Do you know what the name of this red-haired girl was? I'd like to—thank her for her kindness."

Walter Durwinski adjusted his hat on his head. "Sorry, sir. I never asked."

"Did she go on to Chicago?"

"I'm sure she did. Can't think where else she would have gone, unless she turned around and came back to Philly."

Slade forced a smile and stuck out his hand again. "Mr. Durwinski, thank you for your help. And if you should ever see that girl again, or remember what happened to her, would you call me? My office is in town."

"I'd be happy to, sir."

Slade watched the conductor get on the train, then he swung to Bull. "I *knew* she was alive! But she couldn't have gone on to Chicago without someone noticing her." He started to walk away, then stopped in mid-stride and turned toward Bull. "The injured would have been cared for somewhere. A hospital, most likely. Someone has to remember seeing her." He grabbed Bull's coat and pulled him close. "Find out for me, Bull. *Now!*"

"How do I find out?"

Slade gritted his teeth and released his hold, shoving the little man backward. "Get on the next train to Chicago, you imbecile. Have the conductor show you where the train derailed. Go to the nearest town and ask questions. Do you think you can handle that or should I hire a twelve-year-old to do it?"

Bull glared at him. "I can handle it."

"You'd better. We've got to find that girl before she gets brave and comes back to Philadelphia to look for the evidence."

*   *   *

Maddie spent the following three mornings posing for her portrait. Jeremy had given orders that no one was to disturb them, and when he had finished each morning, he had her slide the canvas under the couch. He wanted to be sure no one saw the portrait until it was finished.

Early afternoons were reserved for practicing her riding skills. The rest of the afternoon she spent in the study with Blaine, learning how to keep records of all the expenses and incomes of the farm. He stood at her shoulder as she sat hunched over the desk, straining to make sense of the columns of figures before her, until her eyes blurred and her head hurt.

On the third afternoon, after ruining a column of figures with a big blob of ink, Maddie's patience finally snapped. She slammed the big book closed and folded her arms in front of her. "I'll never get this right. I don't know why you're even bothering to show me."

"You have to learn it," he said evenly.

"We'll hire someone to do the books, then."

"And have him steal you blind? You helped Mrs. Harrington keep records on the art she collected. It can't be all that much different."

"They weren't the same kind of records." Maddie pushed out the chair and rose abruptly from the desk. "I'm going to get an apple." She turned and marched out of the room.

"We'll resume your lessons tomorrow," Blaine called out.

"If you can find me," Maddie retorted, stamping up the stairs.

"I'll find you, Maddie," he called.

"Hah!" she replied from the top of the stairs.

"You don't know how good I am at hiding."

"That's what I'm afraid of," Blaine muttered.

Zebediah came back from town just before supper, bringing a wagonload of supplies, a letter for Jeremy, and another for Blaine. Blaine finished washing at the pump behind the house, dried his hands on his pants, and opened the letter.

It was from the Mother Superior of the convent in New York. She was writing first of all to thank him for informing the sisters of Amelia's well-being.

Blaine looked up. Maddie *had* grown up in a convent then. She hadn't lied about it. He read on.

The Mother Superior was also writing to thank him once again for his kind invitation, and to inform him that Sister Mary Josephetta and Sister Mary Margaret, both of whom had been very fond of Amelia, were planning on journeying to Chicago to interview potential novices within the week and wondered if a visit would be convenient at that time. Their plans hadn't been finalized yet, but the Mother Superior would send a telegram in a day or two to let him know the specifics.

Blaine folded the letter and tucked it in his pocket, debating whether to tell Maddie of their forthcoming visit. It was strange that the sisters had reportedly been fond of her, when Maddie's own memories of their affection were not so kind. Perhaps it would be better not to tell her and risk upsetting her. There was always the possibility they would not come.

Blaine started toward the house at a rapid pace, but as he neared the back door, his steps slowed. He thought he should feel some relief in having verified one of Maddie's stories. Instead he felt guilty for going behind her back.

With Blaine's assistance, Jeremy hobbled down the hallway to join them for supper that evening. Maddie noticed at once his unusually high color and watched him curiously from the corner of her eye as they waited for Evelyn to take her seat at the head of the table.

Evelyn nodded to one of the girls. "I think we're ready to begin, Daisy."

Within minutes, steaming bowls of chicken noodle soup were placed before them. Maddie lifted her soup spoon to her mouth and jumped when Jeremy's spoon clattered into his bowl.

Evelyn stared at him in concern. "Jeremy, are you ill? Your cheeks looked flushed. Do you feel warm? Daisy, fetch Mrs. MacLeod. Hurry!"

"N-no, Mother. Wait, Daisy. I'm not ill, only excited. I wanted to wait until after the m-meal, but I c-can't seem to c-concentrate. I just received word from Mrs. Harrington. She wants to buy m-more of my paintings!"

Evelyn clapped her hands together. "Oh, Jeremy, that's wonderful!"

"Zeb brought the l-letter back from town today. So I've decided to write her and describe my latest works." He turned shyly to Maddie. "Would you write the l-letter for me? You know her so much better than I."

Maddie froze. Mrs. Harrington would know immediately that her handwriting was not Amelia's. Her stomach churned as she searched for a way out. "I'm not sure I remember her street number." She blushed at the feeble excuse.

"I'm sure Jeremy can find it upstairs somewhere," Blaine offered. "Perhaps in your letters."

Maddie stared at Jeremy. "My letters?"

Jeremy's ears turned red with embarrassment. "I have all your l-letters stored away in my desk. Perhaps we can answer her this evening."

Maddie's heart leaped. Jeremy still had Amelia's letters! All she need do was practice copying the handwriting until she could mimic Amelia's style well enough to fool Mrs. Harrington.

"Reverend Williams is due in town today," Evelyn informed them. "Amelia, you will accompany us to church tomorrow, won't you, dear? We only have a service every three weeks when the traveling preacher comes through our part of the county."

"Yes, thank you. I'd like that." Maddie glanced guiltily at Jeremy. Church would be a big improvement over spending another dreary morning posing for her portrait.

"Good." Evelyn looked at her oldest son. "You're going, aren't you, Blaine?"

Maddie glanced at Blaine hopefully and met his dark, brooding gaze.

"Yes, I'm going."

Maddie looked down at her soup, chagrined that it should matter so much what he did.

"Jeremy?" his mother inquired.

Jeremy shook his head. "It's too tiring."

Blaine hurriedly swallowed his bite of food. "I forgot to tell you. I set Earl to work on a pair of crutches for you yesterday. They should be done by now. You can try them out after you've written your letter to Mrs. Harrington."

At the reminder of the letter, Maddie put down her spoon, placed her napkin carefully on the table, and stood up. "Excuse me, won't you please?"

All three glanced at her in surprise. "Aren't you hungry, dear?" Evelyn asked. "You haven't eaten much."

"I don't seem to have much of an appetite this evening."

"Shall I have Mrs. MacLeod bring up a tray later?"

"Yes, that would be fine, thank you," Maddie called from the hallway. As soon as she was past the dining room, she glanced over her shoulder, lifted her skirt, and hurried up the stairs. She stopped at the second floor landing to catch her breath, then darted up the stairs to the third floor, slipping quietly down the hall to the north room where Jeremy had his studio.

The room was stuffy and warm from being closed up. Maddie took off her shoes and placed them by the door, then tiptoed across the floor and opened a window to let in fresh air. Beside the window was the big rolltop desk. Maddie sat down before it and quietly rolled the top back to peer inside.

She found a pen and bottle of ink at the back of the desk and the stack of letters in a lower cubbyhole. She cast a nervous glance over her shoulder to make sure the door was still closed, then untied the string that bound them and opened the top letter.

For the first few moments Maddie concentrated solely on copying Amelia's fine script, but then she began to read the words Amelia had written to Jeremy. With growing interest, she finished the first letter and skimmed the second, then the third. By the time she had read the fourth her interest had changed to alarm. Each letter became increasingly more personal, containing details of Amelia's life that Maddie had never known, details that could easily betray her. She stared in dismay at the tall stack of letters.

She would have to memorize them all, just as she had Jeremy's letters.

Maddie heard her name being called from below and glanced out the small window by the desk. Blaine was standing in the yard two stories below, his hands on his hips, looking in all directions.

Maddie turned back to the letters. She didn't have time for Blaine now. Her eyes widened as she read of Mrs. Harrington's visit to the farm, and then, in another letter, of her second such trip. "Bother!" Maddie said softly. "All I would need is for her to show up."

When the door opened suddenly an hour later, Maddie looked up with a gasp. Mrs. MacLeod poked her head in and smiled. "I wondered if ye'd come up here."

Maddie stared at her blankly. "I—I came up here to—to look at Jeremy's work." She tried to unobtrusively cover the discarded pile of letters with her hands. "I thought I could recommend one to Mrs. Harrington."

"There's a good lass. You'll find your food tray in your room when you're ready." Mrs. MacLeod moved toward her, her eyebrows raised. "What have ye got there, lass?"

"Oh, just my letters to Jeremy. I—I found them while I was hunting for—stationery."

"Maddie!" she heard Blaine yell from somewhere in the house.

Mrs. MacLeod met her panic-filled gaze. "He'll be up here in a minute, lass. He's looked everywhere for ye. Ye'd best go quickly before he loses his temper."

Maddie chewed her lower lip as she glanced at the stationery spread out over the desk. She had been so caught up in reading the letters that she hadn't adequately practiced copying Amelia's handwriting. There would be no possibility of fooling Mrs. Harrington unless she had more time to practice. "But I—"

"Go on now. Quickly. I'll put away the letters."

"Maddie!" she heard again, closer now, and growing angrier by the minute.

Maddie hopped off the chair and darted to the door, snatching up her shoes before calling back, "Thank you, Mrs. MacLeod."

"Where were you? I've been calling for an hour."

Tilting her chin up defiantly, Maddie brushed past Blaine on the stairs and continued down, holding a hunk of bread in her hand which she had hurriedly snatched from her room. "I was looking at Jeremy's paintings."

"For an hour?" He started after her. "Jeremy has been waiting for you to help him write his letter."

"Really?" she said absently, nibbling at the bread.

Blaine charged after her and pulled her to a stop at the bottom of the stairs. "You've been worried about something ever since supper. What is it?"

Maddie searched his dark eyes, wishing suddenly she could tell him everything, confess all her lies. She dropped her gaze. Blaine wouldn't tolerate dishonesty. He would never forgive her if he knew how she had deceived them.

Think, Maddie. What can you tell him? What had Amelia written about Mrs. Harrington? "The thought of writing to Mrs. Harrington makes me—'' Maddie paused to twist her fingers together. ''—anxious. She was very demanding, a bully, actually. She has always intimidated me.''

One dark eyebrow lifted. ''It's only a letter, Maddie.''

She gave him a sheepish grin, her father's grin. ''I know it sounds silly, but there it is. I'll go help Jeremy right now.'' She hurried away before he could question her further.

Blaine shook his head as he walked toward the kitchen. What a puzzle she was. Headstrong and feisty with him, yet intimidated by a woman hundreds of miles away. He should have pointed out the incongruity of it, but when she looked at him with those big silver-green eyes . . .

He came to a sudden stop. With those big silver-green eyes and that little wrinkle in her forehead. Maddie was lying.

He whirled around and stormed back to the study, where he stood just outside and listened as Jeremy began to dictate.

''M-my dear Mrs. Harrington.'' There was a pause, and then Jeremy asked, ''W-what is it, Amelia?''

''Just a cramp in my hand. I must have worked too hard on the bookkeeping this afternoon.''

''C-can you write?''

There was another pause, and then she said hesitantly, ''I'm afraid it will be somewhat stilted.''

''Then l-let's wait until your h-hand is better.''

Blaine heard a rustle of petticoats. ''Thank you, Jeremy. That's so kind of you.''

Blaine moved quickly away from the door. The little manipulator! Maddie wasn't intimidated by

Mrs. Harrington. She just didn't want to write that letter. But why? He wondered if he could find a clue in the remaining letters.

He took the stairs three at a time, then nearly collided with Mrs. MacLeod at the door to Jeremy's attic room.

"Ach, ye frightened a year's growth out of me!" The housekeeper held her hand over her heart and took deep gulps of air.

"I didn't know you were in here, Mrs. MacLeod. I apologize for frightening you."

"I was just freshenin' up the place a bit is all."

Blaine stood aside as she bustled past him, muttering to herself. He crossed directly to the desk, opened the top, sat down, and began to hunt through the letters. By the time dusk had settled, he'd finished the last one, but still hadn't uncovered a clue as to the reason for Maddie's reluctance to write to Mrs. Harrington. According to the letters Mrs. Harrington had been somewhat eccentric, yet Amelia seemed to have enjoyed a fairly good relationship with her.

The other oddity was that he could not find any letter that mentioned Maddie's mother's name. Unless it had been removed.

"I was looking at Jeremy's paintings."

Was that all Maddie had done in the attic, or had she also rifled through the letters and taken out any that might prove she was lying? Blaine quietly closed the desk. He was beginning to suspect everything she did. Perhaps it was time to discuss his doubts with his brother.

But as he stood in the back parlor doorway watching Jeremy paint, he could not bring himself to accuse Maddie of lying. Jeremy seemed to have no qualms about marrying her. What right did he have to put their relationship in jeopardy?

Jeremy suddenly twisted to look behind him. "Blaine?"

"I see you've decided not to write the letter."

"Amelia's h-hand was cramping. You worked her too hard today." Jeremy grinned mischievously.

"Sorry. By the way, did you ever come across the letter that mentioned her mother's name?"

"Damn. I forgot about it. The l-letters are up in my desk in the attic if you want to get them for me."

Blaine shook his head. "It's not that important. I was just curious."

He strode outside, heading for the barn, the muscles in his neck taut with frustration. Why did Maddie keep lying to him? Perhaps it would take the shock of seeing the sisters from the convent to get her to tell the whole truth.

Chapter 17

Bull sat in the high grass at the top of the ravine and stared dismally down the railroad track. His brown derby sat squarely upon his wide head and from under the brim perspiration ran down his red cheeks, soaking his stiff white collar. His shoulders were slumped forward. His soot-covered brown suit coat lay limply across his stumpy legs. He had no idea how long he'd been waiting, or how long he had yet to wait before another train came by. All he knew was that the sun was miserably hot and he was hungry.

He cursed Vincent Slade and the train conductor for his present situation. Hadn't he done what Slade had told him? Hadn't he asked the conductor to let him off where the train had derailed? Was it his fault there wasn't a town waiting for him there?

And just how was he supposed to find the people who had cared for the injured when he couldn't even get to town? Hah! He didn't even know where the town was! Bull sighed and removed his hat to wipe the sweat off his forehead. The boss was going to be very angry when he reported back with no information.

He heard a train whistle in the distance and struggled to his feet, cursing his rotten luck. He wanted to go home but he knew better than to return to Philly with no news. The boss was angry enough already. Bull had no wish to end up like Crandall, lying in the bottom of the river. Of course, Bull knew better than to blackmail Slade. No one blackmailed Vincent Slade and lived to tell about it.

Damn that girl anyway! Bull waved his coat over his head to flag down the train. If she had stayed in the kitchen where she belonged, he wouldn't be in this mess now. It was too bad Slade had reserved the pleasure of killing her. Bull would gladly wring her neck himself.

The giant steam locomotive belched black smoke and ash and the brakes squealed as it ground to a stop. Bull climbed on board the first passenger car and threw his satchel in a seat, then sauntered down the aisle to find the conductor. He opened his pocket watch to check the time. *Shit!* It was already three o'clock in the afternoon. His orders were to wire Slade with the information by nine o'clock Saturday evening. He didn't have much time.

Half an hour later, Bull hopped down from the train at yet another stop and looked around, then smiled in relief. Across the boarding platform was a tiny depot with a window facing the tracks where a clerk sat with his tickets and money box. Across the street was a flour mill where wagons were being loaded and unloaded. A buggy passed by and two men in baggy denim overalls stood talking on the platform next to the train. Civilization!

He swaggered over to the window of the one-room office and cleared his throat. An elderly man wearing a faded blue visor turned to scrutinize him. Close scrutiny always made Bull edgy. He tugged at his collar. "I need some information about the Pennsy train wreck that happened near here about a week ago."

The old man peered at him peevishly. "What about it?"

"I need to find out where the injured passengers were taken."

"Why?"

Bull's mouth tightened angrily. He tugged on his collar again. " 'Cause I need to, that's why."

"Don't think I can help you." With a disdainful sniff, the old man turned away.

"Look," Bull ground out, "I got five dollars for you if you tell me where they were taken."

The old man glanced over his shoulder and eyed the money greedily.

"My boss's daughter was killed in the wreck," Bull hurried to explain. "We're supposed to pick up her things."

The old man sniffed again. "They shoulda sent them things to you."

"Well, they didn't, so I gotta pick them up." Bull was fairly shouting now and he had to calm himself so he didn't frighten the old man. "Okay, I'll make it six dollars. Do you want the money or not?"

"Marshall County Hospital." The ticket clerk snatched the money and shoved it in his pocket. "That's where the people were taken."

"Where is that?"

"Other side of town."

"How do I get there?"

The ticket clerk glared angrily. "Rent a horse

from the livery stable. What d'ya think?''

"Son of a bitch!'' Bull murmured as he stalked away. He hated horses. Because of his squat, heavy legs, he'd never mastered the stupid animals. He glanced down at his expensive kid shoes and cursed viciously at the sooty coating on them. Goldarn trains. He hated trains, too. He stamped down the dirt road, kicking up little swirls of dust as he went.

Maddie sat between Blaine and Evelyn, squirming uncomfortably in her green calico dress as the black-clad preacher stood in his pulpit and raged against the sin of deceit. The narrow one-room church was packed with farmers and their families all listening spellbound to the Reverend Josiah Williams' fiery sermon. Fans fluttered furiously before over-warm faces. Maddie's fluttered more out of guilt than heat.

At the front of the narrow sanctuary was a tall stained-glass window depicting Jesus with a lamb at his feet. Maddie tried focusing on the window to block out the preacher's condemning words, but it even seemed as if Jesus was frowning down at her. It was with great relief, therefore, when she finally opened the hymnbook to sing the last hymn of the day.

"What did you think of our preacher?'' Evelyn asked as they rode home in the surrey.

"He was—forceful,'' Maddie said as tactfully as possible. Blaine laughed and she shot him a frosty look. Blaine had been a large part of the reason for her discomfort. She had felt his eyes on her throughout the sermon, watching her every movement, every facial expression, until she was almost afraid to blink for fear of giving away her guilt.

But she found she couldn't stay angry with him for long. The day was sunny and pleasantly cool, and Blaine looked too utterly handsome in his black suit and embroidered waistcoat, white shirt and patterned silk scarf tied at his neck in the latest four-in-hand knot. It was the first time she'd seen him dressed in anything but his work clothes, and the surprise was that he didn't look stiff in them at all. Instead, he looked quite dashing.

But then Blaine looked dashing in anything—or practically nothing, she thought with a blush, re-membering the sight of his bare chest that night when he'd held her close. She'd wanted so much to run her hand over the coarse black hair, but just laying her cheek against the hard musculature had been daring enough.

Evelyn patted her hand. "You'll like him when you get to know him better."

Maddie gave her a puzzled look. "Who?"

"Why, Reverend Williams, of course. He'll be coming to start your religious instruction tomor-row."

Maddie sighed, wondering how she would make the preacher believe she was Catholic. Another lie to act out. She was so weary of lies. And after that morning's sermon, she was sure she would burn in hell for them—right beside her notorious father. She wondered briefly if she should confess her deceit to the preacher, but dismissed the idea instantly. As the family's minister, Reverend Williams would feel obligated to alert Jeremy to the fact that he was mar-rying an imposter.

Dismally, she watched a group of children play-ing with hoops in the front yard of a farmhouse as they passed by.

"Blaine, did you tell Maddie our surprise?"

Maddie turned quickly to look at Blaine. "What surprise?"

Evelyn laughed her tinkling laugh. "We're having a picnic today."

"We are?" Maddie smiled, her glum mood lifting.

"And we're going to bring Jeremy, too," Evelyn added.

Maddie's spirits dropped again. She didn't want Jeremy to accompany them. With him there she would feel obligated to sit at his side and urge him to talk to her. She glanced at Blaine, his dark hair ruffled by a warm breeze. With Jeremy there, she wouldn't be able to spend as much time with Blaine.

Her own thoughts shocked her, and she blushed in shame that it was Blaine she wanted to be with. Not the man she was going to marry.

They ate on a blanket by the stream near the copse of cottonwood trees. Mrs. Small had made a feast of cold chicken, potatoes cooked with bits of fried onions and butter, buttermilk biscuits, and ginger cookies. Maddie sat dutifully beside Jeremy, laughing at Evelyn's tales about her sons' child-hoods. But she had eyes only for Blaine.

Her heart swelled with love as she watched him. He was lying on his side in the long grass beside the blanket, his dark head propped on his hand. He had on brown canvas pants and his unbleached cotton shirt, the same shirt he'd worn when she first met him, when she'd been so frightened by him. Now she wished she could stretch out beside him, feel his strong arms around her, hear his husky voice near her ear.

Blaine's eyes shifted suddenly to her face, catching her watching him. She quickly looked down, hoping the brim of her white sunbonnet would hide her blush.

"And then, of course, Blaine went off to the Dakotas to fight the Indians," she heard Evelyn say. Maddie lifted her head, eager to hear more.

"I believe I told you he fought at Wounded Knee, didn't I, Amelia?" Evelyn sighed. "So many brave young soldiers were killed in that battle."

Maddie glanced at Blaine and saw that his features had turned stony. He stood up abruptly and walked to the stream.

"M-mother, you shouldn't h-have br-brought that up," Jeremy said quietly.

At Maddie's puzzled look, Evelyn leaned close to whisper, "Blaine hates to talk about the battle."

"H-heroes don't like to speak of their accomplishments," Jeremy added.

Maddie turned her head to gaze at Blaine in the distance. "What did he do?"

"Saved his commanding officer," Jeremy boasted. "Received a m-medal of honor for it, too."

Maddie got to her knees. "Where is it? I'd like to see it."

Evelyn shook her head sadly. "Blaine has it tucked away in a chest in his room. He won't display it. He says it's a memory better left alone."

Maddie watched Blaine crouch beside the stream and skim small stones across the surface of the water. He held himself rigidly aloof, but Maddie sensed an aching loneliness in him. She longed to go sit by him and wrap her arms around him, but she didn't dare leave Jeremy to join his brother.

"Amelia, h-have you ever s-seen a baseball game?

I hear t-tell it has quite a f-following in New York."

Maddie smiled, remembering the sandlot games she'd seen in South Philly. "I've only seen children playing it, but it seems to be a simple game, really." She spotted a branch lying nearby and hurried to get it, then swung her improvised bat in imitation of the batters she'd seen. "It does seem like fun. I wish I had a ball."

"Will this do?"

Maddie turned as Blaine walked up to her holding a large oval pinecone. She smiled and stepped back. "Toss it underhand." She held her "bat" on her shoulder, her backside wiggling in readiness. Blaine tossed the pinecone and she swung hard, but missed.

Evelyn gasped, clapping her hands to her face. "Good heavens, dear, you'll twist your spine!"

"Toss another," Maddie called excitedly.

Blaine found another cone and tossed it. She smacked it across the stream, pieces of cone flying in all directions, and laughed in delight. "What do you think, Jeremy?" she called, poised to swing again. "Does it look like fun?"

"Yes. I w-wish I could play."

"You can when you're better. I'll teach you." She turned back toward Blaine, ready for another try, but at the look of misery in his eyes her smile dissolved. She stared at him for a moment, trying to discern the reason for his sudden despondency. "Why don't you try to hit it, Blaine?" She held out the branch.

At the sound of rapid horse's hooves, all four of them turned toward the road. Zeb came riding toward them on one of the big draft horses. "Mr. Jeremy, there's a lady up at the house wants to see you," he called in a breathless voice.

Blaine walked toward him. "Did she give a name?"

"Yes, sir. Said her name was Mrs. Harrington. Said she come all the way from New York City to see Mr. Jeremy's paintings."

Chapter 18

The branch slipped from Maddie's grasp. She took an involuntary step backward, her heart slamming against her ribs. Her breath felt trapped in her lungs. *It can't be Mrs. Harrington! Oh, please, God, not Amelia's Mrs. Harrington!*

"Help me up, Blaine," Jeremy was saying. "We have to get b-back to the house."

Maddie turned her head and found Blaine watching her. She forced herself to move, to walk toward the blanket on shaking limbs. She knelt and began to help Evelyn pack the leftover food as Blaine sent Zeb back with word that they would be home shortly. Her hands shook as she wrapped the dishes in cloth towels and it felt as if all the blood had drained from her head. What was she going to do?

She folded the blanket slowly, stalling for time, as Blaine stowed the baskets and handed his mother into the surrey. From the corner of her eye she saw him turn and knew he was waiting for her.

"Coming?"

Maddie forced a wooden smile. "Why don't you

go on without me? I'm still so full from the food I'd rather walk back."

Jeremy gave her a puzzled look. "D-don't you want to s-see Mrs. H-harrington?"

"I'll be along directly. You'll want to show her your paintings first anyway. I'm sure she's eager to see them."

Blaine studied her for a moment, then climbed up into the surrey and took the reins. "Let's go."

Maddie walked along the stream until they were out of sight, then she sank down onto the ground and stared hopelessly at the cool, gurgling water. What could she do? Dear God, what could she do? Her thoughts swirled in frightened confusion. She couldn't go back and give away her identity. They'd never forgive her for lying to them, for responding to their kindness with deceit. She blinked back tears. She was just beginning to feel a part of the family, just beginning to forget Vincent Slade. She should have known her lies would catch up with her eventually.

Maddie's throat tightened as she imagined the shocked looks on their faces when they discovered the truth about her. Her deceit would appall them. She had never forgotten her conversation with Mrs. MacLeod. *They don't tolerate dishonesty, do they?* she had asked. *Not at all, lass,* Mrs. MacLeod had replied. And she *was* dishonest. She was a liar—her father's daughter. The daughter of the smoothest liar in Pennsylvania. But it was Blaine's scorn she dreaded the most. She couldn't go back and face that.

Yet if she didn't return to the house, where could she go? To the barn? To her apple tree? To town? It wouldn't matter. Blaine would know where to look for her. There was simply no way out.

Maddie rose wearily and began to trudge home, her heart heavy with grief. Where would she go when they turned her out? On to Chicago? St. Louis? And then where? Where could she hide that Vincent Slade would never find her?

By the time Maddie reached the lane leading to the house her face was streaked with dust and tears and her white sunbonnet was lying on her back, her red hair coming loose from its knot. She didn't care. She would soon be found out anyway. What difference did her appearance make now?

She gazed longingly at the house as she grew closer. It was such a fine house, such a warm, cozy house. It would have been a good house to raise a family in. Swallowing the lump in her throat, Maddie walked slowly up the steps onto the veranda. Voices floated through the open windows. She identified Jeremy's first, then Evelyn's, and finally the booming voice of their visitor, the lady who would seal her doom. She did not hear Blaine.

Maddie closed her eyes and leaned her forehead against the door, fighting tears. Fragments of Amelia's letters slipped unbidden into her mind, bits of gossip written about Mrs. Harrington.

She's quite fussy and particular, but has an excellent eye for talent . . . For her age she is extremely robust, but she must wear very thick spectacles due to her deteriorating eyesight.

And in another letter: *It is so very amusing to see Mrs. Harrington inspect a painting. She stands before the canvas, bent at the waist, wearing her thick spectacles and holding a monocle before one eye in order to see it at all. It is all I can do not to break into a fit of the giggles, which, of course, would be devastating for us both.*

Maddie drew in her breath. Mrs. Harrington had very poor eyesight. Perhaps there was a way to fool Amelia's employer after all! She clapped a hand over her mouth to stifle a joyful laugh. "Bless you, Amelia!" she whispered to the heavens.

She tiptoed down the steps, hurried around to the back, and pumped water onto her hands, splashing her face with it. Slipping into the kitchen where Mrs. Small was preparing a tray of small cakes and cookies, Maddie vigorously scrubbed her face with a towel until her fair skin was nearly raw, then she pulled off her sunbonnet and unpinned her hair, shaking it out until it was full and crackling with energy. She was banking on the fact that Amelia had never worn her hair loose in Mrs. Harrington's presence. Indeed, Amelia had probably never even taken off her hat.

Mrs. Small stopped what she was doing to stare at Maddie in amazement. "Good gracious, Miss Amelia! You're not going into the parlor looking like that, are you?"

"Indeed I am, Mrs. Small." Maddie gave her a smile and pushed through the door, marching resolutely up the hallway to slay her dragon. But as she paused outside the front parlor door to listen to the conversation within, she had an attack of conscience.

She was behaving just as her father would have. And her father had gone to prison for his deceit. But the alternative for her wasn't prison; it was death. Maddie closed her eyes and said a brief prayer for her soul.

She stepped into the doorway of the parlor and held her breath. She didn't dare barge in. Amelia would never have boldly walked into a room without being invited. She glanced quickly around and noted with relief that the heavy gold draperies had been drawn over the windows to keep out the mid-day sun, making the interior of the room dim.

She saw Blaine in profile as he stood near one of a pair of tall draped windows. He held a glass in one hand and held back the side of the drapery with the other to stare outside, a grim expression on his face. Evelyn sat in a straight-backed chair opposite the maroon velvet sofa where Jeremy was seated with his injured leg outstretched. Both Evelyn's and Jeremy's attention was riveted on the lady seated adjacent to the sofa, peering closely through a mon-ocle at one of Jeremy's canvases.

This, then, was Mrs. Harrington.

The lady looked very imposing. She wore a black cheviot wool suit and sweeping black hat with three tall, red ostrich feathers on top. She was holding her monocle to her eye with the stateliness of a mon-arch. Maddie let out her breath and prayed her courage wouldn't fail her.

Blaine was the first to notice her. He turned his head to stare at her, his astonished gaze settling on her red hair, which framed her face in a halo of color and streamed over her shoulders and down her back in wild abandon.

Evelyn noticed the direction of his gaze and turned also. "Oh, here is Amelia now. Come in, dear, and greet your former employer . . ." Her sen-tence trailed off as she, too, stared in disbelief at Maddie's disarray.

Maddie forced her trembling limbs to carry her forward. She repeated over and over in her mind, *You're Fast Freddy's daughter. You remember what*

Amelia wrote about Mrs. Harrington. You can convince her you're Amelia.

"Mrs. Harrington, it's so very good to see you again," she said, imitating Amelia's soft-spoken, genteel manner of speaking. "You're looking quite well. Your rheumatism must not be bothering you as much as when I last saw you."

The lady stared at her in bewilderment, her fleshy jaw hanging open. Maddie leaned over to press her flushed cheek against the lady's cool, dry one, then quickly took a seat beside Jeremy.

"Young lady, I have never seen you before in my life!" Mrs. Harrington turned to glare at Jeremy. "Who is this person?"

Maddie could feel three pairs of shocked eyes on her and her stomach tightened in dread. From the corner of her eye she saw poor Jeremy's face turn a sickly, ashen color. Evelyn had half-risen from her chair in alarm. She dared not even look at Blaine.

"Mrs. Harrington, surely you remember me. I worked evenings for you for over a year. Perhaps the light is too dim for you. And good heavens, of course! I've forgotten to put up my hair." Looking abashed, Maddie smoothed it with her hands, then quickly hurried on.

"I apologize for my appearance. We just returned from a picnic and—oh, my, perhaps that's it! I'm not as pale as I was, and without a hat on or my hair put up it's easy to see why you might not recognize me. How is your dear friend Mrs. Lewis? Has she recovered from her stroke?"

There was a long, expectant silence. Maddie saw that everyone's gaze was now fixed on Mrs. Harrington. She held her breath, knowing Mrs. Harrington's next words would decide her fate.

"Why, yes, she has recovered," the lady replied, her confusion registering on her heavily jowled face. She raised her monocle to one side of her spectacles and peered at Maddie through it. "Perhaps it *is* the lighting. And you know how bad my eyesight is."

Evelyn sat down again with an audible sigh. Jeremy, too, relaxed and color came back to his face. Blaine, however, was watching Maddie skeptically.

"Amelia, have some tea, dear," Evelyn offered.

Maddie accepted gratefully and raised the cup to her lips, trying not to betray the trembling in her hands.

"I must say, Amelia, country life seems to suit you," Mrs. Harrington commented. "I've never seen such color in your cheeks. And you seem to have filled out, too."

Relief washed over Maddie. She had done it. She had convinced Mrs. Harrington that she was Amelia. She gave her a bright smile. "Mrs. Small is a wonderful cook." She reached for a piece of cake and bit into it hungrily.

Amelia's employer turned to Jeremy, dismissing the matter entirely. "Now, Mr. Knight, let's see another painting. That last one was quite the thing."

Jeremy handed her another canvas, and, as the woman bent to examine it, he leaned toward Maddie and said softly, "She wants to h-have another d-display of my work in three weeks."

"Oh, Jeremy, that's wonderful!"

"She came personally because the m-mail moves too slow."

Mrs. Harrington lowered her monocle. "I do wish you would reconsider coming to New York to study, Mr. Knight. Your talent is unmistakable. You shouldn't bury it out here in the farmland."

"Oh, I c-can't leave," Jeremy replied instantly. "I have responsibilities. And I'm to be m-married in a m-month."

"So much the better. Amelia would gladly return to New York with you, I'm sure." Mrs. Harrington trained her monocle on Maddie once again.

"Of course," Maddie quickly answered, but even she could hear the lack of conviction in her voice. She cast Blaine a covert glance, but he was staring out the window again.

"I'm s-sorry," Jeremy said quietly, looking chagrined. "I j-just c-can't—"

Maddie watched him struggle to explain and her heart went out to him. Evelyn came to his rescue. "You see, Mrs. Harrington, the farm is Jeremy's livelihood. He can't abandon it for a hobby."

Mrs. Harrington shook her head. "It's too bad for you, Mr. Knight. I'd have gladly taken you under my wing. My opinion carries great weight among the art critics, you know, and I have contacts with the best teachers in New York and Paris. But perhaps someday you'll reconsider."

"I th-thank you for your k-kind offer, Mrs. Harrington," Jeremy said unhappily, keeping his gaze on his knees.

Maddie ached for him, knowing Jeremy's sense of duty to his mother and to the farm would keep him from receiving the acclaim from the art world he deserved. How ironic that the very thing holding Jeremy back was keeping Maddie safe.

Maddie sat on the veranda in a rocking chair, rocking restlessly, distractedly, while Jeremy fidgeted in silent misery beside her. Evelyn sat peacefully on his other side sipping her favorite mint tea.

Maddie wished she could have gone to town with Blaine. If he had been taking anyone but Mrs. Harrington she would have asked to go along, but she couldn't risk the woman getting a clearer look at her. In the daylight Mrs. Harrington might begin to get suspicious.

She sighed dispiritedly, hoping Blaine would not see Penny Tadwell while he was there. Penny was definitely the wrong woman for him, whether Blaine knew it or not.

The crickets began to chirp, breaking the monotonous silence. It seemed to spur Jeremy into making another halfhearted attempt at conversation.

"The air is st-still tonight. R-rain must be on the way."

In her cheerful manner, Evelyn picked up the thread of conversation. Maddie ignored them. Her fists clenched in her lap as she imagined Blaine sitting with Penny on her veranda, his arm around her shoulders, her blonde head leaning against his chest. She was startled when Jeremy stood suddenly, apologized for being such poor company, and hobbled slowly into the house on the crude crutches Earl had made.

With a sigh, Evelyn leaned her head against the high back of the rocker. "I hope Mrs. Harrington doesn't come back. Her visits always upset Jeremy."

Maddie looked down at her hands, feeling guilty because she had been so caught up in her own thoughts that she hadn't even considered how Jeremy was feeling. But at least she understood his feelings. His mother seemed to have no inkling as to how important Jeremy's painting was to him. Maddie decided she would have to become more

aware of Jeremy's feelings or she would make a
very poor wife.

She sighed again, admitting to herself that she
could not imagine being married to Jeremy. They
were simply ill-suited. But if she didn't marry him
there was no reason for her to continue to stay.

Evelyn rose to her feet and adjusted the black lace
shawl around her shoulders. "I think I'll have Mrs.
MacLeod make Jeremy some of her honey milk. Perhaps that will have a soothing effect on him. Excuse
me, won't you, dear?"

Maddie was only too happy to oblige. She listened for the soft patter of Evelyn's slippers to fade
away, then she dashed upstairs to change into her
shirt and new split skirt and hurried to the barn to
saddle Pepper. She trotted the little mare down the
lane and felt her spirits lift once again.

They wandered the country roads surrounding
the fields until Pepper tired, then Maddie took her
to the stream and watered her. She led the little
mare a short distance away to the picnic spot to
nibble grass, while she lay on her back with her
arms folded beneath her head. With a contented
smile, she gazed up at the thick, billowing gray
clouds and inhaled the heavy damp smell of the
coming rain. She never ever wanted to leave the
farm. She felt more at home here than she ever had
in Philadelphia. In fact, she hoped she never saw
Philly again.

She was still amazed that she had fooled Mrs.
Harrington so easily. It almost seemed as if she had
a guardian angel watching over her. First there was
the coincidence of meeting Amelia, then the good
fortune of finding Jeremy's and Amelia's letters,

and then the stroke of luck of remembering that Mrs. Harrington's eyesight was poor.

She was beginning to feel truly free of her past.

At the snort of a horse, she turned her head and saw Blaine walking his chestnut toward her. He still wore his unbleached cotton shirt and canvas pants from the picnic. His hair was windblown and there was a lazy grin on his tanned face. He looked so very handsome that Maddie's heart began to flutter. She smiled up at him. "Isn't it a beautiful evening tonight?"

He dismounted and walked toward her. "I'm surprised you're not sitting in the apple tree." He stopped beside her, his eyes traveling the length of her prone body.

Maddie laughed with carefree joy. "Not tonight. You know I only go there to think, and tonight I don't feel like thinking about anything at all."

Blaine sat down beside her and plucked a long stem of grass, slipping it between his lips. "Not even about going to New York with Jeremy?"

Maddie's smile dissolved. She sat up and stared across the stream. "Jeremy isn't going to New York."

"Mrs. Harrington said it would further his career. Don't you want that for him?"

"He can't go; you know that. You said yourself he has to run the farm."

"Why don't you want to go back to New York, Maddie?"

She tensed, suddenly on her guard. As casually as possible she replied, "I didn't say that."

Blaine shifted the blade of grass in his mouth. "That was quite a show you put on this afternoon."

Maddie felt her heart beat faster. She lifted her

chin and gave him a disdainful look. "I don't know
what you're talking about."

Blaine smiled lazily, but that old mistrustful look
was back in his dark eyes. "You convinced Mrs.
Harrington she knew you."

"She did know me. She didn't recognize me for
a moment is all."

"Because she'd never seen you before."

Maddie's heart leaped to her throat. She fought
to control her rising panic. "Don't be ridiculous!"
She started to rise, but Blaine gripped her arm and
pulled her around to face him, his dark eyes intense
and suspicious.

"Who *are* you, Maddie?"

Chapter 19

Maddie's heart was pounding so hard she was sure Blaine could hear it. Her voice was strained. "What do you mean?"

Blaine leaned closer and peered intently into her eyes. "I saw your face today when Zeb brought the news about our visitor. You were terrified."

Maddie moistened her lower lip. "I was not terrified. I was surprised is all. Indiana is a far distance to travel for someone Mrs. Harrington's age. And besides that I looked a fright. My hair was—"

"You had time to fix your hair before you joined us."

Maddie stared at him mutely, frantically searching for another excuse, another lie.

His voice was harsh and accusing. "There is no Amelia, is there?"

Maddie tried to swallow but her throat was too dry. "What?"

"She's a product of your imagination. You invented her to win yourself a husband."

Maddie was stunned. "You think I made her up?"

208

His answer was a wry smile.

"Then who wrote those letters for Mrs. Harrington?" she demanded daringly.

"I haven't figured out how you pulled that off."

Maddie turned away from him, pretending indignation, thinking hard. Blaine was clever, yet he still didn't know to what extent she had lied. Perhaps it would be wise to let him believe she had created Amelia to throw him off the track.

She heaved a little sigh and shrugged unhappily. "I made her up."

"Why?"

She bent her head and brushed the soft grass with her fingertips. "Because Amelia is everything I've always wanted to be. Delicate constitution, perfect manners, well versed in art and literature . . ." She shrugged again, keeping her head lowered.

"Who wrote the letters?"

"I did." The lie rolled off her tongue so smoothly Maddie winced. Lying was becoming second nature to her. Her mother's voice rang in her ear. "*A leaf never falls far from the tree.*"

Blaine's reply was silence and Maddie knew he was not convinced. Somehow she had to make him believe her story. She turned to face him. "I *did* work for Mrs. Harrington, Blaine. But she knew me as Amelia. She wouldn't have hired me if she had known the truth."

Blaine searched her eyes mistrustfully, but this time his voice was gentle. "What *is* the truth, Maddie?"

"The truth is," she said slowly, "I never attended a finishing school as I had claimed." She paused and glanced at him sidelong. He was waiting for more. Nervously, she licked her lips. "I—I don't swoon at heights either, and I can barely sew. I don't do any needlework at all and what I know about art is what I've seen on Jeremy's canvases. And the books he and Amelia discussed I've never read." Maddie drew a breath, feeling somewhat vindicated. He had asked for the truth and she had given it to him, at least as much as she dared.

Blaine still looked skeptical. "Then how could you have possibly discussed them?"

"Book reviews," she answered honestly. "I had no time to read novels."

Blaine scrutinized her features in close detail. "You did all that so Jeremy would fall in love with you."

It wasn't a question, but a statement. A false statement to be sure, but Maddie didn't deny it. Instead, she looked down at the ground, letting him believe what he would.

"Why did you think he wouldn't fall in love with the real you?"

Maddie sighed and rubbed her forehead. Her head was beginning to throb from the strain of answering his questions. "Because I'm not a lady. I can't hold a candle to the girl I made up."

"Are you in love with Jeremy, Maddie?" Blaine asked gently.

She stiffened with resentment. "You're interrogating me again."

Blaine was maddeningly persistent. "You're dodging the question."

"I like him very much. Jeremy is a good person."

Blaine reached out to turn her face toward his. With a surprisingly affectionate touch, he traced the wrinkle in her forehead. "You like him. But you don't love him." His fingers lightly skimmed her jawline, sending a tingle down her spine. He leaned closer to her, his hand coming to rest on her shoulder, his dark eyes searching her own. His face was so close that she could see the different shades of brown in his eyes, the little curved scar on one side of his chin, the day's growth of beard.

Was Blaine going to kiss her? He was looking at her just as he had before he kissed her the last time. His gaze roamed over her face, searching out each tiny detail before dropping down to fasten on her mouth. Maddie trembled with anticipation, vividly remembering the raw, potent hunger in his kiss, the heat of his mouth. She yearned to feel his arms around her, holding her close. She yearned for his kiss. What she yearned for most, however, was his love.

"You have to tell Jeremy about Amelia, Maddie," he whispered, barely an inch from her lips.

Maddie felt as if a bucket of ice water had been poured over her head. She pulled back, blinking in surprise. "I can't tell Jeremy I made up Amelia! He would be crushed."

With an exasperated sigh, Blaine rose and dusted off his pants. "It isn't right to keep lying to him, either."

Maddie jumped to her feet and hurried after him as he strode toward his horse. "I'll tell Jeremy, but not yet. Blaine, please swear you won't tell him. I'll be a good wife to him. You must believe that. Give me your word as a friend, please!"

Blaine paused beside his horse and turned to look at her, an expression of infinite desolation in his dark eyes. But then a curtain seemed to drop behind his gaze, shutting out any glimmer of emotion. He swung up into the saddle and picked up the reins.

"All right, Maddie," he answered wearily. "I give you my word. As a friend. I won't tell him about Amelia."

Maddie's shoulders sagged in relief. She hurried to her horse to ride back with him.

"But you're wrong, you know," Blaine said as she mounted.

Maddie turned in the saddle to glance at him curiously. "About what?"

"About Amelia." He swung his horse to face the road. "She can't hold a candle to you."

Maddie stared at Blaine in surprise as his chestnut reared on its hind legs and galloped away.

Vincent Slade opened the telegram as he strode back to his desk, his eyes quickly absorbing the news. HAVE NEWS ABOUT GIRL STOP LIVING IN INDIANA STOP BE HOME BY NIGHT STOP BULL.

Slade laughed out loud and threw the wire into the air. Bull had found Madeline in Indiana! He sat down in his Moroccan leather chair, lit a big cigar, and propped his feet on the desk, puffing contentedly. Should he kill her there in Indiana, Slade mused, or bring her back to Pennsylvania and have her dig up the evidence first?

"The evidence," he hissed with a smirk. Then perhaps he'd sample her luscious body. And *then* he would kill her.

On Monday afternoon the preacher arrived for Maddie's religious instruction. Maddie was so nervous she passed up the little ginger cakes Mrs. MacLeod served them in the parlor and had only sweetened tea instead. She listened wide-eyed to the preacher's lecture and answered what she thought he wanted to hear. By suppertime the Reverend Josiah Williams was so pleased with Maddie's "conversion" that he pronounced her sufficiently prepared to become a Methodist and joined them in a hearty evening meal.

After supper, Maddie was called to the sewing room for a final fitting of her formal gowns. Immediately afterward she took the two gowns to Jeremy's makeshift bedroom in the back parlor to show him.

Jeremy rejected the emerald green satin gown out of hand for reasons only he knew, but his blue eyes lit up at the sight of the copper-colored watered silk. He held the dress in front of him, studying the cut of the deep, square, ermine-trimmed neckline, the fluidity of the material, and then he regarded Maddie carefully, one long finger tapping his chin. "Sir Frederic Leighton," he murmured.

Maddie tilted her head. "I beg your pardon?"

"He's an artist I admire," Jeremy replied absently. "This portrait will be very similar to his style." He studied the dress again and a smile spread across his face. "Yes! This is perfect. Wear this gown for your sitting tomorrow morning." He suddenly blushed a bright red and looked down, chagrined. "I'm s-sorry. I d-didn't mean to s-sound s-so demanding."

"Jeremy, you weren't demanding." Maddie sat beside him on the sofa and placed her hand on his arm. "You were *com*manding, Jeremy. You sounded very much like your brother."

"I d-did?"

"Oh, yes. Didn't you notice? You were wonderful, Jeremy."

They both turned at a knock on the door. Evelyn

poked her head into the parlor and smiled. "I'm sorry to interrupt, but if you're finished, I need Amelia. I've managed to convince Blaine to help me with her dance lesson, but he's growing impatient."

Maddie jumped to her feet, an excited blush coloring her face. "We're finished, aren't we, Jeremy?"

He blinked at her, noticing the high color in her cheeks, the excitement in her eyes, then he dropped his gaze. "We're f-finished."

"Thank you, dear." Evelyn's skirts rustled as she moved toward the hallway. "Amelia, I'm afraid you'll have to endure my piano playing. I don't keep up with it as I should."

Jeremy held up the copper gown and stared at it thoughtfully, remembering the sudden light in Amelia's eyes at the mention of his brother's name. He leaned over to pull the canvas from underneath the reclining couch.

Yes, it was there, too, that same light in her eye. He had captured it perfectly. Was it coincidence? Or had she been thinking of Blaine then as well?

"Follow my lead," Blaine instructed. "Don't look at your feet."

Maddie gave him a scowl. "I'll trip if I don't look at my feet."

"I've got you. I won't let you fall. Count out loud: one, two, three—that's better—one, two, three."

Blaine watched Maddie as she counted and tried to keep her gaze on his face at the same time. His mother played a slow waltz on the piano as they moved around the room together. The furniture had been moved back to clear a space for dancing. Blaine held Maddie with one hand on the small of her back, his other hand lightly clasping her fingers.

The light rose scent he'd bought her wafted seductively from her skin, sending tiny currents of electricity to all his nerve endings.

Maddie had on her aqua-and-gray checked dress, the gray emphasizing the silvery color in her eyes. Her hair was pulled loosely back from her face and tied with an aqua ribbon. Stray wisps of cinnamon red hair curled beguilingly at her temples and her cheeks were pink from the exertion. She chewed her bottom lip with every mistake and counted with grim determination. Where her hand rested in his, her skin was warm and soft, heating his blood to a rolling boil. He couldn't take his eyes off her.

"Now a turn," Blaine warned, and when he led her through it with no mistake, Maddie laughed joyfully and promptly stumbled into a chair leg.

"Oh, I'll never learn it!" She pulled away from him with a pout.

"That's what you said about the accounting," Blaine reminded her, "and look how you've mastered that."

Maddie heaved an exasperated sigh. "All right. One more time." She held out her hand. Blaine accepted it with a wry grin and nodded to his mother. As Evelyn played, he swept Maddie around the small clearing, moving smoothly to the music, their steps in perfect harmony. Maddie looked up at him in amazement.

"You're a quick learner," Blaine commented, his eyes searching her face. *Almost too quick for a girl raised in a convent.*

She smiled at him, an ingenuous smile that warmed him all over and almost made him forget the lies she had told. "You're a good teacher."

He led her into another turn, watching Maddie's

face as they danced, trying to find some clue to the mystery of Amelia Madeline Baker. He knew now she didn't love Jeremy. She was merely marrying him out of necessity, out of need for the anonymity of the countryside, which he guessed was why she hadn't wanted to contact anyone in or return to New York. Again he wondered who it was she feared so much that she had to run across country to escape him.

Blaine's fingers tightened possessively around hers and he pressed his palm firmly against the curve of her back, drawing her closer to him. His fury rose at the thought of another man chasing her, frightening her, driving her to such desperate measures. If only he knew who the man was . . .

Blaine saw Maddie's eyebrows draw together questioningly, saw her lips purse, and he realized he had been frowning at her. He lifted his gaze to hers and felt his anger fade away, felt his desire for her swell into life, hot and demanding, consuming him with need. He slipped his arm down around her waist and pulled Maddie against his hard frame, ignoring her gasp of surprise.

Damn, how he loved her.

He couldn't bear the thought of her marrying Jeremy. Maddie was beautiful and passionate and free-spirited. She deserved more than to be buried on a farm with a husband who thought of nothing but his next painting.

But how could he take away Jeremy's only prospect for marriage?

Blaine was suddenly aware that they had stopped moving and that he was staring deeply, longingly, into her eyes, his hand gripping hers with painful intensity. He saw a sudden flicker of startled comprehension in her eyes as Maddie stared back, and he knew she could read his thoughts as clearly as if he'd spoken them.

Blaine's heart thudded heavily and his gut twisted in agony. Did she love him? Did she feel the same futile longing that he did? He wanted desperately to crush her mouth with his own, to find out for himself what her feelings were. But as he stared at Maddie, her dark lashes quickly lowered and she bent her head to hide the blush that instantly colored her cheeks.

And then he noticed that the piano had stopped and that his mother was staring at him in openmouthed astonishment. He dropped Maddie's hand and stepped back. "I think that's enough for tonight," he muttered hoarsely, guiltily.

Evelyn closed the cover on the piano and cleared her throat. "You've done very well for your first attempt, Amelia."

"Thank you," Maddie murmured, keeping her gaze lowered.

"Perhaps we'll practice again tomorrow night." Evelyn rose and smoothed her skirts. "Blaine, I need to speak with you about the taxes. In the study." Her gaze suddenly darted to the doorway and a look of alarm flashed in her eyes. Blaine swung around at the same time Maddie did and found Jeremy standing there watching them, leaning on one crutch, an odd expression on his pale face.

Blaine's stomach lurched painfully. He opened his mouth to explain—what he would say, he didn't know—but Maddie shot him a warning glance and rushed forward. "Oh, Jeremy, I'm glad you're here. My lesson is finished and I'm quite overheated from dancing. Will you sit outside on the veranda with me?"

"Of c-course." Jeremy glanced at Blaine briefly before turning to leave with Maddie, but it was impossible for Blaine to read his thoughts. *How much had Jeremy seen? Had he seen the longing, the desire that Maddie had read so clearly in his face?*

Evelyn moved past him into the hallway, her face set in a cold mask. "Are you coming, Blaine?"

He straightened his shoulders and followed his mother to the study.

As the train steamed westward from Pennsylvania, Vincent Slade glanced sidelong at the squat man on his right, and his thin upper lip curled in a sneer, belying his relaxed posture, his fingers calmly interlaced over his vest. Bull was a liability. He had bungled in getting rid of Crandall and now he couldn't locate a stupid kitchen girl. *A very clever kitchen girl*, Slade corrected himself—Fast Freddy's daughter. Madeline had already proved she was as cunning as her father. Somewhere in Indiana she had managed to hide herself, posing as another woman.

And Bull was too stupid to find her. Slade leaned his head against the seat back. He shouldn't be taking time out to hunt for her. Too much was happening in Philadelphia. The election was only three months away. But all Bull had managed to find out at the hospital was that a girl matching Madeline's description had been met by two young men, one of them purportedly her fiancé.

Slade looked up as the conductor came down the aisle calling in a booming voice, "Plymouth. Next stop Plymouth."

He jumped to his feet and snarled down at his companion, "Get the bags."

Money talked. It was that simple, Slade thought to himself as he stood on the train platform and waited for Bull. All he had to do was put up some posters offering a big fat reward, spread a little information, and sit back and wait.

He gnashed his teeth. As if he had time to sit back and wait. If he'd had a competent assistant he wouldn't be standing in the middle of nowhere—waiting. As soon as the girl had been taken care of he was going to have to get rid of Bull, too.

"How could you do this to your brother?" Evelyn paced the study from one side to the other, the hem of her lavender calico dress sweeping the carpeted floor.

Blaine sat hunched over the desk, his forehead resting on his fingertips, his eyes closed. His voice was flat, defeated. "I didn't intend to fall in love with her. It just happened."

Evelyn stopped pacing to glare at him. "Is Amelia in love with you?"

Blaine sighed. "No, Mother. All she wants from me is friendship."

"So you've talked to her about this? Have you—made any advances toward her?"

Blaine's head jerked up and his dark eyes flashed angrily. "Have I made love to her, do you mean? No, Mother, I haven't. Would I like to? Yes, Mother, I would. Very much. But I won't. You should know I would never intentionally hurt Jeremy. But why don't you ask me if *I* hurt, Mother? Have you ever thought that maybe *I* could be hurt?"

Blaine pushed to his feet and stalked to the window, ignoring his mother's astounded look. He stared into the darkness, feeling as though he were looking into the yawning emptiness of his soul. "Did it ever occur to you that I had plans of my own when you called me back here?" He swung to face her, his face taut with emotion. "Did you ever stop to think that I might not have wanted to come back? That I might resent having to interrupt my life to teach Jeremy what he should have learned from his father long ago?"

Evelyn shook her head, her eyes wide, shocked. "No, I—"

"No, you didn't. You thought only of Jeremy. He's been the focus of your life since he was born. You called me out of the army so I could come back here and teach Jeremy how to run the farm, how to manage the accounts. Damn it, I even had to outfit Jeremy's future bride because he was too damn scared to face her himself. Why shouldn't I fall in love with her? I've been more of a companion to her than he has! All he wants to do is *paint*. He doesn't want to farm, Mother. He wants to paint."

Evelyn clasped her hands together in a gesture of supplication. "Yes, he wants to paint, but the farm is Jeremy's life, Blaine."

"What about Amelia's life? What about *my* life?" Blaine asked, hands outstretched. "Don't you care about *anyone* but Jeremy?"

Evelyn sat down heavily on the chair and stared blindly at the floor. "I don't know what to say," she whispered tremulously. "I never imagined you felt this way. You've always looked out for your brother; I suppose I just assumed you'd want to again. If I had known—"

"If you had known, would it have changed anything?"

Tears leaked from Evelyn's eyes and ran down her white cheeks. "Yes," she whispered. "Yes, Blaine, it would have, whether you believe me or not."

Blaine closed his eyes, his shoulders sagging under the weight of a twenty-four-year burden. They both knew it wasn't true. Jeremy had always come first. Jeremy *would* always come first through no fault of his own, and Blaine couldn't even hate his brother for it. "It doesn't matter anymore, Mother," he answered wearily.

He felt his mother's hand on his arm, a light, hesitant touch. "How can I make it up to you, Blaine?"

He sighed, feeling cold and empty and dead inside. "Let me go. Let me leave here without feeling as if I were deserting you and Jeremy. I can't stay here any longer, not with the way I feel about— Amelia."

"No," Evelyn said softly, sorrowfully, "you can't." She turned and moved slowly to the doorway, pausing there. "Where will you go?"

Blaine looked through the window to the darkness beyond, imagining the wheat fields blowing in the wind, the rustling of the corn stalks, the rolling hills of oats. His fields. He would have to leave them behind, and with them, the one person who meant more to him than even the fields. "I don't know," he said in an emotionless voice.

"Could you at least wait until after our social evening? For appearance's sake?"

Four more days of being near Maddie. Of wanting her, of aching with need and loneliness and desolation. Blaine sighed raggedly and tunneled his fingers through his hair. "Yes."

When Blaine finally turned from the window his mother was gone. He stared at the empty doorway and his gut twisted at the thought of leaving his fields. Of leaving Maddie. He opened the cabinet and took out the decanter of whiskey. His hand shook as he sloshed the liquor into a glass. He held the glass to his lips, drained it, felt the liquid heat warming his insides. He had to leave. He had to forget Maddie.

He waited impatiently for the whiskey to numb the pain that writhed like a snake inside him. He poured another glass and downed it, closing his eyes as the fire seeped into his blood and dulled his thoughts. Still, Maddie was there, just behind his eyelids, halted in the midst of their dance, her silver-green eyes gazing at him in stunned silence. And regret.

He held the decanter to his lips, letting the whiskey flow down his throat, dribble over his chin and onto his shirt. He swiped at the wetness with the back of his hand. *Damn it, why couldn't he get her out of his mind?*

There was a way. He'd visit Penny, bury his misery in her welcoming arms, drive out his torturous thoughts between Penny's soft thighs. He set the decanter down with a bang and turned, storming out of the room, down the hall, shoving the back door open with a crash. He had to get away from Maddie before he lost his mind.

Chapter 20

The night air was warm and heavy with humidity and there was no breeze to relieve it. Thick purple-gray clouds passed in front of the moon and obliterated the stars from view. On the veranda, Maddie sat rigidly on the wicker settee, her fingers bunching and twisting the material of her skirt. Jeremy sat silently beside her, staring straight ahead, one long-fingered hand tightly clasping the arm of the settee.

Maddie had asked Jeremy to sit with her with the intention of smoothing over whatever he might have seen, but as yet, she hadn't been able to say a word. They were both listening to the murmur of angry voices coming from the study.

Maddie felt sick inside, knowing she was the cause of the argument between Blaine and Evelyn. She closed her eyes to block out the memory of Blaine's face as they had danced, of the naked, hopeless longing in his dark, passionate eyes. Why hadn't she seen it before?

Because she hadn't wanted to see it. Because acknowledging Blaine's feelings would have meant acknowledging her own feelings, and she could never do that. Her love for Blaine had to remain a secret. Now she understood why they couldn't be friends. She thought of how she had stubbornly insisted on it, insisted because she needed Blaine's companionship, and he had suffered in silence—all the time wanting her, yet because of his sense of honor unable to do anything about it.

The irony was that she didn't love Jeremy at all. She felt an affection for him she thought she might feel for a younger brother. She loved Blaine. But her lies had irrefutably bound her to his brother. To confess her feelings for Blaine would require the truth, and truth meant death.

"Amelia."

Jeremy's voice startled her. Maddie turned her head to look at him. His face was strained, his fingers white-knuckled on the arm of the settee. She had no way of knowing how much he had seen or how much he had guessed about Blaine's feelings. She didn't want to know. She only prayed he would not ask her what her feelings were for Blaine. It was the one thing she knew she could not lie about.

"I've b-been thinking about N-new York."

"Yes?" she said quickly, sharply.

"And about w-what Mrs. Harrington said. P-perhaps I should accept her offer."

Maddie felt her heart stand still. Leave the farm? Leave Blaine? "Then you'll have Blaine run the farm for you?" she asked.

"S-something like that."

She stared blankly at Jeremy, then her eyes came into sharp focus. Yes, that's what they should do: go to New York. Then Blaine could stay on the farm. He wouldn't have to give up the land he loved. And she could hide in New York. It was a big city; there would be no reason for Vincent Slade to look for her there.

"Will you help me with a l-letter?"

"Yes," she said, nodding. "I'll help you. You *should* consider going to New York. You'd have wonderful opportunities there. You'd be close to the galleries and the museums. We could take a small apartment. Mrs. Harrington mentioned finding a teacher for you. You could paint as much as you liked. All day."

Jeremy looked at her for a long moment, longer than he'd ever looked at her before. "What will *you* do all day, Amelia?"

Maddie opened her mouth, then quickly shut it. She looked away, remembering the times she had watched Jeremy painting in the attic. When he was creating, he wasn't aware of anyone else in the room. He was so absorbed in his painting that he missed meals. What *would* she do all day while he painted? There would be no reason for her to work; she would be married to a wealthy man.

Jeremy pulled his crutches to his sides and rose carefully. "Well, it's s-something to think about, isn't it?"

Maddie hurried to hold the door open for him. He hobbled inside, pausing to glance back at her as she stood on the porch. His blue eyes were somber. "Good night, Amelia."

Maddie let the door shut softly as Jeremy moved slowly down the hallway. Beyond Jeremy, she suddenly saw a tall, shadowy figure lurch toward the back door and knew instinctively it was Blaine. She jumped when the door crashed angrily behind him.

Maddie dashed down the veranda steps and around the side of the house where she could just make out Blaine's dark shape lunging toward the barn. Her heart thudded heavily as she hurried across the uneven ground after him. Blaine was upset. She had to go to him, had to find out what his mother had said about her.

"Blaine," she called softly.

She saw him pause just outside the barn door, but he didn't turn to look back. Maddie picked up her skirts and ran. "Blaine, wait."

She slipped into the barn after him and stood just inside the door, waiting for her eyes to adjust to the darkness. "Blaine?"

Still he said nothing, but she could hear him moving around. She felt her way along the row of stalls until she came to the end where he kept his horse. As the moon came from behind the clouds and light filtered softly through the long row of windows, she could see him heaving the heavy leather saddle over his chestnut's back.

Her throat tightened. He was leaving. The argument between Blaine and Evelyn must have been even worse than she thought.

"Blaine?"

His voice was harsh, his words slurred. "Get the hell outta here, Maddie."

"Where are you going?"

He crouched to tighten the cinch. "Away."

When he straightened, Maddie moved to his side and laid her hand on his sleeve. "Please don't go."

"Why th' hell shouldn't I? There's nothing for me here."

She recoiled at the strong smell of liquor around him. "You're drunk."

He chuckled dryly. "It won't matter to Penny."

"Penny?" Maddie's heart twisted with jealousy. "You're going to see Penny?"

He fastened the bridle then turned his head to glare at her. "Somethin' wrong with that, Maddie?"

She shook her head though her chest ached in misery at the thought of Blaine being with Penny. He started to lead the horse out of the stall, but Maddie stepped in front of him. "Blaine, you don't need to leave. Jeremy and I are—"

He swore viciously, cutting off her sentence. She stared at him openmouthed as he clenched his teeth and glared down at her. "Damn it, Maddie, you don't know what I need. Stay away from me."

He started past her, but Maddie caught his arm and held on with fierce determination. "Yes, I do know, Blaine. You have to listen!"

With another curse, Blaine swung around and backed her against the wooden wall of the stall, gripping her shoulders in his strong hands. Whiskey fumes fanned her face as he leaned close to speak to her. "You know what I need? You really know what I need?"

Maddie stared up at him mutely, stunned by the fury, the desperation in his eyes. This wasn't the Blaine she knew. This was a stranger, a drunken stranger, unpredictable and frightening. She turned her head away, unable to bear his piercing gaze any longer.

His fingers loosened from one shoulder and gripped her chin, forcing her to face him. "This is what I need, Maddie." His lips crushed hers, hard and relentless. His arms were like ropes of steel around her back, binding her to his lean, muscular body.

Maddie pushed against his solid chest, whimpering in fright, as his other hand slipped down from her shoulder to cup her breast, gently kneading it with his fingers, molding it to his palm. His mouth left hers to leave a trail of hot kisses down her throat. He whispered against her warm skin, "I want you, Maddie. Damn, how I want you." Despite her fear, tremors of desire raced up her spine.

It was madness. Blaine wasn't thinking clearly. She had to stop him before all his constraints were gone. "Blaine," she whispered hoarsely, "Please, don't. Remember Jeremy."

She felt him stiffen, felt the rage, the impotence vibrating inside him. He raised his head to glare at her, his eyes red and furious. "Why?" he asked, his voice a thin, bitter whisper. "Why should I remember Jeremy? You don't love him."

Maddie shook her head, swallowing hard. "No. I never said that. It's not true. I'm going to marry him, Blaine."

Blaine's upper lip curled back. "You're a liar, Maddie. The biggest goddamn liar I've ever met."

Maddie stared at him, her throat too dry to speak. He was right.

"Tell me," he said in a low growl, his hands tightening on her arms. "Tell me the truth. Do you love Jeremy?"

"I told you—"

He released her suddenly. His voice was thick with disgust. "You told me lies. I'm sick to death of your lies."

Maddie sagged weakly against the wall as he led his horse out of the stall and through the silent barn. She sank to her knees in the straw and wrapped her arms around her body, fighting tears, shaking so hard her teeth chattered. She heard the rapid pounding of horse's hooves and knew he was going straight into Penny's arms.

Because she couldn't love him in return.

Because of her lies.

Vincent Slade sprawled on his back on the lumpy hotel bed, his feet aching from the miles he had walked that day. He and three of his men had traveled throughout Marshall County, hanging reward notices in every podunk town, speaking to anyone who might have seen Madeline Beecher, or whatever she was calling herself.

Bull swaggered into the room, a bottle and two glasses in his hands. He kicked the door shut with a bang. Slade jerked, raising his head to glare at him.

Bull merely grinned. "I got the whiskey."

"Thank God you're good for something." Slade groaned as he rolled to a sitting position and swung his long, gaunt legs over the side of the bed. He slapped the back of his neck and glanced up at the ceiling for bedbugs. "I don't know how long I can take this place."

Seemingly oblivious to his boss's ill humor, Bull handed Slade a full glass. "A couple o' days ought to do it. A couple o' days more and we can go home."

A couple of days in hell, Slade thought, sipping steadily at the liquor. But someone would recognize Madeline's description. Someone would want the thousand-dollar reward badly enough to contact him. He chuckled to himself as he held out his glass for another drink. And then Madeline Beecher was his.

*   *   *

Blaine didn't come back the next day. Maddie sat alone in the dining room trying to choke down her supper while Evelyn nervously paced the hallway from the front of the house to the back, as she had done most of the day. Mrs. MacLeod looked worried, too, as she bustled about her duties. Only Jeremy seemed unaffected by Blaine's disappearance. After the noon meal, he had announced with a sort of nervous excitement that he did not wish to be disturbed and had closeted himself in the study, where he had been ever since.

Maddie thought back to the morning spent in the back parlor with Jeremy while he finished her portrait. He had been unusually calm and lighthearted, and now that she thought about it, he hadn't stuttered at all. She supposed she should be glad that he finally felt at ease around her, but it didn't seem to matter anymore. Nothing mattered. She felt hollow inside, drained of energy and emotion. She deserved Blaine's contempt. He had given her friendship at great cost to himself, and in return she had given him nothing but lies.

But soon she would be out of Blaine's life forever. Jeremy had decided that day to accept Mrs. Harrington's offer. He had sent her a wire early that morning informing her that he would be leaving shortly for New York. Maddie knew it had taken great courage for Jeremy to make such a bold decision and she silently applauded him for it. At last he would have the opportunity to do what he had always wanted to do without worry or guilt. And Blaine could stay on the farm.

Blaine. Tears burned the backs of Maddie's eyelids. She lowered her head and squeezed her eyes shut, thinking back to the day he had taken her around on the big draft horse to see the vast farm fields. She remembered the pride she'd seen shimmering in his dark eyes. She thought of how he had looked sitting beside her in the apple tree, gazing out at the land he loved. She recalled the time he had stooped to dig out a handful of black earth to show her, squeezing it in his palm as if it were the finest silk. She remembered the look of triumph in his eyes when he tore an ear of corn from the stalk and peeled back the husk, pressing a thumb into a juicy kernel until it burst. And she imagined the pain he must have felt when he decided he had to leave.

Maddie wiped a stray tear on her cheek with her fingertips. If Blaine would just come home, Jeremy could convince him there was no reason to leave. But what if he never came back? What if he had already taken Penny and left Marshall County for good?

At the rustle of petticoats, she looked up. Evelyn stood in the doorway, her small, heart-shaped face pinched with worry. "May I join you for coffee?"

Maddie nodded. Evelyn moved quietly to the sideboard and poured two cups. Maddie watched her curiously, knowing she seldom drank the strong brew. Evelyn placed one cup at Maddie's elbow, then sat in her usual spot and took a sip from her cup, grimacing comically at the taste. She gave a short, nervous laugh. "I never did acquire a taste for coffee."

Maddie sipped steadily at her own cup, waiting for Evelyn to speak what was on her mind.

"Jeremy tells me he's decided to go to New York. I'm not happy about his decision." Evelyn stared despondently into her cup. "Nevertheless, it's his decision. I only hope his nerves will hold out."

Maddie knew that she was worried about her younger son, and already missing him.

Evelyn drew a shaky breath. "Jeremy intends to leave shortly after the social, while he's still got his nerve, he says. I suppose you'll want to find a minister or justice of the peace to marry you once you get there. You wouldn't want a scandal." She picked up her cup and set it down again without drinking. "I wish I knew where Blaine was. He promised me he wouldn't leave home until after the social. I told him it just wouldn't do to leave before. You know how people talk."

Maddie put down her cup with a clink. Relief washed over her. Blaine hadn't left Marshall County, not yet, anyway. He would never break a promise. But she knew he was still with Penny. "He's at Miss Tadwell's." Maddie felt Evelyn's eyes on her face, but she didn't meet her gaze, fearing her feelings would be too easily read.

Evelyn spoke again, her voice hesitant. "Did you talk to Blaine before he left?"

Maddie remembered Blaine's bitter words and felt a sting of tears behind her eyelids. "Only for a moment."

Evelyn sighed wearily. "Then I should tell you that we talked at some length about—" She waved a dainty hand in the air. "—the situation. We decided it would be for the best if Blaine left as soon as possible. But that was before I knew Jeremy's plans. Blaine will have to stay now. Who will run the farm if he doesn't?" Evelyn pressed her fingertips to her temples. "Oh, I wish Blaine were here. I just can't think what to do."

Maddie put her hand over Evelyn's. "If Blaine promised he'd be back for the social, he'll be here. You can talk to him then."

It was sound advice. But could *she* wait that long to talk to him?

Maddie sat in the chair by her bedroom window, staring dejectedly at the barn below, hoping Blaine would come back before she went to sleep. She heard the door open behind her.

"Miss Maddie," Mrs. MacLeod called gently.

With a sigh, Maddie turned to glance over her shoulder. "Yes, Mrs. MacLeod?"

"Ye hardly ate a bite o' yer supper." The housekeeper gave her a sympathetic smile. "Can I bring ye a wee bit o' food or some honeyed milk perhaps?"

Maddie resumed her watch over the barn, knowing it was in vain. "I don't have much appetite, Mrs. MacLeod. But thank you anyway." After a moment, she felt a hand on her head, stroking the long hair streaming down her back.

"Ye mustn't torture yerself so, lass."

Maddie's throat tightened. "It's my fault Blaine left."

"Ach, 'tis nobody's fault. Did ye come here knowing ye'd fall in love with him? Do ye think *he* planned for it to happen? Love is a curious thing. There's no accounting for it."

Maddie twisted her head to look at the housekeeper, and at the compassion shining in the kindly blue eyes, a sob welled up inside her. "You know," she whispered.

The housekeeper smiled. "Aye, I've known for some time. Yer bonny eyes light up like a lighthouse beacon when Mr. Blaine is around. And as for him . . ." She paused for a moment, then resumed stroking Maddie's hair. "Well, the thing now is to decide what to do about it."

Maddie turned around to face her. "I'm going to New York with Jeremy, Mrs. MacLeod," she said with a determined lift of her chin. "We'll be married there. Blaine can stay here where he belongs. This land is his life's blood. He'd be miserable if he left. The only thing is—" She paused and looked down as tears filled her eyes. "—he still thinks he has to leave. He won't come back because I'm here, not until the night of the social, and only because he promised his mother he would."

"Then ye must go find him."

Maddie looked up in surprise. "But he's at Miss Tadwell's."

"Does it make a difference where he is?"

Maddie stared at her. *Did* it make a difference? She was leaving Marshall County. Did she care what Penny Tadwell thought of her?

"Hold still while I braid yer hair," Mrs. MacLeod ordered, her fingers already making two channels through the heavy locks. "Then ye can slip into your riding clothes and be in town within the hour."

Chapter 21

The boardinghouse was quiet when Maddie dismounted from her mare and walked up the two wide, wooden steps. She opened the door and looked around the interior, her pulse racing expectantly.

She was standing in a large entranceway redolent with the aroma of beeswax and cloves. Straight ahead was an oak staircase, its treads scuffed from constant use and darkened with age. To the right of the staircase was a gleaming dark oak counter. Past the staircase was an open doorway, through which she could see the red-checkered tablecloths of the restaurant. To her right was a small parlor furnished in heavy, wine-red upholstered furniture. Maddie glanced inside and found it empty. The restaurant was also empty. She lifted her gaze to the top of the stairs, gathered her courage, and reluctantly began to climb.

A door opened somewhere above her as Maddie moved steadily upward. She paused at the top of the stairs and saw Penny moving swiftly down the hallway. Her long blonde hair was unbound and she was tying a brightly patterned silk wrapper at her waist. On her feet were red satin bedroom slippers which slapped her heels at each step.

Penny's eyes widened in surprise as she drew nearer and then a smug grin crossed her smooth-complexioned face. "Looking for someone, honey?" she asked in her syrupy voice.

Maddie lifted her chin. "I'm looking for Blaine."

Penny folded her arms under her full breasts and looked Maddie up and down, her brown eyes mocking and hard. Finally, she nodded her head toward the door at the far end. "He's in there."

Maddie moved quickly down the hallway. She could hear the *slap-slap* of Penny's slippers as she followed at a leisurely pace. Maddie opened the door and stepped inside, glancing around at the narrow, crowded sitting room decorated in red velvet. Beyond the sitting room was a door. A door to a bedroom.

Maddie closed her eyes and clenched her jaw. Blaine was in Penny's bedroom. The thought made her stomach turn. She pressed her lips together in grim determination and moved toward the door.

He was half sitting, half lying in her bed, his head and shoulders propped against the blue, silk-tufted headboard, a whiskey glass in one hand. A blue satin sheet covered him from the waist down, but from the waist up he was nude. Maddie's gaze moved from the dark, springy hair on his chest to the lazy grin on his unshaven face to the tousled hair on his head. A bitter stab of jealousy pierced through her so fiercely she pressed her hand to her heart to ease the pain.

"Well, if it isn't m' dear friend Maddie." Blaine

lifted his glass to her. "Welcome, friend. Come in and have a drink with us."

He was drunk. Stinking, disgustingly drunk, and had probably been so since the evening before. Maddie heard Penny slip in behind her and knew if she turned she would find the woman grinning at her with that same self-satisfied look on her face. Maddie moved around to the side of the bed, closer to Blaine. "I came to tell you something."

"Is that right?"

Maddie glanced at the half-empty bottle of whiskey on the bedside table. Blaine followed the direction of her gaze and tried to reach for the bottle, missing by inches. "It's m' second bottle today."

"You must be so proud," she said evenly.

She saw anger flare in his eyes. "What did you want to tell me?" he snarled.

"Jeremy has accepted Mrs. Harrington's offer. He and I are leaving for New York right after the social. We're going to be married by a justice of the peace as soon as we arrive."

Blaine's eyes narrowed in disbelief and when he spoke, he didn't sound drunk at all. "My mother knows about this?"

"Yes." Maddie looked down at her hands. "She thought it would be best to avoid a scandal."

He snickered. "Of course she would. But best for whom? Jeremy and Amelia? Or Jeremy and Maddie? Which one does the lucky groom get to marry?"

Maddie tensed, aware of the prying ears behind her. "I just wanted you to know that there's no reason for you to leave Marshall County. Jeremy and I will be gone in three days. You can go home." She lowered her voice. "You don't need to stay here."

Penny moved around to the other side of the bed and slithered across it to lie close beside Blaine. She smiled coyly as her hand moved familiarly up and down his bare arm, further stoking Maddie's smoldering jealousy. "Why should he go home?" Penny purred. "He likes it here. Don't you, Blaine?"

Maddie coldly ignored her. "Your mother is worried sick, Blaine. You have to come home."

Blaine's hand shot out and closed around Maddie's wrist, dragging her to his side. "My mother," he ground out slowly, "doesn't give a damn about me."

"No." Maddie shook her head rapidly, trying to pry his fingers from her wrist. "That's not true. She's so worried she hasn't eaten all day."

He laughed dryly. "Still can't tell the truth, can you, Maddie?"

"Let go of me," she said firmly.

Blaine stared into her eyes for what felt like an eternity, and then he released her, sinking back against Penny's shoulder. "So you're leaving. Taking Jeremy to New York. I'm surprised you agreed to go. But maybe the danger is over now. Maybe *he's* not looking for you anymore. Or is it that you've done what you came here to do—win yourself a rich husband—and now you're ready to go back with your prize in tow?"

Seething with anger, Maddie shot him a contemptuous look and swung to leave, her heavy braid slapping her shoulder. "Go to hell."

With a curse, Blaine flung back the sheet and rose. Maddie turned with a start and stared at him wide-eyed as he advanced toward her dressed only in his cotton drawers. For a moment she stood her ground, but at the murderous look in his dark eyes, she backed away until a wall stopped her.

"Tell me the truth, Maddie, if that's possible." He came to a stop inches away and reached out, fingering the braid of hair on her shoulder. "Was I your backup in case Jeremy didn't pan out? Were you counting on at least one of us to be gullible enough to fall in love with you to save you from your predicament?"

Angry tears filled her eyes. How could Blaine believe that? How could he believe she had plotted to make him fall in love with her?

Because you lied to him about everything else. Blaine believed she had used him, and there was nothing she could do to prove otherwise. Choking back a sob, Maddie turned and fled the room, dashing down the hallway, flying breathlessly down the stairs and onto the porch.

"Maddie!" she heard Blaine shout angrily, his footsteps loud on the steps.

She kicked her horse into a gallop. Blaine's bitter words gnawed at her insides, constricted her heart, squeezed the air from her lungs. She hoped he didn't come home until she and Jeremy had gone. In fact, she didn't ever want to see him again.

Blaine stood on the porch and watched Maddie until she was little more than a speck in the distance. "Damn!" he muttered, swaying as he turned. Penny was standing in the doorway, a knowing grin on her face.

"I need a drink." He pushed past her into the boardinghouse and strode toward the staircase.

"I think you need more than that."

He swung so fast the room tilted beneath him. "What do you mean?"

"You really have fallen in love with her, haven't you?"

Blaine closed his eyes, his chest tight with misery. Maddie was leaving with Jeremy.

"Are you all right, honey?"

He clenched his teeth and fixed his blurry gaze on Penny. "Don't *ever* call me 'honey.' " The room spun and he sat down hard on the bottom step. "Damn," he muttered, rubbing his temples. "Why did I say those things to her?"

"She's engaged to your brother," Penny reminded him sharply. "It's best that she leave."

Blaine felt his throat close, felt his stomach tighten. Maddie would be gone in three days. Out of his life forever.

Penny lifted Blaine's arm and helped him to his feet. "Come on upstairs with me. There's more whiskey in my room."

He pulled his arm from her grasp and pressed his hands to his temples. A vague thought hovered on the edge of his memory. There was something he had to do, something he had to tell Maddie. "I have to go back."

"No, you don't." Penny's voice dropped to a lusty whisper. "You don't need her." She ran one hand over his bare chest, down the flat stomach to his groin. "You have me."

Maddie tossed restlessly in her bed, drifting in and out of a series of dreams: Blaine holding her in his arms as they danced to a waltz, gazing at her with desperate longing; lying in Penny's bed, taunting her, smirking at her. The vision changed suddenly and it was Vincent Slade smirking at her, reaching out to touch her, his hands long, gnarled claws. "No," she moaned. "Stay away. I don't know anything."

And then she was back in the wine cellar, listening from her hiding place as Slade and his henchman, Bull, forced a confession from Crandall.

"*A servant girl knows about the letter? Damn you, Crandall, what girl? What was her name?*"

"*He's gone, boss. Crandall is dead.*"

"*Dammit, we've got to find that servant, Bull.*"

"*Want me to round 'em up and bring 'em down here?*"

"*Are you mad? There's a dinner party going on upstairs. I've wasted too much time as it is. No, Bull, we'll have to wait until after the dinner to question the servants. I'll have Hawkins make sure none of them leaves before the end of the evening. In the meantime I want the Crandall farm searched for that letter.*"

"*Crandall's parents are bound to be there, boss. Want me to get rid of 'em, too?*"

"*Because you've done such a stellar job this evening, Bull? No, goddamn your runty hide! Tell them Crandall needs the evidence he hid. Tell them he sent you to find it. Try using your brain for a change, if there is any brain in that square head of yours. Now get out and take the body with you. Dump it in the river. And use the outside entrance, for God's sake. I've got to get back upstairs before I'm missed.*"

From her hiding place Maddie could hear the sound of something heavy being dragged from the wine cellar into the root cellar, up the steps and outside. And then there was only empty silence around her. Maddie's heart was beating so fast she was light-headed. Her stomach heaved from the blood under her shoes and her legs were so weak she couldn't stand. She knew it wouldn't take Slade long to figure out which servant Crandall had told. And then her life wouldn't be worth a penny.

She knew she had to run. But run to where? She had no relatives that she knew of. Her only hope lay in losing herself out west somewhere. She would have to slip back to the rowhouse, gather her belongings, and get to the train station before the dinner party ended. She would have to take the next train out and hope that she could stay one step ahead of Vincent Slade.

In the darkness of her bedroom, a hand suddenly clasped her shoulder. Maddie gasped and opened her eyes as a dark shape loomed over her. *Slade*. She tried to scream, but no sound came out. "Please," she cried in a ragged whisper, "I can't hurt you. Please don't kill me."

A shadowy face floated closer, hovered above her. Her heart raced, beating so hard against her ribs she knew it would have to give out.

"Maddie," she heard the vision whisper. She whimpered and tried to draw away from it, but it reached out, stroked her cheek.

"Maddie," it said again in Blaine's voice. "Maddie, I'm sorry."

"Blaine?" she whispered. She rubbed her eyes to clear her vision. It *was* Blaine. Relief washed over her. She pressed her hands to her face and wept softly. It had only been a dream.

"Don't cry, Maddie." Blaine stretched out beside her on the bed and lay his dark head on her breast, his arm across her waist. He whispered drunkenly, "I didn't mean those things I said. I didn't mean to hurt you. I need you, Maddie."

She tried to pry his arm from around her, but he

was too strong. "You don't need me," she said bitterly. "You have Penny."

"Just let me hold you," he murmured drowsily, his breath hot against the thin material of her chemise. "Just hold you."

Within seconds she heard the sound of heavy, even breathing. "Blaine," she whispered, "you have to go to your own room." She shook his shoulder. "Blaine." She looked around for some way to move him, some way to disentangle herself from him, but short of calling for help and waking the entire house, she could think of no way. She heaved a tremulous sigh and wondered how she was going to explain his presence in the morning.

He groaned suddenly, startling her, and settled one long leg over hers. Maddie tried to shift away from him, painfully aware of the feel of his body pressing intimately against hers, trying to deny the sudden heat coiling deep within her womb. For a moment she allowed herself the luxury of imagining it was Blaine she was marrying and not Jeremy. Hesitantly, she reached out to touch the dark stubble on his cheek, to run her fingers through the heavy silk of his hair. A warm glow spread through her, swelling her heart with love.

But she was not marrying Blaine. She was leaving him, leaving to keep him from finding out how she had deceived him. She closed her eyes and wept silently until she fell asleep, one hand resting gently on Blaine's head.

Blaine awoke sometime in the middle of the night to a pounding headache and dry mouth. He moved slightly and was surprised to feel the warmth and softness of a woman's body beneath his. He lifted his head and stared at the face on the pillow, the delicate features lit by moonlight, and tried to make sense of it. Where was Penny? Why was Maddie in Penny's room? And lying with him in Penny's bed?

Carefully, he eased away from her and lay on his back, blinking up at the white plaster ceiling. It wasn't Penny's room, he realized suddenly. He was home. Damn it, how much whiskey had he drunk? He swung his legs over the edge of the bed and groped for the pitcher of water and glass Mrs. MacLeod always kept on the bedside table in each room. The last thing he remembered was Penny helping him up the steps to her room.

Blaine drank thirstily, then shut his eyes as the cool liquid ran down his parched throat. He was still drunk from the whiskey and he wished now he hadn't imbibed so heavily. He rubbed his temples, trying to remember what had happened, why he was there. He had left Penny's house and come back to tell Maddie something—that he was sorry for being deliberately cruel, perhaps. No, it was something more important. His forehead wrinkled. What was it? Damn the heavy fog in his brain!

Blaine turned his head to study her. He vaguely remembered stumbling into her room, shutting the door quietly so as not to wake his mother, feeling his way in the dark to her bed. He remembered wondering why she was so frightened of him. What was it she had whispered? *"I can't hurt you. Please don't kill me."*

He lifted the sheet and slid underneath, moving until he lay even with her. He put his head next to Maddie's on the pillow and reached out to lift a silken lock of her red hair and wind it around his finger. She was still hiding from her demons, whatever or whoever they were. Why couldn't she tell him? Why wouldn't she trust him?

"Maddie," he said in a whisper, "trust me. Tell me who you're hiding from."

She moaned deep in her throat and even in the shadowy darkness of her room Blaine saw the grimace of fear that flickered across her pale features. He leaned over to press his lips against her satiny cheek, across her jaw to her ear in gentle kisses. "Maddie," he whispered. "You can trust me."

She sighed and turned on her side, facing him. Blaine leaned closer and pressed his lips against hers, kissing her gently until she began to kiss him back. Her hand snaked around his neck, sharpening his desire. Damn it, he wanted her so much he throbbed with it. He tossed the sheet aside and slid his hand down over the curve of her hip, gathering the soft material of her chemise in his hand and moving it up over her hips to her waist.

"Maddie, I love you," he murmured in her ear as he cupped her naked derriere and pulled her tightly against him.

Maddie came wide awake with a gasp and pushed him roughly away. She scrambled to her knees, struggling to cover herself. "What do you think you're doing?"

Blaine pressed his hands to his temples, his head pounding fiercely. "Don't yell, Maddie. I didn't mean to frighten you. I thought—"

"You said you just wanted to hold me," she whispered furiously, pulling the sheet to her chin. "Get out! Get out before someone finds you here."

He stumbled to his feet. "Damn it, Maddie. I didn't mean for this to happen. I just came back to tell you something."

"What?" she said in a shaky voice. "Tell me what?"

Blaine shook his head. "I can't remember."

"You're drunk, that's why you can't remember. Go back to Penny's bed. I'm sure she'd be happy to help you remember."

Maddie watched him move unsteadily from the room, then she sank weakly onto the bed and closed her eyes. *"Tell me who you're hiding from."* He had caught her unawares, and she had almost given away her secret. It was good she and Jeremy were leaving. Blaine was much too dangerous.

For a long while she lay in bed thinking about everything that had happened over the last twenty-four hours, and finally she rose with a sigh and went to sit at the window. The sun was just beginning to light the horizon beyond the wheat field. There was no sense trying to go back to sleep—not that she would sleep anyway.

Maddie, trust me. Tell me who you're hiding from. She shut her eyes against a sharp sting of tears. She wanted so much to tell him. But Blaine wouldn't understand the lies. He wouldn't understand why she just hadn't gone to the authorities with her information. She turned her back on the sunrise. How could she convince him that it was impossible for her to go to the police? How could she explain about her notorious father without giving Blaine even more reason to suspect she was lying?

Maddie went to the armoire and took out her riding outfit. After breakfast, she would go to town and buy the two tickets for New York. She would be safe with Jeremy in New York. Safe from Slade and Blaine.

Chapter 22

⎯⎯⎯∞◯◯∞⎯⎯⎯

The hotel restaurant buzzed with noisy conversation and the clank of metal utensils. A heavy, greasy smell hung in the air and flies dotted the windows. Vincent Slade ignored it all to smile at the lady sitting across the table from him. His eyes flickered briefly over her full, ripe curves in the tightly fitted yellow satin dress, moving to her pouting red lips and slanting brown eyes. She had traveled all afternoon to get to his hotel in Plymouth, but she certainly didn't look any worse for the wear. In fact, if she were willing, he just might invite her up to his room for the evening. She looked like a woman well versed in the art of pleasing a man.

He reached for the decanter. "More whiskey?"

"Why, thank you, honey." Penny Tadwell slanted him a coy glance.

"So you say the description on my reward poster matches this girl who claims to be Amelia Baker."

Penny ran one manicured fingertip around the rim of her glass. "Yes, I'm sure of it. She calls herself Maddie."

Maddie. Short for Madeline. Slade took a drink of whiskey and rolled it around his tongue, eyeing the lady speculatively. "What else can you tell me about her, Miss Tadwell?"

Penny frowned thoughtfully, her long, tapered fingers sliding up and down her glass, as if deciding whether she should reveal anything else. He waited confidently. Money always talked.

"Well, I can tell you that she and her fiancé, Jeremy Knight, are leaving for New York after the social gathering at their home." Penny smiled complacently.

"A social gathering?"

"This coming Saturday night. From what I hear it's going to be quite a big to-do."

Saturday. Two days away. Slade's pulse raced in anticipation. "Are you invited?"

Penny grinned. "Naturally."

"Would you like an escort, Miss Tadwell?"

Penny raised the glass to her red lips and took a sip, glancing at him cagily over the rim. "How kind of you to offer, Mr. Slade."

Slade raised his glass to hers. "Miss Tadwell, I don't know how to thank you for your information."

She touched her glass to his. "Here's to you, Mr. Slade."

"And to you, Miss Tadwell. May this day be pleasurable for both of us."

The morning sun was bright as Penny sashayed down the narrow hallway of the hotel in her yellow satin dress, humming softly to herself. She smiled at the old man standing behind the counter and nodded to an elderly female guest who huffed and turned her head away. *Let the old bitch toss her chin in the air*, Penny thought with a grin. It was nobody's business but her own that she'd spent the night with Vincent Slade.

For a moment her full lips thinned with distaste and a shudder shook her as she remembered the things Slade had forced her to do. But no matter. Blaine Knight was worth every minute of it. Once that interloper had been taken back to Philadelphia and thrown in jail, Blaine would forget all about her.

Yes, spending the night with that cruel skeleton of a man was worth getting Blaine back. Of course the thousand-dollar reward didn't hurt any either. She patted the thick bulge between her breasts, threw back her blonde head, and laughed out loud.

"Blaine, wake up."

Blaine groaned and tried to roll away from the voice. An insistent hand shook his shoulder. "Blaine, we have visitors. They said you were expecting them."

He cracked his eyes open and squinted at his mother. "What visitors?"

"Two nuns, Blaine. From New York. They've come to see Amelia. I wish you had let me know in advance."

And then Blaine remembered what he had wanted to tell Maddie. On his way to see Penny, young Daniel from the telegraph office had hailed him with a wire from the Mother Superior informing him that the sisters were on their way.

Damn it, why hadn't he turned back? Why hadn't he ridden home with the wire? But he hadn't been thinking clearly. He'd wanted only to distance himself from Maddie, not go back to her.

Blaine realized his mother was speaking, lecturing him about the scare his absence had given her.

"I've been beside myself with worry, Blaine. With Jeremy and Amelia leaving, how will I manage the farm?" She was holding out a cup of coffee and trying to look irate and helpless at the same time. As usual, she was expecting him to come to her rescue. But damn her, this time he was not going to do it.

Blaine struggled to raise himself to his elbows, gulped the hot coffee, and winced when it singed his tongue. "Where is she? Where's Amelia?" he rasped.

"She went to town sometime after breakfast to buy train tickets. She should be back any minute."

"What time is it?"

"Eleven o'clock. But you haven't said yet what we're going to do."

"You're going to go downstairs and entertain the sisters until I can get some clothes on. We'll talk about the other matter after this mess is cleared up."

"What mess, Blaine? Would you please tell me what is going on?"

He closed his eyes and dropped his head back against the pillow. Maddie was going to walk right into a trap, that's what was going on. A trap he had set in motion. That was what he'd come back to tell Maddie. He'd wanted to explain that the sisters had been invited to come well before her arrival, that it hadn't been his idea to invite them. He wanted to give her time to prepare.

His mother's dress rustled crisply as she moved toward the door. "All right, Blaine. I can see you're not in any frame of mind to discuss anything now. Hurry and get dressed. We'll be in the front parlor."

Blaine cursed his clumsiness as he fumbled with the buttons on his shirt. He'd made a mess of everything. It wasn't enough that he had revealed his feelings for Maddie in front of his mother, and possibly his brother as well, but then he had to blunder into Maddie's bedroom to apologize and end up trying to make love to her. Damn it, she was going to marry Jeremy in a matter of days. What kind of man was he?

He remembered the way Maddie had looked at him as she stood beside Penny's bed, her chin high, her shoulders stiff. *"He and I are leaving for New York right after the social. We'll be married by a justice of the peace as soon as we arrive."* Each word had knifed through his heart. He'd retaliated by lashing out at her, and even in his drunken condition he had seen the damage he'd inflicted on her with his spiteful words. Now, on top of that, she would find the sisters here.

He hurried down the staircase, running his fingers through his hair, feeling the stubble of beard on his face. He must look a sight. What would he say to the sisters?

Both women rose as he strode into the room, their white hats flapping like wings, their hands hidden beneath the voluminous black sleeves of their habits. Jeremy sat in a straight-backed chair, his eyebrows drawn together at the sight of Blaine's unshaven face. His mother sat on the blue velvet settee smiling with her usual graciousness. "Sister Mary Josephetta, Sister Mary Margaret, this is my eldest son, Blaine Knight."

Blaine nodded his head awkwardly. "Sisters."

"Mr. Knight," the older of the two said with a kind smile, "we can't tell you how much we appreciated receiving your letter."

He took a breath. "I think you should know that I—"

A flash of color passed the window. Footsteps sounded on the veranda outside and the front door squeaked as it opened. Blaine's stomach clenched. Maddie was home.

He turned as Maddie stepped into the parlor in her riding skirt and blouse, her long red hair tied back with a white ribbon, her cheeks blushed pink from exertion. She was completely unaware of what awaited her.

She seemed not to notice the nuns standing to one side. She ignored Blaine to look straight at Evelyn, smiling curiously. "Zeb said you wanted to see . . ." And then she stopped, frozen, her wide silver-green eyes sliding to the two figures in black, her fingers gripping the material of her skirt so tightly her knuckles turned white.

Blaine waited helplessly, wanting to know the truth and yet wanting to protect her from it at the same time. He watched her and hated himself for what he had started, feeling sick and powerless to stop it from happening.

"I'm sure you remember Sister Mary Josephetta and Sister Mary Margaret," Evelyn said quickly. "Blaine wrote them to let them know you were safe."

Maddie stared at the sisters for a moment, then quickly turned her head to look at Blaine. *Why?* she asked silently. *Why did you do this?* At the stark panic in her eyes, he knew that she had never seen the nuns before.

Blaine looked down, his chest tight, his mouth a grim line. Damn it, why *had* he done it? Why had he encouraged the nuns to come before the wedding? What difference would it have made to anyone where she grew up? He could think of no justification for his actions and was filled with remorse.

Blaine looked up as the two women moved across the room. He saw Maddie cringe as they stopped directly in front of her.

"My dear child," the older one said, leaning close to kiss her cheek.

The younger nun hugged her affectionately. "We were so relieved to hear you were safe."

They smiled at her, smiled into her astonished gaze. And all Maddie could do was stare at them.

Evelyn rose. "I think we should let Amelia get reacquainted with her friends," she said to her two sons.

Maddie refused to look at Blaine as he passed. Clenching his teeth together, he strode down the hallway and out the back door, heading for the barn. She had been telling the truth. And he had hurt Maddie far beyond what her lies had ever done to him. He had betrayed her. He doubted she would ever forgive him for it.

The parlor doors were closed. The room was silent. Maddie sat on the blue settee between the two sisters, her head bent in shame. "Why did you let them think you knew me?" she whispered in a ragged voice.

The older nun spoke first, her voice low and compassionate. "You must have had a very good reason for needing to hide behind another's identity."

Maddie's throat tightened. "Amelia is dead."

She heard two gasps of dismay and glanced at them, flinching at the sorrow in their eyes. "She died in the train wreck. We had become friends. She told me all about her fiancé, and I—" Maddie let out her breath. "—needed to hide. When I saw she was dead, I took her belongings." A tear rolled down her cheek. "I wish I hadn't done it. I wish I had died instead."

The younger sister took her hand and squeezed it, her own eyes misty. "It must be terribly difficult for you to have to pretend to be someone else. Can you tell us why you needed to hide?"

Maddie dropped her gaze and shook her head. She could not tell these kind nuns the horrors she had seen.

"Is there any way we can be of help?" the younger nun persisted.

Maddie gave her a faltering smile. "You've already helped."

"It took a great deal of courage for you to come here," the older nun remarked kindly.

Maddie stared past her, remembering the heart-stopping terror she had felt as she ran back to her little rowhouse, gathered her few belongings, and dashed to the train station. It had taken no courage to do what she had done. Only fear. Only cowardice. If she were truly courageous she would have gone back to Philadelphia to find the evidence. But she was a coward. A coward and a liar.

The older nun rose and looked around the room. "Amelia would have loved it here."

"Yes." Maddie gazed fondly at her surroundings. "She told me she'd always wanted a home of her own. A good, safe home just like this one."

"Perhaps," said the sister holding her hand, staring into her eyes, "perhaps there was a reason for what happened. Perhaps you needed a good home more than Amelia did."

Maddie blinked back fresh tears. "I'm sorry you came all this way for nothing."

"There was a purpose," the older nun said. "We may not understand it yet, but there was a purpose."

Yes, Maddie thought guiltily, there was a purpose. The sisters had helped her continue her deception.

Blaine sat at the dining room table and waited, his soup untouched, his hand curled tightly around the handle of his spoon. It had been two hours since the sisters had left. Two hours since Maddie had retired to her room and locked the door behind her. His mood was bleak. Since the night he had danced with Maddie his life had fallen apart, piece by piece, and he felt powerless to do anything about it. Maddie was leaving with Jeremy for New York. And his mother was expecting him to stay and run the farm. As usual, he was left with nothing.

Jeremy and Evelyn ate quietly, sensing his mood. Silence hung over them like a shroud. The only sounds were the ticking of the clock and the soft clink of metal against china. He heard footsteps and turned his head expectantly.

"She doesn't want supper," Mrs. MacLeod reported quietly. "I couldn't get her to come down, the poor lass."

"Take a tray up to her, then." Blaine frowned into his soup, remembering the sight of Maddie's shocked, hurt face. What kind of man was he? Lusting after his brother's fiancée, hurling drunken insults at her, climbing into her bed in the middle of the night. What had happened to his honor?

The door between the dining room and kitchen swung open and Daisy came in with a platter of sausages and thickly sliced boiled potatoes. The smell nauseated him. He dropped his spoon and scraped back his chair.

"You should eat something, Blaine," his mother scolded gently.

"I'm not hungry," he muttered as he strode from the room.

"Blaine?" Jeremy reached for a crutch. "C-could I see you in the study before you go?"

Evelyn stared at her younger son in dismay. "Jeremy, aren't you going to eat either?"

"This will only take a few minutes," Jeremy called as he hobbled from the room.

"D-damned thing." He sat down at the desk in the study and propped his crutch beside the chair. "I probably don't need it anymore, but I'm too scared to walk without it."

Blaine watched curiously as Jeremy drew out a paper from the drawer beneath the desktop and slid it across to him. Blaine picked it up. His eyes skimmed over the neatly written words in growing disbelief, and then in anger. "What the hell did you do this for?" he snarled, and tossed it back.

It was the deed to the farm. Made out to him.

Chapter 23

M addie stood at her bureau plaiting her long, heavy hair with fingers that shook uncontrollably. The thought of how close Blaine and Jeremy had come to learning her secret sent waves of nausea crashing through her. What if the sisters hadn't been so compassionate, so understanding? What then?

She pulled the long braid over her shoulder and tied the end with a white ribbon, pausing to stare at her reflection. Her face was ashen, her mouth pinched with worry. Her eyes—she bent closer to the glass—no, they were not her eyes. They were her father's eyes, shameless and deceitful. She twisted away, unable to bear the sight of her own face.

One more day to get through before the social. Maddie looked around her room and a lump formed in her throat. She'd be leaving it all behind—her pretty pink-flowered room, her high feather bed, her new home, her little mare . . .

Her heart.

Maddie knelt at the window and looked down at the deserted yard below, remembering how she had knelt in that exact spot on her first night there. What great expectations she'd had that night: a real home, a family, a fiancé who thought he loved her. Until she had come here, she hadn't realized how lonely she had been or how much she had needed a family.

Now her future seemed murky and frightening. She would be alone in a city she was supposed to know, with nothing to do all day but keep house while Jeremy painted.

Tears misted her eyes and Maddie blinked to disperse them. As much as it had hurt to lie to Blaine, nothing could have been worse than discovering that he had written to the sisters and asked them to come. He had tricked her, hoping to catch her at her lies. He'd said he loved her, but he couldn't love her and betray her.

Maddie rose woodenly and looked around. There had to be something she could do to keep her mind off Blaine. She thought of her little mare in the barn, and decided she would ride. She passed up her new riding outfit in favor of the more comfortable blue cotton shirt and boys' pants. Then, snatching the two buttery slices of bread left from the tray of food Mrs. MacLeod had brought up, Maddie slipped quietly into the hallway, pausing halfway down the stairs to be sure no one was there. She opened the front door slowly to keep it from squeaking, then dashed down the front steps and around to the side of the house, holding her breath as she darted across the yard to the barn. A long ride down the country roads was just what she needed.

*   *   *

Jeremy pushed the deed back across the desk toward his brother. "The land is yours, Blaine."

"For God's sake, Jer, your land is worth a fortune. You'd be a fool to give it away."

Jeremy smiled sadly. "If I died tomorrow and left you my paintbrushes and oils, what would you do with them?"

Blaine stared at him a moment. "I don't know. Pack them away, I suppose. Or give them to someone who could use them."

"It's hard to p-pack up a farm. This land is worth a fortune to you, Blaine, not to me. I have no love for these fields. But you do. So I'm giving them to you."

Although Jeremy's intentions were good, his generous gift stung Blaine's pride. Oliver Knight could have left a portion of the farm to Blaine; he knew as well as anyone how much Blaine loved the land and how ill-equipped Jeremy was to manage it, yet he had left everything to Jeremy, and perhaps rightly so. But now Blaine felt as though he were accepting charity from his brother. "What makes you think I want it?" Blaine asked crossly.

"Can you deny that you do?"

Blaine's temper flared. He slammed his fist against the desk. "I won't accept it. Oliver wanted you to have the farm. *You're* his heir."

"He left it to m-me to do with as I pleased. You should have had it anyway. You worked hard enough on it. I can barely manage to hitch up the plow. I've been useless around here my whole life, yet you've never held that against me. No, don't argue, Blaine. I know I can't do anything well but paint. I can't even c-court a woman, so I may as well go to New York and do the only thing I can do. I don't want the land, Blaine. I want you to have it. Please."

Blaine rubbed his eyes. He'd wanted the land for as long as he could remember, but now that it was within reach, he was hesitant. "Hell, Jeremy, I don't know what to say. I had thought to go away and make a fresh start, find myself a wife . . ."

"I think you've already found one."

Blaine's head came up sharply. "What did you say?"

"I'm n-not taking Amelia to New York."

Blaine was suddenly aware of his own pulse jumping in his neck, of the dull, steady thumping of his heart beneath his ribs. "Not taking her?" he repeated stupidly.

"She loves you, Blaine. I didn't s-see it at first, but it's there, in her eyes. It's even in her portrait. I finished it today, you know. It's one of my best works, but of course I'll leave it here. I p-promised her I would. You'll have to come to the back parlor this evening to see it. I'm going to hang it in the front hallway. I want it to be up in time for the social."

Blaine stared at him blankly, Jeremy's words little more than muddled sounds in his ear, while his own madly racing thoughts were a cacophony of noise. Somehow from it all a single thought emerged, a thought so unexpected, so extraordinary, that he had to sit down.

Maddie was free to marry him.

His fingers tightened around the arms of the chair. "Jer," he choked out, "she's your fiancée. You have to be sure about this. I can't marry her if you love her."

Jeremy suddenly looked lost as he sat in the big,

brown leather chair behind the desk. Lost and mournful. "She's not Amelia, Blaine," he said softly. "She's not the girl I fell in love with; she's not the girl who wrote those l-letters. I'm not even certain Amelia exists, but I *am* certain that someone wrote them for Maddie. The odd part is that I sensed the difference the first time I met her, but I dismissed it as ridiculous because she knew everything I had written to her. She even had the l-locket I sent her with a miniature of me in it."

Blaine rubbed his chin, thinking back to his first impression of Maddie: standing in the hospital in her too-small blue dress, her silver-green eyes wary and apprehensive, searching both of their faces for recognition, her only possession a solitary brown satchel. A satchel belonging to a girl named Amelia Baker. A satchel containing a dress that didn't fit and letters from a fiancé in Indiana who had never met her.

A satchel that could have been picked up by anyone after the train wreck.

A dull ache started in Blaine's chest and spread slowly through his body, wrapping tentacle-like around his heart, making it difficult to breathe. His fingers curled so tightly around the arms of the chair that the brass tacks on the underside gouged his flesh.

Amelia Baker had perished in the train wreck. Maddie had survived, and for whatever reason, had assumed Amelia's identity, down to the locket around her neck. Damn it, why hadn't he seen it before? Maddie knew everything Jeremy had written *because she had the letters.*

Suddenly it all made sense—all the little inconsistencies that should have given her away but hadn't, because none of them had expected her to be anyone other than Amelia. He ground his teeth in vexation, remembering how astute he had thought himself, believing she had invented Amelia's personality to gain a husband. And clever Maddie had let him believe it. She had fooled them all. Hell, she had even fooled a woman who had known the real Amelia.

But the most incomprehensible part of the whole charade was that despite his irritation, despite his disappointment, despite everything, he still loved her.

And he didn't even know who she was.

Blaine suddenly realized that Jeremy was speaking to him, had been speaking to him for some time. He tried to focus on his brother's pale features, his mind turning at a dizzying speed.

"Please understand, Blaine, if I don't do this n-now, I may never have another chance to be someone. I've already informed Mother. I suppose the only thing left to do is tell Amelia."

"Would you let me tell her, Jer? I want to be sure about her feelings for me. She knows I sent for the sisters, you see. It may take some talking to patch things up."

Jeremy grinned. "I saw her walk by the window a little while ago, n-no doubt on her way to the barn. You might still be able to catch her there."

Blaine ran his fingers through his hair, his mind too numb to absorb everything. "I think I need a drink first."

Jeremy laughed shakily. "P-pour me some, too, will you?"

Blaine took the whiskey from the cabinet, sloshed

the amber liquor in two glasses, and handed one to his brother.

"To your land, Blaine," Jeremy said, holding out his glass. He stopped suddenly and smiled. "How good it feels to say that."

Blaine drank until the whiskey was gone, then sat staring down into the glass, watching the last drop roll around the bottom. The land was his. The wheat fields, the corn and oat fields, the grape arbor, the apple orchard—all of it was his. *His!* He wanted to throw back his head and laugh in triumph. He wanted to shout it out so loud that Oliver Knight would hear it from his grave.

But most of all he wanted to share the news with Maddie.

"Maddie?"

Maddie froze at the sound of Blaine's voice calling, then quickly hefted the heavy saddle up onto its peg and hurried to one of the small four-paned windows in the side wall of the barn to look out. Blaine was standing near the water pump at the back of the house, his hands on his hips, looking around the yard. And suddenly he started toward the barn.

Her heart leaped to her throat. She didn't want to see him. Her wounds were too raw, her nerves strung too tight. She glanced around and spotted the ladder to the loft. It was so obvious a hiding place Blaine would never think to look there. With sweating palms she scurried up the creaking rungs of the ladder and knelt in the hay, hardly daring to draw a breath as Blaine walked into the huge building and looked around.

"Maddie!" he called sharply.

Her foot cramped and she winced, trying to ease it out from beneath her body without disturbing the hay. She heard him mutter to himself as he hoisted his saddle from its peg and carried it to the stall where the big chestnut stood. She didn't move until he'd left the barn, and then she let out her breath in a rush and closed her eyes, tugging off her shoe to massage her toes.

If only she could hide from Blaine until it was time to go to New York.

The evening air felt so cool on her foot that she removed her other shoe and peeled off the thick wool stockings. Digging her bare toes into the hay, Maddie lay on her back, her knees up, her hands folded across her stomach, listening to the soothing sounds of the animals below settling in for the night.

She loved it here in the barn; loved the nickering of the horses, the soft lowing of the cows, the sweet, musty smell of the hay, the chirping of crickets in the dark corners. She would miss it terribly. Maddie turned her face to the side as tears gathered in her eyes. She wouldn't think of it. She would concentrate instead on what New York City would be like.

A yawn took her by surprise. It had been a long, trying day, and she was exhausted. If she just shut her eyes for a moment, maybe she would feel better.

Blaine tied his horse to the iron hitching ring in front of the house and strode inside. "Mrs. MacLeod?" he called softly.

In a few moments the housekeeper came bustling down the hallway from the kitchen. "Ye didn't find her?"

Blaine sighed wearily and ran a hand over his

eyes. "Her horse is in its stall; she wasn't in any of her usual places. I don't know where else to look."

Mrs. MacLeod patted his arm. "I wouldn't worry about her. No doubt she's right under our noses, curled up fast asleep."

Blaine gave her a tired smile. "You're right. She's probably in the most obvious place—" He stopped and swung to stare through the screen door. *The most obvious place.* Maddie had told him herself where it would be. The hayloft.

As he had guessed, Maddie was fast asleep in the loft, her head turned to the side, one hand on her stomach, the other lying limply at her side, palm up. In the fading evening light, her long lashes looked dark against her pale skin and there were purple rings beneath her eyes. Her red hair lay in a thick braid over the shoulder of her blue shirt and her bare toes peeked out from beneath two small mounds of hay.

Blaine smiled, the sight warming his heart. He stepped quietly onto the floor of the loft and sat down cross-legged to study her. He wanted to hate her for deceiving them, for pretending to be Amelia Baker, for making him fall in love with her. But he couldn't. God help him, he couldn't.

Who are you, Maddie? he thought. *Why did you steal another woman's identity? Who are you hiding from?* He reached out to touch her hand, letting the tip of his index finger trace the lines in her palm, remembering her nightmares. *"I can't hurt you. Please don't kill me."* If only he knew who or what she was so desperately trying to escape, maybe he could help her.

How can I get her to trust me?

Maddie's fingers curled around his and suddenly

she turned her head and looked at him, her eyes growing wide. With a little cry, she rose to her elbows.

"Sh-h-h, Maddie," Blaine whispered. "It's only me." He bent over her, lowering his mouth to hers.

She twisted out from beneath him and sat with her back turned to him. "Leave me alone, Blaine. Go away."

Blaine reached out to touch her shoulder, but she jerked at the contact. He dropped his hand. "Maddie, I'm sorry I didn't tell you the sisters were coming."

"Why did you write to them?" she asked accusingly.

He sighed. "To find out when they intended to pay us a visit. They had been invited a month before you arrived, but they weren't sure when they were coming. I thought it would be best if they came sooner rather than later."

She turned her head and he saw the determined set of her jaw, the flashing of her eyes. "Because you figured I lied about them."

Blaine looked at her for a moment, then bent his head. "Yes."

"Well, you were right," she said defiantly. "I *am* a liar. The sisters weren't unkind to me at all."

"Then why did you lie about them?"

"It was because I—" Maddie paused, and in that split second Blaine saw all her bravado slip away. She chewed her lip.

Blaine held his breath and waited. *Tell me the truth about Amelia, Maddie. Trust me.*

She straightened her back, lifted her chin resolutely. "It was because I didn't want to be reminded of my past. I didn't want any ties. I wanted to start fresh here."

Blaine's shoulders sagged and he sighed. She was still lying. What had he done to make her afraid to tell him the truth? "Then I apologize again for not telling you about their visit. I never meant to hurt you. I wouldn't do anything to hurt you."

Maddie kept her back toward him. "It's not important now. I'll be gone in another two days."

Blaine's stomach tightened. What if she were counting on going to New York? What if she didn't want to stay on the farm and marry him? He ran his fingers through his hair. He could not tell her about Jeremy's plans until he was sure of her feelings.

"Maddie," he said huskily, and reached for her, only to have her jerk again at his touch. Determinedly, he moved closer and pulled the end of her white ribbon, letting it slip softly to the hay.

"What are you doing?" she whispered hoarsely.

He began to unbraid her hair, his fingers slipping through the heavy plait to loosen it, letting the thick locks cascade over her shoulders and down her back like a satin waterfall. "Making love to you," he murmured against her ear.

Her body went rigid, yet she made no move to stop him as he pressed soft kisses beneath her ear. "Maddie, I don't care that you lied about the sisters." Blaine ran his hands slowly down her arms and up again. "Will you forgive me for going behind your back?"

She said nothing, but he felt her shoulders relax as he gently kneaded them. He tugged her shoulder, turning her toward him. "I love you, Maddie."

She resisted for only a moment, and then she

went willingly into his arms and buried her face against his neck. Blaine closed his eyes as the light rose scent of her skin reached his nostrils. His hands moved down her back. He felt her fragility, her vulnerability, and his heart swelled with love. "Maddie, do you love me?"

She shook her head. "I can't answer that. You know I can't."

"Yes, you can."

Maddie started to push away from him, but he held her tightly. "I won't let you evade the question this time."

Maddie closed her eyes. How could she admit to feelings that were wrong? How could she face Jeremy in the morning after confessing her love to Blaine? "No," she whispered.

"More lies, Maddie?"

Her hand tightened on the material of his shirt. "Why is it so important for me to say it?"

"Because I want the truth for a change."

She pushed herself away from him. "You demand I answer your questions, yet you never answer mine."

"I didn't know you had any."

She toyed with a piece of hay on the floor. "Is Penny going with you when you leave here?"

He chuckled and tugged a lock of her hair. "Would you be jealous if she did?"

Maddie sniffed disdainfully. "Jealous of that hussy?"

"The truth, Maddie."

Tell him the truth about how terribly jealous she was of Penny Tadwell? Never! He would think her childish and petty. Or worse yet, he might begin to think Penny was the better of the two women. Maddie changed the subject instead. "Tell me about your medal of honor."

She felt him release her hair and she turned her head to glance at him curiously. His eyes were no longer warm, but were cold and shuttered, his face a stony mask.

Maddie turned fully to face him and reached out to push back that errant lock of hair falling over one eye. "What happened in South Dakota, Blaine?" she said softly. "Your mother said you were a hero. Why won't you talk about it?"

His fingers suddenly gripped her wrist, but he only brought her hand to his lips. He kissed the sensitive skin of her palm, staring at it with unseeing eyes. "It's in the past. Nothing that concerns you. Leave it be, Maddie."

"Then don't ask me to answer your questions." She tried to pull her hand away, but his grip held. Slowly, he looked up at her, revealing in that one glance something completely unexpected, something so foreign to his nature that she could only blink in surprise.

Shame.

"Tell me, Blaine," she whispered.

For a moment he studied her intently, as though evaluating his risks, weighing something deep inside himself, then he raked his fingers through his hair. His movements were agitated, his body tensed like a tightly coiled spring. And then he began to talk, quickly, as if he wanted to get it out and be done with it.

"We were given orders to take our troops out and round up the Sioux, to bring them back to a cavalry camp on Wounded Knee Creek. After Sitting Bull was killed, the Indians had fled the reservation to join Big Foot's band on the Cheyenne River, and the government was afraid the Indians would make trouble if they were left there. I argued with my commanding officer. I told him I'd had dealings with the Sioux and I knew that to herd them back like cattle would be intolerable to their pride. But he wouldn't listen. Instead, I was accused of being an Indian sympathizer and a coward. I was interrogated for hours and then confined to my quarters while my men rode out with another troop."

Blaine inhaled deeply, as if to relieve the tension, then blew it out. When he spoke again, it was in a flat voice. "The Indians were brought into the camp and penned like animals, stripped of their dignity and then ordered to surrender their weapons. They resisted, as I knew they would. A rifle was fired. The soldiers panicked and began to shoot—men, women, children, it didn't matter who or why. When I heard the shooting start, I tried to break down the door of my quarters, and finally had to break the glass of a window to get out."

He paused to lick dry lips, to wipe the sweat off his brow. "The first thing I saw was my commanding officer crouched behind a water barrel, the muzzle of his gun aimed at a young Indian boy hiding under a wagon. The boy couldn't have been more than five years old. I shouted at my commander to stop, but he didn't move, didn't respond, just kept aiming at his target as if he were out on a deer hunt. I took out my pistol, walked up behind him, and pointed it at his head. Damn, how I wanted to kill the bastard!"

Through gritted teeth Blaine admitted, "But I couldn't pull the trigger." His jaw muscles clenched and his fists tightened as he stared straight ahead, seeing what Maddie could not see. Then, as if all his anger had suddenly drained away, Blaine's shoulders sagged and his voice fell to an almost inaudible whisper. "He shot the boy. Over two hundred Indians died that day at the hands of the soldiers. And I couldn't save one little boy."

Maddie's throat ached from holding back tears. She wrapped her arms around his shoulders and held him, feeling his violent shaking and the chill that raised goose bumps on his skin, and she knew what that admission had cost him.

After a few moments, she felt him shudder as he finished his story. "Another officer saw me standing there with my pistol drawn." Blaine gave a sharp, humorless laugh. "He thought I was trying to protect my commander. I was awarded a medal of honor. Do you know the significance of a medal of honor? Very few are ever awarded, maybe two a year. And yet twenty-seven medals were handed out for that massacre alone. Twenty-seven! I still can't fathom it. And one of them was mine. A medal of honor for letting a young boy die."

Maddie stroked his hair. "Sometimes we do things in a moment of panic that we regret later. We just have to put it behind us and—"

He pulled away from her, glared at her, a muscle in his jaw twitching angrily. "Damn it, Maddie, don't you see what I did? I froze. I couldn't pull that trigger to save an innocent child because I *froze*. What kind of soldier can't pull a damn trigger? What kind of man would let a child die?"

"You knew you'd be killed yourself if you shot an officer," she reasoned.

"Damn the consequences, Maddie," he ground out. "It was a matter of honor."

Maddie blushed ashamedly and looked down. Honor. She had no honor. How could he expect her to understand a matter of honor? If she had honor she would have let Amelia die in peace, instead of stealing her identity and deceiving good people. At least now she understood why Blaine didn't like to talk about it.

"You need to know, Maddie," Blaine said quietly, "that I will never get out of my mind what happened there. It's something that will always shadow me. I can't pick up a gun without remembering that little boy's frightened face." He looked down at the barren boards of the loft. "I can't pick up a gun without becoming physically ill. Do you know what that does to a man? It paralyzes him with fear. What if I had to defend myself or a loved one? What if I froze at the crucial moment?"

"Yet you were planning to go back to the army," she reminded him.

Blaine sighed. "I was hoping for a desk job somewhere. What else did I have? There was nothing for me here."

Maddie hung her head, regretting that she had reopened the wound, but somehow knowing he had carried the burden alone far too long. "I'm sorry, Blaine," she said softly. "I'm sorry for what you've gone through."

"I'm sorry, too, Maddie. I didn't mean to be so harsh with you." He paused and then said, "Come here."

Maddie looked up in surprise. Blaine opened his arms to her and she went into them, holding him tightly, her arms wrapped around his rib cage, her cheek pressed against his chest. He was such a good man. She loved him so much she thought her heart would explode.

"I can't expect you to understand what I went through," he murmured against the top of her head, his hand moving in slow circles on her back. "I only hope you don't think less of me now that you know."

Less of him? Maddie closed her eyes, listening to the reassuring beat of his heart. Not less of him; less of herself. She tilted her head to gaze up into his dark eyes, saying the words he'd been waiting to hear, for once giving him the truth. "I don't think less of you, Blaine. I love you. With all my heart."

He stared at her for a long moment. "Then marry me."

Her eyes widened in surprise. "You know I can't."

"If you could, would you?"

"It's pointless to answer that."

"You're evading again, Maddie."

She pulled away from him. Why was he pressing her for an answer to a cruel, pointless question?

Blaine's hand ran down her arm. "Jeremy made some decisions today."

Maddie grew still. "Decisions?"

"He gave me the farm." Blaine moved her heavy hair aside and bent to kiss her neck. "It's mine now."

"Yours? The land is yours?" Maddie smiled joyously and turned to face him.

"Ours, Maddie, if you'll marry me."

Her smile dissolved as she gazed at his serious face, and tears slowly filled her eyes. She looked down and shook her head. "I can't, Blaine. I can't desert Jeremy."

He cupped her chin with his hand. "Jeremy knows how I feel about you, Maddie. And he's also figured out how you feel about me. He admitted not half an hour ago that it would be a mistake for the two of you to marry."

Fresh tears blurred Maddie's vision and rolled down her cheeks. "Poor Jeremy. I never wanted this to happen, Blaine. I tried to mask my feelings." She used the heel of her hand to dash away her tears. "Bother! I've never cried so much in my entire life."

Blaine produced his handkerchief to wipe her face. "Some things can't be hidden, Maddie."

"Is Jeremy badly hurt?"

"I'm ashamed to say I was too caught up in my own joy to notice."

She started to rise. "I should go talk to him."

Blaine caught her hand and pulled her back. "You haven't given me an answer yet."

Maddie rested her hands on his shoulders and searched his dark eyes. Then she gave him a quick nod. "Yes. I'll marry you."

A broad grin split his face. "Ah, Maddie, you don't know how much I wanted to hear you say that." He cupped her face in his big hands and kissed her.

Maddie didn't know whether to laugh or cry. She could have sung out with the sheer joy of knowing she could love him openly now, of knowing he returned that love.

He took her back with him to the hay, pressing light, teasing kisses along her jaw and down her neck, where he began to work the buttons of her blue cotton shirt, swiftly moving from one to the next until they were all undone. She drew in her breath as his warm palm slid inside the shirt and cupped her breast, gently molding it with his strong fingers, strumming the sensitive nipple with his thumb.

He captured her mouth once again. She moaned deep in her throat at the sensual stroke of his tongue against hers, and trembled from the extraordinary feelings flooding her body. She struggled to control the riot of thoughts and emotions whirling in her head, but Blaine's mouth was too hot and insistent and his touch too intoxicating for clear thought.

He pushed the shirt off her shoulders and let it slip down her arms, baring her breasts to his hungry gaze. She held her breath as he bent his head to cover one supple crest with his mouth and she whimpered with sudden apprehension as powerful surges of desire rippled through her from breast to belly.

Blaine moved up quickly to kiss her, to reassure her. "You're beautiful, Maddie. There's nothing to be frightened of. Will you trust me?"

Maddie searched his eyes and found only tenderness there. She nodded and he kissed her, then bent his head to her other breast, nipping it lightly, teasing it with his tongue until it puckered and tingled. A soft moan slipped out as Maddie dropped her head back, reveling in the sweetness, the sensuousness of his touch. She felt his fingers on the buttons of her pants and suddenly the canvas material parted, exposing bare skin to the sultry night air.

The rough stubble on his chin scratched her as he moved lower to press kisses around her navel and onto her smooth abdomen. Her flesh quivered under the heat of his breath. She gasped and reached for him as he moved lower still.

Then Blaine rose up again, smiling into her eyes as he lowered his mouth once again to claim hers. Maddie clutched his back and kissed him in return, as hungry for the taste of him as he was of her. She felt his hand slip between their bodies to caress the satin skin of her belly and then she swallowed a gasp as his fingers probed lower, stroking her gently and relentlessly—a shockingly intimate, yet exquisitely arousing touch that made her flesh throb with desire, until she was so overwhelmed by it that rational thought was hopeless.

Maddie broke the kiss and clung to him, panting, as her passion built to a fever pitch. "Blaine," she cried, arching against his hand. "Oh, dear Lord, what's happening to me?"

"Exactly what should happen, Maddie."

He moved apart from her and began to rid himself of his clothing. Maddie's eyes widened fearfully at the sight of his engorged sex springing from the dark hair of his groin, but he was immediately beside her to reassure her.

"Maddie, you said you would trust me. I'll try not to hurt you, I promise." He covered her with his body and Maddie felt the sudden heat of his shaft between her thighs. She swallowed hard. "Kiss me," she whispered fearfully.

Blaine kissed her as he entered her, slowly, gently, until she gasped, tensing as her maidenhead tore. He waited, letting her adjust to the feel of him inside her; then he slowly thrust deeper and paused again while he kissed her and murmured soothing words against her ear.

Maddie felt him shaking and knew he was holding back, trying to make it easy for her. She wrapped her arms around his strong back and kissed his neck, letting him know by her actions that she was all right, loving him so much her heart felt as if it were swollen to twice its size. A tear slipped out from beneath her closed eyelids. She was giving herself to Blaine, taking him into herself, joining her soul to his, letting him get closer to her than anyone ever had before.

Indeed, she had never felt as close to another human being, not even to her mother. Blaine seemed to understand her simplest needs and deepest fears, seemed to see inside her soul to the lonely spirit hiding there. Yet that same closeness frightened her.

Blaine was breaking down her defenses—yet she had to keep him from learning the whole truth. If he knew she had taken Amelia's identity for her own purposes, if he knew her father was not dead but in prison for deceit of his own, Blaine would realize exactly what kind of person she was. Maddie was desperate to prevent that from happening. For no matter how much Blaine professed to love her, if he knew how deceitful she was he would leave her.

That was why her mother had left Freddy.

It was not going to happen to her.

For a long while afterward, Maddie lay quietly with Blaine in the loft, savoring their newfound intimacy. She nestled against his bare chest, running her fingers over the dark, coarse hair. Jeremy had been right. It would have been a mistake to marry a man she didn't love. Yet it still bothered her to think that Jeremy would be alone in New York— and she didn't even know anyone there who could help him. A sigh slipped out before she could stop it.

Blaine's voice rumbled low in his chest, vibrating softly against her ear. "What is it, Maddie?"

"I was thinking about Jeremy going alone to New York."

Blaine's hand ran down her bare back. "If I know my mother, she'll be going with him."

Maddie lifted her head to stare at Blaine. "Do you really think so? I'd feel so much better if she did."

Blaine toyed with a lock of her hair and watched her. "I think you'd feel even better if you told me the truth about Amelia Baker."

Chapter 24

Maddie felt as if the breath had been knocked from her lungs. She stared at him wide-eyed, her mind frozen.

"Amelia died in the train wreck, didn't she, Maddie?"

He knew. Oh, God, he knew! The blood drained from her head so quickly Maddie had to brace her hands on the floor to keep from swaying. How did he know? How had she failed? Her head spun. There was no way out this time; she had run out of lies. Blaine would leave her just as surely as her mother had left Freddy.

Maddie opened her mouth to speak but the words caught in her throat. She couldn't breathe. There was no air left to breathe. She closed her eyes as the floor came up to meet her.

Vincent Slade closed his traveling bag and turned to regard Bull sprawled in a chair in the hotel room, sipping steadily at a glass of whiskey. "Do you have everything?" he snarled.

Bull grinned and patted his frock coat pocket. "Right here."

"Where's Potter?"

"Waiting at the saloon."

"Let's go then. I want to get to Miss Tadwell's boardinghouse in plenty of time to change."

Bull gazed at him through slightly unfocused eyes. "Wouldn't want to be late to the party, would you?"

Slade glared at him. "Lay off the booze. You have to look like a federal marshal, not the town drunk. And try to mind your manners around Miss Tadwell. I don't want her to suspect anything and go running to the Knights."

Bull snorted. "Don't worry. I always come through for you, don't I?"

Slade turned to check his appearance in the small oval looking glass over the cheap pine bureau. "Yeah, you've come through for me all right. And when the time comes, I'll make sure you're justly rewarded."

She was hot, so hot her skin was on fire. The train. She was back in the burning train. Jeremy was there, too, searching through the bodies, calling a name. Oh, God, he was looking for Amelia. She stumbled toward him, the black smoke blinding her, the smothering heat paralyzing her legs. "Here I am," she cried.

"You're not Amelia!" he said, pushing her away. "You killed Amelia so you could marry me."

She shook her head frantically. "No, Jeremy, Amelia died in the wreck. I didn't kill her. Please, you have to believe me."

"Believe you?" He threw back his head and laughed, and suddenly his face was Blaine's face. "How can I be-

lieve you? All you've ever done is lie to me."

"Blaine, I love you."

"It's no use, Maddie. We know all about you. Your clever scheme is over. We're sending you back where you came from."

"You can't!" She fell on her knees, her hands clasped before her. "Vincent Slade will kill me. I saw what he did. I know about the murders."

"Another lie?" He shook off her hands, looking down at her with utter loathing. *"You were right, Maddie. You should have died in the train wreck. It would have been better for everyone."*

She put her hands to her face and sobbed, bending her head down to the floor, curling her body into itself. She should have let Amelia die in peace. She never should have tried to deceive them. Now she was alone, alone in a dark, frightening place where only Vincent Slade could find her.

"Maddie, sweetheart, don't cry. I'm here."

Blaine's voice penetrated the darkness, reached through her fear, and drew her back. Her eyelids opened slowly and she looked around in confusion. She was lying in the hayloft, Blaine hovering over her. A blanket covered her, the wool scratching her bare skin.

"Drink this water." He held a tin cup to her lips and she gulped thirstily.

"Maddie, have you eaten anything since lunch?"

She raised herself to her elbows. "Bother! I don't faint . . ." Her words trailed off as she remembered the dream. The dream about Amelia. Her heart began to pound as everything came back to her, Blaine's confession, his slow, sweet seduction, and then—the awful question: *"Amelia died in the train wreck, didn't she?"*

Blaine knew about Amelia's death. He knew Maddie had lied once again. Why, then, had he asked her to marry him? She glanced quickly at him and saw that he was waiting patiently for her to finish.

Tell him the truth, her conscience commanded. *He'll understand. He loves you.*

But her mother had loved Freddy, too. And she had come to despise his deceitful ways. Her mother's words rang in her ears. *"A leaf never falls far from the tree, Maddie."* She gulped back a sob. How would she live without Blaine? How would she survive knowing he despised her?

But wait! He couldn't know everything. He couldn't know about her notorious father; Freddy was in prison. And Blaine didn't know the true reason for switching places with Amelia, either. If Blaine knew everything he wouldn't have asked her to marry him. He despised dishonesty.

Desperation engulfed her. She *had* to keep him from finding out the full truth.

"What is it, Maddie?"

"I was dreaming about—" She took a steadying breath. "About Amelia."

Blaine moved closer, staring deep into her eyes. "I want to know what happened to her."

If only he knew what he was asking. Maddie chewed her lip. "All right," she said at last. "I'll tell you." She shifted to a more comfortable position. "We were traveling together—"

"From New York?"

"Yes." A story was forming in her mind, a way to keep him from knowing how selfish her actions had been. Maddie rushed on. "Amelia knew I lived alone—my father had died when I was twelve and my mother died only last year, you see—and so she talked me into coming west with her so I could start fresh, only I had decided to go on to Chicago to try to find work there." She glanced quickly at Blaine to judge his reaction, but found his expression unreadable.

"When the train went into the ravine I tried to hold onto Amelia, but we were thrown apart." Maddie clenched her fists, her nails digging into her palms, seeing again in her mind's eye the horror of the wreck, the flames, the bodies. Her throat tightened, her voice becoming as hoarse as it had been that night. "Someone was yelling at me to get out. The train was on fire and the smoke was so thick I could barely see, but I could hear Amelia calling to me, and I couldn't leave her there to die. She had a brand-new life waiting for her. I had to find her."

Maddie choked back a sob, remembering the sight of Amelia's broken, lifeless body. She closed her eyes and tilted back her head, the pain and guilt of what she had to say knifing through her heart. "Amelia was lying under a seat. Her legs were pinned and her chest was crushed by timber from the train. She was—dying. I knew she was dying. I could hear her breath rattling in her lungs. She tried to tell me something, but her voice was so weak I had to press my ear next to her lips. She—she asked me to take her locket and her satchel with the letters."

Maddie bowed her head, twisting her fingers together in her lap, swallowing the bile in her throat. "She asked me to take her place—as Jeremy's fiancée."

She turned, gazing at Blaine with pleading eyes. "I refused at first, but Amelia begged me, begged me with her last breath. She was so worried that Jeremy would never find anyone else to marry. She didn't want to let him down. And I kept thinking how much I wanted a home and a family, and so I agreed to do it." Guiltily, Maddie looked down, unable to bear his penetrating gaze.

"Didn't you realize sooner or later someone would discover the truth?"

"Yes, but it was too late then. I couldn't bear to hurt Jeremy by admitting Amelia was dead."

From the corner of her eye, she saw Blaine rub his jaw. His dark eyes studied her skeptically, as if he couldn't quite believe her. "Tell me about the person in your dreams, Maddie. The one you're always hiding from."

Maddie tensed. She thought she'd covered everything, but of course Blaine would remember that. How much could she safely tell him about Slade? Would Blaine demand they go back to Pennsylvania for the evidence to prove Slade was behind the murder? She thought it best to test the waters before she told him everything. "He was a man I worked for. I learned some things about him so I left."

"Who was he? What was his name?"

Maddie shivered, a violent shiver that reached down to her soul and wrapped around her heart like a viper. "Vincent Slade."

"Did you work for him before you took a job with the seamstress?"

She glanced away guiltily. "I never worked for a seamstress. Amelia did. I worked as kitchen help for rich families."

Blaine was silent for a moment, then asked evenly, "Was Vincent Slade one of those you worked for?"

Maddie nodded unhappily.

She felt Blaine studying her. "Were you afraid for your life, Maddie?"

She nodded again.

"Why?"

"I told you why. I learned some things about him that I shouldn't have."

"What *things*, Maddie?" he asked firmly.

Maddie felt cold all over, thinking about those *things*. "I learned he was responsible for a murder."

"Do you know that for sure?"

She nodded quickly, afraid he would think she was lying again. "Oh, yes! I know what he did."

"Did you go to the police?"

She was afraid he would ask that. If Blaine knew there was proof of a murder, naturally he would want to find it. It was the honorable thing to do. But Blaine didn't know Slade's capabilities or his influence or his depravity. Blaine didn't know the mortal danger he would be putting them both in.

She took a deep breath. "I couldn't go to the police. I didn't have any proof and no one would take the word of—" Maddie caught herself before she mentioned her father. "—of a kitchen helper over someone important."

"That's why you left then? Because you were afraid of Slade? Is that also why you agreed to switch identities with Amelia?"

Maddie glanced at him guiltily, dropped her head, and gave a short nod. "Vincent Slade is an evil man, Blaine," she said in a choked voice, fighting back tears of remorse. "I was frightened of what he might do to me if he found out I knew. I wanted to find a place where he could never find me."

Blaine wrapped his arms around her and held her

to his chest. "It's okay, sweetheart. You're safe now. Besides, as you say, you had no proof. You weren't a threat to him. I only wish I had known sooner so I could have allayed your fears and put a stop to your nightmares. There was no reason to keep that from us, Maddie. You know we wouldn't have held it against you."

"I wanted to forget about it, Blaine, just as you wanted to forget what happened at Wounded Knee. I never meant to hurt any of you."

"You were hurting yourself, too, Maddie. You were about to marry a man you didn't love just to keep up false pretenses."

"But I would have been a good wife to Jeremy," she murmured against his shoulder. "You must believe that, Blaine. It's just that I hadn't counted on falling in love with you."

Blaine pressed kisses on the top of her head. "I hadn't counted on falling in love with you, either, sweetheart."

"Does Jeremy know Amelia died in the wreck?" Maddie asked.

"He only told me he was sure you were not the girl who had written to him."

"I'm so sorry for Jeremy," she whispered.

"He'll have to know, Maddie."

She nodded.

Blaine stroked her hair. "I'll tell him if you want me to."

"No." She let out her breath. "It has to come from me."

"I'll tell my mother, then. She'll understand you wanted to help Amelia." His arms tightened reassuringly around her. "It will be all right, sweetheart."

Maddie wrapped her arms around his solid rib cage and breathed in the male scent of him, feeling the coarse, curly hair against her cheek, loving him so fiercely she thought she would die from it. It would be all right now. There was no need to run any longer. Blaine believed her story and she knew Jeremy would, as well. And it was so close to the truth that she didn't fear a slip of the tongue.

"I don't want you to be afraid of Vincent Slade anymore, either," he said firmly. "Do you hear me? You don't have to dream about him hurting you ever again. He's out of your life forever."

His warmth and strength enveloped her, seeped into those dark, frightened places deep inside her and made her believe he could protect her. He took her down to the hay with him and kissed her, his tongue boldly meeting her own, his arms around her back. She threaded her fingers in his hair as his kisses became more passionate, more demanding, more possessive, rekindling the flames of her desire. She felt his hand slide down her back, pulling her tightly against him, and she moved in answer to him, feeling his manhood throb and swell at the apex of her thighs.

"Damn, Maddie, I need you," Blaine said, trailing hot kisses down the slender column of her neck, running his hands over the silken mounds of her breasts, following with his mouth. One hand slid up her thigh, finding heat and arousal, his own passion burning out of control as she gasped and writhed at his touch.

Blaine covered her with his body, seeking entrance between the damp folds, seeking deliverance. He thrust inside and felt the tightness of her sheathing him, his own desire heightened to an unbearable measure by her passionate response. He drove himself faster, deeper, his breathing labored. He heard her gasp and cry out his name. He felt her fingers dig into his back as her body went rigid beneath him, as she found her own blissful release. And then he shuddered as his seed spilled into her womb. Maddie was his. He loved her. Nothing else mattered.

When the roosters began to crow, they dressed and hurried to the house, slipping quietly upstairs, their shoes clutched to their chests. They stopped outside Maddie's bedroom for a lingering kiss.

"I love you, Maddie," Blaine murmured in her ear, trying to kiss her again.

Reluctantly, she pushed him away. "Go, before we're caught." She opened the door, but he pulled her back.

"You haven't told me your real name. I can't ask you to marry me properly until you tell me your name."

"Madeline," she whispered as he pressed kisses against her ear. "Madeline Anne Beecher."

"Will you marry me, Madeline Anne Beecher?"

"Yes," she whispered joyfully. "Yes, I'll marry you, Blaine."

He kissed her deeply, thoroughly, then sent her into her room with a gentle push. "Close your door and lock it before I lose all control and come after you." At Maddie's giggle, he grinned recklessly. "I'll see you at breakfast, Madeline Anne Beecher."

Maddie closed the door and leaned against it, smiling with happiness. But her happiness quickly dissolved at the thought of the task that still lay ahead. She had to tell Jeremy about Amelia. She had to tell him the same story she had told Blaine, a new lie to explain her previous lie. Her fingers curled into her palms, her nails digging into her flesh. If she had any honor she would admit the whole truth and suffer their hatred. But that would mean leaving the safety of the farm. That would mean leaving Blaine.

Maddie straightened her shoulders and pushed away from the door. She would have to stick with her new story. It was the only way. She hurried through her ablutions, changed into a fresh dress, and went up the stairs to the third floor, where Jeremy had resumed painting. Taking a deep breath, she opened the door to his attic room.

"Jeremy?"

He was standing at his easel, a paintbrush in one hand, his palette in the other. He didn't hear her at first, and when he finally looked around, he blushed and began to stutter. "G-good m-morning, Amel . . ."

Awkwardly, he let his sentence trail off. Maddie gave him a weak smile. "It's Maddie. Madeline Beecher."

He stared at her as if he didn't know what to say.

"May I talk to you?"

"Of c-course."

He cleared off a chair and she perched on it, her fingers nervously bunching the material of her skirt. She stared at the floor for a moment, gathering her courage, and then she raised her head and said quietly, "I want you to know about the girl who wrote the letters, Jeremy. I want to tell you about Amelia Baker."

He seemed more confused than surprised. "There really is an Amelia then?"

Maddie hesitated a moment and then sadly, ashamedly, nodded. "Amelia and I were traveling west together. She was on her way here to marry you and I was going to Chicago." Maddie bowed her head and a small sad smile flitted across her face as she remembered the events of that morning. "Amelia talked of nothing but you all the way to Indiana. She must have shown me the miniature of you in her locket a dozen times. She was beside herself with happiness. Her fondest dream was coming true at last. She was to have a husband who loved her and a home of her own." Maddie's throat tightened and tears burned her eyes. "And then the train jumped the track."

She closed her eyes and told him the story just the way she had told Blaine. When she finished, she raised her head and found Jeremy standing rigidly in front of his easel, his eyes moist, his face ashen. She wiped tears from her cheeks with the backs of her hands. "I'm so sorry, Jeremy."

He moved suddenly to a dry sink against one wall, where he began to clean his paintbrushes. His back was stiff, his shoulders straight, and his movements quick and tense. For a long time he said nothing, so long that Maddie wondered whether she should leave him to mourn alone.

But finally Jeremy began to speak, keeping his back to her, his voice low and thick with emotion. "I'm g-glad you told me. And even though it was Amelia's wish for you to take her place, it would have been a m-mistake for us to m-marry. My brother loves you. You belong together."

Maddie said quietly, "I have wished many times that I had died instead of Amelia."

He swung to face her, his features strained, his

voice strident. "It wasn't your fault Amelia d-died. You shouldn't think that way." And then he bent his head and covered his eyes with one hand. Maddie saw his shoulders begin to shake and she looked away.

After a while, she heard Jeremy sigh and she glanced up to find him systematically wiping each of his brushes on a white cloth. He put them carefully in a container, walked to his easel, and stood staring at the painting he had just begun. In a quiet voice he said, "I've always believed that it helps to look for something g-good in every adversity, something that helps make sense out of the senseless. In this case I no longer have to feel g-guilty about wanting to paint and about being such an incompetent farmer. I've come to realize that I don't have to meekly accept my lot in life. For the first time I'm truly free. And who can say what lies ahead? Perhaps one day I'll become f-famous."

Maddie went to him and took both of his hands, squeezing them affectionately. "You will, Jeremy. I'm sure of it."

He stared at her, desolate blue eyes searching her own. "Was Amelia—" He paused to draw a shaky breath and then said in a voice thick with pain, "Was Amelia pretty, Maddie?"

Maddie's throat was so tight she could barely say the words. "She was beautiful, Jeremy. Inside and out."

Tears filled his eyes and ran down his cheeks. He turned back to the easel and bent his head, his hands gripping either side of the canvas. Maddie left him then and moved silently to the door.

"Thank you," she heard him whisper.

She leaned against the wall outside his room and

wept for him. She had been wrong to think Amelia would have been disappointed in Jeremy. Amelia would have loved Jeremy.

As she walked toward the stairway a sudden tremor ran through her. Maddie stopped and pressed her fingers to her temples, feeling something dark, something menacing reaching toward her. She shook her head and continued on, dismissing it as nothing more than the product of a tired mind. She hurried to her room to splash her face with cold water and pinch her cheeks for color. It was time to face Blaine's mother.

Chapter 25

Blaine sat at the dining room table with his chin resting in his palm and his forehead wrinkled. His mother sat opposite him in a similar position. Mrs. MacLeod stood leaning against the sideboard, staring heavenward, her plump arms folded across her chest. By Blaine's estimation, they had been in those same positions for a good quarter of an hour. The half hour prior to that he had spent explaining to his mother the reason for Maddie's deception and his decision to marry her.

What worried his mother now was what to do about the social. The express purpose of the event had been to introduce Jeremy's fiancée to their friends and neighbors. They could hardly do that anymore. Evelyn had finally called in Mrs. Mac-Leod to see if a bit of sound Scottish wisdom could help solve the dilemma. As of yet a solution had not presented itself.

Blaine looked up when his mother heaved a frustrated sigh. "I don't know what to do, Blaine. This is such an awkward situation."

"I told you, Mother," Blaine said, rubbing his eyes, "if you want to cancel the social, I'll ride out right now and let your guests know. Zeb and Earl can help me. We should be able to reach everyone in time."

"Ach, can ye imagine the questions ye'll raise?" Mrs. MacLeod shook her head. "And the talk sure to follow?"

Evelyn reached for the teapot and poured the steaming liquid in her cup. "She's right, Blaine. We'd best face the questions openly and all at once. We'll just have to see the social through and hope for the best."

Blaine sat back and folded his arms across his chest, deep in thought. His mother's reaction to the news had been entirely what he had expected. As always, her main concern had been for Jeremy. She had decided nearly at once that since Maddie would remain at the farm with Blaine, then it was her duty to accompany her younger son to New York to look after his welfare.

As for Jeremy's inheritance, Evelyn had worried at first that he was making a big mistake in giving up the farm, but had finally conceded that Jeremy was happiest when he was painting and would never be as good a farmer as his father had been. Indeed, she had actually seemed happy for Blaine.

Now Blaine sighed at the thought of the upcoming social. It would be a difficult evening for Maddie, he was sure. He knew the other farmers well enough to realize what conclusion they would draw about Maddie's role in Jeremy's sudden decision to leave. He also knew that Maddie's acceptance into the farming community hinged upon their impression of her that night.

"I'll do the talking," he told his mother. "I'll announce the news about Jeremy going to New York first, then muddle my way through some explanation about Maddie and me."

"I can't help but feel sorry for that poor girl, Blaine." Evelyn shook her head. "What she's had to go through. First suffering through that dreadful train wreck, then having to keep her identity a secret. I certainly couldn't have done it." She stirred sugar into her tea. "Not unless I was in desperate straits. Of course I don't have her fortitude."

Blaine scowled down at his plate. His mother's remark about desperate straits prodded something that had been hovering at the back of his mind all morning. Was it likely, he kept asking himself, that Maddie would have tried as hard as she had to fool them in order to honor a friend's last wish and to protect herself from a man to whom she was no real threat? Or, as his mother had suggested, had desperation pushed Maddie to it?

He kept coming back to one idea: that Vincent Slade was somehow still a threat to her. Maddie had told him she had no proof, but he was beginning to realize that when she didn't want him to know something, she was very good at hiding it.

"If I might offer a wee suggestion," Mrs. Mac-Leod said slowly, "yer social evening could be made into somethin' of a farewell party for Mr. Jeremy and yerself."

Evelyn looked up at the housekeeper and her hazel eyes slowly widened. With a laugh she rose and clapped her hands together. "What a wonderful idea! That's exactly what we'll do. We'll invite everyone to join our farewell celebration." She pushed back her chair and started for the door.

"Blaine, apologize to Amelia for my absence, will you, dear?"

"It's Maddie, Mother."

"Yes, of course—how silly of me. Tell Maddie I'll speak with her later. Mrs. MacLeod, come with me. We'll need to make a big banner to hang in the doorway, and, good heavens, a giant cake decorated with . . ."

Blaine could hear his mother chattering excitedly as she headed toward the kitchen, totally absorbed in her new project. As the clock struck eight, he rose and went to the sideboard for a dish of hotcakes. Maddie had been upstairs for an hour. He wondered how his brother was taking the news of Amelia's death.

"Blaine?"

He spun around and saw Maddie standing in the doorway, her red hair pulled back into a neat chignon, her hands clasped tightly together at the waist of her pink-and-white sprigged dress, her eyes large and expectant. "Where is your mother?"

"Busy planning Jeremy's farewell party. She apologized for missing you. Did it go all right upstairs?"

Maddie nodded and suddenly her eyes were bright with tears. Blaine opened his arms and she walked into them, burying her head against his shoulder. He closed his eyes and wrapped his arms tightly about her. "What did Jeremy say?"

Blaine heard her sigh. "He took Amelia's death as well as could be expected. It was painful for him to hear what happened to her, but he was very brave about it."

Blaine leaned back to look down at her. "As painful as it may have been, the truth is always best."

Maddie gave him a weak smile and stepped back.

Averting her gaze, she moved quickly to the sideboard. "I'm famished. Have you eaten yet?"

Blaine watched her pick up a plate and begin to fill it. Something coiled inside him, gnawed at him. "You did tell Jeremy the truth, didn't you, Maddie?"

For a moment she stilled, then she calmly turned and carried her plate to the table. "I told you I would," she said as she sat down. Her expression was composed but she wouldn't meet his gaze. And there was the tiniest trace of a wrinkle in her forehead.

Blaine's stomach twisted. Maddie was still lying.

The sky was a bright, clear blue and the sun was intense as Maddie tied her white sunbonnet under her chin, arranged the skirt of her pink dress on the upholstered bench, and waited for Blaine to climb into the black buggy beside her. He looked as lean and handsome as always in his canvas pants and white cotton shirt, and her heart swelled to think that soon she would be married to him.

"Ready?" he asked.

She nodded happily. "Ready."

They had decided to take a trip into town to buy a going-away present to give to his brother and mother after the social that evening. The thought of facing all of their neighbors still caused Maddie's stomach to flutter anxiously, but she knew with Blaine at her side she would be all right. A quick frown crossed Maddie's brow at the thought of how easily her new story had been accepted and how readily they had forgiven her for lying, but at least this time what she had told them had been very close to the truth.

Maddie knew, however, that the Knights would not be so forgiving if they learned she had stolen Amelia's identity for her own selfish purposes and not for the unselfish reason she had given. And she was sure she would still suffer eternal damnation for it.

Maddie watched Blaine pick up the reins. "Why are you using your chestnut instead of the farm horse?"

"The draft horses are out in the fields today." He glanced at her with a grin. "Don't worry. The buggy is light and you don't weigh more than a bushel of corn."

Maddie gave him a scowl. "A bushel of corn indeed!" She folded her arms across her chest, then glanced at him sheepishly. "Is that a lot?"

With a wide smile, Blaine clicked his tongue at the horse. "Ho, Fred."

Maddie glanced at him in shock. "Fred?"

"I had to name him something. You never did decide."

"*Not* Fred. How about Charlie, or Lightning, or—"

"I take it you don't like Fred."

"I hate that name," she said sharply.

Blaine turned his head to regard her curiously. "Pick out another, then."

Maddie closed her eyes tightly, then opened them with a smile. "Prince," she declared.

Blaine wrinkled his nose. "Aw, Maddie, *Prince?*"

"Why not? He looks regal, like a prince."

Blaine sighed resolutely. "Prince it is."

Maddie squinted at the blue sky overhead. Anything but Fred. Anything to keep from being reminded of her father.

* * *

No other vehicles were parked in front of the general store this afternoon. Blaine tied the horse to the hitching rail, helped Maddie down, and escorted her into the store. They wandered the narrow aisles together, conferring with heads bent until they'd determined the right gift for both Jeremy and Evelyn. Blaine sent Maddie to the front to pick out a peppermint stick while he paid for their purchases in the back.

Maddie could hear Blaine talking loudly to Clement Spriggs at the rear of the store as she stood in front of the glass case by the door. She looked around, bored, and noticed a new poster propped in the window. For lack of something to do, she picked it up and turned it around. Her heart lurched violently as her own name stared back at her.

Maddie pressed her hand to her mouth. *Vincent Slade knew she was alive.*

"Thank you, Clem," she heard Blaine call.

With shaking hands, she hurriedly crumpled the heavy paper and stuffed it into her drawstring handbag. *Slade knew she was in Marshall County. Oh, God, he was going to find her!*

"Did you pick out some candy?"

Maddie swung to face Blaine. "No, I—I don't care for any."

His dark eyebrows drew together. "You don't care for any?"

She swallowed, staring up at him with huge eyes. "Maybe next time. We should go now. I have to get ready for tonight."

"Maddie, you're as white as a sheet. Are you going to faint?"

She shook her head. "No. May we please go?"

Giving her a puzzled frown, Blaine held open the door. Maddie climbed into the buggy and sat staring straight ahead, her hands clasping and unclasping the handbag in her lap. Vincent Slade had offered a thousand-dollar reward for information as to her whereabouts. It was an unheard of sum! No one would be able to resist such a large amount of money. What was she going to do? Her mind raced, her fear a cold lump in her chest. How many people had already seen the poster? How many had already wired him with information?

Maddie dug her nails into her palms and took deep, slow gulps of air. *Think, Maddie,* she cried inwardly, fighting the blind terror that blanketed her mind. The poster had recently been put in the window, perhaps only the day before. She was in Indiana. Slade was in Pennsylvania. Even if someone had recognized her description, they would still have to contact Slade. And he would have to travel all the way to Marshall County. That left her a few days to come up with a plan before he showed up at the farm, a few days to think of some way to protect Blaine and his family from Vincent Slade.

But first she had to get through the social evening. Then she would decide what to do.

Blaine stood in the front hallway beside his brother and stared at Maddie's portrait. Zeb had hung the large, gilt-framed painting on the tall wall beneath the staircase earlier that evening while Blaine was dressing for the party. He vaguely remembered Jeremy describing it to him, but nothing his brother had said had prepared him for the reality of it.

Jeremy had captured Maddie perfectly, from the sensuous curve of her coral-tinted mouth to the sparkle in her incredible silver-green eyes. He had even managed to recreate the deep, rich cinnabar-red color of her hair, which had been pulled loosely to the top of her head and fastened with mother-of-pearl combs, *his* combs. Long graceful wisps of hair trailed down her elegant neck and floated around her face, giving her a look both innocent and provocative.

His eyes traveled down to the copper-colored satin gown with its outsized cap sleeves topping long, tightly fitted, ecru lace gloves. The square-cut neckline trimmed in ermine revealed a tempting swell of ivory breasts. Her waist was narrow, her skirt bell-shaped, the ermine-trimmed hem swirling about her coppery satin slippers as if she had been caught in the act of turning to look over her shoulder, the expectant look on her face as if someone had just called to her. A black lace fan was clasped in one gloved hand and the other rested gracefully against a stone pillar. A pot of ivy spilled over the top of the pillar and trailed languidly down one side.

It was the most beautiful painting he'd ever seen.

"Wh-what do you think?" Jeremy asked nervously.

"Damnation," he whispered, his throat dry. "I expect her to step down out of that painting at any minute."

Jeremy laughed and slapped him on the back. "It's your wedding present, Blaine."

At a slight movement to his right, Blaine's eyes shifted suddenly to the staircase. Maddie stood there in person in her shimmering copper gown, her hair exactly as it was in the portrait. His heart flip-flopped.

"Do you like it?" she asked breathlessly, and he wasn't sure if she meant her gown or the painting.

He walked toward the stairs and took her hand as she stepped down. "It's beautiful," he whispered hoarsely, "and so are you."

Blaine saw love blaze brightly in her eyes as she smiled at him. Madeline Anne Beecher. He didn't care that she had deceived them. He knew who she was now. She was his. He pushed aside that niggling worry that she was still lying, tucked her hand through his arm, and escorted her to the front parlor where his mother was waiting. His life couldn't be any more perfect. At last he had everything he wanted.

At least fifty people filled the brightly lit parlor, talking, laughing, eating, some gathered around the upright piano singing. The mood was gay but Maddie felt no joy in it. She stood quietly at Blaine's side and pretended to listen as he talked to several of his neighbors. His hand held hers, his long, strong fingers tightly entwined with her own cold ones. She was cold clear down to her toes. She was so cold she had to clench her teeth together to keep them from chattering.

Vincent Slade was getting closer.

Maddie felt Blaine's hand squeeze her own and she glanced quickly at him. He gave her a puzzled look and she managed a smile, knowing he must have felt her trembling. It was unfair to spoil his happiness, so she forced her mind away from Slade. She thought of how skillfully Blaine had handled the surprise announcement of Jeremy's move to

New York, and how, after everyone had congratulated his brother, Blaine had brought her up to stand beside him and had announced proudly that he had fallen in love with her and that she had consented to marry him.

There had been a few whispers at his news, but mostly everyone seemed genuinely happy for all of them and had welcomed her warmly to their farming community. She had even been invited to join a quilting circle, though she hadn't had the heart to tell the ladies she hated to sew. But now, as she glanced around at the unfamiliar faces, she worried that if someone had noticed the poster, they might recognize her by the description on it. But would they contact Slade, knowing Blaine was going to marry her?

Would they pass up a thousand-dollar reward for the sake of Blaine's friendship?

Maddie eased her hand from Blaine's grasp, whispering to him she would be back in a few minutes, the four glasses of punch she had consumed presenting a pressing concern. She wove her way through the crowd, moved silently down the hallway to the back door, lifted the hem of her skirt, and made a quick dash to the backhouse.

Mrs. Small and Mrs. MacLeod were in the kitchen talking when she returned. She smiled at them as she passed by the doorway, but as she drew closer to the front parlor, she heard a man's voice in the front hall that stopped her dead in her tracks. Only one man had a voice like that.

Vincent Slade had found her.

Chapter 26

Maddie stepped into the back parlor, her heart thumping so loudly she was sure it would give her away. *It couldn't be Slade! Oh, God, how could he have found her so quickly?* She pressed her hand to her breast to still the wild beating and held her breath as Evelyn came out of the parlor to greet the latecomers. She heard another voice, a familiar syrupy voice introducing her guest to Evelyn. And then she knew how Vincent Slade had found her.

Penny Tadwell had contacted him.

Maddie closed her eyes and leaned weakly against the doorjamb. Vincent Slade was in their house and only she knew the atrocities of which he was capable. No doubt his odious counterpart was lurking somewhere nearby, ready to assist him. Now they were all in danger and it was her fault.

She heard the voices move away and she peered out, watching in horror as Evelyn unsuspectingly led the devil himself into the crowded parlor. What would Slade tell Blaine? Not the truth, surely. But he knew enough damning information about her to say almost anything and make Blaine believe it. Why wouldn't Blaine take the word of a wealthy, smooth-talking politician over a girl who had never told him the truth?

But I did tell him the truth. The most important truth. That I love him.

Or would Blaine doubt that as well?

Forcing her trembling legs to move, Maddie darted down the hallway, around the corner, and up the stairs, pausing at the landing to catch her breath, the tightly laced corset squeezing her lungs. She flew down the hallway to her room and looked around in a panic. Where could she hide? What could she do to save herself from Vincent Slade?

No matter where you hide, he'll find you. Maddie covered her mouth to stifle a frightened sob. He *would* find her again. She knew that now. He had money and resources. He would never give up until he had killed her.

Unless she could stop him first.

She pressed her fingers to her temples to drive out the unwanted thought. She couldn't stop Vincent Slade. To do that, she would need to find the incriminating letter and money hidden in a barn west of Philadelphia.

The train tickets to New York were in Jeremy's room. She need only take one from his bureau.

No! she cried silently. Slade would come after her. She was too frightened to carry off such a foolhardy plan.

What was the alternative?

Maddie's stomach knotted in terror. The alternative was Slade finding her tonight, in this house, where Blaine and his family would also be in danger. She'd seen how easy it was for Slade to end a life. He would have no qualms about killing all of them.

She closed her eyes, tears squeezing from the corners, and in the blackness behind her eyelids she was once more in Vincent Slade's wine cellar. Her stomach cramped as she smelled again the stench of burning flesh, heard the sound of tortured screams, felt the sticky blood that had run across the floor, staining the bottom of her shoes as she crouched unseen in her hiding place. But most of all, she remembered Slade's hideous laughter.

How could she risk the same fate befalling Blaine?

Maddie darted across the hall into Jeremy's room, stopping directly in front of his bureau. She closed her eyes and pressed her hand to her heart. She had to do it. She had to stop Vincent Slade before he hurt Blaine.

For a brief moment her hand hovered over the tickets, then she snatched one, dashed back to her room, and pulled the satchel from the armoire to stuff her boys' clothing inside. She opened her handbag, frantically shook out the crumpled poster, and replaced it with her coin purse and the train ticket.

With shaking hands, Maddie took a piece of stationery from the writing desk, removed the pen from its ceramic holder, and opened the bottled ink. She shut her eyes tightly, thinking hard. Blaine would be downstairs now speaking with Slade. In a few moments he would come looking for her, demanding answers. What could she write that would not only keep him from following her, but also absolve him from any duplicity in Slade's eyes? For if he suspected Blaine of helping her escape, there was no telling what he might do.

Quickly she scratched out a message and folded the paper, placing it on her bureau. Clutching the satchel in one hand and her handbag in the other, she closed the door of her room, crept down the stairs, dashed past the closed doors of the front parlor, and fled down the back hallway.

Pepper was startled by her agitated movements and kept sidestepping as she tried to saddle him. She led the mare out of the barn, snatching Zeb's brown cap from a peg as she went. She closed the big barn doors and swung onto the horse, pushing her billowing skirts as far down around her stocking-clad legs as she could.

Instead of using the front lane and risking being seen, Maddie cut through the grape arbor, skirted the wheat field, and followed the stream to the apple grove. She glanced back once at the brightly lit house in the distance and felt a lump come to her throat. Would she ever return? Would she ever see Blaine again? She turned away from it, turned away from her home and her new life. Blaine was in the house with Vincent Slade. She had to pray her plan worked.

Blinking back a fresh sting of tears, she bent low over the saddle and kicked the horse's sides. "Run, Pepper!"

Blaine leaned against the mantelpiece of the fireplace and watched suspiciously as the tall, gaunt, stylishly dressed man walk into the room with Penny on his arm. It wasn't so much the man's arrogant demeanor and dandified style of dress that made Blaine suddenly leery, but Penny's gloating, secretive smile.

Blaine bent his head as his mother hurried across the room to whisper in his ear. "Miss Tadwell's guest wishes to have a word with you in the hallway. He says it is a matter of great importance."

Blaine looked down at her and saw a flicker of alarm in her eyes. His gaze shifted back to the man. "What is his name?"

"Vincent Slade."

"Who was he? What was his name?"

"Vincent Slade."

This, then, was the wealthy employer who Maddie thought was responsible for a murder, the man who haunted Maddie's nightmares. What the hell was he doing in their parlor? Blaine's cold gaze returned to Penny Tadwell and narrowed. What role did she have in Slade's surprise visit?

Penny suddenly noticed Blaine's attention and her full lips curved into a flirtatious smile. But when he continued to study her with accusing eyes, her gaze slid away and a guilty blush stained her already rouged cheeks. Blaine's jaw clenched. Whatever Slade's reason for being there was, Penny was directly responsible.

Casually, he glanced around the crowded parlor for Maddie, but she had not yet returned. He threaded his way through the guests and stopped directly in front of Slade. "You wanted to speak to me?"

Vincent Slade smiled. "In the hall, if you don't mind."

They stepped outside and Blaine closed the doors behind him. When he turned, Slade was staring at

Maddie's portrait, his thin lips curved up at the corners in a cruel smile.

Blaine remembered Maddie's desperate words. *"Vincent Slade is an evil man. I was frightened of what he might do to me if he found out I knew. I wanted to find a place where he could never find me."*

It was all Blaine could do not to wrap his fingers about the man's skinny neck and strangle him, but his fury was evident only in the twitch of a muscle in his jaw. "What is this about?" he said in a low, barely civil voice.

"She's a beautiful creature, isn't she?" Slade rocked back on his heels, his hands crossed in front of him. "Your artist captured Madeline's sensuality quite well."

Hatred and jealousy flared red-hot inside him. A creature—Maddie was nothing but a creature to him. Blaine took a step toward him, his hands balled into fists at his sides. "Look, Slade—"

"But perhaps you know her as Amelia." Vincent Slade turned slowly, a heavy eyebrow raised speculatively.

"I know her real name."

"Then I suppose you also know she stole two thousand dollars from my house."

Blaine's nostrils flared and his mouth thinned to a harsh line. "No," he said, "I didn't."

"Then perhaps I should enlighten you. I hired Madeline to work in my kitchen this summer. The night I hosted a dinner for a group of prominent Philadelphia politicians, she sneaked into my wife's bedroom and pried open her strongbox."

Philadelphia. Not New York. *Damn it. Maddie had lied about that, too.* A cold knot of dread formed in his stomach. Had she lied about the murder as well? "Go on."

"I shouldn't have hired her in the first place, especially knowing who her father was. Fast Freddy they called him. He was a renowned con artist, sent to prison ten years ago.

"I took pity on her because her mother had died and she was desperate for work. So I gave the little thief a break and she robbed me blind. I put out a reward and hired a detective to find out where she was headed. And then I heard she had been killed in a train wreck. To tell you the truth, I'd forgotten about her until your friend Miss Tadwell happened to notice one of my posters and contacted me." He paused, then added, "A U.S. marshal is waiting outside now to accompany Madeline back to Philadelphia to stand trial."

Blaine wanted to strike him. Maddie couldn't have stolen the money. Not the passionate, gentle girl he had held in his arms last night. Not the Maddie he knew. But did he really know her? He turned sharply and strode to the front door, open now to catch the cool evening breeze. A short, husky man in a brown suit and derby leaned against a post, whittling a piece of wood with a pocketknife. He looked up and nodded coolly.

Blaine spun, his dark eyes flashing. "You're not taking her anywhere."

Slade smiled silkily. "I have a warrant, Mr. Knight. And a U.S. marshal."

"Maybe the marshal would be interested in hearing about a murder you were involved in," Blaine said evenly.

"A murder?" Slade asked, looking bewildered. Then he smiled knowingly. "It would seem Madeline is telling stories again, Mr. Knight. No doubt she also told you she had no proof to back up her— ah—story. Yes, I can see by your expression you were completely taken in by her. She's rather good at that. Let me assure you, Mr. Knight, that I move in the highest political circles in Philadelphia. Murder is simply not my style. Political ostracism, public embarrassment—now that's a different story." He paused and looked toward the door. "If you would fetch her for me . . ." He let the sentence trail off.

"I'm going back with her," Blaine told him.

Slade lifted his shoulders in a careless shrug. "Suit yourself."

"I trust this can wait until morning." Blaine gestured stiffly toward the parlor. "I'm a little busy at present."

Slade smiled. "In that case I'll have to leave the marshal here. Just in case." He waved his hand. "You understand."

Blaine's dark eyes narrowed. "He can sit on that porch all night if he wants to. But I want *you* to get the hell off my property."

Vincent Slade raised both eyebrows. "Very well, Mr. Knight. I'll be back in the morning." He paused to stare at Maddie's portrait, then took his black hat from the hat rack and strode out the door. Blaine shut it behind him and turned.

Everything Maddie had told him had been a lie. Everything but her name. He was surprised she had even told him the truth about that. He stood in the hallway beneath Maddie's portrait and stared at the face of the woman he loved. He was numb.

His mother slipped quietly from the parlor and stood beside him, her eyes wide with worry. "What is it, Blaine? What did Mr. Slade want?"

"Maddie is in trouble," he said in a flat voice. "Slade has accused her of stealing two thousand dollars from his home. A marshal is posted outside. He intends to take her back to Philadelphia in the morning."

Evelyn shook her head vehemently. "I can't believe it of her, Blaine. She wouldn't do that. Why, just look what she did for Amelia."

"Did she do it for Amelia? Or did she do it to hide from the law?"

"You believe Mr. Slade's story then?"

Blaine sat down heavily on the bottom stair and rubbed his eyes with his thumbs. "Maddie has told so many lies I don't know what to believe anymore. If Slade is telling the truth, Maddie was running from the marshal when she took the train west. It was just by chance that she met Amelia."

He lifted his head and looked around. "Where *is* Maddie? She should have been back long before now."

He stared at his mother and saw the same suspicion flash in her eyes.

"I'll check in the kitchen," Evelyn said, and hurried away.

Blaine took the stairs two at a time, his heart thumping with dread. But even before he opened her door, he knew the room would be empty. He strode across the floor and tore open the armoire. Her satchel was gone and so was her handbag.

Blaine sat down on her slipper chair and dropped his head to his hands. She must have seen Slade enter the house and panicked. Was she guilty? *Could* she have stolen the money? He wasn't sure anymore. Everything he thought he knew about her had been turned upside down.

"I can't hurt you. Please don't kill me." Were those words, a plaintive cry from the depths of a dream, the words of a thief?

He suddenly noticed the crumpled paper lying on the floor near the bed. He reached for it and smoothed it out, his eyes narrowing at the bold, black words at the top. ONE THOUSAND DOLLAR REWARD FOR INFORMATION ON THE WHEREABOUTS OF MADELINE BEECHER.

One thousand dollars for a two-thousand-dollar robbery? It didn't make sense. Slade would have spent nearly half again that amount hunting her down. His eyes moved over the notice once more. There wasn't even a mention of a robbery. Blaine looked up as his mother swept in.

"Madeline stopped at the kitchen after she came back inside the house," Evelyn said breathlessly. "Mrs. MacLeod hasn't seen her since."

"She came up here," Blaine told her. "Her satchel and handbag are gone. She must have seen Slade come in."

"But where would she go?"

Jeremy limped into the room, still favoring his injured ankle. "What's going on? Penny T-tadwell left in a rush and the whole room is abuzz."

Blaine strode to the window to stare at the ground below while Evelyn explained the situation to Jeremy. Where would Maddie go? Would she hide in the apple tree or the hayloft until Slade left? He sighed wearily, braced his hands on the sill, and peered through the darkness.

Why did you lie to me, Maddie?

He had given her every opportunity to tell him

the truth. He had bared the ugly secrets of his soul to her, telling her what no one else in the world knew, hoping it would help her trust him. And still she had lied to him, over and over again. His fist slammed against the windowsill.

"Sometimes we do things in a moment of panic that we regret later," Maddie had once told him. *"We just have to put it behind us."* Is that what she had done? Had she simply made a mistake and tried to put it behind her?

"She left you a n-note, Blaine."

He spun around. Jeremy stood by the bureau holding a letter in his hand. Blaine stared at it, his heart thudding heavily, his hands feeling suddenly too unsteady to reach for it. Jeremy held it out and Blaine forced his arm to stretch, forced his fingers to clasp it, to open the folded paper. His eyes slowly focused on the hastily scrawled handwriting.

Dear Blaine, kindly inform Mr. Slade that I have returned to Philadelphia. He will understand why. Please believe that I never intended to hurt you or your family. I hope someday you will forgive me for deceiving you. It was signed simply *Maddie.*

I hope someday you will forgive me.

The words blurred, ran together. She wasn't coming back.

Blaine gripped the note and brought it closer, as if by sheer force of will he could wring more information from it—a logical reason for her stealing the money, a valid excuse as to why she couldn't have confided in him, an explanation as to how she could have so easily left him. Had she lied about loving him, too?

Questions swirled in his mind, questions that demanded answers. What was Maddie planning to do when she returned to Philadelphia? Why did she want Slade to know her plans? Why would the man who had frightened her, who had haunted her dreams, understand why she was returning? What was the secret between them?

Blaine slowly crumpled the letter in his hands. If he had to chase Maddie to the ends of the earth to get his answers, then, by God, he would do it. She was not going to sneak out of his life like a thief in the night.

Even if she was one.

"Blaine, where are you going?" his mother called, hurrying after him as he charged into the hallway.

"To find Maddie."

Evelyn stood in the bedroom doorway, wringing her hands helplessly as Blaine stuffed clothing into a traveling case. "If she did steal the money," he said through clenched teeth, "I want to hear it from her myself. If she didn't . . ."

If she didn't, then why did she leave?

"But what shall I tell our guests?"

"I'll h-handle it, Mother. Blaine has a more p-pressing concern right now than our guests."

Blaine's eyes met Jeremy's over his mother's head and he gave him a grateful nod. He finished packing and turned, his eyes falling on his mother's distraught face. He grabbed her shoulders, startling her. "Mother, I want you to do something for me. There's a U.S. marshal waiting on the front porch. You've got to distract him so he doesn't follow me. I don't want Slade to know Maddie and I are gone until morning. Will you do that? Will you help me?"

For a moment Evelyn stared helplessly at him. Then suddenly her expression changed, her mouth firmed, and her eyes glittered with an inner strength that gladdened him. "Leave it to me."

Bull sat in one of the rocking chairs on the front porch, swatting the insects buzzing around his head. "Damned mosquitoes," he grumbled. He hated mosquitoes. He hated farms, too, with their smelly barns and piles of manure sitting where you least expected them. He picked up one of his once-fine leather boots and examined the sole. Damned smelly animals.

He took out his pocket watch and checked the time. Ten-thirty. The last guest had left just fifteen minutes before. There would be nothing to keep him occupied until dawn. He yawned and rubbed his eyes, then opened them wide and vigorously shook his head. The boss would never forgive him if he fell asleep.

The front door squeaked open and a silver-haired lady in a fancy plum gown stepped outside.

"Good evening, Marshal," she said in singsong voice. She held out a glass of punch and a piece of cherry pie. "I thought you might like a little refreshment before I retire for the night."

Bull sauntered across the porch toward her, smiling broadly. "Thanks," he said, trying to take them from her hands. His brows drew together when she refused to let them go. "Hey—"

A heavy *thunk* from behind sent him sinking slowly to his knees. He buckled over onto the porch and rolled onto his back.

Evelyn nudged his shoulder with the toe of her slipper. "My goodness, Mrs. Small. The marshal seems to have fallen asleep."

The cook gave a satisfied smile. "These cast-iron

skillets are good for a lot more than cooking." She looked down at the unconscious man and huffed, then stepped over the body and marched into the house behind her employer.

Chapter 27

∽◦◦∽

Maddie left Pepper at the town livery stable
and hurried down the dark street to the
train depot. The wooden platform was empty and
the clerk's window dark. She squinted at the train
schedule posted on the outside wall of the depot,
trying to make it out by the faint light of the moon.
She wished she knew what time it was.

An eastbound train was due in at nine o'clock.
She closed her eyes and tried to remember if she'd
glanced at the clock on her bedside table. Had it
read eight-thirty? Had the train already come? She
sank down onto a wooden bench in front of the tiny
building and leaned her head against the rough
wall.

Her worst fears had come true. Vincent Slade had
found her and, if Blaine had delivered her message,
he would soon be after her again. She prayed Slade
would do nothing to harm Blaine or his family. She
imagined how hurt and angry Blaine would be
when he read her note, and a lump rose in her
throat. Whatever Slade had told Blaine her crime

was, that letter would surely make him believe it.

But it was imperative that Blaine not try to follow her. Slade would have no qualms about killing him as easily as he had murdered Crandall. She had to find the evidence and take her chances with Slade. Alone.

In the distance Maddie heard a train whistle. She jumped to her feet, clutching her satchel in one hand, the cord of her handbag around her other wrist, and cast nervous glances into the darkness around her. If Slade found her now they were all lost.

As soon as the giant locomotive wheezed to a halt, Maddie climbed onto the first car and slipped into a seat. There were only three other people in the car with her, an elderly man and woman and the conductor, a heavy man in his middle fifties. As the train pulled away from the station, the conductor stopped at her seat and smiled down at her. "Ticket?"

She handed him her ticket without a word.

"Miss, your ticket is for a sleeping compartment."

An embarrassed blush colored Maddie's cheeks. She'd forgotten Jeremy had requested compartments. He had insisted they travel in the highest style. "Where would the compartment be?"

"The Pullman car, next car back. Compartment four."

"Thank you." Maddie waited until the conductor left the car, then she picked up her satchel and moved quickly down the aisle, nodding politely to the old couple. She crossed the noisy vestibule between cars, stepped into the Pullman car, and walked down the aisle between the compartments until she found the narrow door marked with a brass 4. She opened it and stepped inside.

The compartment was very small but elegantly furnished. The floor was covered with a dark burgundy patterned carpet and the walls in hand-rubbed wood paneling. At the end of the room burgundy velvet draperies framed a small window. Beneath the window, facing each other, were two long benches upholstered in a plush burgundy fabric. Just behind the door was a tiny convenience. Looking around, Maddie spotted leather straps in the wall above each bench. Pulling on one produced a foldout wooden berth complete with thin mattress, gray wool blanket with the word "Pullman" woven into it, and a pillow.

For a time Maddie sat and stared out the window, listening to the rhythmic sounds of the wheels clattering along the iron rails. Then her thoughts drifted back to the farmhouse and she tried to imagine what was happening there. Surely by now Blaine had noticed she was missing. Her throat tightened as she remembered the way he had clung to her hand all evening, as if he somehow sensed they would soon be parted.

Maddie bit her lower lip to stop its trembling. Had Blaine found her note and taken it directly to Slade or would he wait until after the social when he could read it over carefully? Was he terribly hurt, or furious with her for deceiving him?

With a heavy sigh, Maddie slipped out of the satin gown and petticoats and laid them out carefully on the opposite bench, arranging them so she could dress quickly if need be. She removed the mother-of-pearl combs Blaine had given her and laid them beside her dress, then ran her fingers through her hair to loosen it. She climbed into the berth and stretched out on the mattress, pulling the blanket up around her chin. She rested her cheek against the hard pillow and closed her eyes, willing sleep to come.

Had it only been a day ago that she had slept in Blaine's arms? Only a day ago that they had made love, that he had asked her to marry him? At that moment, she had thought herself the happiest woman on earth. And now she was running for her life. Again.

Tears flooded her eyes. "Blaine," she whispered into the darkness. "I'm frightened."

Blaine pushed the chestnut hard, riding for town. At the livery, he hopped down and strode inside. Pepper was tied up in one of the stalls. "Damn!" he swore, and ran back outside to his horse, galloping to meet Zeb who had followed him in the black buggy. "I'm going to the depot," he told him, turning his horse around, "but she's probably already on the nine o'clock train."

Just as he thought, the depot and boarding platform were deserted. Blaine stood with his hands on his hips, staring up the train tracks into the dark void beyond, feeling the same sense of helplessness that he'd felt locked in his army quarters while the world outside his door went mad.

Only this time there were no locks to torment him. There were only his doubts.

He spun and strode toward the black buggy waiting in front of the depot. "Zeb, I'm going to ride on to the next stop to see if I can catch the train there. If I can't, I'll try the next one. I'll stable my horse, so don't worry about following me."

"You want me to take Pepper back with me or leave her stabled here?"

Blaine picked up the reins. "Take her with you, but don't ride up to the house the front way. I don't trust Slade or his marshal friend. And if one of them should stop you, don't answer any questions about Maddie or me."

Zeb gave a short nod and turned the buggy around. "I don't know a thing."

Blaine kicked Prince's sides and the chestnut took off at a hard run. Zeb wasn't the only one who didn't know a thing, he thought bitterly. But before he returned home, he *would* have some answers.

Bull rolled over onto his side with a groan. He was definitely going to have to have his mattress restuffed. Damned thing was as hard as wood. His pillow was no better. For God's sake, it was as stiff as a hat. His fingers reached up and moved along the curve of a rolled brim. He raised his head and stared at the object beneath him. It *was* a hat!

Bull pushed himself to his knees and looked down at the porch beneath him, groaning at the sight of his squashed derby. He picked it up and hit the inside with his fist, hammering it back into a facsimile of its original shape, then rose to his feet. His joints were stiff, his head throbbed, and he winced as his fingers touched a large, egg-shaped lump on the top of his head.

He'd been hit! Bull clenched his teeth and glared at the front door of the house, remembering the lady who had brought him dessert. His hand sought out the reassuring coldness of his knife in the pocket of his frock coat. He ought to go in there and slit her sneaky throat, that's what he ought to do.

Why had she hit him? He hadn't done anything to her. He'd only been following orders. Damn sneaky farmers. He hated farmers. Grumbling under his breath, Bull took out his pocket watch and glanced at the time. Eleven-thirty. He'd been unconscious for over an hour, and still there were six and a half hours to go before dawn.

He sat down on a wicker rocking chair, folded his short arms across his chest, and carefully leaned his head against the back. Wait until the boss heard what that lady did to him. Bull slid the knife from his pocket and switched it open, running his thumb over the blade. Slade wasn't going to like it one bit.

Bull had no sooner settled himself into a reasonably comfortable position when a hired buggy came careening up the lane. Vincent Slade hopped down and strode rapidly up the steps to the porch. Bull jumped to his feet, his hat in his hands, a nervous smile flitting across his flat features. "Evening, boss," he muttered, shifting from one foot to the other under Slade's shrewd stare.

"Evening, boss," Slade mocked, glaring down at him. "Would you mind telling me what you've been doing for the last two hours?"

"Someone hit me. Knocked me out cold." To prove his story, Bull turned and pointed to the top of his head, his fingers gingerly prodding the lump on his head. "I just came to a few minutes ago."

"You *let* someone sneak up on you?" Slade sneered sarcastically.

Bull puffed out his chest and lifted his square chin defensively. "A lady brought me a piece of pie.

How was I supposed to know she was gonna whack me?"

"You imbecile," Slade ground out. "Madeline got away. Potter saw her get on the train headed east."

"He did? Shit!" Bull exclaimed, throwing down his hat.

"Shut up and get in the buggy. We've got to catch the next train out of here."

"I hate trains," Bull muttered as he scurried after Slade. He barely had enough time to climb into the buggy before it lurched off down the gravel drive.

Vincent kicked the buggy. "Damn it to hell, Madeline's got a two-hour head start on us!" He turned to snarl at his companion, "She's going back to Philadelphia for the evidence, Bull, and you know what's going to happen when she finds it?"

Bull sighed miserably. "We'll both hang."

Vincent's thin lips curled into a sneer. "You won't hang, Bull. I'll kill you first."

Chapter 28

Maddie dozed fitfully for the first several hours, her heart lurching in terror at each footfall outside the compartment, until exhaustion finally took over. When she awoke, the first rays of the sun were streaming through the small window. She glanced outside at the passing scenery, wondering how close they were to Philadelphia. She put on the copper-colored gown, ran her fingers through her tangled tresses, and refastened the knot in back with the mother-of-pearl combs. Her coin purse in hand, Maddie opened the door to her compartment and cautiously peered out. The aisle was empty save for a conductor at the far end of the car.

"Excuse me, sir," she called. When he looked back, she closed her door and hurried toward him. "Can you tell me if the next stop will have a refreshment station? I'm so very hungry." Maddie gave him a helpless smile.

"It sure does, little lady, but we won't reach Pittsburgh for another half hour. But if you continue on up through the parlor car and the coach after it, you can buy yourself a hearty breakfast in the dining car." The conductor smiled at her over his thin spectacles.

They were in Pennsylvania. The thought of it made Maddie's stomach tighten. "Thank you," she said quickly, and hurried past him. Only a few more hours until they reached Philadelphia.

The parlor car was furnished exactly like a parlor in a home, with carpeting, comfortable chairs, tables, and even a small sofa. At one end was a pantry presided over by a porter, who was busy setting out a tray of pastries and cups of coffee. At the opposite end of the car, a group of gentlemen in dark frock coats and hats sat around a table playing a game of cards.

Maddie glanced quickly at the men's faces as she passed to be sure Slade wasn't among them. She reached for the handle to open the door into the vestibule.

"Madeline?"

Maddie froze. *She knew that voice.* She turned back slowly as one of the gentlemen rose from his chair, staring at her as if she were an apparition. He wore a brown tweed suit and matching vest with a white shirt and stiff collar beneath. He had a full red handlebar mustache and wavy, faded red hair topped by a brown derby which had been pushed to the back of his head. He had a wide face, a prominent nose with a round tip, and a cleft in his chin. A smile spread slowly across his face, his gray-green eyes crinkling at the corners as Maddie gaped at him openmouthed.

"Madeline," he said in his richly timbred voice, holding out his arms. "My dearest daughter."

Maddie backed up against the door. *It couldn't be*

Freddy. He was in prison! She spun around and twisted the handle, darting out into the vestibule between the trains. Not Fast Freddy. Not now! She pushed open the door to the next car and moved hurriedly down the center aisle.

"Madeline Anne!" a voice thundered behind her.

Maddie stopped cold. No one had called her that since she was in pigtails. Yet even now there was no doubt as to what it meant. She was in trouble. "Oh, bother!" she exclaimed, and turned reluctantly as her father strode up the aisle toward her, looking nearly the same as when she had last seen him more than ten years ago.

He stopped directly in front of her and folded his arms across his chest, lowering his red eyebrows accusingly. "Is that any way to greet your father?"

Maddie planted her hands on her hips and scowled up at him. "I suppose I should have thrown my arms around your neck, kissed your cheek, and told you how happy I was to see you again!"

One bushy eyebrow lifted ruefully. "You did when you were little."

"Well, I've grown up. I'm not so foolish anymore."

"You're still my daughter."

Maddie frowned down at her shoes. She didn't want to remember that. She didn't want to remember when she was little, either. She didn't want to remember waiting by the door night after night listening for the sound of his carefree whistle. She didn't want to remember being swept up into his arms, being happy for a few short hours before he would be off again on another of his vainglorious pursuits.

Her fingers curled tightly at her sides. She wanted to remember the sounds of her mother sobbing long into the night. She wanted to remember the shame of learning why her father had been taken to prison. She wanted to remember the harsh work her mother had been forced to do in order to support them.

But when Maddie looked up into those twinkling gray-green eyes that looked so very much like her own, what she remembered instead were the bright red peppermint sticks he always had hidden in his vest pocket just for her.

She looked away; she looked at her fingertips; she looked anywhere but at her father.

Freddy removed his hat and held it against his vest. "Ah, Madeline," he said softly. "You've become a real beauty. And a lady, too."

She wanted to laugh in his face at that last remark, but she could barely see him through the sudden film of tears in her eyes. She blinked to clear her vision and said gruffly, "I thought you were in prison."

"Released just three weeks ago," Freddy said proudly, throwing back his shoulders. Then his expression sobered and his voice grew husky with emotion. "I heard about the train wreck, Madeline. I thought you were dead."

"I was supposed to be," Maddie muttered dryly.

He raised his eyebrows in surprise, then glanced around. "Can we sit somewhere and talk?"

Talk. As if he'd never been away. As if they could just pick up from where they'd left off ten years before. Maddie shook her head and took a step back. "No. I—I can't. I have to—find the dining car. I haven't eaten."

"I'll take you." And before she could protest, her father had tucked her arm in his and was leading her down the middle of the aisle.

The long, wood-paneled dining car was nearly full and quite noisy at that time of the morning. Diners' voices competed with the sound of silverware clanking against metal dishes and waiters calling out orders. In the midst of it all, Freddy maneuvered Maddie skillfully around other passengers to a vacant booth at the far end.

Maddie settled onto the bench opposite Freddy and sniffed the air, her stomach growling at the smell of smoked meats, freshly baked breads, fried onions, and butter which hung heavily in the air. A waiter immediately scurried to their table.

"Good morning, Mr. Beecher."

"And a good morning to you, Efram," Freddy called in a booming voice. "Madeline, what will you have?"

Maddie winced at his loudness and peered nervously over his shoulder. "Just a dish of oatmeal, please," she said quietly to the waiter.

"Hardly enough to keep a flea alive," Freddy remarked, "and I've become something of an expert on fleas. Order up, daughter."

"Toasted bread with jam," Maddie said in a low voice, and at her father's look of displeasure, she added, "And a cup of tea."

"My usual," Freddy said with his twinkling eyes and charming smile. Maddie stared at him in bewilderment. His usual?

When the waiter had gone, Freddy smiled across the table at her. "I've developed an affection for steak and eggs since I left prison. Can't get enough of them."

Maddie leaned across the table to keep her voice low. "What are you doing on this train?"

"I've taken up a new occupation. Cards."

Maddie blanched. "You're a *cardsharp?*"

He grimaced. "Must you phrase it that way? I play an honest game, you see. I've no desire to do a repeat engagement behind bars." He leaned across the table. "Why are we whispering?"

Maddie sat back and smoothed the sleeves of her gown. "No reason."

His shrewd gaze quietly assessed her. "Pretty fancy traveling outfit, that."

"Yes, well, I was pressed for time."

"On the lam is more like it."

She narrowed her eyes at him. "You know what they say. A leaf never falls far from the tree."

Freddy frowned as he shook out his linen napkin and laid it in his lap. "Now you sound like your mother."

"My mother," Maddie said icily, "died a year ago, in case you hadn't heard."

"Ah," he said sadly, "but I *had* heard." He smiled, but his smile didn't reach his eyes. His hands moved across the table to cover hers. "I looked for Sarah the moment they let me out, Madeline. I wanted to tell her that I'd reformed, that I'd take care of her the way I should have from the beginning. Then I learned that she had died, and that you had perished in a train wreck." He squeezed her fingers. "You'll never know the guilt and the pain I felt when I discovered that the only two people I cared about in this entire world were dead."

Maddie searched his eyes, wanting desperately to believe him, to forgive him for his deceiving ways.

Then her eyes narrowed and she pulled her hands away. "Still trying to pull a con, aren't you, Freddy?"

He looked stung by her words. "Madeline, I—"

"Don't," she said sharply. "It doesn't work on me." She paused as the waiter brought their food to the table. "I've learned to play the game, too," she continued, calmly stirring brown sugar into her oatmeal, "almost as well as you."

Maddie could feel his eyes on her as she ate her oatmeal. The lumps seemed to stick in her throat and she had to wash each bite down with tea, but she refused to let him see that what he'd told her had affected her more than she was letting on. She scoffed at her own gullibility. Freddy was such a good liar that he had nearly convinced her his feelings were genuine.

"Will you at least tell me why you're running?" he asked in a subdued voice.

Maddie stared down into the dish and found herself wanting to tell him, wanting to pretend that he really was a good father and that somehow he would be able to help her. "Do you remember Vincent Slade?" she asked.

"Slade?" he repeated warily. "Yes, I remember him."

"He remembers you, too," Maddie told him, "and not fondly, by the way."

Freddy's eyes darkened ominously. "Has he threatened you because of that one hundred dollars I took from him?"

"That was only the beginning."

Freddy sat forward, listening intently as Maddie recounted the horrors of that evening in Vincent Slade's cellar. She told him of the money and incriminating letter hidden on the Crandall farm. She told him of meeting Amelia, of switching identities, of Slade's appearance at the social, and of her own plans to find the evidence. But Maddie stopped short of telling him about falling in love with Blaine.

Freddy sat back and studied her skeptically. "You're going to the Crandall farm alone?"

At her quick nod, he scowled. "I'm coming with you."

Maddie shook her head furiously and leaned toward him. "No, you're not! It's much easier for one person to sneak around than two. And besides," she said, "I have a disguise."

Freddy's eyes widened and she could have sworn she saw a glimmer of pride in them. "A disguise." He twirled one end of his mustache and studied her.

"If you want to help," she told her father, "think of a way to get the police up to the Crandall farm. The only problem is that I'm not sure exactly where it is other than west of Havertown."

"Then how do you propose to find it?" he asked.

"I'll rent a horse at the livery there and ask for directions. Someone is bound to know where the farm is."

"Rent a horse?" Freddy spluttered in amazement. "Madeline, have you learned to ride?"

Maddie looked down at her hands on the table, remembering her riding lessons, remembering the feel of Blaine's arm around her waist, remembering her surprise at his gift of the small spotted mare. "Blaine taught me," she said wistfully.

"Jeremy's brother taught you?"

Maddie jerked her head up to find her father's curious gaze on her. "Jeremy didn't ride well," she hurriedly explained. "And Blaine insisted that I learn. He was such a tyrant. You don't know how glad I am to be away from him."

Freddy cut a bite of steak and chewed it, watching her thoughtfully. After a moment he asked, "Does Slade know where the evidence is hidden?"

"He knows it's at the farm. But he obviously didn't find it or he wouldn't be after me. A farm is a big place. There would be a thousand places to look."

"What makes you think you can find it?" Freddy asked, stabbing a fresh bite of steak with his fork.

"I know where to look."

"And where is that?"

"In the barn."

Freddy put down the fork and leaned toward her. "Madeline, if Slade knows you're headed back to Philly, don't you think he'll make a beeline for the Crandall farm?"

Maddie sighed miserably. "I hope by the time he figures it out I'll have the evidence. And if you do your part, the police will get there before him anyway."

"And just how do you think I'll be able to convince the police to make this trip out to the country?"

Maddie smiled humorlessly. "You'll think of something. It's what you do best, Freddy."

Suddenly, over her father's shoulder Maddie saw a man walk into the car and pause to look around. She gasped and slumped down in her seat.

"What is it?" Freddy glanced over his shoulder.

"Blaine!"

Chapter 29

✦◦◦✦

Maddie's heart sank. Blaine had followed her. How would she elude him now? She couldn't risk his life, too. *Think, Maddie, think!*

"You've got to help me," she whispered to her father. "You've got to keep Blaine on the train all the way to Philadelphia." She peered around her father and saw Blaine striding toward them, his stormy eyes fixed on her face, his features stiff with rage. "He's working with Vincent Slade, but he thinks I don't know. I don't care how you do it, just don't let him get off until the train reaches Broad Street Station."

"Madeline," her father said sternly, "I don't like your plan. You're dealing with dangerous men, men who would—"

"Freddy, you owe me this," Maddie said through clenched teeth. "Here he comes. Go along with whatever I say."

She picked up her cup with both hands to keep it from shaking and betraying her nervousness. Carefully, she brought it to her lips, gazing out the window as she sipped. From the corner of her eye, she saw Blaine come to a halt beside their table. She turned her head, tilting her face up to his with an innocent expression even while her heart was pounding frantically.

Blaine still had on his black suit and white shirt from the previous evening, though it now looked crumpled and dusty. His hair was wind-tossed and his eyes as dark as obsidian. His fingers clenched the brim of the black hat in his hand as he glared down at her.

Maddie gave him a sheepish smile. "Hello, Blaine."

His eyes slid to the man sitting across from her, then returned to her face. She saw a muscle twitch in his jaw. "I'd like to talk to you," he said in a low, steely voice. "In private."

Her father cleared his throat. "Madeline, perhaps you'd like to introduce us."

"Yes," she said, giving Freddy a hard look. "I think I would. Freddy, this is Blaine Knight, Jeremy's brother. Blaine, Frederick Beecher." She paused and let out her breath. "My father."

The shock and confusion on Blaine's face pierced Maddie's heart, but she forced her features to remain emotionless. She watched as his gaze darted from Freddy back to her and she cringed inwardly from the angry reproach in his dark eyes. She had led him to believe her father was dead.

Now her sudden flight, combined with the fact that she was with Freddy, would obviously convince Blaine that whatever lies Slade had told him were true. But she didn't dare let him know otherwise, or he would never let her hunt for the evidence alone.

Freddy sprang to his feet, his charming smile in place. "Please sit down and join us, Mr. Knight. You look like you could use a hearty meal."

Blaine's face took on that familiar stony look. He stared at Maddie as if waiting for her to say something. She sipped her tea and looked away.

"Yes, I believe I could use a good meal." Blaine slid onto the bench next to her father. "I've been riding half the night trying to catch a train." He paused to give the waiter his order. "I thought I'd lost something of great value last night, you see, and I wanted to get it back. But perhaps I was wrong. Perhaps it was never mine at all."

Maddie couldn't swallow past the lump in her throat. She kept her gaze fixed out the window so he wouldn't see the tears in her eyes.

"Tell me something, Maddie," Blaine said in a voice heavy with sarcasm. "Had you planned to rob us, too, or was marrying into the family enough for you?"

Maddie's head jerked around in surprise. "*Rob* you?"

"We didn't believe Slade," Blaine told her as he spread a white napkin on his lap. "We didn't think you were capable of stealing his wife's money."

Maddie shot her father a startled look.

"Even knowing that everything you'd told us was a lie, we still didn't believe you stole that money." Blaine's hand curled into a fist. "I told him I wouldn't let him take you back to Philadelphia without me. I thought if I swore to your innocence, the police wouldn't hold you. And then you ran." He leaned toward her, his upper lip pulled back to reveal his even, white teeth. "You tell me what I should believe, Maddie."

Beneath the table Maddie's hands clenched her knees. She had to convince Blaine of her duplicity. She had to make him hate her or there was no way he would let her out of his sight until he took her back to Philadelphia and discovered the truth for himself. And by that time Vincent Slade would have caught up with them.

Maddie raised her chin and said coldly, "You should have believed Slade. It's all true, you see. I took the money and ran. I just happened to meet Amelia on the train that day. And after the accident—" She shrugged nonchalantly. "—everything fell into place. It was the perfect escape. Only I hadn't counted on Slade tracking me down so quickly." She turned toward her father and forced a stiff smile. "Vincent Slade very nearly ruined our plans, didn't he, Freddy?"

Freddy looked at Blaine and shrugged sheepishly.

Maddie shoved her chair back and rose. "I'm going to my compartment to rest. I have a headache." She gave her father a meaningful look. "Wake me when we reach Broad Street Station."

Freddy's eyes locked with hers for only a second, but it was enough to read the message of concern in his gaze. "Are you sure you'll be all right?" he asked, and she knew he wasn't referring to her headache.

She gave him a fleeting smile. "I'll be fine."

Maddie left the dining car and moved quickly through the parlor car, wanting to distance herself from Blaine. How clever Vincent Slade had been to invent the story of his wife's robbery. It was the perfect reason to take her back to Philadelphia.

And now Blaine was in danger, too, because he

had refused to believe her guilty of stealing the money. Maddie bit her lip as tears sprang to her eyes. The pain in his eyes at her phony confession had nearly been her undoing. Now she had to trust that her father would be true to his word at least once in his life and keep Blaine on the train.

She slipped into the empty compartment and started to close the door, but it was shoved open and Blaine stepped in behind her. She gasped and took a step back, pressing herself against the wall. "Get out!" she cried. "I told you I have a headache."

He shut the door and braced his hands on either side of her shoulders, his eyes searching her face. "You'd never make a good poker player, Maddie."

Damn that wrinkle in her forehead! Maddie forced herself to relax, to concentrate on her words. "All right," she said. "I don't have a headache. I just don't want to see you."

"Why, Maddie?" Blaine said in a bitingly cold voice, his face inches from hers, his breath hot on her cheek. "Is your conscience bothering you?"

She turned her head away. "Yes."

"Well," he said. "The truth at last."

"I didn't want to deceive you," Maddie told him stiffly, "but I'm afraid of Vincent Slade. He's a powerful man. I knew he'd hunt me down. That's why I had to leave Philadelphia."

Blaine gripped her chin and turned her to face him, studying her features carefully. "Why did you take the money from Slade's wife?"

Maddie blinked, swallowed, opened her mouth to reply. But what could she tell him? If she told him a lie, he'd know it instantly. She pushed his hand away, ducked under his arm, and went to stand by the small window at the end of the compartment. "I've had to work hard since my mother died. She had no savings. There were funeral costs, rent, food . . . And the money was just lying there." She shrugged. "It was too much of a temptation."

"It was just lying there?"

"Yes. On Mrs. Slade's dressing table. She always left money lying carelessly about."

"I see." Blaine walked up behind her and gripped her arms. "You told me you loved me. You agreed to marry me. Were those lies, too?"

Maddie closed her eyes and pressed her lips together to keep from turning and throwing herself in his arms. She drew a steadying breath. "I didn't want to go to New York with Jeremy. Slade has connections. I was afraid he might be able to find me there." She exhaled slowly. "That's why I agreed to marry you."

For a long moment, there was nothing but silence behind her. When Blaine finally spoke, his voice was so quiet she had to strain to hear him. "That was the only reason you agreed to marry me?"

"Yes."

"Look at me and say it, Maddie."

Maddie's fingers curled into her palms. She steeled herself to meet his penetrating gaze and slowly turned to face him, her heart melting at the sight of his handsome, intense features. She wanted to stroke the hard stubble of his beard and smooth back the dark lock of hair on his forehead and tell him she had lied. Tell him that she loved him and always would. She dropped her gaze. "That was the only reason."

He lifted her chin and brought his mouth down over hers with surprising intensity, drawing her against him, enfolding her in the warm circle of his arms. Maddie closed her eyes and tried to resist the love that surged through her. She put her hands against his chest to push him away, but stopped. This was the man she loved, the man to whom she had given her most precious gift. She couldn't deny herself this one last kiss.

She slipped her arms around his neck as Blaine's tongue seared the line of her lips, seeking entrance. Her lips parted and he plunged inside, melding his taste with hers, igniting her passion until her blood sang with it, hot and sweet and insistent. She felt his hand slide along her ribs to the underside of her breast, his thumb teasing the soft crest until it puckered and tingled, until she moaned deep in her throat and pressed her hips against his, seeking his hardness.

And then he broke the kiss and leaned back, his breathing ragged. "Are you sure, Maddie?" he asked huskily. "Are you sure love had nothing to do with it?"

Maddie shuddered inwardly from the desire coiling deep inside her and fought to pull together the scattered strands of her emotions. *Lie, Maddie, but lie carefully.* She forced a blank expression on her face. "I'm Fast Freddy's daughter, Blaine. Do you want me to tell you that I love you? That I want you? I will, if that's what you want to hear. I'm good at making up stories. I studied under the best con artist in Pennsylvania."

Blaine stared at her in disbelief, and then he stepped back, removing his hands from her shoulders as if it pained him to touch her. Maddie's heart felt as though it were shattering. She had never felt such deep self-loathing as she did at that moment.

From the hallway she heard the conductor's voice. "Next stop—King of Prussia."

Her stomach knotted. Havertown would be coming up soon and she still hadn't changed into her pants and shirt. She forced herself to walk calmly to the door and open it. "I'd like to rest, if you don't mind."

"Ah, here you are!" Freddy said from the hallway, quickly meeting Maddie's panicked gaze with a reassuring nod. "Look here, Mr. Knight, I don't know how far you intend to travel, but as long as we're going to be on the train for another half hour or so, how about a game of poker to while away the time?"

Blaine glanced back at Maddie, and when she wouldn't meet his gaze, he said in a hard voice, "That would suit me fine."

"Madeline," her father said, "close your door and rest now."

"Thank you, Freddy," she managed.

Blaine studied the cards in his hand and threw two on the table. More than fifteen minutes had passed since he'd left Maddie's room, yet he could not get her words out of his mind. He was certain she was still lying, but he was at a loss to know why. Slade had said she'd stolen the money from a strongbox. Maddie's version was that she had taken it from a dressing table. Blaine didn't believe she had done either.

Why then had she run? And how had she happened to meet up with her father on the train? He eyed the man sitting across the table from him in the parlor car. Fast Freddy the con man. Not a bad card player, either, Blaine thought dryly, giving Freddy's considerable pile of coins a quick, appraising glance.

He suddenly remembered Maddie's response to the name of his horse. *"Not Fred. I hate that name."*

Had she lied about her father, too? Had she schemed all along to meet him? Had Slade's timely arrival foiled her plans to rob the Knights, as well?

"What's the bet?" he asked Freddy.

"Two bits."

Blaine tossed the money on the table. "How long have you been out of prison?"

Freddy's eyebrows lifted. "Did Madeline tell you about me?"

Blaine discarded two cards. "Slade did."

"Ah, yes. Vincent Slade." Freddy eyed him warily as he dealt two new cards. "I've been out three weeks, Mr. Knight."

Blaine kept his gaze fixed on Freddy. "Slade was pretty upset about Maddie stealing five hundred dollars from his wife."

"I can imagine," Freddy muttered dryly.

"Did she tell you what she did with the money?"

With a flourish, Freddy laid down three aces and two tens and reached for the coins in the center of the table. "Paid off her debts."

Blaine threw down four jacks, bringing a sudden halt to Freddy's movements. "It was two thousand dollars, Mr. Beecher, not five hundred."

Freddy's face turned bright red. Sheepishly, he pushed the coins toward Blaine. "My memory isn't what it used to be."

"Maddie didn't steal the money, did she?"

"She did what she had to do, Mr. Knight."

Blaine laughed dryly. "I can see where she comes by her skill for evasion." He sat forward, his face serious and intense. "Look, I don't know what's going on here, but I do know that neither one of you is telling me the truth."

"Why is it you feel such a need to know the truth, young man? Madeline is out of your life. No harm done. Why can't you just let her be?"

"No harm done?" Blaine repeated with an incredulous laugh. "I asked her to marry me, Mr. Beecher, and she accepted."

Blaine Knight had offered for Madeline's hand? Freddy's eyes narrowed. Either Blaine was more cunning than he thought or Madeline had conned her own father. He nearly laughed aloud at that thought. Would Madeline con him? It would certainly be a novel turn of the tables. "I thought your brother was supposed to marry my daughter, Mr. Knight."

"That was the original plan. In any case, I'm not going to let her simply walk out of my life with no explanations. Would you let the woman you loved walk away from you so easily?"

Freddy considered Blaine's question, his gray-green eyes shifting to the window and seeing far beyond it, seeing into his past. He slowly shook his head. "No, Mr. Knight. Never again." After a moment, he rubbed his eyes. "Ah, but have I? Yes, I have." He turned a sorrowful gaze back to Blaine. "It's something I'll regret for the rest of my life."

"Why don't you tell me what's really going on?" Blaine said quietly.

The train chugged to a stop. Freddy sighed. The last stop before Broad Street Station. From his window, Freddy watched the passengers mill about on the platform outside. He thought of the slender boy in denim pants and a blue cotton shirt who had disembarked less than a quarter of an hour ago, a brown tweed cap on his head and an old satchel in his hand. Freddy smiled, recalling the unmistakable wisps of red hair trailing from beneath the boy's cap.

But as the train pulled away again, his smile dissolved. His daughter *was* in danger. If he didn't help her, she could very well be killed. Yet he had promised her that he would keep Blaine on the train. But what if Madeline *had* conned him? What if Blaine really did love her? How could he be sure? Freddy sighed wearily and shook his head. Being a father was a tough business.

"Deal the cards, Mr. Knight."

Blaine stared at Freddy as if he had lost his mind. "What?"

"We've a few minutes yet to kill, don't we? Five-card stud, five-card draw, blackjack, your choice."

Blaine scraped back his chair and jerked to his feet, his face taut with anger. "I've had enough of your games."

Freddy jumped up. "I'll make you a wager, Mr. Knight."

Blaine regarded him with dark, mistrustful eyes. "What is it?"

"If you win, I'll tell you what you need to know." Freddy resumed his seat and picked up the cards. "Choose your game." He began to shuffle, counting on Blaine's curiosity to keep him at the table.

"What happens if I lose?"

Freddy tipped back his hat with his thumb. "If you lose I don't tell you a thing."

Blaine's eyes narrowed and Freddy knew he was weighing his options, deciding whether to take the bet. One thing was certain, if Blaine Knight truly cared about his daughter, losing a card game wouldn't stop him from learning what he needed to know.

"You're on, Mr. Beecher." Blaine sat and scooted in his chair. "My choice?"

"That's right."

Blaine folded his arms across his chest. "Gin rummy."

Freddy's hands halted in mid-shuffle. *Gin rummy?* Did the man think he had no pride? He shook his head. He should have guessed as much, coming from a farmer, although Blaine had been more than adequate at poker. But still, *rummy?* "Rummy it is. First man to reach one hundred points wins."

Ten minutes later, his frock coat off, his shirt-sleeves rolled to his elbows, Freddy smiled to himself when Blaine threw down his cards and said quietly, "Gin."

Freddy pretended disgust. "It seems you've won the wager, Mr. Knight. Gin rummy is not my game." He gathered the cards. Losing had gone against every fiber of his being. He hoped Madeline would someday appreciate the sacrifice he had made. He looked up and found Blaine studying him speculatively.

"Start talking, Mr. Beecher."

Freddy leaned back in his chair, pushed his hat to the back of his head, and hooked his thumbs in his belt. "Madeline got off the train at Havertown."

Blaine's fingers gripped the edge of the table. "What did you say?"

Freddy scratched the back of his neck. Blaine Knight was a big man and he didn't relish the idea of tangling with him, but he had given his word to his daughter, and, for possibly the first time in Madeline's lifetime, he intended to keep it. "I said she's off the train."

Blaine lurched across the table and grabbed Freddy by his shirtfront, his teeth bared. "Where the hell did she go?"

"She mentioned something about a barn in Havertown."

"Damn!" Blaine lunged for the emergency cord.

Freddy grabbed his arm. "It's no use stopping the train here. We'll be pulling into the station in another few minutes."

"Why the hell did you let her get off?" Blaine snarled.

"Unfortunately, I had very little say in the matter."

"Damn!" Blaine sank into his seat and tunneled his fingers through his hair. He stopped and glared at Freddy. "I want some answers, Mr. Beecher, or I swear I'll toss you bodily from this train and take great pleasure in doing it."

Freddy held up both hands. "There's no need to resort to violence. The barn belongs to folks by the name of Crandall. Madeline went there to dig up some buried money." He rose and picked up his frock coat.

"The *stolen* money?" Blaine sat forward as Freddy prepared to take his leave. "Wait a minute. You haven't told me how Slade fits into the picture."

Freddy smiled. "The wager was, Mr. Knight, that if you won, I would tell you everything you needed to know, and I have done just that. Now, if you'll excuse me," he said, politely lifting his hat, "I must fetch my traveling bag before the train stops."

Blaine jumped up, but Freddy managed to slip among the passengers now filling the aisle before he could stop him. Blaine pushed through the crowd to the end of the parlor car only to find that Fast Freddy was nowhere to be seen.

He'd lost both the father and the daughter.

Chapter 30

Vincent Slade sat on the edge of his train seat, staring through the window at the passing scenery. Bull sat on a seat across the aisle, whittling a piece of wood with his knife. The *scritch-scritch* of the blade was getting on Slade's nerves, but he held his tongue. There would be time later to settle his differences with Bull.

He took out his watch and snapped it open. Five-thirty in the afternoon. By his calculations Madeline had at least a two-hour head start. Fortunately, he had thought to wire ahead to have a man waiting at each station between Villanova and Broad Street. All he had to do was check in at each stop down the line and he'd know where she got off.

He closed his eyes and leaned his head against the back of the seat. *Oh, yes, Madeline Beecher, I'll find you. You'll pay for leading me on this merry chase.* He recalled how luscious she'd looked in the portrait and he felt his body respond. He'd waited a long time for this. She was going to pay dearly.

* * *

Maddie pressed herself flat against the back side of the barn and held her breath, waiting, listening, her heartbeat drumming in her ears. She had tried to open the single door at the rear of the barn, only to have it screech loudly on ancient hinges. Cautiously, she peered around the corner to see if anyone in the house had heard the disturbance. When no one appeared at the door, she forced herself to move quickly down the long side and around the corner to the big double doors at the front.

Finding the Crandall farm had proved to be more difficult than she had expected. She'd gotten lost twice on the winding country lanes, losing at least an hour's time. When she finally located the farm, she'd hid in a stand of elm trees and watched the house and surrounding property for signs of life. Finally she'd stolen up to a window to peer inside, where she'd seen an elderly couple sitting in the kitchen eating their supper. She had not seen any farmhands outside.

Maddie wished she knew how far behind Slade was. She gently eased the heavy wooden latch up out of its holder and tugged one door open wide enough to fit through, wincing at each tiny noise. She glanced back at the farmhouse, then slipped inside and paused to get her bearings.

The quickly fading daylight shone dimly through the row of small windows on one side of the barn, barely illuminating the large pen that housed at least a dozen cows. She saw a wooden feeding trough that ran down the middle of the front end of the barn and a row of single stalls near the back. Pitchforks, shovels, and coils of rope hung from iron hooks on the wall near the front door and two ladders on either side led to a loft directly over the cows.

Maddie moved forward cautiously, straw crunching under her feet. The barn smelled of musty hay, manure, and animals, familiar smells to her now. She stumbled over a three-legged stool and quickly righted it, then spotted an oil lamp and a box of phosphorous matches on an old table against one wall. She looked around, her forehead wrinkling. Where would Crandall have hidden the evidence?

"In the most difficult place to get to."

Maddie bit her lower lip, knowing she had little time left. She moved silently toward the stalls at the far end where she could see the heads of two draft horses. Four of the stalls were empty, but from the last one she heard the sound of heavy blowing and hooves pawing the ground. The stall had higher, sturdier walls than the others and only a narrow door into it. She opened it cautiously. Her eyes widened in alarm as a bull raised its heavy head and glared at her. She slammed the door and backed away, her heart thundering like a cannon.

The most difficult place to get to.

It had to be in the bull's stall.

Maddie closed her eyes and clenched her fists, pushing back her fear. There was no time to be afraid. She dragged the stool over to the stall and climbed onto it to peer over the top of the wall. A door at the back of the stall appeared to lead outside. Maddie jumped down and hurried to the window. Sure enough, the door led directly into a paddock some twenty-five feet square.

She looked around, thinking hard. How could she lure the bull into the paddock? Spotting a sack of grain at the front of the barn, she took two handfuls from it, slipped outside to the paddock, and circled around. She found a gate, but it was chained shut.

"Bother!" Maddie muttered in frustration. She looked around for something to hold the handfuls of grain and finally poured it into the pockets of her pants. She climbed the slatted fence, dug the grain out of her pockets, and made a line with it leading to the corner farthest from the barn. Then she quickly unlatched the stall door and ran for the fence.

In a few moments the bull stuck his huge, horned head through the open doorway and sniffed the air. He turned to fix her with his ill-tempered glare and shook his head in warning. Maddie made a hasty exit down the other side of the fence. She hurried into the barn, back to the bull's stall, opened the narrow doorway, and peeked through to the paddock beyond. Spotting the bull in the far corner contentedly eating the grain, she rushed through the stall to the outside door and closed it.

Straining to see in the semidarkness, Maddie carefully knelt in the stall, avoiding the fresh piles of manure, and scraped through the straw covering, pulling and clawing at the floorboards in the corners, driving splinters of wood deep into her fingertips, only to find the floor solidly nailed. With a groan of frustration, she pushed to her feet. How much time had she wasted? She felt her way back to the table, found the matches, and lit the lamp, turning down the wick so the flame would burn as low as possible.

Where else could Crandall have hidden the evidence? She gave the loft overhead a cursory glance, then dismissed it as too obvious. Hands on her hips, Maddie slowly turned in a circle. *Where would be the most difficult place to get to?* She examined every corner of each stall; she overturned the feeding trough; she moved heavy bags of grain to check the floor beneath them; she wove through the cows to check the corners of their pen, and still she found nothing.

What if it isn't here? Maddie's stomach knotted in dread. What if she couldn't find it? From the corner of her eye, a tiny square of yellow appeared. She turned toward the window with a gasp to see the front door of the farmhouse standing open.

In an instant, she had turned down the wick of the lamp and was scurrying up one of the ladders to the loft above. Holding her hand over her mouth to stifle the harsh sounds of her breathing, Maddie knelt beside the large, shuttered opening at the far end of the loft and peered out.

"Tie them up."

With a sneer of contempt, Vincent Slade turned away from the elderly couple huddled together in a corner of their kitchen and glanced at Bull. "These people don't know anything. Let's start searching for Madeline."

He left his man Potter standing guard over the Crandalls and walked out onto the farmhouse porch. "Start with the barn. I'll check the outbuildings."

Bull lifted his hat and scratched his head. "We searched the barn already. The evidence ain't there."

Slade gritted his teeth. He was tired and dirty and had no time for Bull's whining. "You're looking for the girl, not the evidence. Search the barn!"

Bull grumbled and shuffled away. Slade strode toward the smokehouse and unlatched the door, lighting a match to see inside. With a muttered curse, he moved to the icehouse and then to the chicken coop, again with no luck. He was on his way to the barn when Bull sauntered across the barnyard toward him. "Nothing in the barn but some dumb animals."

Slade kicked the dirt with his boot. "Damn it! She could be anywhere."

"Ain't there a cellar behind the house?"

"A cellar? Yes, I would say there is. And she does have a preference for hiding in cellars, doesn't she?" Slade smiled and strode back toward the farmhouse with Bull hard upon his heels.

Her heart pounding in terror, Maddie backed away from the opening. Her whole body shook with fear as she crawled to the edge of the loft. Vincent Slade was there and she still hadn't found the evidence.

"Please, Lord, help me," she whispered tearfully, her hands folded together, her gaze raised to the huge rafters above her. "I don't want to die. But I don't know where else to look . . ." Maddie blinked and stared harder at the rafters. She wiped her eyes on her sleeve and blinked again.

Sitting atop one of the huge beams halfway across the open side of the barn was a deserted swallow's nest made of mud and grass.

The most difficult place to get to.

Hope flickered inside her. An old nest would be the perfect place to hide a small bundle. No one would ever think to search the rafters, let alone to search an empty nest. She jumped to her feet and looked around. A coil of rope lay near the back end of the loft and a three-tined hayfork rested against one wall. Maddie tried using the hayfork to reach the nest, but the tool proved to be much too short.

She picked up the rope, tied a knot at one end, and tossed it over the rafter directly above her, but it dangled just out of reach. She tried again, heaving it up with a grunt and grabbing it as it slithered down the other side. Holding onto both ends of the rope with one hand, Maddie leaned out from the loft and stretched toward the nest with the hayfork. It was still beyond her reach.

With a smothered cry of frustration, she sank down onto the hay. There seemed to be no way to reach the nest without crawling across the rafter. She was stuck in the loft, unable to reach the evidence, and unable to climb down for fear of Slade coming upon her. "Freddy, where are you?" Maddie whispered.

She wondered if her father had told Blaine the truth about Slade. The thought made her laugh. *Her* father tell the truth? She knew Blaine would be furious when he found out she'd gotten off the train before him. And after all the lies she had told, she wouldn't be at all surprised if he got back on the train and went home. At that moment, however, Blaine's fury was the least of her worries. She eyed the nest again.

"Bother," she muttered, and got to her feet. No one was going to come to her rescue. She had to save herself.

Maddie reached for the two ends of the rope still dangling from the rafter, twisted them together, and knotted them at the base. Hand over hand she began to climb, her legs wrapped tightly around the rope, until she could grasp the top of the beam. Her arms shaking from the effort, she hauled herself up and lay stomach-down upon it. Hugging the huge wooden rafter with both arms, she gazed at the floor far beneath her.

When she felt steady enough, Maddie pushed to her knees. She glanced down again and nearly lost her balance. "Don't look down," she whispered. She hauled up the rope and wound it around her waist, then focused on the nest ten feet away. Slowly, she moved forward—an inch, two inches, a foot. Perspiration beaded her forehead and trickled into her eyebrows, but she didn't dare lift a hand to wipe it. The rafter creaked ominously under her weight. Maddie swallowed and continued forward.

When the nest was within reach, she put out her hand and gingerly felt inside. The dried mud nest was filled with a mixture of feathers and brittle grass. Her fingers probed further and felt something flat and hard covered by cloth. A tremor of excitement shot through her. Quickly, she wrapped her fingers around it.

Suddenly, the barn doors opened below her and Vincent Slade walked in, accompanied by his sidekick. Maddie held her breath and watched as they stopped directly beneath her.

"What do we do now, boss?"

Slade spotted the old lamp on the table and lit it. The wavering light threw shadows across his craggy face, giving it a diabolic cast Maddie knew to be all too true. "We're going to tear apart this farm until we find her," Slade sneered. "I know Madeline Beecher is somewhere on this property, Bull. I can feel her."

Maddie bit down on her lip to keep from whimpering in fear.

"What about the Crandalls?" Bull asked.

"We'll take care of them later."

Maddie's arm began to tingle from holding it out so long. Slowly, she lifted the cloth package out of the nest and stuffed it in her shirt. Stifling a panicked gasp, she watched helplessly as a light shower of grass and feathers fell from the nest to the ground below. She froze as Slade and Bull tilted their heads back and looked up at her.

"Someone is up there, boss."

"Hey, boy! What are you doing up there?"

Maddie closed her eyes. It was all over now.

"Did you hear me, boy?"

"Maybe he's deaf, boss."

Maddie ventured a peek and saw Slade move to one side to get a better look at her. "No," he said slowly, his hand stroking his long chin, "I don't think that's the problem, Bull." He began to chuckle, then threw his head back and shouted with laughter that bounced off the high roof and turned the very marrow in Maddie's bones to ice. She wanted to clap her hands over her ears, but she didn't dare let go of the beam.

His laughter died suddenly. "Madeline, my dear," he jeered softly, "I've waited a long time for this moment."

Slade nodded his head and Bull immediately hurried to one of the ladders. Maddie couldn't move. Her breath felt trapped in her lungs, and fear such as she had never known before wrapped its sharp talons around her heart. Not even when she had watched Crandall die had she felt such absolute terror. Then at least she had been hidden from sight. Now there was nowhere left to hide.

Vincent Slade had finally caught her.

"Come down, my sweet Madeline," Slade called

in a deceptively pleasant tone. "You've been excep-
tionally clever until now, but you can't escape me
anymore."

A small sob escaped Maddie's lips. She glanced
back at Bull, who was halfway up the ladder, huff-
ing with exertion as he struggled to gain the next
rung with his stumpy legs. She closed her eyes and
called up an image of Blaine, remembering the feel
of his strong arms around her.

*"I love you, Maddie. I don't want you to be afraid of
Vincent Slade anymore."*

Maddie inhaled slowly, trying to draw strength
from the memory. She opened her eyes and looked
down. Slade was glaring up at her, his long, cruel
hands on his hips, a leering grin on his evil face.

"Madeline, I'm growing impatient. I have a gun.
Do you want me to use it?"

Maddie swallowed and looked forward. The
wooden rafter ended above the bull's stall. If she
could make it to the stall, she could escape through
the door to the paddock. It was her only hope.
Slowly, she began to crawl away from the loft.

"Madeline, look at me, dammit!"

Maddie ignored him and kept moving. Suddenly
a shot rang out and a bullet splintered the edge of
the rafter in front of her. With a gasp, she jerked
back. Another shot hit where her hand had just
been. With a cry of terror, she fell to her stomach
and clung to the rafter with both arms, her eyes
tightly shut, her legs so rubbery she knew they
would never support her. "Don't shoot," she cried
in a hoarse voice. "I can't move."

"Get up on your knees," Slade hissed. "Start
crawling backwards."

Maddie glanced over her shoulder. Bull stood at

the edge of the loft, a smug grin on his flat face. A tiny voice sounded in her mind: *You're Fast Freddy's daughter. Use your head. Talk your way out.*

"The—evidence," Maddie called weakly. "It's—just a little farther on."

"Do you see anything, Bull?"

"It looks like there could be somethin' up on the rafter, boss, but it's too dark to see what it is."

Maddie pushed to her knees. "It's in a flat pouch—" She swallowed the lump of terror in her throat. "—on top of the rafter." She forced herself to crawl toward the bull's stall. Her hands were clammy and she was shaking so hard she was afraid she would slip.

From far below Slade cursed profusely, but he didn't shoot again. "Bull, get down here."

Maddie eyed the end stall and licked her upper lip. What was her plan when she reached it? *Think, Maddie!* The cloth package was stuffed inside her shirt. If she could distract Slade by tossing it into another stall before Bull reached the bottom, there was a chance she could shimmy down the rope into the bull's stall and escape before either one noticed she had gone.

But then where would she go?

"Do you have it yet?" Slade called.

"Almost." She was nearly over the stall. She reached inside her shirt and slid out the package. The evidence was her only hope of proving Slade was a murderer. But it was also her last hope of escaping with her life. She closed her eyes and whispered a quick prayer. Holding it out for Slade to see, she called in a shaking voice, "I have it."

"Drop it."

Maddie looked down at Slade, the package

clutched in her fingers. She had to make her move now. But suddenly, at the front of the barn, Blaine stepped quietly through the big double doors.

Maddie sucked in her breath. Blaine had come after her! Freddy had told him after all. But Blaine wouldn't be carrying a gun, not after his experience at Wounded Knee Creek. He would have no way to defend himself against Slade; he would surely be killed! Somehow she had to distract Slade to give Blaine an advantage.

Quickly, Maddie tossed the package into a far stall. As the two men rushed forward to claim it, she slipped the rope from around her waist, looped it over the rafter, and dropped down into the bull's stall.

"Get her!" she heard Slade snarl. Maddie sprang to her feet, pushed open the door, and slipped into the paddock, her heart thundering in her ears. In the moonlight she saw the bull turn and lower his head threateningly. He dug at the ground with one hoof, his breath coming out in angry snorts. Maddie darted behind the door just as Bull stepped outside and looked around.

Quickly, Maddie slammed the door behind him and ran for the fence. The beast charged, hooves pounding the ground. The little man cried out and dived to the side, rolling over in the dirt. He scrambled to his feet as the animal turned and charged once more. With a cry of terror, Bull raced for the fence, scrabbling for a foothold, but his short legs foiled him. Maddie pressed her fingers to her mouth in horror as the animal gored him in the back and tossed him over his huge head. She heard a sickening crunch as he landed. His head lolled to one side, his eyes open and sightless. Bull was dead.

But Blaine was inside the barn with a murderer.

Chapter 31

Blaine was halfway across the barnyard when the first shot rang out. He had just come from the house, where through the window he had seen an elderly couple being guarded by one of Slade's men. Seeing no sign of Slade or Maddie, he had skirted the house and started off to find them. At the second shot, he set off at a hard run. He slipped inside the double doors and paused to take in the scene before him. He saw Slade and the man who claimed to be a marshal rush into one of the far stalls. And then Blaine saw a slender form in canvas pants fall from the rafters into the last stall.

"Dear God, no!" he whispered in a strangled voice. He had arrived too late. Slade had shot Maddie.

A terrible blinding rage surged through his body. He wrenched a pitchfork from the wall and started across the barn after Slade. He'd kill the bastard.

"Get her!" he heard Slade snarl. Blaine stopped in confusion when a door in the last stall suddenly swung toward the outside. He looked up and noticed a rope dangling from the rafter directly above it.

She was alive! Maddie hadn't fallen at all. She had used a rope to lower herself into the stall. Blaine backed out of sight as the smaller man ran after her. He waited until Slade strode out of the stall, a smile of victory on his craggy face, and then he stepped out in front of him. "You shouldn't be so careless with your gun, Slade. You could have killed her."

Slade's eyes widened in surprise as Blaine's fist connected with his jaw. He dropped the package in his hand and reeled backward into the empty stall, hitting the end wall and sinking to the ground. Blaine tossed the pitchfork aside and started toward his opponent just as Slade reached for the gun tucked in his waistband. Blaine tackled him, gripping Slade's wrist with all his strength until the gun slipped from his grasp. Blaine jumped to his feet and kicked the gun out of the stall, his dark eyes glittering with rage.

"Get up, you bastard!"

With a grimace, Slade touched his fingers to his bleeding lower lip and climbed to his feet. "Listen, Mr. Knight, Madeline came here to get the money she stole from my wife. I was only trying to get it back."

"Step out of the stall."

Slade glared at Blaine, then straightened his soot-damaged frock coat and walked out. "You're making a huge mistake, my friend."

"Move over there," Blaine said, jerking his head toward the front of the barn, "against the ladder." He saw Slade eyeing the gun on the floor, and knew he should pick it up. But the thought of handling the weapon brought out such revulsion in him that he couldn't move. Beads of sweat broke out on his forehead and his vision wavered and blurred. And once again he saw in his mind's eye the carnage at Wounded Knee.

Pick it up! his mind commanded. *Quickly! Before Slade goes for it.* Blaine made a quick swipe of his sleeve across his face. Why couldn't he pick up the damn gun?

Slade started past him, then turned and pulled one elbow back hard into Blaine's ribs. As Blaine grunted in pain, Slade stooped for the gun. Startled into action, Blaine used his foot to shove Slade forward, sending the man tumbling to his hands and knees. Gritting his teeth, Blaine retrieved the weapon and shoved it in the back of his waistband.

Slade jumped to his feet and backed away. "Look here, Mr. Knight, if you're smart you'll persuade Madeline to turn herself in. It'll go much easier on her than if the marshal has to take her in by force."

Blaine picked up the cloth package and followed him. "Is that right?"

Slade walked up to the ladder and turned around. "Damn it, Knight, you'll be charged as an accomplice if you let her escape!"

Blaine pulled a rope from the wall. "Tell me something, Slade. Why did you go to so much effort to find her? Offering a thousand-dollar reward for a two-thousand-dollar robbery doesn't make a whole lot of sense to me."

"Nor to me. If I'd had to come up with the money myself it wouldn't have been nearly that amount. But you see, Mr. Knight, Madeline had stolen before she came to work for me. After she ran away I contacted a few of her victims, and they were more than happy to add their money to the pot. If you don't believe me, ask the marshal. He'll verify it."

Blaine stared at Slade's harsh features and his stomach tightened. What if Maddie *was* a thief? What if he had come all this way only to discover that Slade was right? Maddie's own father had admitted she had left the train for the purpose of retrieving the money.

No. He wouldn't believe it. He loved Maddie. He had been as close to her as a man could be to a woman. He would know if she were truly a thief. He would know it in his heart.

Wouldn't he?

Blaine tossed the rope at Slade's feet. "Tie your legs at the knees to the ladder."

Suddenly, a loud crash sounded behind Blaine as one of the doors hit the wall. He swung around as a tall, solidly built man hauled Maddie through it, one thick arm around her neck, the other holding a long, slim knife to her throat.

The man grinned stupidly. "Look who I found outside, boss."

Blaine's insides twisted in misery as he stared at Maddie. Her pants were torn at the knees and one tail of her blue shirt hung out of the waistband. Her arms were badly scratched, her fingertips crusted with blood. Her hair had come loose from its pins and tumbled over her shoulders in disarray. Her face was streaked with dirt and tears and her silver-green eyes were wide with terror. Blaine snarled at her captor, "Let her go."

Suddenly, Maddie's gaze shifted to a point behind him and she let out a muffled gasp of fear. Blaine swung around just as Slade slipped his hand inside his frock coat, and this time Blaine knew the man intended to kill him. Clenching his teeth,

Blaine forced himself to pull the gun from his waist-band and take aim at Slade's chest. "Get your hands up!"

With an amused smile, Slade obeyed, easing his hand from his coat and then raising both hands, palms outward. "They're up, Mr. Knight."

Sweat began to trickle down the sides of Blaine's face. He gripped the weapon tighter, trying to stop his hands from shaking. But all he could see was the terrified face of the Indian boy just before his captain shot him. *Concentrate on Maddie,* he told himself. She was defenseless, just like the child. He had to protect her. But what if he froze again?

He wanted to wipe away the wetness on his face, but his fingers were clenched too tightly around the butt of the gun. "Tell your man to release her," Blaine commanded hoarsely.

"No, Mr. Knight. Either you put the gun down or my man will slit her throat."

Blaine tried to swallow but his throat was too dry. Could he bluff Slade? Or would they find out what kind of a coward he really was?

Maddie felt the tip of the knife dig into her flesh. She whimpered in fright, her eyes watching Blaine's every move. She heard the sound of the gun cocking and she knew Blaine was preparing to shoot.

"If you want to live, Slade," Blaine called, "release Maddie *now!*"

As Maddie watched Blaine, she suddenly became aware of a tremble in his hand and drops of per-spiration running down his face. Her skin crawled with fear as realization swept through her. *Blaine couldn't shoot the gun!*

She felt light-headed and closed her eyes, remembering Blaine's account of the massacre at Wounded Knee Creek. He would not be able to kill Slade even if her life depended on it. She prayed that his bluff would work. Because if it didn't, Slade would kill them both.

Freddy, where are you? Tears gathered behind Maddie's eyelids. Why had she thought she could trust him? Ten years of prison had not changed her father. He had let her down again.

"Tell your man to let her go!" Blaine repeated through clenched teeth. Maddie watched him fearfully. The strain was evident on his face. Surely Slade saw it.

"I'll give you to the count of ten."

"Listen here, Knight," Slade said quickly. "Madeline is cunning, just like her father. She'll try to convince you she's innocent. How many times has she lied to you already?"

Maddie saw Blaine dash away the sweat on his face with his arm, both hands still gripping the gun. Her eyes darted to Slade, who continued to taunt him. "Ask Madeline to tell you the truth about the money. Ask her if you dare, Mr. Knight."

Blaine's dark gaze shifted momentarily to Maddie's face and she flinched at the doubt there. *Trust me*, she pleaded silently. But how could she expect him to trust her when she'd never been honest with him? And still couldn't be honest with him, for fear of seeing them both killed? Tears pooled in her eyes and ran down her cheeks. Vincent Slade knew exactly what he was doing. He knew she wouldn't jeopardize either her or Blaine's life by telling Blaine about the murder. Her eyes beseeched him, *Please trust me*.

"What's the truth, Maddie?" Blaine whispered hoarsely.

She caught her lower lip between her teeth and gazed at him through a veil of tears. "I—" A sob escaped and she fought for control. She dared not say anything that would provoke Slade's anger. One look from him and Potter would slit her throat. "I—love you," she finished in a whisper.

For a long expectant moment Blaine stared at her, and then understanding flared in his dark gaze. With a quick, subtle drawing together of his eyebrows, Blaine warned her to be silent, then he lowered the gun in mock defeat and turned slowly to face Slade. "It seems I was wrong, Slade."

"Hah!" Slade shouted gleefully. "I told you she couldn't tell the truth." He motioned to Potter, who removed the knife from Maddie's throat. She started to run toward Blaine, but Potter gripped her arm. "What do you want me to do with her, boss?"

"Hold on to her. We'll take her back to Philadelphia with us tonight. Mr. Knight," he said, striding forward, "I'll take the gun and that little package, too."

"Stay where you are." Blaine's hand shot up, leveling the gun at Slade's chest, bringing the man to an immediate standstill. "The police are on their way here. We'll let them handle the matter, including this little package."

Maddie glanced fearfully at Slade. As long as Blaine still held the evidence, Slade couldn't afford to let the police get involved. She paled as Slade's smug look changed to one of diabolic fury. "Blaine!" she cried out in warning.

"Potter, kill her!" Slade snarled as he launched himself at Blaine.

Maddie heard the gun fire, but before she could see what had happened, a heavy arm wrapped around her throat and pulled her back. She clawed at the arm and struggled for air. White flashes of light filled her vision. She prayed for unconsciousness so she wouldn't feel the cold sting of the blade sear her flesh.

Instead, she felt Potter go rigid.

"That's right, my good man," she heard a familiar voice say, "now drop the knife or you'll feel the impact of this rifle clear through your spine."

Freddy! Suddenly, the arm around her throat went slack and the knife in Potter's hand fell silently to the straw. Coughing and wheezing, Maddie stumbled to the wall and leaned against it, dragging air into her starved lungs. A sob welled in her chest. Her father had come after all.

Maddie glanced at Blaine and saw that he was tying Slade's hands to the ladder with a rope. Slade cursed viciously and winced in pain as his hands were dragged behind him. One shoulder of his coat was bloodstained where Blaine had wounded him.

Blaine had fired the gun! She closed her eyes and sagged to the ground. *He had fired the gun. He had conquered his fear. They were safe.*

"Well, well!" Freddy called jovially as he pushed Potter toward the ladder with the handle of a pitchfork. "How good to see you again, Mr. Slade." He held up the pitchfork while Blaine tied Potter's hands behind his back. "How do you like my rifle?"

"Damn you, Freddy!" Slade snarled. "You're supposed to be in prison."

"Oh, I've served my time, Mr. Slade. It's your turn now." Freddy smiled at Blaine. "I'll stand guard here. You'd better see to my daughter. She seems to have fainted."

Blaine handed Freddy the gun and strode to where Maddie had collapsed on the ground. He knelt beside her and gathered her in his arms. "Maddie, sweetheart. It's all right. Maddie, can you hear me?"

Maddie struggled to open her eyes, and for a second gazed at him blankly.

Blaine smoothed back her tangled hair. "You're safe, Maddie. Slade and his man are tied securely."

With a cry of relief, she wrapped her arms around his neck. "Oh, Blaine, you didn't freeze! Thank God, you're all right! You don't know how dangerous Vincent Slade is. That's why I didn't want you to follow me. I knew he would try to kill you."

"Hush, Maddie," Blaine said gently. "Don't upset yourself further. We'll talk about it later."

Maddie buried her face in his strong shoulder and clung to him, shaking from the aftereffects of her ordeal. She felt Blaine shaking, too, and knew it had been terrible for him as well.

Blaine began to rub her back with soothing strokes. "The police will be here soon, thanks to your father."

Maddie lifted her head and peered at Freddy over Blaine's shoulder. He was standing on the other side of the barn keeping watch over Slade and Potter, his arms folded across his chest, his brown derby pushed to the back of his head. She still couldn't believe Freddy had come. And that he had contacted the police, just as she had requested.

Freddy looked over at her and smiled his wide, infectious smile. Maddie couldn't help but smile back.

Blaine helped her to her feet and brushed the hay off her clothing. "I should go check on the people in the house. Will you be all right?"

Maddie gave him a wavering smile. "I'll be fine. Go ahead."

He handed her the cloth package. "Hold this until the police come."

She watched Blaine stride toward the big doors. She couldn't have loved him any more than she did at that moment.

"Well, daughter, that was quite a con you tried to pull on me."

Maddie swung around to find Freddy behind her, his eyes twinkling with a mixture of pride and amusement. "You're good, pet, but I'm better. I figured out your little scheme right away."

Maddie wagged her finger at him. "Oh, no, you didn't. I had you fooled and you know it."

Freddy lifted one red eyebrow in reproach. But before he could say anything, the sound of pounding hooves and clattering wagon wheels made them both turn toward the doors. "Must be the police," Freddy murmured, stroking his red handlebar mustache thoughtfully. His gaze darted to Maddie's face. "You might want to wipe some of that dirt off your cheek and tuck in your shirt before they get here." With a smile he produced his handkerchief. "I'll hold that package for you."

Maddie snuggled closer to Blaine's warm body and sighed in contentment. His arm lay possessively across her shoulder. One long, muscular leg was draped over her thigh. The first faint light of dawn slithered around the edges of the velvet drapery covering the window, and outside their tiny sleeping compartment other travelers were just beginning to stir. Maddie thought of the breakfast she had eaten with her father in the dining car a day earlier and her stomach growled, demanding food.

She shook Blaine's arm. "I'm hungry," she whispered.

A warm hand slid slowly down her naked back and cupped her backside, pulling her against his aroused body. "So am I," he growled, and bent his head to press hot, lingering kisses in the curve of her neck.

Maddie smiled as his mouth moved lower. "That's not what I meant."

Blaine covered one velvety peak with his mouth and gently suckled. Maddie groaned and dropped her head back, threading her fingers through his thick hair as desire coiled deep in her belly.

"Let's take care of my hunger first," Blaine said huskily, raising passion-darkened eyes to hers, "then we'll work on yours."

"But my stomach—" She gasped as his fingers sought out the damp heat between her legs.

"Your stomach what?"

"I—forget," she managed between breathless gasps.

Blaine laughed and raised himself over her. "Mrs. Knight, you're trying to con me." He parted her thighs and entered her swiftly.

"Oh, no, Mr. Knight," she panted, digging her fingers into the firm muscles of his back. "Never again."

When they finally climbed down from the narrow bed, Maddie shivered as she reached for her corset and petticoats lying on the opposite bench. "Why is it so cold this morning?" she said through chattering teeth.

"Autumn is in the air." Blaine pulled on his black suit pants. "Turn around, Mrs. Knight, and I'll lace your corset."

Maddie presented her back and pulled her long hair out of the way. *Mrs. Knight.* She liked the sound of that very much. She smiled to herself, remembering the shocked look on the face of the justice of the peace when she and Blaine had awakened him in the middle of the night and pleaded with him to marry them. Considering Blaine's somewhat battered appearance and her own disheveled copper gown, the poor man probably would have refused had she not put her inherited talent to use. There were times when being the daughter of a con man had its advantages.

With a sudden scowl, Maddie thought back to the events of the previous night. In the confusion of the police's arrival Freddy had mysteriously disappeared, along with the money from the cloth package, leaving only Crandall's incriminating letter inside to back up her story. Luckily, it had been enough to convince the police to arrest Vincent Slade and Potter.

But that didn't excuse her father's actions. Indeed, it only confirmed what she had believed about Freddy all along: he was nothing but a con man, out to make an easy dollar. And no amount of jail time would change that.

To think Freddy had almost convinced her he cared about her. She blinked back a prickle of tears. Now she knew why he had followed her—to get his hands on the money.

"Done," Blaine said, and gave her an affectionate pat on the backside.

With a tremulous sigh, Maddie donned her petticoats and fastened them at her waist.

Blaine's hands halted on the buttons of his shirt and he gave her a curious look. "What is it, Maddie?"

"He stole the money right out from under our noses. He's shameless."

"Your father?"

"He just got out of prison, too. Why would he take the chance?"

"Maddie, other than you and I, no one but Slade knew there was money in that package. Freddy knew he wasn't in any danger from us, and the police certainly wouldn't believe Slade's claim after learning what he had done. Your father was very clever about it."

"Bother!" Maddie muttered angrily. "He even had the gall to try to convince me he cared about me."

"I'm certain he does care about you."

Maddie scoffed as she snatched the copper-colored gown from the bench. "If he truly cared he wouldn't have stolen the money. Obviously, what he cared about *was* the money." She lifted the gown over her head. "I knew he didn't *really* care about me. It was just another one of his many lies." She stopped guiltily. Until she had confessed the truth to Blaine last night, she had told more than her share of lies as well.

Blaine stepped behind her and began to fasten the tiny buttons down her back. "Freddy cares about you, Maddie. He let me win a game of rummy so he'd have an excuse to tell me where you'd gone."

"It doesn't change the fact that he stole Crandall's money," Maddie insisted stubbornly.

"Crandall is dead, sweetheart. And even if he were alive, he blackmailed Slade to get that money."

Maddie swung around, her expression strained and intense. "Did you believe Vincent Slade, Blaine? Did you believe I stole his wife's money?"

Blaine framed her face between his large hands. "I believed that you loved me, Maddie. That was the only truth that mattered."

"I meant what I said, Blaine. I'll never lie to you again. I won't be like Freddy."

"I know you won't, Maddie." Blaine gave her a quick kiss on the forehead, then turned her around. "Get your shoes and let's get some breakfast."

Maddie reached into the satchel and felt for her brown suede slippers. Her fingers closed over a heel and she pulled one shoe from the bottom. The other was wedged inside the tweed cap with her silk stockings. She sat on the edge of the bench and rolled one stocking onto her foot. In the second stocking her toes hit something hard, and she reached inside to retrieve it.

"Oh, bother!"

Blaine finished fastening his collar and turned to look at her. In Maddie's open palm lay a thick wad of one-hundred-dollar bills. As she fanned out the money, Blaine threw back his head and laughed. "And you thought Freddy didn't care."

She gave him an indignant glare. "Blaine, this isn't funny. Freddy stole this money!"

Blaine grinned down at her. "For you, sweetheart. He stole it for you."

"Of all the nerve!" Maddie shoved it at Blaine. "Take it. I don't want it."

Blaine quickly counted it. "Two thousand dollars. It's all here. I'll send it back to the police as soon as we get home."

Maddie snatched a suede slipper and slid her foot inside. "What kind of father steals money and gives it to his daughter as a gift?"

"Don't be so hard on him, Maddie. He's being the only kind of father he knows how to be."

"A damn lousy one, if you ask me." She slipped her toes in the second shoe. "I used to wait and wait for him to come home, and when he finally did . . ."

There was something in the toe of her slipper. Maddie pulled her foot out, picked up the slipper, and shook it. A slender, three-inch-long, paper-wrapped object fell into her lap.

"And when he finally did?" Blaine prompted.

"And when he finally did . . ." Maddie's throat tightened. She removed the paper covering and pressed her hand to her mouth. Tears flooded her eyes, nearly obliterating the shiny red object in her palm. ". . . all he would bring me—" She swallowed a sob. "—was a red peppermint stick."

Tears coursed down her cheeks. Freddy had remembered.

Blaine knelt down in front of her and cupped his hand beneath her chin. "I told you he cared about you."

"Bother!" she whispered. "I think I'm going to cry."

Blaine chuckled and pulled her into his arms. "Cry, sweetheart. I'll be right here to hold you."

Maddie slipped her arms around his ribs and

pressed her face into his shirt, weeping silently. When she had emptied her heart of its grief, she inhaled the comforting male scent of him and closed her eyes, letting his strength and love seep into her. Blaine would always be there for her, unlike her father.

"Blaine," she mumbled tearfully against his chest.

"Yes, Maddie."

She sniffled. "Can we go eat breakfast?"

With a sigh, Blaine slipped his hand beneath Maddie's legs and rose, holding her in his arms. "For a slender woman you have one hell of an appetite, Maddie."

She wiped her wet cheeks with the heels of her hands. "That's not true at all! Why, once I went three days without eating."

Blaine opened the door and paused to look down at her. "Madeline Anne Knight, are you making up another story?"

Maddie tapped her chin thoughtfully. "You know, you never did tell me if you were planning to take Penny Tadwell with you when you left the farm."

"Of course I was. We were going out to California to mine gold together."

Maddie gaped at him. "With that hussy?"

He kissed her. "You see, you're not the only one who can make up stories."

"Then you weren't going to take Penny with you?"

Blaine grinned and stepped outside. Maddie kicked her feet. "Blaine, answer me!"

He laughed harder as he carried her down the hallway.

At the opposite end of the car, a man stood outside his compartment and watched the departing couple. He tipped his brown derby back with his thumb and smiled at their playful banter. Then, whistling cheerfully, he stuck his hands in his pockets and headed off toward the parlor car in hopes of finding a few bored gents ready to lose a few coins to a game of cards.

If he was lucky, he might even find another farmer who thought he could win at gin rummy.

Dear Reader,

If you're looking for a sensuous, utterly romantic historical love story, then look no further than November's Avon Romantic Treasure *So Wild a Kiss* by Nancy Richards-Akers. It's filled with all the unforgettable passion you're looking for! A young woman needs protection and help to keep her family together, so her little brothers and sisters arrange for her to drink a love potion—and it seems to work when a dashing man enters her life...and steals her heart.

There's nothing like a sexy lawman to steal a working woman's heart, and in Cait London's Avon Contemporary romance debut, *Three Kisses*, you'll meet Michael Bearclaw, the strongest man in Lolo, Wyoming. He sweeps Cloe Matthews off her feet...and together they discover the secrets of Lolo. Learn why *New York Times* bestselling author Jayne Ann Krentz calls Cait, "...An exciting, distinctive voice."

Lovers of historical westerns won't want to miss the latest in Rosalyn West's exciting series, *The Men of Pride County: The Rebel*. A former Confederate soldier travels west, and finds love in the arms of a Union colonel's daring daughter.

And Danelle Harmon's delicious de Monteforte brothers make another appearance in *The Beloved One*. An English officer spirits a young American woman to his English home, only to discover he feels much, much more for her than he ever dreamed.

You'll find the very best romance here at Avon Books. Until next month, happy reading!

Lucia Macro

Lucia Macro
Senior Editor

AEL 1098

Avon Romances—
the best in exceptional authors
and unforgettable novels!